BLAZE IGNITES

SCOURGE SURVIVOR SERIES - BOOK ONE

JL MADORE

Copyright © 2013 by JLMadore

JL Madore

www.jlmadore.com

Cover Design: Book Cover Artistry

Copy Edit: Jenn Wood, All About the Edits

Note: The moral right of the author has been asserted.

This is a work of fiction. Names, characters, places and incidents either are the product of the author's imagination or are used fictitiously, and any resemblance to actual persons, living or dead, business establishments, events, or locales is entirely coincidental.

No part of this publication may be reproduced, stored in a retrieval system or transmitted, in any form or by any means without the prior written permission of the author, nor be otherwise circulated in any form of binding or cover other than that in which it is published and without a similar condition being imposed on the subsequent buyer.

The scanning, uploading, and distribution of this book via the Internet or via any other means without the permission of the author is illegal and punishable by law. Please purchase only authorized electronic editions, and do not participate in or encourage electronic piracy of copyrighted materials.

Your support of the author's rights is appreciated.

Blaze Ignites / JL Madore – 2nd ed.

ISBN 9798201244040

CHAPTER ONE

Gun versus wand.

Lexi and I saw the standoff escalating beyond the crush of half-naked, leather-clad bodies on the dance floor. The patrons of the tavern, human and not, ceased shimmying to the techno-rock of the house band and drew wands and daggers in every direction.

"Let us *through* people." Raising my palms, I called my powers. "Castian, come to me." A surge of arcane energy lifted my hair as my affinity awoke. "Down!" I shielded Lexi and avoided the white-gold energy bolt zinging past our heads. It hit the mirrored wall over the bar, bursting into a shower of sparks and jagged shards.

A shot rang out. *Shit.*

Magic buzzed and crackled in the air like a bug-light in August. I threw out some heat to part the remaining sea of bodies. Ignoring the sneers of rubberneckers, we pushed through, and my sister and I joined the altercation.

A scruffy, brute of a man sporting a bandana stood, gun poised, staring straight into the wand-tip of one of the Academy of Affinities' fifth-year wizardry students.

"Problem, gentlemen?" I asked, easing into their circle.

With shoulders rigid and wand steady, the student, Nash Blackpaw, focused straight ahead. "Jade, this asshole thinks he's dragging my friend back to the Modern Realm."

I assessed the native girl shielded behind his back. She looked shaken but unharmed.

"I don't think," the brute hissed. "This is a family matter. *Jade*, is it?"

Pushing down the urge to wipe the amused sneer off the bastard's face, I remained professional. "Jade is what friends and students call me. You can call me Blaze. That is my official *nom de guerre*."

I held up my wrist and revealed my Talon brand. Cold, sharp eyes narrowed on my copper skin as the trademark golden hawk of a Talon enforcer appeared. "Sir, you are armed with intent to do harm on Haven grounds. This entire mountain is a sanctuary. According to Fae law, the girl is welcome to claim refuge here."

"Screw the laws," he spat, shifting the business end of the gun toward me. "Fae laws force our race to live in the Modern Realm—force us to hide who we are as if we're worth less than those fucking *humans*. The gods won't care about one worthless runaway. Tell your boy here to lower his wand, and we're gone."

Catching Lexi's eye, I glanced toward the girl, and my sister dissolved into the crowd.

"Again, that's a *no*." The muzzle of the gun pointed at my chest at an almost point-blank range. My skin tingled warmly. I pushed back my temper. "I know how you must feel—"

"You know *nothing*," he snapped, spittle flying. "You *are* human."

With his full attention on me, I wove more persuasion into my words. "As a Talon enforcer, I ensure the laws of both realms are upheld. You smuggled a gun from the Modern Realm onto sanctuary grounds. There's no chance you're leaving with the girl. The Portal Gates were sealed for the summer solstice, and you have things to answer for. Your only option here is to lower your weapon."

My suggestion had the barrel wavering, but he clutched the grip with both hands to stabilize it. His jaw clenched as his index finger tightened on the trigger. I gave another push of energy, and when I thought I was at my limit, I pushed further. Perspiration beaded across his furrowed brow. I held on. Needles of pain ran through my jaw as I clenched my teeth. After another minute, the Glock clattered to the tavern floor.

He lunged.

My feet left the ground as his shoulder caught my cheek. Something solid connected with my ribs, and I hit the dance floor in an awkward half-twist. My back met the wood plank right before my head bounced. White splotches burst in front of my eyes when the brute's staggering weight lifted, and two Were-lion bouncers took control.

One snatched the weapon and shoved it into the waistband of his jeans. His litter-mate grabbed the guy's thick arms and wrenched them back until I expected to hear the snap of bone. Rumbling like a storm cloud, the pair of Weres cable-tied the guy's hands and signaled to everyone that the show was over.

"And a good night was had by all." Lexi rolled her eyes and offered me a hand up. "You good, girlfriend?"

I nodded, wiping blood from my cheek as the crowd dispersed. Once the band resumed, everyone went right back to their evening.

"Remove his bandana, or he'll shift." The native girl peered from behind Lexi, then squealed as the brute surged.

"Are you snitching little *bitch*," he snapped.

Lexi drew the knife from her thigh sheath, and the lion tightened his hold on our now-squirming, cursing prisoner. When the tie of the bandana was severed, the glamour—the illusion which made it appear as if his cloak were nothing more than a piece of cloth—shattered. What looked to be a worn black cloth-covered in flames and a rebel flag dissolved, leaving Lexi holding a floor-length fur pelt.

"Finfolk?" Lexi asked.

Long chestnut hair shimmered in the tavern's lantern light as the girl nodded. Definitely First Nations—Inuit maybe? I scanned the fringed cape draped to the thighs of her jeans. It was probably glamoured, too.

"Two weeks ago," she said, "my parents were killed off the Alaskan

Coast, and my uncle took over my raft. He's a bastard, even by Finfolk standards, but was next in line to rule."

"And what race of Finfolk are you?" I asked, studying the thick, grey pelt in Lexi's hand.

"Otterkie," she said. "At first, I believed my parents were netted and killed by human poachers while in their animal form. That's what my uncle reported to the council, but last night I heard him in the den whispering with that man." She pointed to our prisoner. "My uncle thanked him for a job well done. My parents were dead, and nobody suspected a thing. Now all he had to do was kill off the whelps."

She flipped her cape back, revealing a dark-haired toddler in a child sling across her chest. "My race has always been proud to be Dark Fae. Dark, but not evil. I believe my uncle has betrayed our people to gain favor with the Scourge."

The pain in her wide brown eyes pegged me in the gut. The slaughter of my parents still ate at me—jagged teeth gnawing my insides—even seventeen years later.

I gazed at the bouncers. *Damn Were-lion littermates are tough to tell apart.* "Boys, take our guests up to the security office at the castle. My brother is on duty and will do the honors with the paperwork. I'll call him and let him know what's happened."

After handing over the guy's otter pelt, Lexi and I headed back to our booth. My call to Julian about what happened was quick, and before I knew it, I was back to our evening.

"You okay, Jade?"

"Fine," I lied, forcing a smile.

Lexi bounced up on her knees and signaled our waitress for another round. "Okay, spill. What's wrong?"

I tipped back what I'd left in my glass and focused my healing affinity on my ribs, cheek, and shoulder. When that was taken care of, I wiped the blood from my face with a napkin. "It just pisses me off. I beat that idiot with my powers. I could've taken him with weapons, but no matter how much we train or over-train, I'm not freakishly strong like you. I'll never out-muscle half the men we come up against.

"You're way smarter."

"Maybe, but that won't convince Reign to treat us as equals in the field."

Lexi bit her lip. "I bet the take down doesn't even register with him. He's gonna go ballistic about a gun on the property—and that it was aimed at you."

I winced. "Gods. He won't let us off-site for a month."

"A month?" She snorted. "If we're lucky. I figure a year."

I accepted two more wide-mouthed glasses from the waitress in the Daisy-Dukes and bit back a smirk. The deep cleavage lean-in went beautifully with the turquoise hair, and the pounds of gold glitter cemented to her eyelids.

Gods, I hope that stuff didn't flake off. After a quick scan of the surface of my Rhapsody Cosmo, I chased a drop of pink nectar down the stem of the glass and inhaled the fruity fragrance. It was dizzying how the heady scent mixed with the tavern's potpourri of tobacco, onion rings, and lust.

Ahhh, the Hearthstone, the Realm of the Fair's very own Vegas. Except, unlike the Modern Realm, what happened at the Hearthstone didn't always stay at the Hearthstone.

"To the summer solstice." I raised my glass, committed to drowning the onslaught of memories tonight had belched up. I swallowed hard, pushing past the lump in my throat. "To my parents. May we annihilate the Scourge from both realms and avenge every innocent who fell victim to their evil." I proceeded to chug what was my fourth—or maybe my fifth drink.

Lexi raised her glass; her light purple eyes glittered a myriad of emotions in the dim light. Reaching across the table, she squeezed my hand. "What happened to your parents sucked Jade—no argument—but you're a survivor. Maybe it's all part of some cosmic plan." She tilted her head, her spiky black hair exploding in every direction. "If they lived, you wouldn't have lived here, and we wouldn't be sisters. Maybe it's destiny somehow."

"Destiny my ass," I snapped. A wave of hurt crossed Lexi's face. *Shit.* I waved my empty glass until our waitress headed to the bar.

"The truth is, when the Fates get bored with life Behind the Veil, they amuse themselves by tossing innocent people and random events into life's blender. You never know what flavor Slushie you'll end up once the hum of the blades stop. You struggle to pull yourself together, and when you finally think you've got control, the little sadists flip the switch, and the whole shitstorm starts again."

Lexi swirled her Cosmo and studiously watched the surface dance. "Remember what Bruin and Julian painted on the clubhouse when we were kids?"

We recited together. "Shitstorm Survivors: Come in peace or leave in pieces."

When Lexi lifted her head, her smile was back in place. "Julian was pissed he had to cover the gates tonight. He wanted to be here for you."

I nodded. "He stopped by the clinic on his way to the Gatehouse. Oh, and he gave me something. . ." I scrabbled around in my purse and retrieved two shiny, touch-screen phones. "Julian's at it again. He's installed a GPS tracker on our SIM cards and downloaded a couple of nifty new mapping apps for when we're in the field. All our mission specs open at a touch and sync up with our comm system when we're on the move."

Lexi scrolled through the upgrades and beamed. "Gods, he's the best."

The little envelope on my screen blinked its message: two missed calls—Bruin and Reign.

Was Lexi right? Was my adopted family my destiny? "Who's on patrol tonight?"

"Who's not?" Lexi jumped on my change of subject and ran with it. "Calls have flooded in from both realms all day: crop circles, people vanishing in plain sight, apparitions, cloud shapes, UFO sightings. We had a dozen exposure risks in the Modern Realm by the time Julian closed the Portal Gates at full dark. Hopefully, that will contain—" Lexi leaned forward, her brow disappearing under inky bangs. "Well, that didn't take long."

"Wha—*dammit*." I ducked behind a menu and slid to the back of our booth. Peeking around my laminated shield, I assessed the leggy brunette Samuel wore around his neck like a pet chimpanzee. Joined at the lips, they stumbled and staggered across the dance floor and tipped, as one, backward onto the bench of an empty booth.

"Is she kissing him or draining his blood? If it's the latter, I should go help. She's nowhere near the carotid." Lexi pulled her dirk from her boot-sheath and spun it in her palm.

"Nah, we've had enough drama for one night."

With her lip pushed out in a pout, she sheathed her weapon. "Fine. We're here to get you smashingly drunk, not dwell on which Succubus your ex has sucker-fished to his throat."

"Right." I glanced over to the lovely couple. Samuel's shabby-chic hair was getting a good mussing, and apparently, he was lapping it up. How long would it be before they headed somewhere more private? My gaze wandered toward the private bathrooms down by the office. I'd never been inclined to use them myself, though the oversized dimensions made them popular when regulars, especially the Weres and Centaurs, had a thirst for something they couldn't order at the bar. I swallowed hard and closed my eyes against nausea churning in my gut.

Well then, Samuel finally gets laid.

I didn't blame him. Samuel was charming, hot, and an unbelievable wizard. A sexual relationship just wasn't in me. After two years of dating, teaching at the Academy, and battling the Scourge together wasn't enough for him. As much as he'd hoped for a physical relationship, he'd never inspired a clear-the-table-take-me-now passion in me. No one had.

As Samuel's hands skimmed over the skank's ribcage and under her breasts, I remembered every nuance of his touch, the warm softness of his wizard hands, the gentle strength of his fingers—Nothing. No weak knees, no racing pulse, no heat liquefying my insides.

There was something seriously wrong with me.

Lexi huffed at the display. "Let's turn him into a zombie and make him dance the Macarena naked."

"Entertaining, but no, Samuel deserves to be happy."

"Ew, how mature." Sticking her tongue out, she refocused on her drink, downing half without taking a breath. How could someone so little drink so much and still be steady with a knife? She claimed it was a superior metabolism. "Okay, forget him. Do you wanna dance?"

I evaluated the hedonistic grind on the dance floor then the action at Samuel's booth. "No. Let's get drunk."

"Wisdom for the ages." Lexi whooped and lifted her glass. "Here's to women everywhere, drinking far too much to be sensible and not giving a shit!"

A high-pitched *clink* signaled the resumption of our evening, and I pushed all thoughts of Samuel and my emotional and sexual deficiencies out of my mind. "So," I said, "are we still going to the—*Shit*." The deep violet of Lexi's pupils was dilating and overtaking the pale purple irises. "Lexi, sit back, hon. You're about to go off-line."

Sliding deeper into the booth, she pressed her back against the wall. "You sure? I don't feel—" Her face blanked out just as her eyes rolled back. When they blinked open, they had done a quick-change to the shimmering violet of a velvet night sky.

I hustled to the opposite bench and slid in. With my back to the dance floor, I set her limp palms over my own and started the mental upload between her vision and my mind…

CHAPTER TWO

The indigo night hung veiled in glistening stars. A group of Elves regarded a stately man speaking at the altar-stone of a ceremonial ruin site. Three men sat on display to the left of the speaker. Two had honey-flax hair, and the third silver. Each of them wore it pulled back and tied, exposing elongated, softly pointed ears.

Looking out over the gathering, every guest shared the same physical characteristics: medium to long hair, in one shade of gold or another, flawless alabaster skin and stained-glass blue eyes. The silver hair of the one at the front was the only exception.

My mind swirled in drunken dizziness that had nothing to do with the Rhapsodies we'd inhaled and everything to do with a race of Elves long believed to be extinct. Of the seven races of Elves, six thrived in the Realm of the Fair. The seventh was exiled eight thousand years ago—Highbornes.

∼

"Tonight," the host said, turning to gesture to the three. "Galanodel, Thamior, and Aust embark on their *Ambar Lenn*—Fate's Journey. As they embrace their passage from cub to wolf, sapling to oak, they seek purpose in the next phase of their lives. Upon their return, each male will assume his station and endeavor to become a male of worth. Blessing and abundance."

"Blessing and abundance," they responded.

The crowd tilted their heads in whispered conversation. The ceremony continued until, after a time, the host dismissed formalities in favor of festivities. Steins were drained, laughter was shared, and everyone ate enough to hold them 'til the autumn rains. When it was over, Galan, Tham, and Aust watched the procession of exodus. Guests flowed down the path in silken waves like smoke on the night breeze. Slim-waisted, blush-cheeked beauties giggled and gossiped while the men conversed about tradition and the days, long behind them, when they accepted their stations.

"And they leave disappointed," Galan, the silver-haired one, deadpanned. "Many of them attended simply to witness our scandalous refusal to quest, no doubt."

"Nonsense, my rapier wit, and stunning charm was the draw." Tham waggled his brow then sobered when Galan failed to laugh. "Regardless. The grains of sand have trickled through the sandglass for the last time. They may force us to abandon youth but become *responsible* males? Never." Tham's body shook with an exaggerated shudder, and this time, Galan did smile. Tham squeezed his friend's shoulder. "Fash not, brother mine." They have endeavored to mold us for a century and have yet to succeed."

Galan pulled the tie binding his hair and scrubbed his fingers through it as it fell loose. "I cannot explain it, Tham. Deep in the knit of my bones, I sense something ill awaiting us. Lia needs me, and Nyssa is close to birthing. My every instinct scream to tell the Elder Council to shove the *Ambar Lenn* into any orifice of their choosing and leave me be."

"Mayhap, speak with your *eda* again."

"No." Galan said. "Disdain and unending criticism are the very bricks and mortar of my relationship with my sire. Our uniting bond from the day *Naneth* passed." He squeezed his eyes shut and sighed. "Whatever the Fates have in store, I am helpless to fight it."

Galan and Tham joined Aust at the altar-stone. The ivory, rectangular slab lay where it had for eons, cracked and eroded from bearing the load of centuries past. This night it lay buried beneath layers of silken, hand-stitched runners, littered with ravaged platters of sweets and loaves of bread.

Galan sifted through dozens of crock jugs tipped on their sides, bellies drained. Finding a half-size still corked, he laced his finger through the loop, swirled the contents, and proposed a toast. "To success on our *Ambar Lenn* and returning to those we love." He drank deep.

Tham corralled the abandoned scraps of food onto one platter, tucked it into the crook of his arm, and glanced around the vacated site while popping pastries into his mouth. "Is Faolan not questing with you, Aust?"

Aust lifted his gaze from the ground and shook his head. "The elders insist she remains in the village to 'allow me the opportunity to expand and embrace my possibilities.' Toeing the dirt, he kicked a rock soaring. "Faolan is vexed."

Tham popped a honey-glaze into his mouth and washed it down with a swig from Galan's jug. "Can you use your ability and explain it to her?"

Aust glanced over his shoulder toward their host and leaned closer. "I have, yet she still refuses to see me off."

"Your wolf and my father have much in common." Galan reclaimed the stone jug and drained it before placing it amongst its fallen brothers. Finding another containing a few sloshes, he smiled. "Mayhap, Faolan should console him while we venture off on our quests."

Tham smiled. "Or better yet, sink her canines into his gem pouch and shake until the old man turns blue."

They all chuckled.

"Did Lia not attend, Galan?" Aust asked.

Galan's jaw flexed. "No, she did not."

The heavy silence that followed ended when their host spoke. "Gentlemales, seek your purpose. Discover the path to personal fulfillment and the enrichment of our community. Inventory your lives as you inventoried your belongings for this quest. Some items were chosen for survival, though equal in importance are the talismans which give your guiding spirit strength. Decide which burdens are worth the weight to bear. Keep your load light and your hearts pure. Blessed be."

"Blessed be," they repeated.

With belts cinched, swords sheathed, and bows slung, the three men grabbed their satchels and bedrolls. The worn path from the ruin site took them away from the village and along the larger of the two rivers heading north to begin their *Ambar Lenn*—Fate's Journey.

My mind spun in a wild vortex of surreal images as I disconnected from Lexi's vision. Breathe. I needed to breathe. How could they—

"Jade?" Lexi whispered, dropping her head forward.

"I'm here, hon."

The summer solstice was more than just the longest day of the year and my personal hell. Fae lore claimed it was the day when the veil between magic and reality was almost non-existent. I'd thought that was superstitious hoo-ha until now. Highborne Elves?

"Jade?" Lexi raised her head as she eased out of the trance. When her vision cleared, she stared at me with the same *Oh-My-Gods* look I wore. "We need to go."

I scooted to the edge of the booth, grabbed my purse, and handed Lexi a piece of chocolate. She peeled the wrapper and popped it in her mouth. When the sugar kicked in, her eyes returned to their usual shade of purple. "Are you good?"

Lexi tossed half a dozen silver pieces onto the table, then bounced down from the booth. Grabbing the edge of the table, she checked her balance. "No, but we need to find Reign."

Damn. "He's at that stupid exposure conference in Hong Kong. Cowboy?"

"On a mission. Savage?"

"Covering up that crop circle disturbance in Vancouver."

"So, who's in charge?"

Ah, double damn. My heart stopped mid-beat. "Samuel." I looked to his booth and fought the urge to bolt. I'd like to think we cared enough about each other to get past the failure of us as a couple... that Samuel wouldn't trash me for the times he'd felt rejected... that we could function on a professional level until the wounds healed.

That, of course, was bullshit.

"You want me to do this?" Lexi asked.

Yes. "No. I've got it." With clenched fists, I made my way to the other side of the dance floor to the booth where Samuel and his date were oh-so-cozy. She was draped over him like a blanket—a horny, skanky blanket—and his face was buried somewhere under her back-teased brown hair, along her neck, maybe or in her cleavage. I *so* did not need that visual.

Steeling myself against what was coming, I knocked on the table. "Excuse me."

Samuel's dark, half-hooded gaze was unfocused when he lifted his head. I knew that look. As he registered the source of interruption, I thought I glimpsed the man I cared about. He vanished all too quickly. "Jade, are ye on for a pint, or are ye on the pull?"

Ignoring the tone, I raised my chin. "I need to speak with you."

"Do ye now? And where's the wee princess?" He struggled to lift his head. Glancing around the crowded tavern, he found her next to the exit. "Oh, there she is. Never too far."

I ignored the one-fingered salute Lexi offered Samuel and the lazy roll of his unfocused eyes in reply. After she pointed at the door and stepped outside, I got back on task. "Samuel, forget Lexi, I need you."

He blinked slowly, his lazy grin widening. "I may be a bit gone in drink, but I recall too well that ye've never truly needed me Jade."

"Look, I need to speak with you. Can I have a moment?"

"I've company at the moment, Luv."

"I see that. However, that's not what this is about."

"Really? Ye're sure?" The brunette looked up from his neck as if noticing me for the first time. Apparently, I held no interest because she went straight back to business.

"Look. Reign isn't here, and I need to speak to you. Lexi had a vision."

Samuel straightened, resting his head against the back of the booth. "A vision? Well, very convenient that your sister had a vision during my date. Very convenient indeed."

"It's not *convenient*, Samuel. Something happened."

He leaned forward, propping his head in his hands. "I'm no so gone that I don't know this is the night of the solstice, Jade. Wallowing in the murder of your parents, are ye? Need a shoulder to weep on?"

"You *bastard*." My fists clenched as a dozen candles on surrounding tables hissed to life. Six-inch flames leaped into the air as diners jumped back. When my eyes began to sting, I spun. *Do not cry in front of him.* Heading for the exit, I fought the urge to break into a run. Using my parents against me was low. Samuel knew how badly I hungered to find the last of those responsible and claim my Right of Vengeance. The need was especially raw tonight.

Everything in me wanted to go back to that booth and smack the sanctimonious scowl off his face. Slamming through the door, I collided with a couple groping hot and heavy at the exit. The duo toppled like pins on a waxed alley.

Lexi took one look at me bowling through lovebirds, cursed, and headed back into the tavern. "What the hell did Merlin say to you?"

I caught her arm as she flew by. "Forget him." I swiped at my cheeks. "Nothing has changed. We need a plan."

My mind cleared as we crossed the grounds back to the castle. Even without a plan, getting our gear assembled was a given. Twenty-five minutes later, we sat in my suite, gear packed and brainstorming. I turned the mug in my hands, studying the butter-caramel surface as if answers might magically manifest within.

"Why did we get this vision, tonight of all nights?" I asked. "What does it mean?"

A flutter of serenity overwhelmed as a warm breeze stirred my locks, and my senses filled with lavender and bergamot. Thank the gods—or *god* was more accurate. I raised my gaze to the ceiling and closed my eyes. "Have you been spying on me, Sire?"

The presence in my mind filled with male amusement. *I prefer to think I watch over you, Mir. Spying sounds invasive.*

Castian's endearment, *Mir*—his treasure—soothed like a hot stone massage after training. "That's some distinction. So, what does the vision of the Highbornes mean?"

I am releasing them from exile.

"You're kidding? After all this time?"

I think eight thousand years makes my point.

"I'm sure it does." Sipping my coffee, I held down the butterflies fluttering in my belly and waited for Castian to continue. Gods were not ones to be rushed.

Ready your mounts. You and Alexannia will make first contact. The information you need will be sent to your phones.

"Us?" I set my coffee on the table. "Alone? There are a dozen enforcers more qualified. Why would you send us?"

Are you questioning the God of gods?

I winced at the cutting edge in Castian's voice. Damn, I was off my game tonight. But that was it, wasn't it? At the Hearthstone, I did everything right and still got knocked on my ass. If the lions hadn't been there, I might've been in serious trouble. Maybe Reign was right. Maybe I should stick to training at the Academy and joining raid parties.

Mir, I'm waiting.

I snapped back to my senses. "No. Of course not, Sire. I am so sorry. It's just—"

What?

I took in wide-eyed WTF glare Lexi was throwing from across the table and shook my head. "Nothing, Sire. Thy will be done."

Good. This task is part of your destiny, Mir. *I have seen it.*

Destiny. I bit my tongue. If he only knew.

CHAPTER THREE

*T*here was a long moment of silence as Lexi, and I caught our breath. We'd only just grabbed our gear and readied our mounts when Castian Flashed us to our destination. In a split second, we dissolved from the Haven stables and stood on a leafy ridge, watching the first tangerine rays of the sun come up over an enchanted rainforest.

"This is where the Highborne Elves spent the last eight thousand years?" Lexi wrinkled her nose. She'd face off against deranged sorcerers and filthy, half-naked barbarians rather than rough it for a few nights in the wild. "Gods, it's *sooo* green."

A warm, wind blew strong in our faces, stirring a lush canopy of emerald-leafed branches high above our heads and swirling the earthy scents of growth and decay. The ground lay overrun with sprawling plants and vines, the rich browns of the tree trunks, buried beneath spongy sage mosses. Even the weak morning light filtered in with dappled mint strobes as the tropical trees danced above.

"Is it possible for something to smell green?" Lexi scowled, running her fingers over the gem-studded saddle spanning the back of her bearded dragon. After adjusting the girth and harness, she patted her mount's scaly head. "Puff and I don't like so much nature.

Do we Puff?" Puff continued chewing a chunk of sweet potato, not giving any indication of his preferences. "Are they Elves or Ewoks 'cause I'm getting a yub-nub feeling here?"

I laughed. "You'll survive."

Lexi pushed the toe of her new Chloé boot into the stirrup and sprang into her saddle. They were three-strap, sable, mid-calf boots with silver buckles. Nice. Her predilection for inappropriate footwear in the field always made me smile. "Imagine being exiled here," she said. "No Victoria's Secret. No BeDazzlers. No Game of Thrones!" She rolled her eyes.

"Don't sweat it. We'll make first contact with the Highbornes and be home for John Snow—" I finished reading the mission spec downloaded to my phone and pulled up short. "Holy hells."

"What?"

"This isn't just first contact." I reread the last paragraph of our orders, waiting for it to sink in. "We're retrieving the lost spellbook of Queen Rheagan. Are we ready for this?"

"Uh… yes." Lexi's body was almost completely shielded behind the frill of her bearded dragon, her spiky black hair bobbing in the affirmative. Gripping the two curved horns coming off the scales of Puff's neck, she turned away. "And even if we aren't, we sure as hell aren't admitting that to Castian or Reign."

After tying my cloak, I secured my backpack to the saddle-horn and swung up onto my ebony panther. The crunch of leather on leather, as I sunk into the saddle, roused Naith from his catnap. Tendons and muscles quivered and lengthened as my mount bowed in a deep stretch and *mrowled* a yawn. His rising rump pitched me forward and then leveled, ready to ride.

Reining north, we crossed a clearing and headed on a course to intercept. No matter how hard I pushed the waves of nausea down, I had a sickening feeling that this mission would bite me in the ass.

Ten minutes into our ride, Lexi stopped. "Um, Jade?"

Naith and I strode alongside her, and my mouth fell open. "What the hell is that?"

On a mossy fallen log, gently flapping, blue, iridescent tennis racket sized wings, sat what I guessed was a pre-historic butterfly.

"This isn't the Ewok village," Lexi muttered. "We're in freakin' Jurassic Park." Both of us scanned the forest, doing a complete 360. Now that I was looking for it, the leaves of the trees higher up were the size of bedsheets. "Jade, what if this doesn't go according to Hoyle and everything craps out?"

"Nothing's going to crap out."

"Could we at least have our full gear?" Her gaze jerked and darted to the shadows of the forest, following every sound, every movement. "Remember that goat getting munched by the T-rex in the first movie? One minute it was there, and the next it was *crunch crunch* in the bushes."

I imagined the trees rustling, hiding the unseen dinosaur. "I remember, but for first contact, we're messengers—knives only and only for defense." I ignored the icy amethyst glare. "When we go for the spellbook, you can wear the entire armory."

"I don't need the entire armory." She patted the hilt of her dagger, where it rested against her thigh. "Over accessorizing is tacky anyway, right, Puff?"

Puff swung his broad, triangular head from the trail and glanced back at us. His reptilian grin gave nothing away. *Puff*. I bit my tongue —only Lexi.

Naith padded along, swaying in a hypnotic rhythm. It was grace in motion that only a prowling jungle cat could pull off. Lying over his neck, I nuzzled deep into his velvety pelt. He smelled like musk and the cedar mulch from his barn stall.

Straightening, I watched the sun continue to rise. The solstice was over for another year.

Lexi slowed Puff until we were side by side. "At least you have memories beyond the bad. More than I've got."

I loosened the drawstrings on my pack and pushed my hand inside. Which was better? Reliving the annihilation of your family over and over, like me, or living in a void of not knowing where you come from, like Lexi?

My fingers found the smooth curve of Castian's royal seal on the Highborne pardon. *'This task is part of your destiny,* Mir. *I have seen it.'* Destiny. Was it my parents' destiny to be slaughtered? Was I supposed to live? Would I ever know the answers?

I drew a deep breath. Time to think about the now. What the hell was I supposed to say to these three men? Hi, I know you've never seen a human before, and your people were trapped in this valley for eight thousand years, but today's your lucky day.

A mint-scented breeze blew my curls away from my face as Castian's silky baritone entered my mind. *Have faith in my judgment,* Mir. *Worry less, smile more, my child.*

Easy for him to say, looking down from the Palace of the Fae. I rubbed my thumb over the royal seal again. "I like the mint. It's a nice touch."

Castian's tone was rock steady and severe. *You need this,* Mir. *I've seen your tapestry. Trust in me. This journey is the path to the answers for which you yearn.*

My mind went numb. "What? Are you sure?" I winced. Of course, he's sure. He's the God of gods for god's sake.

Lexi met my gaze and cocked a brow. "Message from on high?"

"Ah . . . yeah." My voice was too high pitched, and I tried to regain my wits before Lexi caught on and started up with an interrogation.

Thankfully, she wasn't paying attention to me. She tilted her head to the canopy and smiled. "I bet Castian's a total jaw-dropping hottie."

I shut my eyes, hoping in vain that Castian had signed off or tuned out or whatever he did to break his connection. The rolling laughter filling my mind made me cringe. "Lexi, you might think about exercising impulse control once in a while."

Having gone through every conceivable first contact scenario, I couldn't see how my destiny linked with the rediscovery of the Highbornes. The entire race was segregated for eight millennia. I was twenty-five and barely qualified to handle this. Other Talon enforcers could do this, but they were off covering solstice exposures and dealing with realm issues instead of being available for what was important.

What a total waste of resources.

Lexi and I were strong in battle, unbeatable in the classroom, and now apparently, we were emissaries? I shook my head. "Hold up, Naith." As he padded to a stop, I pulled up the topographical map Castian had sent to my phone. Tracing my finger over the screen, I calculated the distance then checked the time. "If they left the coming-of-age ceremony last night here and took the side path along the north river, they should be intersecting this part of the forest soon."

"Unless they hopped the river and went off on a tangent."

Great. Then we'd have to track them, instead of letting them discover us. I pulled the hood of my cloak back so Lexi saw my face.

"What?" she snapped. "Don't give me the skunk eye, Medusa. It's possible."

On a sigh, I stashed my phone into my pack. Rain was falling. Thankfully though, it didn't make it through the weave of the canopy. I squinted skyward. What sounded like a thundering downpour in the distance was nothing more than a patter and sprinkle to us.

"Jade, no offense, but your hair is seriously scaring me."

I pulled the hood closer, so it hung over my eyes. "It's this soupy humidity. I need a bottle of frizz controller."

"A bottle? Hon, you need a freakin' case." Lexi laughed and laughed as I rolled my eyes. "Just keepin' it real." She patted her chest, then held out her fingers in a peace symbol. I had to laugh. How could anyone stay annoyed with her?

"Okay," she said, shifting in her saddle. "My turn. How about this one. Would you rather drink two shot-glasses of Centaur spit or pick up Naith's warm, steaming poo with your bare hands for a week?"

"Really? Those are my choices?"

"Yep."

I thought about my options as the maze of trees pressed closer, and we shifted to single file. *Spit or poo? Hmm.* The distant rumble of thunder joined the screech of cicadas, the caws of unseen birds, and the howl of monkeys.

"I'll go with the poo," I said. Lexi nodded as if she agreed, and that gave me an idea for my turn. "Okay, would you rather—*urghh*"

Steel arms grappled my shoulders and slammed the breath from my lungs. Knocked from my saddle, we crashed to the dirt. Entangled in a mass of arms, legs, and hair, we rolled into a snarl of brush. The impact of the forest floor shot through my hip. A tree root jutted into my shoulder blade. My pulse raced in my ears. As my mind struggled to catch up with my body, I lay pinned beneath the silver-haired Highborne, both wrists manacled above my head.

Naith snapped at a wolf positioned between him and our struggle. The beast crouched to pounce when a velvet voice barked a command from beyond.

Both animals fell instantly silent.

The razor edge of Galan's dagger pressed against my throat as he yanked back the hood of my cloak, taking a handful of hair with it.

"A female?" he gasped, in Elvish. His bold, blue eyes narrowed and then flared wide. Tightening his hold on my wrists, he removed the knife and placed it on the ground beside my head. He rubbed my curls between thumb and fingers, then traced my cheek with the touch of a feather. "No. A goddess."

I shook my head and grappled for words. The instant his ocean blue stare met mine the plug in my brain pulled, and my thoughts had circled the drain.

He was uber-hot, no one with eyes would argue that, but it was his touch that had me mesmerized. It tingled across my cheek, where he brushed me skin to skin. For the first time in my life, I wanted to kiss a man senseless.

"My name is Jade," I replied in his language, swallowing as the tingle on my skin grew into a zing. "Jade Glaster."

Flat on my back with that stupid root still pressed into my shoulder, I stared at the cut of his jaw, the depths of his blue eyes, and the curve of his full lips. He smelled wild and woodsy, a heady blend of suede and male sweat. His hips rested dead center between my thighs, every hard, taut inch of him pressing intimately against every soft, pliable inch of me.

Oh, my. I swallowed. My breasts grew tight as heat bloomed in my belly, smoldered, and moved south like the steady creep of a brush fire. His lips were moving. I didn't hear a word.

Dwinn. My voice whispered in my mind. *Dwinn.*

Warm breath brushed my cheek. Again, I tried to focus, my mind swimming. A curtain of silver tickled my neck as he dropped his head to the side of my face and inhaled. Pulling back, his mouth hovered inches from mine, his eyes practically glowing.

Above my head, I pulled against his hold in a vain effort to regain control. *Say something, Jade. Just open your mouth and say something.* "Please, Galan, let me up."

The spell was broken.

Galan's eyes narrowed as he released my wrists and reclaimed his blade. "How do you know me?"

"I know a great deal." I pressed my unsteady hands firmly against his chest, softening my tone. "I know Tham, Aust, and you are on your *Ambar Lenn.* I know Castian Larethan asked us to escort your journey as it ties in with *His* plans." I lifted my mouth to brush the pointed tip of his ear. "And I know you lying over me has grown far too intimate for a first encounter."

Galan pulled his hips back and rolled off me. He looked away as he sheathed the blade, and when he looked up, a mask of calm covered his face.

After brushing bits of forest off my ass, I straightened. "I see you two have met my sister, Alexannia Grace."

Engaged as I rolled across the forest floor, I missed when Aust and Tham secured Lexi. Well, *secured* overstated the situation since she remained mounted on Puff and fully capable of liberating herself at any moment. She was, however, flanked by Naith and a large silver wolf with ebony points.

Tham stood beside Lexi, feet braced, and arrow nocked. After a moment, he lowered his bow, and I swear he winked at her. "And are you a friend, little one?"

Her double-take was priceless. "Umm, pardon hotness? *Sprechen sie English?*"

"Lexi's Elvish is spotty," I said. "She speaks Draconic, though. If you do."

He nodded and tried again. "Merry meet, Lexi. I am known as Thamior." He gathered her hand from her dagger hilt and raised it to his lips. "If it pleases, address me as Tham. This is Aust, his wolf companion, Faolan, and the silver-haired male accosting your sister is Galan." Galan threw him a lovely scowl, and Tham laughed. "What brings such beauty to our valley?"

"That is the crux of it, is it not?" Galan snapped. "Mayhap you could refrain from overtures until we discover the why of things?"

Ignoring the fact that their Elvish lilt was like warm chocolate melting in my mouth, I fished the parchment from my backpack. "Castian Larethan, God of Fae gods and ruler of The Realm of the Fair, is setting the three of you on a task." I set the missive in Galan's hands and stepped back. "When it is complete, Lexi and I will accompany you back to your village to deliver this pardon of exile to your people." I plucked a piece of grass from my hair and dropped it to the ground. "As of last night, midnight on the eve of the summer solstice, the enchantment on your valley was lifted."

The three of them staggered, staring from one to another. Dropping to one knee, Tham and Aust touched their foreheads, mumbling a prayer.

Galan stood tall, brow arched. "And Castian Latheron, Father of Fae, chose two *females* to be the envoys of this momentous news?"

Rude much? "Sorry to disappoint. But yes, we are your welcome wagon."

After tossing me a do-you-think-I'm-an-idiot look, Galan cracked the seal and gave the document a cursory once-over. "What did you mean . . . as it ties in with *His* plans?"

"Well, the five of us are setting off on a little adventure. If we're successful, the Highbornes will be reinstated in the Realm of the Fair with honor restored and Castian's blessing."

"And if not?" Tham asked.

I flipped my hair behind my shoulders. "Failure is not an option."

CHAPTER FOUR

Tham scooped his sleeveless leather slicker from the forest floor, shrugged it on, and pulled his blond waves free to fall behind his shoulders. Circling to a stand of trees behind Faolan, Naith, and Puff, Galan, and Aust retrieved their belongings as well.

The three of them were like something from an erotic Elven dream, exuding a rare masculine grace that had Lexi and me both biting our lips. In suede pants fitted to sleek, powerful thighs and bare sculpted chests, they stole our breath. Built like male gymnasts, their lean muscles rippled and shifted beneath brown leather vests and sleeveless thigh-length coats.

Devastating.

A deep thrum burned through my body. This couldn't be happening—not now—not on a mission. *Eyes down Blaze.* Better. Breathing deep, I studied their feet. Well-tailored, fitted leather boots were laced below their knees, soft-soled I assumed, because when they moved, not a twig snapped, not a blade of grass rustled.

"And what is our task?" Tham asked.

Damn. After a *holy-hotness* grin of approval, Lexi reached behind Puff's frill and angled down the path. I nodded, slipped a toe into my stirrup, and swung up onto my panther. "We'll get to the quest in a minute. First, you need a 411 on what you've missed."

"Apologies, a what?" Tham asked.

The Elves started an easy jog just outside the narrow, north forest path, maneuvering the surrounding trees as if without thought.

"How much do you know about your exile?"

"I would wager more than you," Galan said, arching a perfectly shaped brow.

"Normally, I'd take that bet. However, for the sake of time, humor me."

Tham jogged alongside me, ducking under a low branch. "Ten millennia past, Queen Rheagan, goddess of the Fae Pantheon, was given rule over the mortal lands of the Realm of the Fair. She had a particular love of the Highbornes and adopted them as her noble children. They stood by her as guardians to the throne and keepers of the peace."

"As time passed," Galan said, "they became complacent in their station and their mastery of arcane energies. They were blind to the Queen's corrupt intent to take over the realm and realized their mistake too late."

Weaving between two trees, Tham strode onto the path with the wolf at his heels. "When they discovered the Queen was using them, they stood against her, though it made little difference. Centuries of arrogance could not be corrected in the final hours. As a result, our people were exiled and secured in this valley, isolated and forgotten, until today."

"That's what it says in the history books." I urged Naith over a ridge and down the smooth slope on the other side. "Let's move on to what's happening now. Almost thirty years ago, a violent siege spread through the western range: villages burned, shops looted, and prominent residents found face down taking dirt naps. It was a maniacal free-for-all."

"Dirt nap?" Tham asked.

"Right. Sorry. They were dead. A sadistic sorcerer named Abaddon is gathering the like-minded scum of the realm, collecting them like souvenirs. He attracts leaders, rogues, and outcasts of the chaotic Dark races, and once they prove themselves vile enough, he transforms them into powerful, undead soldiers known as Scourge."

"Not without paying his price, though," Lexi said. "The cost of immortality and a free reign of terror is to forfeit their souls to their master. Abaddon makes them faster, stronger, and meaner, but their living organs decay. They become an awful funk of rot and evil."

I nodded. "And every soul Abaddon collects makes him stronger."

"Unless," Lexi grinned, "we expire the Scourge scum it belongs to and send him back to hell. Then the power of that soldier is lost to him."

"To what end?" Galan asked.

I shifted in my saddle. "The same as eight thousand years ago, greed and power. We believe Abaddon is making a play for the throne in the absence of a royal figurehead. If he succeeds, he's promised to rid the Realm of the Fair of what he considers the weaker races. That's one of the reasons why we're here."

Galan stopped short. "You consider us a weak race?"

"*I* don't." I reined Naith to block the path and waited for our procession to close in. "Abaddon's definition of *weaker* includes whoever stands in opposition. He's a manipulator bent on getting what he wants."

"And your point?"

Pain in my palms made me look down. I was strangling my reins, my nails cutting into my skin. Releasing my fists, I forced a smile. "My *point* is that Dark Elves hate Highbornes. Your people lived a life of privilege with the Queen while they felt slighted. In essence, you stole their destiny. With a nudge from Abaddon, the more volatile members of the Dark Elves might be convinced to join the Scourge and come knocking on your door looking for payback."

Tham barked a dry laugh. "Stole their destiny? If they wish to be exiled for millennia and restricted to a home range of nothing larger than a moon cycle's run, let us trade lives now."

The hairs on my nape stood on end, and I pivoted.

Aust circled my panther, stalking with such a hardened intensity I curled my hand over my dagger hilt and readied to dismount. In a blur, his arm speared at my head. I rolled off and landed in a crouch, dagger drawn.

In the next heartbeat, Aust spun away, a six-foot serpent with a triangular head coiled around his hand. As its spike tail furiously flailed, Aust crouched off the path and tossed the snake into the tangled growth of the jungle floor. "What does this mean for us?" he asked, brushing his hands against the thighs of his pants.

I swallowed, my mouth remained dry. The Elves seemed unfazed, but I might have peed a bit. I didn't dare look at Lexi. "Uh . . . it means that since the enchantment was lifted, others will come. Your village must transition back into the realm."

"And you two females will protect us?" Galan cleared his throat. The corners of his mouth twitched as his shoulders bounced. "Are you daft? Did I not just have you flat on your back with a knife to your throat? Did Aust not just save you from a stinger serpent?"

I urged Naith north and tried not to react to him. *Tighten up, Jade. You're working here.* "We don't pretend to be experts on your world, Galan, but as for your ambush . . . Lexi thought meeting on your terms might go smoother if we let you get the drop on us."

His face turned from pale amusement to rosy disbelief.

"Forgive me," I said, sweetening my tone, "you have no experience defending against a Scourge raid. You know nothing of their strategic strengths, tactics, or training. That's why Castian wants us in place."

"You and your sister?" Galan scanned Lexi with unveiled insolence. "Forgive *me, wen,* but how could that diminutive halfling offer anything in the way of protection?"

Lexi tensed to dismount, and I raised my hand. By her compliance, it was obvious she hadn't understood what was said, maybe just the tone. I could ignore him calling me *wen*—an Elven equivalent of a damsel—however, Lexi would skewer him for calling her a halfling.

"I assume your view on the capabilities of women is based on the Pollyanna flowers you grow in your village. I assure you, they don't represent women today, Galan."

"A female who fights and strategizes alongside a male cannot be much of a female."

"*Oh?*" Lexi drew her knife from her garter.

Great. *That* she understands.

Spinning the knife in her palm, the perfectly weighted steel swiveled and danced. Its jeweled hilt gleamed while the blade caught the morning light. "Jade, let me kick his ass."

I shot her a glare before she dismounted. "Since the start of the uprisings, the security of the realm has been policed by a group of elite warriors called the Talon. Lexi and I are both branded Talon enforcers. Believe it or not, we can fight and strategize and if you recall lying over me earlier, Galan," I glanced down his front to the lacings of his pants, "I carry *all* the attributes you seem to find attractive in a female."

Galan's ears flushed a brilliant pink. *Ha.*

Tham whistled between his teeth. "Might I ask where those brands are hiding?"

Lexi and I raised our wrists and revealed our tattoos. The Highbornes bristled as our marks appeared then disappeared. I brushed a wayward lock of hair out of my face. "Trust us. You'll have plenty of time to evaluate our abilities while we quest."

"And what *is* our quest?" Galan unsheathed his dagger and spun it lazily in his palm, matching Lexi's action. He was extremely coordinated, considering we were moving again, and he was also jogging along a forest path.

"Castian wants to recover a book."

"What book?" Galan frowned.

"Your ancestors studied the arcane arts under Queen Rheagan for thousands of years. They recorded the amassed knowledge of spells, from wizards and sorcerers, as well as Fae gods. During the Highbornes' exile, they retained possession of that spellbook. To eliminate the possibility of history repeating itself, Castian wants the book out of circulation and secured with him Behind the Veil."

"He is a god," Tham said. "Why not take it himself? Why send us?"

"Castian remains neutral in realm conflicts. He wants the three of you to retrieve the book and present it as an offering of good faith for your reinstatement."

Galan vaulted over a decaying tree, landing in line with me as he spoke. "Assuming we believe you, where might this compendium of the ancients be?"

"Sealed in a tomb in your northern mountains."

"That is a three-day journey each way," he bitched.

"Oh, sorry, there goes your weekend."

Tham ducked below a low hanging branch. "If the use of magic concealed the book, we have no way of retrieving it. Once our people began their life in exile, magic was forbidden. Our people have long forgotten the art of wizardry."

"Get us to the location, hotness," Lexi said. "We have people who will retrieve it." Lexi's gaze met mine, and I knew what was on her mind.

I groaned, urging Naith on. My stomach churned. "We'll travel 'til dusk then make camp. What kind of pace can you three manage long-term?"

"The same as you, resting atop your beasts of burden." Galan sheathed his dagger and secured his hair with a leather cord. "And what if we wish no part of this?"

Is he serious? "I'll take it up with Castian the next time we speak, though he gets a little testy when people challenge him."

"Testy?" Lexi snorted. "You'll lose body parts, Highborne."

"Speak to *Him*?" Galan shook his head. "You must think us beyond gullible to believe you, personally, have the ear of the gods."

I scowled. "No. Not gods. Just Castian."

Galan broke stride to glower, and I halted the group. "I am a bard in his service, Galan. My powers come from him."

He scrubbed his palm over his wide harsh smile. "Verily, if this is so, you should be able to offer some proof to that effect."

Whatever. I tilted my gaze to the canopy above. "Castian. It's a tough crowd down here. I'm getting heckled."

One would think that an emissary carrying my seal would be accepted on my word. No?

"I don't believe he means disrespect." I looked at Galan's cocky scowl. What an ass.

Yet he shows you disrespect, Mir.

"I'm a big girl."

You are generous to a fault.

Images of a story filled my mind. "Really? This is what you want me to use?" When nothing else came, I shrugged and met Galan's hard blue glare. "You sure you want to do this?"

"I am certain."

"Okay." I swung my leg over Naith's haunches and dropped to my feet. "On the night of your birthday celebration two months ago, you returned from dinner at your friend Nyssa's a little drunk and looking forward to getting to bed."

Galan stepped closer, subtle disbelief on his face. "Go on."

"In your room, you found an unexpected present waiting for you in, shall we say . . . an unwrapped and somewhat opened condition."

Galan looked stricken. His ears flushed pink as his hand came up to stop my narration. "Apologies, your point is made."

Tham's brow rose. "Wait. What was your gift? Carry on, Jade."

With his hand still up, Galan looked abashed. "Tham, be done with this. I concede. Indeed, she knows that which cannot be known. Let us continue our travels."

"His gift wasn't a *what*, Tham, it was a *who*." I pressed on, enjoying Galan's discomfort more than I should. "So, Galan's little birthday present wasn't to his liking. He and this Yavanna woman had words."

"Yavanna? Unwrapped?" Tham's grin grew ridiculously full, exposing a dimple on his right cheek. "Sweet Shalana, what did you do?"

Galan dropped his hands and shifted rolled back on his heels. "Fine. If the story must be told, I shall do the telling. You know, I will not entertain within my home. My sister sleeps in the adjoining chamber and is a young female of virtue."

"However," Tham interjected, "Yavanna is ambitious."

Galan nodded. "I asked her with a gentlemale's grace to clothe herself and leave. When she refused and proceeded in her advances, I placed her garments into her lap, wrapped her in the coverlet she sat upon, and tossed the entire bundle out my chamber window."

"Is that what happened to the ganderberry patch?" Tham's mouth gaped open while he shook with laughter. "Your father accused half the young in the village of breaking the stalks."

Aust turned to tie his hair back, hiding his grin.

"I imagine Yavanna was vexed." Tham wiped tears from his eyes. "And that she retaliated?"

He glowered at me and clenched his teeth.

Tham turned to me. "Oh, Jade, let us hear the entire tale."

I had to laugh at the sheer enjoyment on Tham's face. "Well, unbeknownst to the two of you, Yavanna followed you to the hot springs the next day and added something to Galan's pants while you were in the water."

Tham choked, sputtering for air. "I remember this. Just after we returned home, Galan had the worst case of male—"

"—That was not humorous at all," Galan snapped. He grimaced as he adjusted himself. "The rash from the *Heca* oil spread until I could neither sit nor appear in public without a tunic. Now, may we continue?"

CHAPTER FIVE

*B*y early afternoon the tropical sun had become a broiling force. Even under the canopy of the jungle, I was a wilting flower trapped under greenhouse glass. Leather pants were great in battle but less than ideal shrink-wrapped to your body. Lifting the length of my hair off my back, I prayed for a breeze. No such luck.

I cursed the Elves. They looked as fresh as they had at the break of dawn. No sweat. No red cheeks. No clothing sticking to their cracks and crevices. Faolan was the only one drooping. Over the past few hours, Aust's wolf had ceased running willy-nilly from one Highborne to another and back again. Now she merely kept pace at Aust's heel, and her long pink tongue lolled out to the side.

"I thought Faolan wasn't allowed to join your quest," I said. Aust broke stride utterly nonplussed, and it took me a moment to understand his reaction. "Sorry. We saw part of your ceremony in Lexi's vision. That's how we came to find you."

"A vision?" Aust said, clearly unsettled.

"Lexi sees things. At your *Ambar Lenn* ceremony, you said Faolan had to stay behind."

He nodded, mussing his wolf's thick silver ruff. "Um, yes, that was my understanding. However, my sire seems to have sent her along regardless."

After another long silence, we came to a clearing beside a stream. I dismounted, rubbing my hands down my thighs to adjust the bunching of my leathers. Chatting about nothing, in particular, Lexi and I pulled at our tank-tops from where they'd shrunk to every curve we possessed. Lexi giggled and tilted her head toward the Elves. They had dropped their gear and eyed us from the water's edge.

Growing up around male warriors, we were neither modest nor self-conscious. Hiding a silent chuckle, I drifted into the forest in the other direction to take care of my more basic needs. When I got back, Lexi was leaning against the flat of a large rock, fanning herself like Cleopatra with a broad, green leaf.

Tham flashed a quirky grin. "I wondered how it works, ladies—the realm, our enchantment, the rest of it?"

Aust and Galan bounded from water and up the bank before leaning against the trunks of two broad trees.

"That is a mind-bender," Lexi said, gesturing for Naith and Puff to go get a drink.

I felt around in my backpack for a water bottle and took a swig. Warm. Gross. I chucked it back in. "Since the exile of your ancestors, our world evolved in some ways and remained essentially unchanged in others. There were periods in time when dragons were slain, witches and wizards were staked and burned, and our way of life was threatened by religion and modernization."

"What was the objection?" Aust stepped to the bank where he'd dropped his quiver and peeled off his vest. After rolling up his pant-legs, he escorted all three animals into the shallows of the nearby stream.

"Over time, people stopped believing in pagan gods, and many new belief systems took root. The followers of these new religions thought it was blasphemous to believe in fantastical creatures and magical powers. To eliminate the problem, they tried to eliminate everything unique about our realm."

"Verily, they did not succeed." Tham rolled his pants and waded into the water as well. He pulled Faolan's ebony ear and snickered when she snapped at his fingers.

"Many races wanted to live without fear or prejudice," I said. "All the Pantheon leaders Behind the Veil, from all sources of power, established protected areas for their more conspicuous realm members. Castian focused on Centaurs, Elves, Sprights, dragons, griffons, etc. In essence, the Realm of the Fair hasn't changed from the days of your exile. We just live unseen by Mundanes of the Modern Realm.

"Mundanes?" Tham snatched his fingertips back from another crack of Faolan's jaws.

"Non-realm humans. Geographically, the Realm of the Fair occupies areas on every continent." Perplexed looks met me on all sides. "What you need to know is this. Our lands are enchanted the same way your valley was. When non-realm humans reach the borders, they are transported across to the opposite side. It's such a seamless journey Mundanes don't realize they've made it. They find themselves traveling the same path in the same direction they were and are none the wiser. At most, they get a sense of déjà-vu, like they've been there before."

"And you can access this Modern Realm?" Tham asked.

"We have Portal Gates, which act as doorways between the two realms."

"Is that how you two traveled here?"

"No, we Flashed." I peeled the muscle shirt suctioned to my chest and prayed, yet again, for a breeze. "Certain races have the natural ability to travel from place to place within this realm or the other by simply wishing to do so."

"Do you?"

"No. Castian Flashed us here." I wiped at the sweat beading down from my forehead. "Unfortunately, the Scourge can Flash too, and now that your exile is over, they will come."

Back on the trail, I leaned from side to side, stretching my aches. It had been ages since Naith, and I took an extended road-trip, and I was saddle sore. If only there were a spa with a hot bath and an even hotter masseur in my future.

Not bloody likely.

"Those are beautiful," I said, admiring the flights of the arrows jostling in Tham's quiver.

"Gratitude. Galan and I fletched them with golden eagle feathers we collected along the jagged ledge of our southern meadow. We were bloodied retrieving them from the nests, yet pleased with the result." Tham slid a sideways glance at me, and his dimple reappeared. "Jade, would you tell us more about your world?"

I pulled my water bottle from my bag and took a long swallow. "Maximus Reign, our adoptive father, is a respected warrior and quite famous in our realm. When the Scourge attacks started, he established a sanctuary on a pristine mountain topped with a castle and called it Haven. Now, there are more than a dozen Haven sites around the world where people of any race can live in peace."

"And what does your Haven offer?"

I listed a dozen things that drew people to Haven, safety, shops, community, but Tham seemed most intrigued by The Academy of Affinities.

"It's a training center," I explained, "for people with gifts from the Fae gods, those studying wizardry or those training to become Talon enforcers. Lexi and I and are instructors and Julian and Bruin, our adoptive brothers, teach when they're available as well."

"Wizardry?" Tham hopped a rock and landed without a sound, his smile fading. "The two of you teach wizardry?" Though his tone was neutral, his eyes narrowed.

"No, not us. I have an affinity for healing, so I teach that and herbology."

Aust tilted his head, pushed off a log, and moved his run closer. Tham regained some of his natural swagger and moved closer to my sister. "And you, Lexi? What do you teach?"

"Weapons and attacks." Her tone remained casual, but the glitter in her purple eyes spoke of her anticipation for their reaction. "Battle armor, weapon mastery, strategic assaults." She drew her dagger and spun it, so the business end pointed at Galan. Batting her eyes, she smiled extra sweet. "And contrary to what some people think, I am all female."

The clearing Aust chose to make camp for the night overlooked the valley to the north. Bordered on two sides by forest, it had several large, jutting rocks for defensive positions and a sheer three-hundred-foot drop at the far end. I hadn't realized we changed altitude.

Then again, I'd never been a Girl Scout.

Thank the gods for the soft grasses covering the hard-packed ground in our camping area and for the nearby stream, which ran clean and refreshing.

From the cliff edge, Tham pointed to a set of distant peaks, violet against a grey-dusky sky. "That craggy formation is Dragon's Peak, a dormant volcano. It is said to be the entry point our ancestors used to access the valley. I would wager the compendium is somewhere within the belly of that dragon."

I nodded. "Good. Then that's where we'll start."

"With Castian's grace," Galan said, stepping in behind us, "we shall retrieve this compendium and be home within a sennight."

Tham patted Galan's shoulder then jogged to the mound of their belongings. After sifting through the pile, he straightened with three wineskins. "Faolan, come."

Faolan bounded after him, ebony nose to the ground, sniffing the wild grasses as she ran toward the water. Galan gathered sticks and dried palm fronds, cleared an area of debris, and then brushed off an area of glittery stone on the ground. He fished around in the leather pouch he wore and came out with something small and dark. Staring at his hand, a secret smile flirted at the corners of his mouth.

"Something funny?" I asked, kneeling beside him to get a better look. The smile disappeared as his hand clamped shut. Ignoring the wave of attitude, I waited, watching the shadows in the forest deepen around us. I smelled the night breeze for any hint of Scourge funk. Nothing came back to me, beyond the pungency of moss, earth, and the rainforest itself.

Finally, he opened his hand and let me study the non-descript green stone in his palm. "A gift for my *Ambar Lenn*. A strike-stone in the shape of a frog is said to bring good fortune."

How one could view the lump of stone in his hand and see a frog was beyond even my vivid imagination. Galan's jaw muscles twitched and tightened as he withdrew to his thoughts and refocused on building the fire.

I could have helped him. I controlled flames in my sleep. Before I decided if he would find it offensive to be aided by a lowly female, he pulled some Pyro-hocus-pocus, and his little flame was glowing like a faerie ring. After adding a mound of dried palm, he coaxed and caressed the tiny wisps of orange until the fire took hold. When he stood to light the torches, I joined Lexi in walking the perimeter.

By the time the light faded, my sister and I knew the ins and outs of the surrounding area and turned Puff and Naith loose beneath a cluster of mango trees. The spot was rank with the super-sweet stench of fruit passed its best-before date. The over-ripened buffet lay scattered and fermenting on the damp ground, just waiting for Puff.

Naith was another story. Reaching into the side-bag of the saddle, I unwrapped and tossed down a lamb joint Cook had sent along for him. While he licked his treat, I loosened the cinch beneath his velvety belly, removed the harnesses, and hefted the saddle off his back.

"May I be of aid?" Aust accepted my burden and straddled it over a wide log. "Astounding creatures, your mounts."

Lexi handed him her saddle, which was half the size of mine, and patted Aust's cheek. "I'll leave you to it then." She skipped off to sit in front of the fire with Galan and Tham.

"Apologies. Have I run her off?"

I laughed, shaking my head. "No. Lexi welcomes any opportunity to escape chores. If it weren't for our housekeeping staff at our Academy, she'd go through life naked and starving. As it is, she lives like a princess."

Aust smiled, drawing closer to my panther. "You are blessed to have siblings."

I nodded. *Was my destiny to lose my parents and be raised by Reign?* Hanging the saddle blanket over a low branch to air out, I followed

JL MADORE

Aust's gaze back to my cat. "Would you like to meet Naith? Officially, I mean."

His smile broadened, and he bowed. "Indeed, I would."

I clapped my hands, and Naith sprang in the air between us. His large bone hung precariously from the corner of his mouth. "Come here, big guy."

As Naith padded over, Aust squared his shoulders and inventoried my feline's black velvet pelt. "He is a powerful beast," he said, his silky voice deep with reverence. "Sinew and bone held in reserve. Yet a cub, he already possesses the strength of a dozen males."

I took the bone, and Naith opened his mouth slightly agape. He curled his upper lip and breathed deep. Aust cocked his head, listening to the breathy chuffing.

"He's smelling you," I said. "Or tasting your scent would probably be more accurate."

"His sense of smell is in his mouth?" Aust raised his hand, holding the back of it to Naith's muzzle. "Astounding."

"He's referred to as a panther but is actually a melanistic jaguar. Normally his breed is gold mottled with brown and black spots. Black is rare. When the sun hits his side at the right angle, you can see his spots, hidden in plain sight."

Aust scrubbed Naith's muzzle and bent to look straight into his amber eyes.

I moved to intercede, but Naith didn't bristle. *Weird.* He always became aggressive when men looked him straight in the eye. It was a dominance thing.

Aust's expression blanked out as subtle energy tingled through my body. The sensation was similar to Lexi's visions channeling. Naith chuffed a satisfied breath, his shoulder muscles easing, as his tail dropped to sway in a lazy arc.

"Aust? What are you doing with Naith?"

He froze, and his shoulders sagged. "Apologies. I, uh—"

"Don't apologize. Do you have an affinity with animals?"

He shot a quick glance over his shoulder. "I speak not of it. In my village, I am considered an aberration."

"What? Why? Affinities are a blessing from the gods."

"Mayhap." He leaned closer and lowered his voice. "My community believes magic is the evil which led to our fall from grace. They see my ability as sorcery lying dormant in my soul." Something flickered across his face, a dark shadow of some painful memory.

Without conscious thought, I raised my hand to his cheek and paused when my palm was about to touch his skin. Meeting his stare with as much encouragement as I possessed, I bit the bullet. "Aust, may I touch you with my gift? It won't hurt."

After a long moment, he nodded. "This is Fate's Journey, after all."

I cupped his cheek. When he met my other hand with his, we laced fingers, and his eyes rolled closed. Aust's affinity surged in strands of energy, extensive, vibrant ribbons of power. The kaleidoscope of colors burst and flickered inside my eyelids like a fireworks finale against a night sky. After who knows how long, I eased out of the connection.

"Jade, I—" His ears flushed right to the tips, his eyes a brilliant, shimmering blue.

It was then I realized we had an audience. Reading the expressions of the peanut gallery, Lexi looked dazzled, Tham seemed amused, and Galan was... flat-out pissed?

Aust dropped my hand and stepped away. "I, uh, shall finish tending the animals."

"What was *that*?" Lexi's eyebrows disappeared under her crown of spiky bangs.

I shook my hands, trying to clear the residual tingle. "He's so strong. And with no training, he's communicating with animals. Can you imagine?"

Lexi shrugged, skipped over to grab her bag, and after rummaging through the disarray of her packing, straightened with the Victoria's Secret catalog in hand.

"What have you there, little one?" Tham sidled close beside her on the log lain close to the fire. Speaking Draconic made Tham's lilt thicker and even sexier.

Lexi giggled and looked across to me. "Hey, Jade, could you hand me that torch? I want to enlighten Tham on a few other things he's been missing."

"Sure." I grabbed the wooden handle, realizing too late that the strapping was loose. As I raised the torch, the burner tilted, slid off, and landed on my bare forearm. I roared and threw the thing to the ground. "*Ow*, for fuck's sake!" The stench of singed flesh burned my nostrils. My arm screamed as an ugly welt appeared. A string of curses rolled off my tongue.

The Elves blinked, and then Aust raced to the tree line, saying something about *yrma* leaf.

Tham grabbed my elbow and thrust my hand to the sky. "Raise it. The receding blood will reduce the throb."

Galan pushed past Lexi with a bottle of unguent from his pouch.

Lexi did an oh-no-you-didn't double take then snatched my arm from his grasp. I hissed as she eyeballed the blister. "Ew, that's gross. Be more careful, Jade. Conjured or not, fire is hot."

I rolled my eyes as she giggled at her rhyming wisdom. "Thanks." Hovering my good hand over the damage for one focused pass, the pain dissolved. Healed. I sighed as smooth, copper skin replaced the pulsing pink blister.

The Elven trio fell silent, their faces unreadable. "Sorry for the swearing," I said, feeling the heat of my cheeks against the cooling night air. "Being raised by a warrior has given Lexi and me a rather descriptive vocabulary." The Elves didn't respond. "What?"

"You are a sorceress." Galan's tone sliced the air.

"No." I stared back, trying not to laugh. He glared at my arm. "That? No, I'm a healer."

"A very talented healer," Lexi said.

As they stared at me, I had the urge to check to see if I'd suddenly grown a second head. "I told you I had an affinity for healing. Is there a problem?"

There was a long silence before Aust cleared his throat. "We simply. . ." He bent and began a gentle massage of Faolan's ebony ears. When he looked up, the suspicion in his expression had softened.

"Fash not, our conditioning regarding magic and its lures to evil are not easily discounted."

"Wha—I, uh, there's nothing evil about what I do. My power comes straight from Castian, like your ability to speak with animals. I am not a sorceress. I heal people."

Tham closed his mouth and nodded.

Torn by the looks of bewilderment, I picked up the discarded torch and turned to repair it. Over Lexi's shoulder, I caught movement in the trees.

It couldn't be.

My heart stopped mid-beat the minute his face caught the firelight. "Oh shit."

CHAPTER SIX

Tham's eyes widened as the warrior approached. A fantastic, brindle mane of hair bounced with each long stride. The multi-colored combination of gold, black, and browns was set off by the glow of the fire. In the dim light, his deep-set charcoal eyes and sharp-cut jaw cast imposing dark shadows. "Should we be concerned?" he asked.

"No," I said, breathing deep. "He's not here for you."

"Who is he here for?" Tham stepped behind Lexi, edging toward his sword.

"*Us*," Lexi and I both said in unison.

Who could blame the Highbornes for staring? Nothing like this man had ever been in their valley. Maximus Reign, our father, was intimidating, from his leather battle-vest sheathed with weapons to his blade-tipped shit-kickers. Scarred and chiseled from a lifetime of fighting, he was brutally striking. He stormed into our camp, leaving a wake of branches and dust swirling in mini sandstorms behind him. When the firelight illuminated the vein pulsing beside his temple, I knew we were in trouble.

"He stands head and shoulders above every male in our village," Aust whispered.

"And as broad as two," Tham said. "Are we to fight him?"

Lexi barked a laugh. "You'll never walk again if you try."

I shook my head. "No, as lethal as he is, he's our father. You stay out of his way."

"I am surprisingly comfortable with that."

My father drew closer as Tham, and the others dissolved into the shadows. Without acknowledging anyone else, he thrust his finger out. "*You* and *you*, over *there*."

Lexi and I hustled our butts behind him, jogging to keep up with his yard-long strides. Reign paced to the edge of the clearing, rebounded, and wheeled on us. "Jade, I don't need a fucking audience. *Veil us.*"

"Castian, come to me." I waited until my bard powers surged then circled my hand in a swooping arch. "Veil of Silence, surround us."

Within our bubble of privacy, Reign let loose. "What the *hell* is this? I get back to the castle, and Julian says there was an attack at the Hearthstone and that Castian sent you out on a mission? Just the two of you? What if you get ambushed? What if Abaddon and his men descend on your party? I don't even have the *fucking intel*. You know the rules, girls. They're in place for your safety. What am I supposed to do about this?" He proceeded to curse a long, colorful rant of things which were crude and though I didn't point it out—anatomically impossible.

It was *sooo* not the time to assert our independence, so we settled in.

It took a bit to calm him down. Only after a dozen 'sorrys', two dozen 'yes sirs,' and three dozen 'it won't happen agains,' did he release us from the intensity of his glower and yank us into his arms. We said nothing about his crushing embrace or the scratchy, whiskery kiss we each got on our cheek. As the tension eased from his frame, the mottling drained from his face. "All right. I'm here now, and I've sent for Cowboy, Sin, and Savage to join us."

"*No!*" I said. "Castian trusted us to do this on our own."

Reign scowled. "It's not about trust. It's about safety."

"If it were Cowboy and Savage escorting the Elves, would you assign three more Talon?"

I had him by the balls on that one, and we both knew it. He would never underestimate his men or undermine their authority in the field. Reign's hard stare glared back at me. "Fine. I'll Flash you a few at a time to your destination, and we'll polish off your mission."

"No. Part of our mission is to spend the week gaining their trust and learning about their lives before we get to their village. They hate magic. Flashing would set us back."

"Trust us, Reign," Lexi said. "We're good."

When he didn't argue, I lifted the veil, and the sounds of the rainforest returned.

"Has everything been worked out?" Tham shot a sharp look from Lexi to Reign to me.

I nodded. "Reign was concerned when he returned to Haven and learned Castian had sent us on a mission without his approval." *Understatement of the century.*

"Without *his* approval?" Tham repeated, raising a brow. "Pardon my inquiring, would the God of Fae need approval to set you on a task?"

"Fucking right!" Reign snapped, lunging right up into Tham's grille. The elf paled and stumbled back. "The Talon is *mine*. These girls are *mine*. No one—not even the all mighty Castian—gets to put them in danger."

Lexi slipped between Reign and Tham and reached up to place a delicate hand on Reign's chest. The father-daughter dynamic of those two was a mountain-molehill kind of thing. However, the four-foot-seven molehill had always had the advantage. Craning her head, Lexi's dark lashes batted over her eyes. "There's no problem here, Reign. We're fine."

Tham bowed his head and offered Reign his hand. "Apologies, sir, I meant no offense. I am Thamior, and these are my brethren, Galanodel, and Aust."

Ignoring the proffered hand, he stepped to Lexi and me. His hand closed over the worn grip of his dagger, and he turned a lethal glare on the Highborne trio. "Gentlemen, we need to have a convo on how my daughters are to be treated this week."

"What might a convo—" Tham choked, as Reign surged forward.

Lexi widened her eyes at me, but I let it play out.

As Reign laid down the law, the three Elves stood stock-still and silent, like children being schooled by a headmaster. Thank. The. Gods.

"Good. Glad we're crystal on what's what." Reign's obsidian gaze danced in the shadows of the campfire. They'd seem cold and dark to those who didn't know better. Hell, to me, too, at times. His knuckles cracked as his fists tightened, and with no attempt at subtlety, he assessed each of the Highbornes. His expression was a mask as his hand slid over the battle-ax hanging at his side. "These women are priceless treasures. If something happens to them, if they are injured, mistreated, or even if you upset their delicate natures, you will learn why I am known as The Reign of Terror. You feel me?"

"Feel you?" Tham frowned. "Am I to lay hands on you?"

"*Fuck no!*" Reign growled, the get-the-hell-away-from-me burning in his eyes.

"Easy," I said, stepping in. "We're good. We've got this."

A shadow fell across his face before he hid it. He took my arm in a firm grip and turned me to face him. "I meant to be back for you. Last night. I left you a message."

"I got it and one from Bruin too. Everyone's busy keeping all the balls in the air."

Reign frowned. "I'm not too busy for my kids. Never."

"I'm fine." I raised my fingers and smoothed the crease from his brow. "Lexi took good care of me. We went out and had a few drinks."

"Yeah, but Samuel was a dick," Lexi said. I tried to drill her into silence with my stare. She ignored me. "The SOB made her cry, Reign, on the solstice of all nights."

I'd seen men crazed with murderous intent in battle, the promise of violence in their eyes, the clenching of their jaw to the point you thought the bones would shatter. They had nothing on Reign. His frame stiffened until I thought he might break out of his skin. A gust

JL MADORE

of cold air blasted me as he zoned in on Lexi. "What did he *say* to her, Princess?"

She shrugged. "I don't know exactly. I was outside by then—"

"Nothing," I said, stepping between them. "He was talking trash. Our dust will settle, and I'll make things right with him." My stomach flipped, seeing the resolve in my father's eyes.

Oh no. No, no, no.

"You will *not* kill or maim him in any way. Promise me."

Reign stroked the head of his battle-ax, a horrifying look of determination solidifying in his expression. "I'll promise you no such thing. Now, I need to get back."

"Reign. I mean it." I chased behind him as he stormed past the fire. "Do *not* fight my battles. Samuel is my problem. I'm a big girl."

Reign stroked a calloused hand over my hair and tugged a lock. "I swore you'd never stand alone, and you never will."

Thank the gods for Maximus Reign.

As he neared the edge of our camp, Reign tipped his head to the starlit sky. "Castian, if you expect my girls to sleep in the dirt with snakes and spiders, think again. Do something about this, or we'll have words."

A sizzle in the brisk night air built to a buzz, then crackled as a tent appeared in the clearing behind us. It was the size of a small shed from the outside but would be a three-roomed royal suite on the interior. Reign pulled back a heavy brocade flap and leaned inside for a quick inspection. "That'll do." He turned a severe scowl to Lexi and me and clenched his jaw. "Okay, I'm leaving you to it. Got your phones?"

Lexi and I produced the sexy new phones Julian gave us.

"Heads on a swivel, right? Scourge are never far away, and they love a good ambush. Don't let your guards down. I'll keep my phone with me. Check-in every couple of hours, or you'll have the entire Talon force here. Got it?" He waited until we nodded then strode off. Marching toward the thick of the forest, he faded into the ether, leaving us staring at nothing.

"Again, with the magic." Galan muttered.

"Don't start." I held up my hand and walked my backpack over to the tent. My patience had worn thin, and I was achy and sore from the ride. "I told you about Flashing earlier. It's a form of transportation, nothing more. I also told you that I had an affinity for healing."

"It is still magic."

Lexi spun a slow circle, her head dropping back to address the heavens. "Castian, babe, could you Martha Stewart us a few refreshments? A girl's gotta eat."

Castian babe?

I raised my gaze to the heavens. "You shouldn't encourage her, Sire."

When no buffet appeared, Lexi crossed her arms tight against her chest. "Would it hurt for you to back me up? Now we'll be sucking on tree bark and crunching grubs all week."

"Nonsense," Tham said. "Give the three of us a moment, and we can surely fill your stomachs. There are fish in the stream, greens in the forest and berries and nuts abound."

"Yum, nuts, and berries." Lexi stuck her tongue out at me. "And me without red wine."

Tham scratched his head. "I wonder what our *Ambar Lenn* might have been, had you, females, not dropped into our lives."

"*Boring.*" Lexi and I answered in stereo.

It was four a.m. when I woke, heated from a restless sleep of bold blue eyes and electric touches. I shook my head and punched my pillow, waiting for my pulse to slow and the mass of estrogen pumping through my body to settle the hell down. What was with me? Never had a man affected me the way this arrogant, coolly self-possessed Elf did. I couldn't fathom why I was responding to him, Tham and Aust were just as hot and waaay nicer.

The *neeeeee* of what I hoped was a simple mosquito singing in my ear, distracted me from insanity. Waving blindly through the frosty night air of the tent, male voices whispered outside. Eavesdropping wasn't my thing but snuggled within the warmth of my blankets with only a layer of canvas between me and the clearing. I couldn't help overhearing.

"—the father simply vanished. Are you saying we should accept magic?" Impressive. Galan's disdain was thick, even in hushed tones. "And what will the release of exile mean to us?"

"I have no answers. Nonetheless—"

"Tham, I know you. You are dancing at the prospect of adventure and change."

"Are you *not*? Galan, we have lived a century of our lives, looking to the stars, dreaming of what lay beyond this valley. We can finally leave it behind, the formality, the pompous judgment, and the narrow mindedness."

"I understand how alluring it seems. Be wary. We know nothing of these females and even less of the lives they lead."

"I know they are witty, passionate, and stunningly beautiful. Tell me you can gaze into Jade's green, gemstone eyes or Lexi's purple and not become entranced. And their hair—not eleventy shades of gold, Galan, *red*, deep elderberry with sparks of copper or black as a starless night sky. It is incredible. Even their father's hair was a marvel, though I would never say so."

"Aesthetics notwithstanding, I find Jade very unsettling."

Tham's chuckle rumbled low. "You were unsettled before you knew she was magical."

The stirring of the trees behind the tent brought soft, almost silent footsteps into play. "I saw her soul, Galan," Aust whispered. "Jade *is* the female she claims to be and more."

"And," Tham said, still chuckling, "you enjoyed yourself well, lying over her in the scrub. Utterly bewitched, you were."

"And by what? Resplendent as she is, she wields magic."

"In Castian's service," Aust said.

There was a long pause before Tham broke the silence. "Imagine the village when we return with two human females and the compendium of the ancients."

Galan laughed. "The Council of Elders will be beside themselves: meetings held, prayers said, offerings lain. Utter chaos. Very undignified."

Tham laughed now too. "And your sire's face when we saunter

into the courtyard with Castian's envoys... and they are females... and they look like that!" The crackle of sparks snapping followed the hollow *clunk* of wood-on-wood at the bonfire. "Galan, six days, and you shall be back with Lia, head held high. Verily, before these females appeared, we had no notion of the purpose of our quest. We may never have found our enlightened path."

"True, though how—"

"How do you suppose that man is their father?" Tham whispered over the croaking of frog songs. "There is no resemblance. Jade is voluptuous and copper-skinned, Lexi, a pale little halfling with the insouciance of an imp, and Reign, a beast of a male and those black eyes—"

"Mayhap humans do not share physical traits as we do," Aust said.

"I would wager the little one is a lightning strike in a skirmish," Galan whispered. "Did you see how her gaze flared in challenge this morn, how she handled her dagger?"

"Her name is Lexi," Tham said. "It would do you well to involve yourself in polite conversation. You have yet to speak one word of Draconic while knowing Lexi cannot understand Elvish well. They are engaging females, and you have been nothing short of rude."

"One of us needs to remain objective."

There was a heavy sigh before Tham spoke. "After seeing their father, do you suppose they are the warriors they claim themselves to be?"

"Irrelevant. They are female. To think themselves enough to best a male is ridiculous."

"Jade can curse as well as a male," Tham said.

"Did you understand what was said?"

"No, yet still, it was fascinating."

CHAPTER SEVEN

"*If* human females are like those of our village, we shall sit most of the day in wait. Females are far too delicate to be warriors and live rough. They need comforts."

What a pompous ass! I flipped back the flap of the tent and painted on a smile. "Now Galan, did you wake up on the wrong side of the bedroll and find yourself in the Middle Ages?" I captured the haphazard craziness of my morning scare-do and bound it with an elastic. "FYI, I told you yesterday not to make assumptions about modern women. We don't like it."

Galan stood at the cliff edge, looking out over the valley. His ears flushed pink, but he didn't have anything more to say.

I was still counting to ten when I inhaled. "Bless you, Castian." The scent of French Caramel filled my senses and practically carried me to the java hut. Well, it wasn't so much a hut really, but a pot of French Caramel and a carton of half and half sitting on a rock beside my tent. I picked up an oversized mug and mixed up a double-double for Lexi and double milk for me. The smell made me moan, the taste…

Mmm, one sip of the caramelotta ambrosia, and I could face anything.

Naith sauntered from the trees and pushed his head against my chest. I staggered back, holding my mug out to one side. "Good morning, puss." I nuzzled my face into his velvety scruff. He smelled like one of those rainforest air fresheners you hang in the closet. I patted him, grinning as the rumble of his purr vibrated in my chest.

"Pay my brother no mind," Tham said. "If warriors can look like you, I shall be delighted to stand beside you in battle."

Faolan pranced over and preened in front of Naith. With her dark tail bristled and held straight as a maypole, the she-wolf scratched at the dirt, showcasing her feminine attributes for the appraisal of my sleek ebony jaguar.

"Faolan is aware she is a wolf, is she not?" Tham passed his hand over his mouth, hiding his smile. "And Naith is an extremely oversized cat."

Aust's gaze softened as Faolan brushed her muzzle against my mount. Playfully mipping his jaw and whiskers, her tail cut through the air like a sword. "Verily she is, yet she cannot tame her affections any more than the rest of us."

Galan finished brooding at the ledge and joined us, his smooth, stalking stride a predator's prowl. Keeping his eyes fixed on me, he scooped up his pack. "May we begin our day?"

"In a minute," I said, then eased Galan's bag from his hand and held it out to Tham. "We need to clear the air first. How about some early morning hand-to-hand?" I smiled, hoping it came off sweet and inviting. "If you're up for it."

Tham's jaw dropped, and he looked from me to Galan and back again. In a hot-minute, he and Aust snatched up the other satchels and bedrolls and moved them out of our way.

Galan scrubbed his fingers through his hair. "This is unnecessary, Jade. Apologies if I offended your delicate nature. I shall endeavor to be more aware of your sensitivities in the future."

I eyed the clearing the boys had made and checked my ponytail. "Sensitivities. Hmm. Well, I accept your snide apology, but actually, I insist."

Galan was athletic and lithe, corded with muscle, and carried himself with total co-ordination. Gods, he annoyed me. Curling my finger, I beckoned him forward. "What are you made of Highborne, other than haughty arrogance?"

After shrugging out of his vest, he sunk into position and slapped away my hand. "Fash not, female, I shall try not to bruise you overmuch." Highbornes had once been the protectors of the realm. I wondered if they'd kept up their skills all these years. Galan started a slow, intricate circle of footwork. "I find it endearing, however misguided, you think yourself competent to challenge a male."

My fury needle jerked out of 'School Him' and buried deep into 'Kick-his-Ass' territory. With Bruin, Julian, and Lexi around, I had thick skin. But Galan wasn't spewing trash—he believed this crap. "It's chauvinistic to judge my competency as a fighter based on me having breasts." I pivoted, positioning to receive Galan's offensive.

Watching. Waiting. Galan's nostrils flared, and he lunged. We covered the clearing, blocking, and batting as we measured each other's strengths. He was good, honestly better than I thought, though I'd never admit that. Fists and feet, knees and knuckles, grunts, and groans.

Galan was poised, muscles rippling. He circled, searching for my weakness. *Keep searching Highborne.* He avoided my backhand and the cuff to his ear but didn't get far enough from my sweeping kick. My knee connected. His breath hissed from his lungs as I nailed his ribcage. Then, capitalizing on his momentary weakness, I thrust a palm strike to his face.

Galan grunted as his head whiplashed back. Blood arched into the air, spraying the feathery leaves of a mutant fern behind him. Wiping his hand along his mouth, he spat scarlet to the grass. "My underestimation of you has been remedied. Ready yourself, female."

Ding-ding-ding. Round two.

We began again, this time with more strength behind his attacks. *Good. Give it.*

Galan made a rookie slip and stepped into a compromised position. Dropping low, I swiped his feet and turtled him onto his back. I slammed my foot toward his solar plexus. His blurring reflexes saved him from the blow. He rolled away then back again, lightning-fast, grabbing my leg. The momentum flipped me on my back.

He straddled my waist, secured my wrists, and pinned me to the dirt. "Do you concede?" A fine sheen of sweat beaded his brow, while his cheeks mottled with a healthy flush. Gods, he was cute. He didn't think that he had me, did he? The gall of this man was astonishing.

"Not even close." My legs came up from behind his head and wrapped across his chest. A solid heave and my shoulder lariat flung him back to the ground. I sprung to my feet as Galan kipped to his.

My roundhouse landed square on his chest, but he managed to capture my foot. Using his body as leverage, I pushed off, flipped backward, and cart-wheeled to my feet.

He stumbled into saving his fall. The corners of his mouth twitched. *Surprised?*

I dove to the door of the tent, grabbed my bullwhip, and uncoiled its twelve-foot length. It was a gift from Reign on my twelfth birthday, along with training three times a week. The *crack* that sliced through the air gave me the warm-and-tinglies.

As I advanced, Galan sprang back into a string of acrobatic spins and flips, gaining distance from the tail of my weapon. His speed and grace sucked the breath out of me. Rolling to his knees he grabbed a good-sized stick off the ground and moved toward me.

Okay, I'll bite. What's the stick for? "I didn't realize you were a gymnast, Galan."

He bowed and twirled the stick in his hand like a baton. Over. Under. Over. Under.

I snapped my whip, and before I saw him move, he'd caught the length of leather with his stick and wound it. A rookie play, but I couldn't help but watch him move. In a blur, he drew me in like a fish on a line. In the next moment, he yanked my body against his, spun me in his arms and slammed me hard against the wide, rough trunk of a massive tree. My shoulder screamed in protest as he pinned me, his thigh thrust between my legs.

I sucked in a labored breath, my excitement having nothing to do with physical exertion and everything to do with Galan's proximity and his raw masculine strength. My pulse thundered in my ears as my heart pounded for freedom. Could Galan hear my traitorous organ misbehaving? Full sensuous lips curved into a half-hearted smile then dipped toward the column of my neck. He inhaled.

The noise of my heart quieted, replaced by a warmth spreading in the pit of my stomach and heading south. When he lifted his gaze, I was transfixed, caught up in brilliant blue eyes just inches from mine. *Dwinn.* The word echoed in my mind. My skin tingled to life.

Something was happening.

I silenced my inner voice and drew a deep breath. Suede mixed with sunshine. Gods, he made my mouth water. The pupils of his eyes flared as he studied me. "Galan." My voice was far too excited for my liking. "I'm impressed. You can bring it for a pampered boy from the valley."

Galan shook his head and stepped back. Without his frame for support, I stumbled, catching myself before I took a header into the scrub. His eyes bore into mine, his face stoic and unamused. "Not much of a challenge. As I expected, you fight like a female."

Seriously? Stepping against him, I trailed a shaky hand up to his bare chest to the smooth ivory column of his neck. His pulse was pounding against my palm, his skin hot and slick from sparring. I took a deep breath. "Galan, if I fought like a girl, I would have done this."

In one motion, I yanked a fistful of silver hair and thrust my knee into his groin. As he sank to his knees, I shoved him away. "Asshole."

"Ohhh!" came the chorus from the peanut gallery as Galan crumpled to the dirt.

My hands were twitching, throwing off sparks like holiday sparklers. I stomped away. *Dammit, what is happening to me?* My sister doubled over laughing, grabbing the tent for support. "Not one word, Lexi. I mean it. Not. One. Word."

The rest of the second day passed without incident. Well, if riding for hours through a rainforest with Highborne Elves could be considered uneventful. Around mid-day, Aust moved us from the path along the water and cut through a section of thicker forest. We pressed on, looking for a rock formation along the western ridge that would signal the place to change direction. Aust assured me we were good, but I thought we'd missed the exit sign for Dragon's Peak.

"You sure you know where we're going, Aust?" I asked.

"I am. It is where I was headed for my *Ambar Lenn*."

"Really? Why there?" Lexi asked.

Aust fell back on the path to keep pace with Lexi and Puff. "Lore from the ancient Highbornes spoke of Mahogany Bears in the farthest reaches of the north. They are said to den along the mountain ridges. Legend claims they stand ten feet when reared." He held his hand well above his head. "I always wondered if my connection would work with a beast so fierce as it does with the animals of our region. I meant to try it."

"Alone? What if you were hurt?"

Aust picked up a stick, mid-stride, and tossed it for Faolan. "That is the very nature of the *Ambar Lenn*: a quest to challenge oneself physically as well as mentally, to find one's inner strengths and purpose."

I rode, wondering what inner purpose Lexi and I would find if we were sent on Fate's Journey. As I considered the possibilities, I found myself peeking sideways at Galan. What had his plans been? He hadn't spoken since I left him palming himself in the dirt this morning. Watching his scowl harden all day, I was quite sure this was a case of *'If you keep making that face, it'll stay that way.'* It had, in fact, stayed that way for the past seven hours. As my stomach knotted, I shook my head. Why should I feel guilty? He was the jerk.

The screeching laughter of a jungle bird had me scanning the canopy. I was no expert in exotics, but I knew that one. A toucan sat in the leaves of a tall palm, watching our procession. Tipping back its broad beak, it cackled as if mocking us.

Over the course of the day, the light filtering through the canopy transformed. What started out as a brilliant lemon-yellow softened to a golden glow. Thankfully with the passing of hours, the sticky heat also faded. If last night was any indication, by around eleven o'clock, the temperature would plummet, and we'd be piling on layers.

I licked over my cracked lips and ignored the tightening of my face. Adjusting my position in the saddle, I fished in my backpack and found water. Mmm, warm and stale. What wouldn't I give to be drinking a cold beer... in a frosted mug... while sitting on a snowbank? Replacing the lid on my bottle, I tossed it back into my bag and promised myself I'd visit the Hearthstone the minute we got home.

Without my permission, my attention drew back to Galan. Long legs propelled him along the path. He showed no signs of tiring, no signs of faltering in the thick heat of the rainforest. His skin wasn't even flushed. And oh, there was so much smooth, ivory skin. He tugged at the lacings of his pants and grimaced mid-stride.

Damn. I really tagged him.

In a moment of pity, I called it an early night and gestured to a small clearing ahead. When his gaze met mine, I offered him a genuine smile. His brow remained creased with the same angry scowl he'd worn all day.

"I should apologize," I whispered to Lexi.

"Of offer to heal what's achin'," Lexi said, wiggling her fingers in the air. "Give him a happy ending to a bad day with those magic fingers of yours."

I rolled my eyes and headed into the wilderness to relieve the pressure on my bladder. Thankfully Lexi didn't follow. *Heal what's achin.* I huffed, stepping over broad-leafed scrub. *Give him a happy ending.* I tromped on, breathing in the solitude. I had no intention of entertaining Lexi by responding to her idiocy. And it was idiocy.

... he was looked at with great admiration for about half the evening, till his manners gave a disgust which turned the tide of his popularity.

Wisdom from Jane Austen's *Pride and Prejudice*.

"Oh shit!" *I did not just compare Galan to Mr. Darcy, did I?* I wiped my brow with the back of my wrist. It had been a long two days. The sun had obviously fried my brain. I hadn't even gotten to wash in the stream this morning after *the incident* with Galan. Lifting my arm, I performed a quick sniff test to assess the damage. Yep, two days in a tropical rainforest. Nice.

As if the universe was listening, a faint rush of water called from a distance. Glancing back toward camp, I wondered how far I'd come. Every tree and every rock looked the same. How long had I been trudging?

Shit, I had broken about five of Reign's rules in as many minutes. I counted them off on my fingers as I pressed on. I was alone in an unsecured location. I had no backup and no weapon. I'd left my charges to fend for themselves, and no one knew where I was. Technically, I could be ambushed at any moment, and who would know?

I scanned the forest.

Surely, if someone were watching me, I'd know, wouldn't I? With the light fading, the forest filled with endless shadows and places Scourge could be hiding. The hairs on my arms stood on end. *Paranoid much?*

I swallowed, listening for anything beyond an insect or a creature of the cute and fuzzy variety. "Get a grip."

Refocused on the noise of the stream, I lifted my feet high and plodded through a tangle of vines and green. Gods, I missed cobblestone paths. After a few hundred yards, the jungle transformed, and trees thinned. Soaring fifty feet before branching into a living umbrella, I stood beneath a vaulted ceiling in a massive natural cathedral.

The sound of running water grew louder, and after a few more minutes of exploring, the trees opened up. It wasn't a river I'd heard at all. The grotto in front of me sat encircled by stone. At the far side, a seventy-foot waterfall plunged into a contained pool. The frothy, white water graduated into an iridescent turquoise as it moved away from the falls. Where I stood, across the pool, it appeared as clear as glass.

Cool mist kissed my face with an overwhelming relief after the swelter of the day. Edging toward the low rocks, I dipped my fingers, confirming my initial thought. It was a limestone pool, warm, clear, and probably rich with restorative properties.

I studied the surface shimmering in the light. Would there be blood-sucking or maybe flesh-eating beasties living within? The underwater inhabitants darted away in streaks of silver, gold, and crimson, too fast to focus on. They would probably be garden variety tropical fishies, right? Feeling somewhat confident that I was not about to become piranha-paté, I toed off my boots, peeled my leathers down my thighs, and pulled my muscle-shirt over my head.

There was no helping the squeal that slipped from my throat as I sank into the water. Logic told me it wasn't cold, the goosebumps tingling across the waistband of my undies, and my hardening nipples said differently. My internal temperature was molten. Gravity took my body as I fell forward, disturbing the mirrored surface. I pushed across the center of the pool. It was deep enough to swim, and I luxuriated in the stretch of my aching muscles.

The silt at the bottom of the pool gave way to fine sand close to the waterfall. Scrunching my toes into the silky soil, I sighed and spun a slow circle, watching the ripples dance away from me. "Gods, this is *so* what I needed." Floating on my back for who knows how long, the sky darkened, and the stars came out one by one.

"If you created this place, Castian, you were inspired."

I floated in half-conscious bliss until male voices invaded my world. My eyes flew open just in time to catch the blur of someone cannon-balling beside me.

"Ahhh." Tham shook his hair like a Golden Retriever. He stood, looking to where Lexi, Aust, and Galan were stripping down and laughed. "Will you three be joining us at any point within our lifespan?"

Galan cast him a dry look. "Mayhap." He pulled off his sleeveless jacket and the tunic they wore and night, folded them and laid them beside Tham's clothing strewn across the rocks. "We need not disrupt the forest in its entirety. There is something to be said for civility."

Lexi held her fingers over her mouth, gawking at Galan and Aust as they undressed. Ignoring my initial urge to get out of Dodge, I retreated to deeper water until the surface lapped above my black lace bra. It became evident in a hot minute that these Elves had no qualms about being naked.

I got the distinct feeling they didn't even realize they were exposing themselves to two women they'd just met. I studied every detail of the waterfall until all male parts were safely in the water. Nice rocks. Very gray.

"Civility is regarded with all too much importance, Galan." Tham laughed.

"True," Galan said, pushing across the pool. "And you are correct. This is perfection."

"Yet, still, my ideas are met with trepidation." Tham feigned a look of insult.

"In truth, this was Jade's idea, not yours," Aust said, swimming over. "How did you find your way here, *neelan*?"

I smiled to myself at his endearment of 'lovely one'. *Oh, I was burning off energy, looking for a place to hide for a while.* Something brushed against my calf, and I jumped. Full-dark had fallen. There was no way to tell what might be down there.

Lexi peeled down to her skivvies and jumped in. "Well, lucky for us, Aust and Galan thought to track you. Otherwise, you might have kept this little oasis all to yourself."

Tham splashed Faolan on the edge of the pool.

All to myself, huh, what a tragedy.

Outwardly, I made every attempt to remain composed. Inwardly, my body was aware—unsettlingly aware—these men were naked. Gods, like, really—everything out there—naked. It shouldn't have mattered; I was a healer for gods' sake. I'd laid hands on dozens of naked men, and nothing stirred within. I was raised around warriors who thought underwear was offensive and often wandered the halls drunk with their parts airing out.

But the Highbornes...

I focused on calming breaths. *Dear gods, they were buff!* Broad shoulders tapered toward washboard stomachs any woman would kill to rake her body down. Forget six-packs, these guys had eight, and their muscles rippled and flexed with every move. They lounged waist-deep, the indent of their hips disappearing below the dark surface.

I regarded Galan, shamefaced. His split lip looked better with the blood washed away, but not much. Considering his feelings about my affinity, I hadn't offered to heal it. "I'm sorry I lost my temper this morning. Are you all right?"

Galan ran dripping hands over his head, smoothing back his silver hair until it almost disappeared against his scalp. "I shall do." In a lazy dive, he submerged himself, and I noticed how stunningly tight and smooth his backside was.

A warm hand fell on my shoulder from behind. "Not that *you* would believe it, Jade, however, Galan is well regarded as one of the sweetest males amongst the females of our village." Tham squeezed my arm and then swished his hands below the surface of the water.

"You're right. I don't."

"Fair enough." Tham nodded. "Regretfully, you have yet to see his true character."

"So, how is it I inspire such disdain?"

Tham's smile looked hopelessly apologetic. "You are a strong, outspoken female . . . with magic abilities, and his mood was already foul."

"You mean there's something or someone other than me that makes him this miserable?"

Tham looked over my shoulder, and I winced.

"Yes," Galan grumbled from behind me. "Surprise. Not everything is about you."

"*I know.*" I inhaled deeply and pushed my hair out of my face. "It's just, I can't do anything right when it comes to you."

Galan inclined his head to Tham, who nodded and waded off to join the others. Galan gestured to the rock wall of the pool. "Would you care to sit?"

My mind flooded with erotic images of him sitting naked on the rocks beside me. Heat flushed from my cheeks to my belly to my core. "Um, no, I'm good, thanks." I stepped backward, letting the water creep further above my bra.

Galan tilted his head and looked down at me. "When my questing age arrived ten years past, to my father's horror and my community's amazement, I opted not to quest. Technically, I was within my rights. A Highborne's transition to adulthood occurs within a ten-year period. We can embrace our station any time within that frame. Most Highbornes," he shook his head, "all, in truth, count the hours until they are eligible to delve into the world of responsibility. I did not. Had I the choice…" He nipped his lip and stared at the white-water, cascading down the falls.

I thought back to some of the comments we'd heard in the vision of the *Ambar Lenn* ceremony. "It's a woman, right? You didn't want to leave her?"

He smiled. "Two, actually."

"Two?"

I don't know what my expression betrayed, but he laughed. The sound was soft and enchanting. "Lia, is the sun of my universe and Nyssa, the strength of my soul. Nyssa, my dearest friend save Tham, is with young and could bear at any time. While I am away, she might well perish. I may miss the opportunity to wish her well in the afterlife."

"Has she had problems with her pregnancy?"

He paled. "Highborne females perish more oft than not when bearing young. It is a curse that makes the blessing of progeny a double-edged sword. The loss of the mother and often the babe weighed against the natural need to procreate."

"When is she due?" He stared at me, blank-faced. "When are you expecting the young?"

"Oh, verily, any moment."

I nodded. "Okay, so you're worried about your friend, what about Lia?"

"Lia." Galan rubbed at his chest, his gaze searching the stars. "Lia is the air in my lungs. I need to be near her, to love her, to provide for her." My gut knotted. I didn't know why his involvement with someone would upset me as much as it did. I only met him yesterday.

His face twisted into a perfect crooked smile as he sighed. "My sire is not a kind male, and in my absence, there will be no buffer between his cruel bitterness and her unsullied joy."

"Can't she take care of herself?"

Galan looked shocked. "She is but five decades and nine."

"She's fifty-nine years old, and you think you need to protect her? How old are you?"

"One century and ten. That is why I must enter adulthood."

Huh, I would have guessed thirty-two. "Well, I'm twenty-five and can take care of myself. I'm sure Lia will be fine. Maybe if you aren't there to smother her with your love and protection, she'll stand up for herself. It might be good for her." The snip in my voice was evident. What the hell was with me?

Anger filled his gaze as his scowl deepened. "I do not smother her, and how would our sire striking out at her with forked tongue be good for her?"

Our sire? Huh, Lia, is his sister.

A flash of all-things-male hurtled off the rocks, and I ducked. Tham cannonballed between Galan and me, sputtering as he resurfaced. "Aust wishes to get back. The animals are restless, and the wind is picking up. A storm is coming."

We waded to where the clothes lay on the outer rim of the pool. Lexi and Aust were dressing when Tham called out. "Another mysterious brand. Is this a Talon mark as well?"

Lexi glanced down at the small dragon tattooed on her hip. "No, Jade and I had these done when we turned twenty-one."

Tham snickered, acting out his wet dog impression again and sprayed water over everyone. Grabbing his tunic, he patted his face and tossed the other one to Galan. "Is yours the same, Jade?" he asked, lacing the front of his pants.

I hadn't made it out of the water yet and wondered how to get leather pants over wet legs in mixed company while they eyed me for my dragon tattoo. Galan must have taken my hesitation for modesty because he held open his tunic as I stepped out of the water and shrugged it around my shoulders. Gods, it was chamois soft and smelled like... him.

Suede and sunshine.

"Thank you," I said, distracted by the mercurial shifts in his moods.

"A basic courtesy, naught more." He turned his back and walked away.

CHAPTER EIGHT

Sitting fireside, I held my shaky palms to the meager but determined flames and willed myself to tighten up. I felt icy inside. Frozen. Just minutes after Aust had us tucked under a rocky overhang to wait out the violent storm he predicted, it spiraled, thundered, and then pelted down. The rainstorm, persistent and loud, made conversation impossible. It left the five of us to stand in the darkness alone with our thoughts. I hadn't enjoyed the company.

Then, an hour later, the crack of lightning had ceased, as though the Fates had gotten bored with their games and shut off the faucet from the heavens. The trip back from the grotto was long and miserable. Goosebumps covered my flesh. The day's warmth had fled and left me stripped to the bare bones.

Tham shifted around the fire and used a stick to pluck out his third wide leaf bundle from the embers. The dozen little packages were stuffed with roasted fish and greens and filled the smoky air with the scent of fish-fry. Aust stepped away to check on the animals, while Galan tossed more wood on the struggling fire.

Unknown to him, though it hissed with a vengeance, his fire had no choice but to succumb to my affinity. I needed heat, and slowly it rose from a lick of smoking amber to the crackling of golden flames.

Tugging at the brambles stuck in my hair, I hoped I didn't scare off any neighboring wildlife. Or maybe it was better if I did.

"So," Tham said, lifting another piece of fish to his mouth, "you have people who keep house and cook for you whenever you hunger?"

I nodded. "Brownies usually. They love to clean and care for people. We've got a whole castle filled with students, instructors, and guests."

"And they are great at it," Lexi said. "Fabulous cooks too."

"You need their aid at your cottage," Aust chuckled, rejoining the group. "Tham is fortunate to have a path from the entryway to his bed-chamber to meditate."

"*Mmph.*" Tham huffed, swallowing his mouthful of food. "Not all of us have perfect home lives. Some of us have had to make do."

Aust paused, and for a brief moment, looked unexpectedly hurt. He reached for Faolan's scruff. "Apologies, brother mine. I meant no—"

"No apologies." Tham tossed Aust a strange pink fruit and shrugged. "I like my cottage. Everything is where I can see it. If I want something, I know where and how it lies. Servants might snigger the whole system."

"I couldn't imagine living without the staff," Lexi said. She handed me a fish bundle and tossed Naith his nightly bone. He snatched it out of the air and trotted over beside the tent to gnaw it in private.

"It must've been difficult for your ancestors." I steadied my dinner leaf on my lap and cut the vine binding it closed with my dagger. "Insulating themselves in this valley after living their lives, productive and vital in the royal palace. They gave up magical abilities, their home, and positions in the realm. I'm not sure I could do it."

Galan raised his gaze to the stars and shook his head. After a moment, he strode to stand over me, an unattractive crease between his brows. "For a woman who claims of making us welcome, you are ever determined to insult. It was never a choice to give up those things. We were *exiled*. Cast out. Thrown away and forgotten."

"I wasn't insulting you, Galan. I was pointing out—"

"Yes." His hand cut through the air. "Pointing out what hollow lives we lead when held up against the productive, vital existence of you and yours."

"That's not what I—"

He was in my face then, and for once, his icy blue eyes weren't icy. They were burning hot and furious. "What right have you to spout sanctimonious judgment on how we, *the poor displaced Highbornes*, live? You know naught of our lives."

He scrubbed both hands through his hair. "Should we bow to you for the chance to live in your realm? Are we so pathetic we should grovel for your wisdom and hospitality? What, pray tell, would we ever do without—*uggh!*"

Galan groaned as his feet tore from the ground. His body reeled and soared across the clearing. The air hissed from his lungs as his head cracked against the packed earth.

My seven-hundred-pound ebony panther landed over him. The resonant bass of Naith's growl rumbled deep and low, filling the camp.

Galan froze, pinned to the ground as ivory fangs tightened around his neck.

Aust leaped into the mix, and his expression blanked out. I bit my lip and waited until his gaze refocused. "Galan, Naith is protective toward his mistress. He demands Jade be treated with more respect."

Galan was in no position to argue. The tensile strength of a normal-sized jungle cat's jaws would crush his windpipe without effort. Naith was twice that or more. "Apologies," he rasped. "My behavior was uncalled for, my tone unbefitting a gentlemale." His strained whisper was barely audible from the forest floor. At Aust's nod, my mount released Galan's throat and prowled over to rub against me.

Once on his feet, Galan massaged the four pink welts on his throat. I sensed his temper still boiling, right beneath the surface. "I may have misspoken, Jade, and I do apologize for my tone. However, you need not lecture me on sacrifice and suffering. You, who know the privileges of royalty, living in your castle, catered to by servants. Doted upon by a father who believes you hung the moon and likely a mother who adores you as well, your opinions on suffering can be kept to yourself."

I heard, rather than felt my breath escape. Without looking down, I was sure a wrecking-ball had plowed into my gut. The fire that stoked my body's warmth through the trials of life snuffed and left me colder than ever. "I . . . uh, if you'll excuse me." I strode, numb, into the tent, and just made it to my pallet before my knees gave away.

"You pretentious prick!" Lexi's snapped, followed by a crack of a fist hitting what I guessed was Galan's face. Lexi wasn't one to hold her temper where her family was concerned.

I almost felt bad for him as I heard another punch land and the dull hiss of a man getting the wind knocked out of him. Almost. Not quite.

"Your Elven logic has Jade's life of privilege all figured out, eh? Well, fuck-you-very-much for your opinion!" Boots shuffled and paced. Lexi was a hellcat and was probably fighting the urge to take a running leap at Galan. When she continued, her voice was strained and tight.

"When Jade was seven years old, a party of Scourge crested the ridge above her family farmhouse. Warhorses thundered down the slope, their riders armed to the teeth. With no time to flee, Jade's mother raced her to the barn and shoved her into a root cellar under the barn floor. Jade was terrified, but her mother didn't have time to comfort her or even tell her that she loved her. She pushed her little girl into the damp room and cast an enchantment immobilizing her until the danger passed. After sealing the trap door and hiding it with loose straw, Jade laid there, alone in the dark."

Inside the tent, I lay on my pallet, pulling to draw air into lead lungs. My chest was tight. I forced my breath to steady. This was history. It happened a long time ago. Unwanted images replayed in my mind as Lexi told the tale, and I had no choice but to watch.

"After her father's belly was Ginsued, the raiders wrapped his intestines around his throat and strangled him on their porch. Then, the Scourge scum came for the women. Jade heard the soldiers ask her mother over and over again. 'Where's the girl?' Jade wanted to answer. She wanted to stop them from hurting her mother. It didn't happen. Every horrified scream that ripped from her mother's soul filled Jade's ears. Every plea for mercy seared into her heart. Jade remained powerless, trapped in a nightmare. She prayed for her mother's screams to stop. *They did*. After the Scourge cut out her tongue."

My knees came up to my chest as I fought the blackness washing over me. Not this time. I closed my eyes and prayed to Castian for strength. His response was instant. An otherworldly sense of peace seeped into my body, warmed me as it spread, distanced me from the memories. I inhaled deep and recited my life's mission.

Track down the five. Save those I can. Never let it happen again.

Six raiders died that day, five escaped. I'd tracked down and taken the lives of three of them, as was my right by law, and would one day uncover the last two from whatever dank rock they buried themselves under. That vow warmed me. Enough that I hears Lexi's words without the fall-apart.

"Locked below the torture, rank male sweat filled Jade's nostrils. The Scourge got a workout, stripping her mother, beating and raping her over and over again. And where was little Jade as they each took their turn? Sitting as close as I stand to you now, unable to wipe the blood from her face as it ran through the barn floorboards, unable to scream, knowing her parents were as good as dead."

I remembered my mother's throaty cries falling silent the moment the barn door shattered. An unearthly bellow of a beast echoed through the building. Guttural sounds of fighting, flesh tearing, and men dying.

I pinched my eyes tight and breathed deep. The next memory I had before everything went black was Reign tucking me under his duster and wrapping his arms around me.

When Lexi spoke next, her voice was a whisper. "When Reign found her, she was catatonic, lost inside her own mind. She trembled uncontrollably for weeks, was mute for months, and unable to perform the most basic tasks. Every morning Reign carried her from her bath where he washed her, to their table where he fed her, to his office where he sat her in the sun of the window seat like a lifeless porcelain doll. Between meetings, Reign would read to her while she stared unseeing out the window. She says she followed the sound of his voice through the darkness and eventually found her way to him. That is why Reign dotes on her."

Lexi's voice moved closer to the entrance of the tent. "Jade Elizabeth Glaster was not born of privilege, Highborne. She was forged from an iron necessity to survive. If you think that living all snug in your valley with daddy being mean to you and having to leave your sister for a week is suffering, think again." There was a long pause. "And the next time you see my sister, be on your fucking knees apologizing, or you'll feel the sting of how lethal I am when I *try* to hurt someone."

Lexi's footfalls were slow as she stepped inside the tent. After wiping my tears, I closed my eyes. I would figure it all out, one day, and when I did, I would get my justice. The shuffling of movement stopped outside my room and waited. When I didn't call her in, she retreated to her room on the other side of the tent.

After everything quieted down, one of the Highbornes left camp.

CHAPTER NINE

'*Keep your words soft and tender because tomorrow you might have to eat them.*' Reign had said that since the four of us were kids. Its wisdom gave me no pleasure the following morning. When I threw back the tent flap and stepped out, Galan was waiting, rubbing the palms of his hands down the front of his suede pants. Seeing me, he took a knee and bowed his head. He looked awful. The black and green shiner Lexi had given him last night now accented the split lip from our sparring match and the purple bags under his eyes.

"Jade," he said, looking up at me, "there are no words to express my regret. My callous words struck a blow not only to you, but to the honor of your family as well. It is unforgiveable. In hopes to begin making amends, I offer you my most sincere apology." He reached into the fold of his tunic and pulled out a small wooden box. It sat in the palm of his hand, my name carved in an intricate flourish of Elven script across the lid.

"It's beautiful, Galan, but I can't accept it."

As I turned, he caught my wrist. "Verily, I have no right to ask your forgiveness, and this is a meager token to repair the insult I inflicted upon, however, please—"

I raised my hands and shook my head. "I can't."

With my sights on Naith across the camp, I strode over and fastened my backpack. It wasn't that I didn't believe his sincerity—it oozed from his every pore. I was just tired of the high-maintenance-Highborne roller-coaster and chose to get off the ride.

Galan wasn't my concern. He was my assignment.

In a week, I would be back at the Academy, and he would be back buttering his sixty-year-old sister's toast.

Naith's head lifted and turned to the stand of trees beyond. When his ears went back, the hair on the nape of my neck stood on end. I scanned the area. Rainforest trees were so stupidly massive an entire raid party could hide behind one of them. Abaddon's seer probably knew about the spellbook by now. If so, the Scourge would intercept. I drew a long breath, filtering for the rotting stench of skunk and decay. Nothing. I strained to hear anything out of place. All I got was the *screeeeee* of cicadas thanking the heavens for another sweltering day to come.

We needed to keep moving.

My sense of unease persisted through the day, and so did Galan's overtures: a perfect feather, a handful of colorful fruits, a bouquet of tropical orchids. I needed to focus, but with Galan around, my emotions vacillated between a rock and a crazy place. He was the most annoying, exhausting man I'd ever met, yet I was drawn to him.

Inexplicably. Undeniably.

My body never responded to anyone, and now, all at once, I threw off heat and hummed like a kettle about to boil. I wished Galan would go back to being obnoxious and self-important. I had no defenses when he was sweet.

"You gotta give him points for effort," Lexi whispered as we dismounted at the clearing below Dragon's Peak.

"I don't need him to make things up to me." I pulled out my phone and sent Reign a text with our position. "I accepted his apology."

"Your mouth said the words, though it's crystal your heart didn't get the memo." Lexi pouted, looking oh-so-disgruntled.

"Since when do you side with the guy?"

"You are priority one, always—" Lexi waved to Reign. "They're here. You gather yourself, and I'll be right back."

Staring at the profile of the dormant volcano, I fortified myself for what was to come: climb to the mouth of Dragon's Peak and, if all went as planned, we'd find the entrance, search the tomb, retrieve the lost spellbook and offer it to Castian. *Easy peasy.*

The tough part would be working with Galan and Samuel in close quarters together. Both of them—at the same time.

They'd each stomped on my heart, and if I was honest, they actually blew a bazooka-sized hole through my pride. That, however, had nothing to do with the task at hand, did it? We had a quest to complete. When it finished, I'd walk away and get back to my life. Whatever that meant.

This task is part of your destiny, Mir. *I have seen it.* What did Castian mean by that? My destiny was avenging my parents. I had to keep it together. I had to find my answers and make sense of their deaths. I just had to.

"All right?" Lexi tugged one of my curls straight and let it spring back into place.

"Sure. Fine."

"Reign is bringing in Rue and Cowboy as sentries, and, uh, Samuel's here."

The strange tone of Lexi's voice had me studying her. It was there, in her eyes, too. "What? We knew Samuel was coming. He's the best wizard we've got."

Lexi shrugged and tilted her head toward Reign and Samuel standing with their backs to us. "You'll see."

Cryptic. Reign had introduced Samuel to the Highbornes and was making small-talk when I joined them. Nothing seemed out of the ordinary. The two of them wore the usual black leather battle gear, an assortment of sheathed weapons, tinted wraparounds—

"No!" I reached for Samuel's sunglasses. He looked even worse than Galan did. I whirled on my father. "Oh. My. Gods. What did you do? I told you—"

"Stop the hissy, missy." Reign pointed to the bruised mess on Samuel's face. "Not my handiwork."

I searched his eyes until I was certain. "Then, who?"

"Forget it." Samuel snatched the glasses from my hand and hid the nasty purple mound swelling over his left eye. When he stomped off, I followed, reaching for his shoulder. At the touch of my fingers, he shrank away and hissed. "Dammit, Jade. Dinna touch me."

He was holding his side. Had he been limping? A wave of understanding flopped like a cold fish in my belly. Ignoring his protests, I pulled open his battle-vest and lifted his muscle shirt. His washboard looked more like someone ran over him with a tanker, then backed up and ran him over again, then did it once more just for kicks.

"What the hell?" I ran a feather touch over purple and yellow splotches in different stages of healing. "This is because of me?"

"No." He shook his head, scrubbing his fingers through his hair. "No. It's on me. I was a dick at the bar, aye?" His chestnut eyes held a glimpse of the guy I'd been crazy about. There was still plenty of pain and regret there, but I couldn't help hoping. "Using your parents against ye crossed the line."

"It did, but *I* should've gotten to beat you for it."

Samuel's dark eyes met mine, and after a minute, we both smiled. Reaching out, he laid a heavy arm across my shoulder and drew me in. "Gods, it feels good to not fight with you." He smelled the same, a mixture of cologne, magic, and *him*. It felt like a million years since we'd been like this. I hugged him tighter until he gasped and grabbed his side.

"Shit. I forgot, sorry." I pushed up his shirt.

Knowing better than to argue with me, he stood still while I fanned my hands over his ribs and summoned my gift. *Huh?* It didn't come. Refocusing my attention, I moved my hands and tried again. Nothing. "What's wrong? Why can't I heal this?"

Samuel's lips pinched in a tight line. "Because Reign dinnae do it." After a long silence, he released a long breath. "Castian was pissed. And when the God of gods breaks ass on ye, it's no good." He picked up my hand, stepped closer, and held it against his chest. "I was a bastard. I am truly sorry, Luv."

"Maybe I could speak to him?"

He lifted my knuckles and rubbed his lips against them the way he'd done a thousand times before. "No. After what I said about your parents, this punishment is on me."

"Wrap up the sloppy shit," Reign growled. "Not like we're on a fucking mission here."

Samuel killed his smile but winked when Reign turned back the group.

"Fine." I scanned the outline of the peaks above. "Where to from here?"

Galan sidled in behind me and pointed over my shoulder toward a jagged rock face up and to the right. It did look like the silhouette of a dragon. "The account of the Highborne journey begins like this," he said, his breath tickling my neck.

Into the valley, the exiled came,
With naught but their lives and selves to blame,
Through a dragon's mouth that held no bite,
The aubergine sky sank into night.

He wrapped a muscled arm around my waist and turned me to face the slope. "The setting sun would have been there when they emerged from the cave," he whispered, his voice deep and smooth, "and so, the mouth of the dragon would be up this way."

Samuel cursed under his breath and unsheathed his wand.

I sidestepped Galan and stepped over to Reign. "Right, then let's get this party started."

As we began our ascent, Faolan chased a weird-looking brown rodent out of a stump. It ran over the patches of summer moss and bracken, and through the leaves. It looked a lot like a groundhog and hopped like a rabbit. It bounced from trunk to trunk, table-topping, scrambling until it scaled a neighboring palm. Safe and out of reach, it squawked.

Whatever the message, Aust's wolf ignored it and bounded through the trees to continue her fun.

Aust shrugged, and we walked in companionable silence.

Our group reached what we figured was the mouth of the dragon just as the sun blazed directly overhead. The rainforest was thick to the south and west, a solid, weathered rock face rose up to the north and a sheer drop to the south.

"It is near." Aust hesitated, arms out, drawing closer to the rocks. Even though there was no sign of an opening, the Elves didn't seem to doubt him. Aust had an intuition about nature that they respected. In every aspect of life he was reserved. In the forest Aust was king.

A soupy breeze stirred my hair. "What do you feel exactly?"

He tilted his head, squinting in concentration. "I am not certain I can describe it."

"May I help you focus?" He wet his lips and, after a moment, gave a slow nod. Sidling in behind him, I lifted the hem of his vest. With one hand on each of his hips, skin to skin, I faced him toward the cliff face. "Now, relax. Let my energy flow through you. It will help you see."

No one stilled like the Highbornes. He closed his eyes and became as immobile as the rock face before us. "Breathe, Aust. It's all good. You're good." His chest was too tight. His tension blocked our connection. A shock of energy jolted back at me. "*Relax*," I whispered. "Trust me, and your vision will come."

I hummed a quiet ballad until his breathing quieted, and his shoulders eased. We moved with deliberate steps along the cliff face, searching, listening, and feeling the sheets of solid rock in front of him.

"Here." He spread his fingers against the cliff face. "The entrance is here, sealed behind this wall." It appeared to be a solid sheet of gray stone, from the mossy ground at our boots, to far beyond the swaying treetops. There was no indication of an entrance or even a crack in the face.

"How do we get in?" Tham asked. "It could be as thick as a tree trunk."

"It is not." Aust closed his eyes and ran his hand ran along the surface of the rock. A faint smile tugged at his mouth.

"Samuel, you're up. How long?" I stepped out of his way as he waggled his brow.

Palms out, he began to assess the rock face, mumbling to himself. "Twenty?"

Aust scratched his fingers in Faolan's ruff then looked up. His ocean blue eyes glittered with excitement. "Did you feel it, Jade?"

"*Mhmm*, your connection to nature is very impressive."

Aust's ears blushed pink, and then a strange puzzlement crept into his expression. With his head cocked to the side, his quizzical look changed into outright alarm. He spun toward the trees, his gaze piercing the heart of the forest. "Everyone, take to the trees. *Now!*"

CHAPTER TEN

*T*ham grabbed Lexi, dragging her with him. Galan moved toward me, but Samuel had my arm, and after a moment's hesitation, the two of us heeded Aust's command and climbed. My jaw dropped slack when Reign followed the order. I'd never seen such a show of compliance from him in all our years together. Aust stood on the forest floor with his arms stretched open and tense concentration covering on his face.

"What is it, Aust?"

"*Mahogany Bears.* Stay in the trees." He pointed to where Naith paced and snarled, and Puff ate the discards from a fruit tree. "Faolan, enough. *Go.*" Faolan snarled and bared her teeth. Aust's head spun at the sound, his eyes wild and wide. Instantly Faolan dropped her head, and her ears pinned back. Growling long and low, she stalked to the other animals, her fur standing straight up at the hackles.

"Ironic," Galan said from the tree across from us. "A fortnight past, this was what you hoped for, Aust."

He didn't seem certain now. What if these bears didn't hear his voice? I wished Bruin had come. My brother could handle this.

"I can put down a couple of bears," Samuel said, offended. "We didna need to shimmy up trees like frightened squirrels."

Aust raised a menacing glare. "Touch these creatures of Shalana, and I will slit your throat and set my animal brothers to pick at your carcass while you drain."

"You and what army, Highborne?" Samuel snapped.

"This one *wizard*." The tip of Galan's arrow gleamed in the afternoon sun, trained on Samuel. His Highborne blue eyes glittered with wild excitement.

Shit. I looked to Tham for help. His arrow hovered nocked as well. *Isn't this going well?*

"Animals of the wild are sacred to our people," Galan hissed. "Senseless violence against them will not be tolerated."

"Enough," Reign barked. "Lock your shit down and—"

Snapping brush and a low *harump* rose from the eastern slope. The noise was deep in the trees, about a hundred feet behind our position. Aust breathed deep and slow, opening and closing his hands as the sound grew nearer.

The lumbering ursine gait of the massive beasts made my pulse race. "Aust, maybe you shouldn't be down there."

"Fash not, *neelan*. Remain where you are."

The colossal lead bear was male, followed by half a dozen smaller —but in no way small—females. They were larger than any species of bear I'd ever seen, including Weres. Their legs were long and muscular on the front and short and thick at the back, giving them an angled, hyena-like stance. As they neared, the male's round head eclipsed the view of Aust's chest. Matted with clumps of shaggy, mahogany fur, he *galumphed* closer, shifting twelve-inch paws. They thudded heavily onto the damp growth as he plodded through the forest brush.

Reaching Aust, he twitched and waggled his long, ebony nose in the air, sniffing the breeze. Morning light glinted off the curved ivory canines extending from his jaw, up the side of his muzzle. Lowering his head, he huffed, pawing the dirt while his females paced behind him.

Aust's far off look of concentration reminded me of a child working on a brainteaser. What was he saying to the beasts glaring down at him? The colossal bear tilted his head to the side as if considering his words. For a moment, I thought it might be as easy as Aust's past encounters with wildlife.

Not this time.

A wild base growl vibrated through the trees as the male shook its head from side to side. Thrusting itself forward, he caught Aust in the gut with his head, flipping him into the air like a worn rag doll. A deranged roar filled the clearing as the Elf came crashing down into the brush. Brittle snaps popped and cracked. I couldn't tell if it was bones or branches.

"*Aust!*" Galan cried, starting a frantic descent.

"*Stay*," Aust gasped. The bear's massive claws scooped him out of the dirt and threw him across the clearing. Aust landed in a tangled thud, then lifted his head and continued to stare at the male. Why didn't he defend himself?

Faolan and Naith were wild, snarling, and snapping empty air. They made no advance, obviously under the same orders as we were, and hunched and paced in a frenzy. Aust coughed, grabbing his side. Scarlet spittle speckled the forest floor and stained his lips.

Galan looked to Tham. "What say you?"

They held their position.

The bear galloped as Aust he staggered to his feet. The beast swiped his paw through the air, thumping him back to the ground. Aust's bloody body was a twig in a hurricane, crumpling as the massive predator straddled and pinned him to the forest floor, enveloped him under the matted brown pelt.

The bear flipped his head up and down, its roar echoing in the trees around us. On a whimper, Faolan fell silent and laid flat to the ground. The bear reared onto its hind legs and dropped its weight onto Aust's crumpled frame. The snap which followed couldn't be mistaken.

Aust's bones were breaking.

Galan started down the tree with Tham right behind him. They were ten feet from the forest floor when the females charged. Reared on hind legs, they clawed up the trees and bared a mass of discolored teeth.

"Aust?" Galan cried, ascending a few feet beyond their reach.

"I-I am... well." The weak cough came from somewhere under the bear.

After what seemed an eternity, the male waddled backward and settled on his haunches. Aust rolled to one side and struggled to sit. Retaining eye contact, he watched his attacker until, to my utter amazement, a crooked smirk covered his blood-smeared face. The male barked a few short grunts, and then the females holding Galan and Tham at bay lowered onto all fours and lumbered over to squat behind their male.

Aust staggered to his feet. Even so, the bear reached the underside of his chin.

Lexi squealed when Aust scrubbed a shaky hand against the male's jowl, the Elf's smirk spreading to a glowing smile. "Verily, all is well. You may join me."

Galan exhaled, scrubbing his fingers through his hair. I couldn't decide if he was furious or in awe. "You astound me, brother mine."

"How bad are you?" Reign asked.

"I am well." Aust coughed, wrapping his arm across his chest. Fresh blood stained his lips as he spoke. "He never wished to hurt me... simply stubborn. All is resolved. Honestly, the interface was *incredible*." He teetered as Faolan pushed through the group to brush against his leg. Her low growl was constant, her fur still bristled.

I bit my tongue, vacillating between the knowledge of how deeply Highbornes hated magic and how badly his injuries required it. This might bite me in the ass, but— "Aust, would you allow me to heal you?"

A wincing smile spread across his marred face as he bowed his head. "I would be honored. Gratitude, *neelan*." When he listed to the side, Galan caught him before he fell headlong into the trunk of the rosewood he was headed for.

Aust's eyes rolled closed, and he leaned his head against Galan's chest. After a couple of shallow breaths, he broke out with the stupidest grin I'd ever seen. *Men.*

"Tham lay your cloaks down on that patch of grass. Galan, lay him down." Kneeling over Aust, I paused. "Before we get started, I need to tell you that when I connect with patients, memories shimmer in my mind. Some are personal, and some are random. I never share them, though, in the past, it has made some people uncomfortable with my touch."

Aust looked surprised, but not unnerved. Taking my hand, he pressed it flat against his chest and closed his eyes again. "I trust you, Jade."

The moment I palpated his side, his eyes rolled back, and he was out. Four broken ribs, lacerations to his hip and back, deep bruising in the shoulder... I shook my head, wiping a gob of muddy blood from his face. "Incredible, my ass."

He was unconscious long enough to get most of the healing done. I was still mumbling about men and their idiotic ideas of what was fun when I sensed he was waking.

"Worth it," he choked, his eyes still closed.

"You enjoyed being molested by a wild bear?" I said, taking considerable effort to be gentle. "Well, don't do it again. From where I was, it was terrifying."

"Verily, it was a pinnacle moment in my life. Besides," he opened his eyes and gave me a look so endearing it rivaled Lexi's best, "I am blessed to have you heal me."

"I'm not a safety net, so you can risk your life." I re-knit Aust's ribs, ignoring the testosterone babble between the men. "You're lucky you didn't puncture anything vital." When he was back to pre-Mahogany bear health, I sat him up. "You'll be sore for today, so take it—"

"*Jade?* You might want to break that up." Lexi pointed to a standoff by the rock face.

Galan and Samuel were glowering at one another. *Fan-fucking-tastic.*

I didn't care what the current pissing match was about. The

tension hung so thick I might need to quarantine everyone for testosterone poisoning. "Enough. Samuel, can you take care of the—"

In one sweeping move, Samuel crushed me against his chest and claimed my mouth. His kiss was passionate, possessive, and completely unexpected. When I drew back, he winked. Beneath that Scottish bravado, though, the anguish in his expression was palpable. "I'm on it."

Galan stalked off to check on Aust.

Pushing off Samuel's chest, I shot him a glare. He dumped me months ago and left me snotting in my suite. I wouldn't be a pawn in a game of King of Dragon's Peak.

Sitting at the base of a stump, I closed my eyes. Aust's healing had my head spinning, and I needed time to recover. When the world stopped turning, I watched Samuel work. Regardless of the past few months, he was an exceptional wizard, thus his Talon title—Merlin.

He addressed the wall, unraveling the enchantment which had been in place for eight thousand years. As his lips moved with quiet utterings, my annoyance faded. A soft smile curved his mouth as he worked. To him, a well-executed spell was one of the greatest tributes to his craft. From his expression, the original Highbornes were beyond good at what they did—they'd been excellent.

His wand waved side to side, dipping up and down like a symphony conductor. The mountain cracked and then groaned as a hairline fissure snaked its way up from the mossy ground. Gradually it widened. Without warning, deafening screams pierced the air around us.

I covered my ears. The jungle swam around me.

A tidal wave of fur cascaded from the crevice, pooling around Samuel's feet. Rats. Dozens and dozens of rats screamed at a pitch that had my head ringing.

Aust was on it. Within moments the rodents scurried into the forest, and the world quieted. He touched his fingers to his ears and came away with blood. "Fash not. I am well."

Samuel continued as if nothing had happened.

My equilibrium stabilized once I healed my eardrums, then I

helped the others. A thunderous crack signaled the coming rush of creepy crawlies: tarantulas, scorpions, black widows, fire ants, and snakes. Lexi squeaked as legs, stingers and scales slithered and sludged down the rock face. The hideous army of evil seemed united in their target.

Samuel.

Aust went back to it. When the mass didn't disband like the rats, he lowered to his knees. An ear-splitting crack signaled the collapse of the enchantment, and the insect sentries vanished into nothingness. With the dragon's mouth pried open, we advanced into its belly.

"Are we there yet?" Lexi asked after an hour of winding through a maze of tunnels.

Thankfully my headache had downgraded from corkscrew-through-your-eye sockets pain to rubber-mallet-to-the-temple ache. The ambient lighting was helping, though. Twenty minutes in, we'd extinguished the torches because the deeper we sank into the dormant volcano, the more brilliant the phosphorescent mushrooms and fungi glowed—aqua blue, grass green, mustard yellow, bubblegum pink. Magical.

The narrow-tube passageway opened into a spacious cavern of molten rock. Forty feet around, it was filled with hot, stale air and the pungent stench of sulfur. By the colorful glow of mushroom light, an altar was visible in the middle of the cavern.

I relit a couple of torches to get a better look.

"The Altar of the Ancients," Tham said, running his hand over the relief. "It has the same proportions ornamented with the same etched vine work as the altar at our ruin site."

Bingo. Lying on the center of the altar stone was an oversized, leather-bound book. Well preserved beneath a layer of sediment, it was hard to believe it was left here over eight-thousand years before. Drawing closer, I looked at the carved figurines standing on the altar along the spine of the book. Twice the size of chess pieces, the two carnelian idols—Shalana, Goddess of the Woodlands, and a fierce tiger at her side—seemed to be keeping watch.

"Astounding," Tham said, as he caressed the cover of the book. "It is the most incredible leather-working I have ever seen. Iadon will go mad—*Aughhh!*"

Tham snatched his hand back. The air sizzled with the stench of burnt flesh as a brilliant silver explosion lit the cavern. When it faded, an iridescent barrier appeared over the altar. Resembling a harmless glass cake cover, it gave off a pulsing glow and a low crackling hiss.

I grabbed Tham's curled fingers and forced open his blackened palm. The sight of the charred digits and the putrid stench made us both gag. "Tham, do you object to me healing you?"

He shook his head. "No. Please do."

Reaching into the injury, I soothed the sting of the burn. In minutes his flesh was milky white, soft, and healed.

"Gratitude, Jade." Tham flexed his fingers in and out, staring at his palm. "Verily, Jade, you are a marvel."

"Check it out," Lexi said, pointing to an intricate scrollwork etching itself into the top of the case. As we watched, a design of vines and leaves danced along the surface, and then a handprint appeared, five fingers splayed and glowing in an inlaid design.

"All right," Lexi said, "who's the next crispy critter?"

"Mayhap, we might apply logic to the situation before another of us attempts to touch it," Aust said.

"I am in no hurry." Tham cradled his hand. "Reign, would you have any insight on this? You look as though none of this has surprised you."

Tham was right. Reign stood, leaning against the stone wall at the mouth of the cavern, arms and ankles crossed. The expression he wore may have been new to the Highbornes, but it was SOP for us. Standard Operating Procedure.

"Give it up, Tham," Lexi sighed. "Reign doesn't shed light on situations once he gets that look. He insists we should stumble in the dark bumping into furniture."

"Not stumble in the dark, Princess," Reign said. "Work through it. It does you no good to be lead through life. The answer is here. This is your quest. Apply what you know."

"Okay, what do we know," I asked. "Protective measures were put into play eight-thousand years ago by your ancestors. They didn't want the book to fall into the hands of their enemies, and they didn't want to be able to access it for themselves, so they entombed it."

"They left it for someone to find, though." Lexi pointed to the altar. "The figurines, the way the book is set on display. It's respectful—a tribute. To who? To what?"

"To Elven magic?" Aust offered.

"To the power of their Elven magic," I said. "That's possible. Who would they trust to reclaim the book and be responsible for safeguarding it?"

"Obviously not, Tham," Lexi giggled.

Samuel rolled his eyes. "Come on, people. I know ye were raised in the land of merry-fuckin-sunshine, but if Castian wanted the girls to bring the three of ye here, there's a reason. If Aust was to find the cave opening and it's not Tham who can touch it," He turned to Galan. "I think the tinsel-haired twit is next up for the barbeque."

Like it or not, I couldn't argue with Samuel's logic. I just didn't want Galan hurt. What if this was Samuel's creative excuse to cause Galan pain? Would he do that? Judging by the expectant smirk on Samuel's face, I'd say yes. Yes, he would.

"Wait," I said. "Maybe we should talk this out—"

"Fash not, Jade," Galan said, stepping up to the altar. "All is well."

As my heart started to hammer and my gut knotted, he laid his palm on the cover.

CHAPTER ELEVEN

The explosion lit the entire cavern. Streams of light burst from the altar, encircling Galan's athletic frame in a vast wave. It built in intensity, sparking around him like fireworks, lighting him from every angle until his silhouette disappeared within the white-hot flames.

"*Galan!*" I lunged forward, but the blazing heat stung my skin and burned my eyes. Strong hands grabbed my shoulders. The treacle scent of old magic and the stench of sulfur made my head spin. A stream of blue energy spewed from Samuel's wand, and from one heartbeat to the next, the cavern fell into darkness. When my eyes adjusted, Galan was standing with his hand flat on the cover of the Elven spellbook.

I scanned him, top to bottom—from his beautiful battered face down every inch of his definition. He seemed unharmed. I resisted the urge to reach out and examine him, certain he would reject my evil magic tainting his life.

"You okay," I choked. "Are you burned? Hurt? Are you dizzy?"

"I shall do." Galan cast me a haunting smile. His deep blue eyes were dark in the mushroom light, but they locked on mine. His gaze

JL MADORE

was intense. It penetrated me, tightened in my chest, and made me acutely aware of my body's more feminine wants.

"Nicely done, brother mine." Tham patted Galan's shoulder and stepped between us.

"Aye," Samuel muttered, waving his wand. "Takes real talent to rest your hand on a glass case once everyone else has paved your way."

Galan turned his attention to the book and traced his fingers along the surface.

The center inlay of the cover depicted a scraggly, ancient Elven face surrounded by a tangle of hair. His wild mane encircled his features, evolving into twigs as it traveled outward. As it reached the edge of the cover, the twigs evolved again, into branches reaching to the top of the book and gnarled roots weaving into the ground below.

Along the left spine ran an intricate vine carving punctured in regular intervals through the depth of the book. "Eight millennia past, a leather cord would have bound it." Galan said.

Samuel flicked his wand toward the book, and the spine was newly bound.

Tham raised the cover, and the group closed in. It was majestic. Powerful. Even as an inanimate object, many Fae items emanated a huge amount of magical energy. This one held more than most. An electrical charge arced in the air and raised the hairs on my arms.

A strange emotional vibration had me scanning the room. Samuel's focus on the book went far beyond reverent curiosity. His eyes were hooded and dark, his stare hungry. He drew closer, like a magnet drawn toward its iron companion.

Galan blocked his path. "Is there something I may aid you with?"

Samuel shook his head and withdrew his hand. "No, but thanks for askin'."

The two stared each other down. The fact that they sported almost identical shiners was kind of funny in a morbid, distracting sort of way.

"Astounding," Tham muttered, turning pages. "Animal Mastery, Concealment, Empathic Links... There are hundreds of spells and enchantments. Everything laid out. Imagine the seduction of it, of commanding the power to change the realm and alter fate." He shook his head and closed the cover.

"Exactly why we need to wrap this up and offer the book to Castian," Reign said. "If Abaddon or the Scourge got hold of this, we'll be up to our eyes in it."

After sliding the book into his satchel, Aust tucked away the figurine of Shalana and reached for the tiger. That's when everything went to hell.

The moment Aust's fingers closed around the idol, a powerful rush surged through the cavern. Sweat broke out across his skin, and he scrambled away from the group. Stumbling on shaky legs, he buckled to the stone floor and crawled backward until he hit the cave wall. Cornered like an animal, he shuddered and began to convulse.

"Jade, what is happening?" Galan asked.

"He's having a seizure."

Aust's eyes rolled back, leaving only the white sclera visible. His body was rigid, thrashing wildly against the stone floor. Galan secured him on his side, holding his head until, after what seemed like ages, he fell still. The stillness was short-lived.

He curled in on himself, screaming through clenched teeth, the tendons on his neck, standing out like cables.

"Jade, *do something*," Galan said.

My hands were on him, tracking what was happening. I leaned back and met Galan's frantic gaze. "I can't fix this. I heal injuries. He's not injured. I think it's his gift. He's—"

"What?"

"I think... His gift is surging through him like he's broken a dam, and his body is flooding with magical energy."

"To what end?"

"It's the figurine," Lexi said. "It started as soon as he picked up the figurine."

I grabbed his clenched fist, prying at his fingers. Aust's eyes flew wide. On a lunge, he knocked me on my back and bared his teeth.

Before I blinked, Aust flew against the cave wall, and Reign crouched next to me, dagger drawn. "What the fuck was that? Did you see his eyes?"

Aust's eyes were—well, they weren't Highborne blue. They were a cold, ice-blue, and when he looked at me, they reflected the torchlight like an animal in the headlights of a car.

Galan scrambled to check on him. "If you cannot heal him, what can be done?"

Not a damned thing. I joined Galan where Reign had thrown Aust and tried to minimize his discomfort. "His vitals are strong. All we can do is ride this out."

Connected as I was, I felt the wave of nausea coil. "Tham, back it up, he's gonna hurl." Tham's boots just cleared the detonation zone before Aust emptied his stomach onto the stone and blacked out for the second time that afternoon.

It took considerably longer to make our way back to Dragon's Peak than it had to get into its belly. Aust was as pale as the undead yet insisted on shuffling along under his own steam. When we finally made it to the brilliance of the afternoon sun, I was rendered momentarily blind. The Elves didn't seem disoriented, maybe because of their advanced vision. I was still blinking away the moisture in my eyes when I felt the change.

Faolan growled low in her belly as the Elves stiffened. The high-pitched keening of unsheathed metal sliced the air.

"*Ambush*," Reign bellowed.

Lunging into formation, Lexi, Samuel, Reign, and I formed an outer circle around the Highbornes. Galan, Tham, and Faolan closed in around Aust and the spellbook. After tossing me his short sword, Samuel stretched his neck side to side and drew his wand, grinning like the Scot he was. Reign and Lexi were amped too, rocking on the balls of their feet as they unsheathed a fricken armory.

A dozen Scourge raiders tightened around the half-acre clearing, gauging our group. No doubt others lurked in the trees. There was nothing to be done about that.

They seemed surprised to be face opposition, so maybe a case of wrong-place-wrong-time. Scouting party? Maybe. Otherwise, we might've been impaled by sniper fire by now.

I could make out traces of what these men were before they gave themselves over to be Scourge. Beneath the reek of their mutations were the long, pointed ears and spiking eyebrows of Dark Elves, the rippling muscles of human barbarians, the beaked faces of Orcs, the drooling obliviousness of a Goblin and the boxy, no neck, barrel body of Trolls.

The Highbornes stared at the group and must have recognized the features of the Dark Elves because Galan took a tentative step forward. "Merry meet cousins. Many lifetimes have passed since the parting of our people. Might we reunite amicably?"

Cue the cackle of evil laughter.

I cringed. Aust was a weak link at the moment, and other than sparring with Galan, we hadn't assessed any of their fighting abilities. They were hunters and trackers. How would they measure up in battle? *Damn.* It was a rookie oversight, and now we were headed into this blind.

Easing off the death grip I had on the hilt of my sword, I twisted my wrist and started windmilling. "Aust, are you up to calling a few friends?"

Aust's strange new gaze cast to the forest. "Consider it done."

Gods, I loved that look.

In one of those slow-mo moments in life, both sides assessed the other. Galan and Tham dropped their cloaks and strung their bows in one graceful motion.

Lexi craned her neck to meet the empty gaze of one of the orcs. Yellow saliva dripped in chunks from a scraggly beard as he curled his finger to coax her closer. "Wanna dance, child?"

"Thought you'd never ask." Lexi crinkled her nose, widened her stance, and then sank into a crouch. His crooked sneer slipped from his face as she swept his legs and pounced, daggers spinning. The snap of bone and a burst of blood left the first Scourge dispatched into a sinewy puddle of tar.

"One for you, Princess." Reign advanced on his opponent. "Shall we keep score?"

"You bet your ornery ass, old man." Lexi grinned and spun to the fight.

A booming battle cry roared through the clearing, and the fight broke free.

"Blaze." The Scourge facing me raised his ax. "I hoped I'd run into you."

I searched passed the stretched, shiny flesh, the distorted sneer, and the blotchy complexion. It was the scar from his mouth to his eye that gave his identity away. "Bloodvine?"

"Still picking up strays, I see," he said, swinging his blade.

I jumped beyond his reach, then jabbed forward and angled left, right, a solid upper block. "You didn't complain when you were the road-kill I scooped from the gutter."

His breath reeked of rot, and his sneer tugged at the gnarly scar at the corner of his mouth. "Times change."

I grunted, pushing against his strike. Arms and legs and weapons connected as we got our game on. The piercing clang of metal rang in my ears. Three wolves raced out of the forest, releasing a flash of teeth as they passed. Aust swayed and took a knee. What would happen if he lost consciousness again? How would we control the wolves?

"Castian, come to me." Power surged in the air around me, arching to my fingertips. I raised my hands, breathing in the bergamot breeze.

Another disfigured grin stretched across Bloodvine's puss. "Won't do you much good, Jade. I've learned to block bard powers since my transformation."

Wonderful. The two of us continued our tango as grunts and smacks resounded around the clearing. I was more than a bard and a healer. I was a warrior's daughter. Bloodvine was a seasoned fighter before his transition, and now he'd be even stronger. He waggled—what I assumed was his brow—as we faced off. He evaded the wolves as they surged forward again.

Two raiders facing off with Lexi weren't so lucky. The wolves flew past us, cannoning them into the ferns. The echo of snarls and tearing flesh vibrated around us. And what do you know the squeals were so freakin' satisfying.

Bloodvine barely turned his head as black ichor spouted into the air behind the wall of macabre fur.

"Nicely done, my brothers," Aust said.

I bobbed left and avoided Bloodvine's backup blade as it sang past my head. A blue bolt of energy sizzled my ear and exploded behind me. The thud of dead weight landed within striking distance of my back.

A barbarian. I'd thank Samuel later.

Bloodvine's rebuttal forced me back, and I had to maneuver quickly to get around the barbarian lying behind me. The relentless hammering of sword on sword jarred my bones and vibrated up my arms to the roots of my molars. Over and over, he came down, until my arms ached, and my teeth rattled.

"Blaze, tighten up." Reign's string of curses highlighted my growing distance from the group. In battle, my father was a beast—truly a Reign of Terror—but when one of his girls faced a threat, he was flat out terrifying. In a mindless fury, he forced his way to me, slicing and splattering through three Scourge.

Bloodvine bombarded me, blow after blow after blow.

The hit came out of nowhere. It caught my shoulder and sent me hurtling over a tangle of roots and onto my ass. I raised my guard cursing as my hip burned like a mother.

Shit, dermabrasion sucked.

The *hiss* and *thwack* of an arrow finding purchase barely registered as I rolled back to my feet and regained my stance. Bloodvine stared down at the lustrous brown shaft sticking out of his chest. Wide-eyed, he reached for the golden eagle flight.

When I moved to strike, he raised his hand. "Kill me, and you won't get the name."

"What name?" I barely had time to pull back.

"Just an insurance policy I've had for a while." He struggled to touch his watch face, and I froze. He coughed, and a spray of blood spewed down his lip and chest. "Remember those conversations long into the night while you tended my injuries? I did some digging on my side and ferreted out one of the men who attacked your farmhouse."

Bloodvine watched me edge forward and smiled. "Let me go, and I'll get it to you." A bolt-hole appeared just behind him. "On my honor."

"Tell me now, or you go nowhere." I heard the juicy rattle as air passed through the hole in his chest. There was a good chance he was walking dead, and I wanted that name.

He shook his head and stumbled backward into the energy field of the bolt-hole. As he disappeared, I heard him repeat his pledge. "On... my... honor."

Reign slew the last Scourge in a decapitating slice and wiped his sword clean of its tarred goo. *Like a knife through molasses.* His shit-kickers gushed and squished through the muck that killing Scourge left behind. He was filthy, sweated out, and magnificent. "Everyone breathing?" Dark eyes assessed each of us before his shoulders eased.

I triaged the group. Reign had a couple of broken fingers, Aust and Tham had some minor magical burns and Samuel had taken a nasty gash to his ribcage. Lexi, as usual, was more offended by the black spray of grossness on her designer boots than any injury she might have sustained. Her theory was, *'Cuts and bones heal. Ripped and ruined leather is forever.'*

"We're good." I grabbed Reign's hand to work on his fingers. "Samuel, could you do something about the stench?"

As Samuel sent a spell around to clear the air, I moved to heal his side.

"Was their objective to secure the spellbook?" Tham asked, helping Aust to his feet and picking up the book.

"No." Reign shook his head. "That was a scouting party. If they had any clue about the book, they would have come at us like a swarm of demons." The air snapped with electricity, and faster than I formed thought to stop them, the Highbornes nocked another round of arrows.

"Hold that thought, boys." Reign held up his hands. "The fight response is a good reflex. In this case, unnecessary. These ugly bastards are with us."

Three Talon enforcers strode from the tree line. They looked like a matching set of hard-core soldiers, armed, stoked, and ready to go off: muscled arms bulged out of leather battle-vests, tree-trunk legs spread in their stance, and expressionless eyes hidden behind mirrored wraparounds.

Intimidating was a laughable understatement.

"Welcome to our band of merry men." I began the introductions pointing from left to right. "Galan, Tham, and Aust, this is Savage, Cowboy, and Rue."

The Highbornes inclined their heads and nodded in turn, their scanning glances capturing the body ink and wide dog-collar Savage wore, the Garth Brook's Southern flare of Cowboy's black hat and boots and Rue's seedy been-there-survived-it-all disposition.

Rue sauntered over to Reign, and his inner fuck-you dialed down for once. "Julian tracked Scourge mobilizing to your destination. A scouting party trailed your Flash signatures about an hour ago."

"You're late on that one." I gestured behind me. "Been there, got the stringy mess of corpses to prove it. We're about to loot the fallen. Want to join the fun?"

"Sadly, not this time, Blaze." Rue scanned the dead bodies scattered around the clearing. "Castian wants that book Behind the Veil and out of Scourge reach ASAP. Reign, you and the girls are to escort the Highbornes back to their village while Samuel watches over Haven."

Reign stiffened. "When the fuck did I become Castian's bitch?"

Cowboy tipped his hat. "Don't kill the messengers, boss. We're just following orders. Figured you'd want to stick close to the girls since the Scourge are in play, so we brought you a warhorse for your travels."

"Is there any movement toward the village?"

"Nada," Cowboy said.

Rue ignored my father's glower spearing him and reached for Rheagan's spellbook. "Gentlemen, if you don't mind."

Tham paused, looking to his brothers before checking with us.

When Reign nodded, he handed it over. In a Flash, Rue, Cowboy, and Savage vanished.

"This is good news," I said, searching the faces of the Highbornes. "With the spellbook in Castian's possession, the Scourge can't access it, and we have one less thing to worry about. Now, let's get you three back to your village and release you all from exile."

CHAPTER TWELVE

Looking to the setting sun two days later, all I thought about was dismounting and closing my legs. We were back at the clearing from the second night, and headed straight for the grotto. My shirt was sweated through and clung to me, the seams of my pants chaffed my inner thighs, and my arms and neck were bitten by a carnivorous insect the size of a fleck of pepper.

The Elves called the little vampires 'no-see-ums'. I might not be able to see-um, but I could sure as hell feel-um.

Oh, and I smelled. No lady-like way to put it. I stunk.

It seemed like I'd been astride Naith for weeks, and wanted to get back to Haven and my students at the Academy. The travel since the battle in the clearing had been uneventful, but the excitement of dropping the reality bomb on the Elders Council had grown to epic proportions with the Highbornes.

If nothing else, tomorrow would be interesting. The Elves had acted out a dozen scenarios. Tham always played the part of the irate, irrational, and irritating council members, and Galan took on the role of the bane of their existence.

Apparently, stirring shit and ruffling feathers was the least the elders deserved.

"Envision the elders' faces when they learn that we have secured our reinstatement to the Realm. The frenzy will be something to marvel," Tham said. "And we three, unworthy and unwanted souls, were chosen by Castian to do it."

They all laughed.

"Unwanted?" I said. "At your *Ambar Lenn*, everyone looked supportive of you."

Tham shook his head. "False appearances, *neelan*. We three are the shame of our community. You are looking at the scoundrel, the disappointment, and the aberration. Those who came to our ceremony, other than Aust's parents and a few friends, attended solely for their own entertainment."

"That's awful." I looked at each of them, shaking my head. Aust caught me watching Galan. His exotic feline eyes lit as his smirk broadened into the first genuine smile I'd seen since his shake-rattle-and-roll on the floor of the tomb two days earlier.

I looked to the trail and told myself it was professional interest drawing my attention. Galan had been scratching the palm of his hand raw for days. Something was up.

When we finally dismounted for the evening, I gave my reins to Aust and went straight to where Galan tossed his bedroll. "Galan, what's happening with your hand?"

Slowly he straightened, lifting his eyes only at the last moment. I reached for his wrist, and he stepped back. "Merely a scratch I received from a jagged rock during the Scourge battle. Gratitude for your concern."

"Will you let me have a look?"

"Again, gratitude, but I respectfully decline your care."

I sucked in a breath. Nothing had changed. Aust trusted me. Tham trusted me. Galan, however, didn't want me or my gift anywhere near him.

"I see." I forced down a wave of nausea pushing up my throat. Pivoting, I undid the strap of my pack and dropped it where our tent would be. Leaning my head forward, I covered my expression with a mass of hair. "Sorry, I wouldn't want to taint you with my evil."

A warm hand secured my wrist. "This is not a reflection on you. It is not personal."

"Not personal?" I jerked my arm back, enraged at the quiver in my voice. "My gift is a huge part of my identity. Nothing could be more personal."

"Jade."

I shook my head, striding from the clearing without a backward glance.

"*Jade!*"

I pulled out of the water and propped myself on the large sloping rock at the edge of the limestone pool. Breathing deep, I wriggled my toes at the tiny fish and tried not to squirm when they came to investigate what intruder had invaded their world. They were cautious and darted away, tentative and unsure of what the unknown might cost them. I could *so* relate.

Somehow, I felt rather than heard Galan arrive behind me. Staring at the pristine water below, I waited. He said nothing.

"What do you want?" I asked.

Leather ties rasped as he unlaced his boots and tossed them to the side. "Mayhap, a moment of your attention." It maddened me how his voice stirred butterflies in my chest. "I would like to explain—"

"Don't bother. Tomorrow you'll be back in your village and done with me. Reign can send someone else to help Lexi reintegrate your village." I drew a deep breath and cursed how good he smelled.

Wrapping my arms around my knees, I became well aware that I wore only my bra and underpants. "Our quest is complete once you three are safely returned, and the Elders are served Castian's release. Won't be long now."

"You need not go."

I laughed. "You can't accept me, and I won't stay where I'm not wanted." Saying the words stung like vinegar in a cut. He rolled up his pant legs, sat beside me, and slipped his feet into the water. I refused to look at him and stared down into the water.

"Not wanted?" he repeated.

My heart broke a little more. "I won't apologize for my affinity—"

"Jade. Please look at me."

My hair swung as I shook my head. "I have nothing to say." Hot tears stung my eyes, but I'd rather he thought I was a bitch than a fatal attraction.

"Very well, I shall speak, you listen." He paused as if picking his words. "I cannot say being with you is easy." As I fought the urge to bolt, he swept back my hair. "*Sweet merciful gods.*" Galan stroked my tears with his thumb. "Oh, Blossom, the last thing I want is to see tears shed because of me."

I stood, brushing off my cheeks, and then my butt. "I don't need your pity." I stepped past him and stopped only when his hand clenched my calf.

Without letting go of me, he rose and took hold of my arm. "Please, hear me out."

"I've heard *enough*." I pulled at my arm. "You can't stand me. I *get* it!"

In a blur, he yanked me to his chest, pinning both my arms behind my back. He held me tight, crushing us together while his breath came fast, and his heart slammed against mine. "I was *saying*. . ." He struggled against me, grabbed a fistful of hair to hold my attention locked on his. "Being with you is not easy. You stir my affections far beyond my comfort. I have fought for control, yet trigger a desire I can neither deny nor ignore."

I stopped struggling and searched his face for any sign he was screwing with me. He couldn't be so cruel. Could he?

He smiled at my expression. "Is it so difficult to believe?"

I closed my mouth. "Between the scowling, disdain, and insults, I must have missed it."

Releasing his hold, he brushed my hair behind my shoulder and inhaled. "Since the moment I laid, poised over you on the forest floor, I was at my wit's end. My body burns with hunger, my heart aches to be near you, and my senses strain to catch your scent on the breeze or hear your silken voice. I cannot explain what it is between us, Jade. It is synergy for certain, the whole larger than the both of us. Physically you are resplendent, beyond that..."

He kissed my exposed collarbone, then burned a trail of seduction up the column of my neck. Silken hair draped over my chest and bra, tickling as he nipped the tender skin behind my ear. I locked my knees as heat engulfed me.

"From out of nowhere, I have the uncontrollable need to claim you as my own. I think of little else save my desire to lay with you, our bodies united. I have struggled to fight it, and in doing so, I have hurt us both. For that, I apologize."

"Why fight? Am I that bad?"

"No." He kissed the bridge of my nose, hovering just inches from my face. "It would be far too easy to lose myself with you." His crooked grin melted me, stoked the fire smoldering low in my belly. "Jade, if I were to give in and take you, we would be bound for eternity. Highbornes mate for life."

I don't know what he read in my eyes, but his smile softened. "You are an exquisite female, spirited, strong, educated, and *human*. I am of Elven blood and have never been outside my valley. I hold no station, no notable skills, and I am regarded in my village as a terrible waste of a male."

What the hell? "Why?"

He ran his fingers through his hair and frowned. "When my *naneth* died birthing Lia, I went against my sire's wishes and our village traditions and raised her myself. The elders demanded she be placed in a home with a female to leave me the freedom to contribute to our society as a male of worth. I refused."

"So?"

His face tightened. "So, I shamed my father and gave up my chance of ever holding any station within my community."

"How does—I'm sorry I don't get what that has to do with anything."

"Do you want to know what my father said on the eve of my *Ambar Lenn*?" '*Galanodel, your life is frivolous, your attitude puerile. My only solace is that your naneth's death prevented her from real*izing *the bitter disappointment you would become.*'"

I reined in my disgust before Galan's gaze captured mine. When our eyes met, I hoped my face was expressionless. In Lexi's vision at the *Ambar Lenn*, he spoke about his father. *'Disdain and unending criticisms are the bricks and mortar of our relationship.'*

His tone was cool and detached. "I expect nothing less from my sire." His eyes focused on the white-water pooling at the base of the waterfall. "If you bonded with me, you would share my shame, and I cannot allow that. You deserve more from a male."

It took a moment before I could speak. "I'm sorry, Galan. To be ridiculed because you chose to raise your sister was wrong. At the risk of overstepping and thrusting my opinion on you again, your father is a colossal bastard."

He laughed louder than I had ever heard, drowning out the rush of the waterfall for a moment. For the first time since I'd met him, his smile lit up his eyes. "I appreciate your opinions more by the moment, yet they change nothing."

"I was raised by a man, a warrior. I'd love to see one of your elders say Reign was a waste of manhood. He'd tear their lungs out their assholes."

Galan's laughter vibrated against my chest. "Gods, you have a wicked tongue."

"Sorry."

He pulled me closer and shook his head. "I have lived a century and ten with those who speak only what is acceptable. I detest it. You, beautiful Blossom, are never to hold back. Promise me."

"You'll live to regret that."

He tilted his head and smiled a crooked smile. "I shall take my chances."

"All right. If I'm honest, I think we should forget about forever for now. Forget about station and shame and your community." I brushed his cheek. His skin was warm, and he pressed a kiss into my palm.

He watched me, his face unreadable. "To what end?"

I held his gaze and pulled the tie at the waist of his tunic. With steady hands, I pushed the fabric off his smooth, muscled shoulders. It dropped to the slope of the rock below with a soft thud. "Let's explore this spark between us and see if it ignites." I left him to think about that and eased into the water. The initial chill of the surface encircled my hips, my ribs, my shoulders. After gliding across the pool toward the falls, I turned to catch a gorgeous glimpse of his pale, yet seriously choice, backside as he dove in to join me.

Galan was as graceful in water as he was on land. After a couple of strong strokes, he caught me up in his arms and swam backward toward the swirling mist of the waterfall. When we came to a shallow spot, he stood, waist-deep, and pulled me up against him. My hands slid flat against his pecs, and he tilted his head back, eyes closed. He arched his back and exhaled, letting my wandering fingers do their thing—that is until I reached his injured hand.

He winced at the contact and blew out a breath. "Jade, might you examine my hand?"

I searched his expression, my heart picking up its pace. "Why now?"

He let out an irritated sigh. "That will be evident in a moment."

"Are you sure?"

A slow grin broke across his face. "My refusal was never a matter of trust." Galan's gaze burned me with its passion. I doubted a human man could manage such intensity. "Gods, you are a vision when your eyes dance, *neelan*. Liquid emeralds."

I rubbed my palms together, slowly raising my hands, allowing my magic to touch his life. I wanted him to trust me, needed it. Soft as the brush of a feather, I dragged my fingertips across his palm. *Desire.* The intensity of his feelings jolted through me. As my ability took hold, a sexual current arced between us. My knees weakened, and the hair on my nape rose. Every nerve ending tingled. Not wanting it to end, I moved to heal his lip and eye.

Raw emotion swirled in my head and coursed through me: attraction, sexual hunger, wanton, burning lust. My body's heat burst into flame. I looked into his wide, wild eyes and bit my bottom lip.

Breathe Jade.

"This is why you didn't want me to heal you?"

"A futile effort to deny what I knew you would see in my soul." With his gaze locked, his lips began an excruciatingly slow trip to meet mine. He closed the distance, a look of absolute conviction glowing in his eyes. Cupping my face, he pulled me against his warm, firm mouth.

Sweet gods of the Veil!

He had a way with his lips that defied explanation. They were silk and satin, moving with a raw fierceness that set fire to my entire body. Everything around us receded, and when I thought I might lose my mind, his tongue invaded my mouth. Penetrating with possessive sweeps, he moaned, and my head spun.

Standing there, skin to skin, under the spray of the waterfall, all I wanted was him. I'd never felt anything like this desire before. It snapped through me like a lightning strike. It ignited every cell in one sudden white-hot awakening. It stole my breath.

Galan's kiss tasted like honeysuckle and sunshine. Sweet and sinful mixed with raw, masculine lust. The pounding of my heart in my ears drowned out the crash of the falls, and my body ignited. Of their own volition, my hands wrapped around his back and laced through his wet silver hair. My fingers twined deep and pulled him closer. With his mouth on mine, he backed us into the edge of the falling water. A cool rush cascaded over us as his lips, silk over steel, met mine. His eagerness verged on desperation, his body incredibly hard.

Moving my lips along his cheek, I gasped for air and then nipped the gentle peak of his ear. His throaty moan told me I was on to something. I exploited the discovery, nibbling, and focusing my attention first on one ear, then the other.

"Sweet mercies, Jade. How is a male to keep a logical mind when you are determined to seduce? Verily, we need to stop," he gasped, shaking his head. "You are far too tempting." When he tried to wrench away, I tightened my grip in his hair and held him in place. "Jade, please. Gods, I want to sheath myself inside you with a madness so uncontrollable I tremble. It is . . . animalistic and primal. We need to stop."

I don't know what had taken over me, but I knew what I needed.

Destiny. I raked my nails down his back and cupped the globe of his ass beneath the surface of the water.

"By the love of all that is holy." His eyes rolled back. "Have you any idea what you are doing to me?"

I moaned as he spanned my ribs, strong fingers pulling me tight against his musculature. His arousal pressed against my navel, strained and ready. Blinding sensation burned through me. My hands slid up his back, across his shoulders, fisted into his silky hair. *Dwinn.*

"Gods help me, Blossom, I want you." My body arched under the flow of water as my core wept for his attention.

Galan stiffened. I didn't notice what he'd seen or smelled or heard. He pivoted toward the edge of the pool. In a blur, he shielded me from the curious gaze of Tham, Lexi, and Aust. Mercifully, Reign wasn't with them.

"Well, we were wrong," Lexi giggled. "You're not about to *kill* each other."

"No, not unless they were to suffocate," Tham said.

Aust at least had the decency to look embarrassed. "Um, apologies. We were concerned when you failed to return and wished to ensure that you were well."

"I'd say they're well," Lexi smirked.

"Doing very well indeed," Tham said.

"How long were you standing there?" I asked, peering around Galan's shoulder, struggling for breath.

"Since Galan wanted to mate you with animalistic and primal madness." Tham rubbed his hand over his mouth as his shoulders shook.

Standing behind Galan, I watched the tips of his ears blush scarlet. "And privacy means so little that you didn't make your presence known?"

"We were stunned by the scene." Lexi barely contained her giggles. "Besides, we've suffered through the past week with you two at each other's throats. We deserved a little voyeurism. Damn Highborne, you've got game."

"Hmph." The muscle in the side of his jaw twitched wildly. "If you would be so kind as to give us a moment, we will join you on the path presently."

When they retreated into the trees, Galan and I swam back to our clothes.

"Great." I fought wet legs into my leathers. "They'll be impossible to live with now."

CHAPTER THIRTEEN

The next afternoon, Naith's massive body swayed beneath me as we made our way through the last of the journey back to the village. We saw the Highborne ruin site in the distance, set atop the plateau beneath the rumbling purple sky. If we were lucky, the storm which threatened to unfurl on us would hold off a little while longer. I tried to anticipate what our arrival would bring as I urged Naith to pull back a bit.

"What kind of response should Lexi, Reign, and I expect from your Elders Council?"

The Elves chuckled.

Tham jogged up beside me. "Imagine a small holding pen with a dozen fat, lazy chickens scratching around, kicking up sand, and looking down their beaks at the rest of the flock. Picture them all puffed up and cocksure. Now, imagine a hungry wolf suddenly dropped into the center of that pen. Can you see the chickens squawking and scrambling as they flail around, clucking madly? That is what awaits us."

"Really?"

All three Elves nodded, looking more amused by the moment.

I waited for a comment from my sister. When it didn't come, I

JL MADORE

glanced over—"Shit! Tham grab Lexi before she falls." I scissored my legs over Naith's head and dropped to my feet.

Thank the gods for Highborne reflexes.

Both Aust and Tham swooped to Puff's side, caught Lexi mid-fall, and lowered her to the ground. I knelt beside her and placed her hands over mine. The deep violet pupils of her eyes had expanded, and now they were swirling solid violet.

"Jade, what is it?" Tham asked. "What is happening?"

"She's having a vision," Reign explained.

Lexi's face blanked out, and her eyes rolled back. When they blinked open, images shimmered in front of my eyes.

∾

Clouds hung thick, and lightning stitched across an angry sky. The village swarmed like a hornet's nest as Scourge raiders sliced their way through Highbornes. Rows of cottages glowed orange while plumes of ebony smoke billowed toward the stars. Attackers tossed torches into buildings and then grappled choking Elves as they staggered into the street.

In the main square, Highborne men were corralled and strung up, hands bound and hooked to posts, trees, and maypoles. As women screamed, the barbed whips of a cat-o-nine descended upon the men. They ripped and mutilated the ivory flesh of those who fought back.

Behind a bench, a boy crumpled over the body of a lifeless woman. His small fingers gathered pink intestines where they spilled onto the cobblestone as he gently pressed them back into place. He knelt in a slick pool of blood, sobbing as his mother's life seeped between the cracks of the walk.

Movement in the center square hushed the chaos.

Abaddon, a deceivingly handsome man with the charm of a viper, held up his hand. He pointed into the crowd, and Bloodvine and another raider seized a young girl. She cried out, delicate hands extending for an anchor in the crowd.

Highbornes sprang to grab hold only to be beaten back by mace and flail.

"You know what I seek." Abaddon's voice was seductive with persuasion. He waited. No one came forward. He loomed over the girl, raking his wand down her body. Wherever he touched, her frame twisted, and a shrill scream pealed from her throat. "Where is the female? Anyone? No?"

No one responded.

A scarlet pulse launched from his wand, crushing her in a cocoon of light. Her delicate body arched, snapped, and crumpled into a contorted heap.

In the echo of silence that followed, Abaddon turned back to the Highbornes. "If you give her to us, we will leave you in peace. You have my word. Now, where is the female?"

∼

I yanked my hands back the moment the vision ended. This was my fault. Bloodvine had found a healer for his wound and gone straight to Abaddon. If I'd killed him when I had the chance—

"Jade? Are you well?" Tham asked.

It was Reign's firm grasp, lifting me that brought me to focus. "Tell me."

"Jade?" Lexi blinked awake. "Did you see? I couldn't—"

"I saw." I ran a quick hand over Lexi's cheek, then strode to Naith and grabbed the M&M's from my backpack. "Aust, will you call in some friends and stay with Lexi until she's steady? The chocolate helps, but it takes a bit before she's ready to roll."

"Certainly, what—"

"Scourge are in your village." I mounted Naith and looked back on the horrified faces of the Highbornes.

"Are they after the book?" Reign slid his foot into the stirrup of his warhorse and vaulted himself into the saddle. "How bad is it?"

"It wasn't a scouting party. It was a raid." I pulled my hair back and tied it as Reign cursed. Aust helped Lexi sit up against his side.

JL MADORE

"Princess," Reign growled, "you and Aust make your way as soon as you're steady and not a second before. If you can't plunge a dagger, you stay away, we clear?"

"Crystal." She nodded, laying her head against Aust's chest.

"We'll see you two in a few. Stay safe."

"And you as well," Aust said, as the four of us raced away.

"Jade, what are you not saying?" Galan hid the stress in his voice well, but I heard it.

"They aren't there for the book." On the fly, I met his gaze. "They want the female with the silver hair. They want Lia."

Galan looked ill as he pushed forward, his sure strides and muscled legs eating up the distance. We moved with the force of a hurricane. I was thankful Lexi, and I had studied the village intel for the mission. There were three points of entry into the village. Two bridges accessed the surrounding forests and a sandy path that snaked down from where their ancient ruin site sat on a plateau above the village proper.

Fifty-six stone cottages radiated in a spoke and wheel pattern, clustered at the crux of two small rivers. Livestock, stables, and barns were located downriver to the west. The watermill, blacksmith, and altar house were along the east. Within half an hour, we spread out, searching a shell-shocked little ghost town. The clouds hung in a wide heavy blanket overhead, rumbling and threatening. There was no rain, though, and there was also no sign of the Scourge.

Reign and Tham raced toward the west river while Galan and I searched for Lia along the east. The streets were empty except for a couple of dozen Highborne bodies scattered among fallen weapons and smoldering homes. Galan looked at the faces of the dead as we passed. A middle-aged man, his eyes clouded with death, caught his attention. He cursed.

"Who is it?"

"Aust's father, Cameron. He was an extraordinary male." He bent, closed his eyes, and straightened his tunic. *Shit.* How much was Aust supposed to take? After a deep breath, Galan led the way. We ran from one cottage, across the courtyard to another, then to a meadow by the river, and back to the courtyard. He looked like he was about to explode. There was no sign of his sister. There was no sign of anyone.

"Where would they go if there was danger?" I asked.

"The altar-building?" And we were off again.

"*Galan!*" Our heads whipped around at the call.

"Durian," he said, racing to where a teenaged boy had popped out from between two cottages. "Where is Lia? Durian, have you seen Lia?"

The momentary excitement of seeing us faded as his expression crumbled. "Galan, they took her. We tried to stop them. But they were many, and we were unprepared."

"Which way did they take her?" he choked. "And how long ago?"

"Mayhap a quarter candle's burning, over the western bridge toward the forest."

"Tell Gisir we are in pursuit." Galan reached for my hand and headed west.

"*Wait!* Galan—"

Galan growled. "Durian, I must—"

He shook his head. "Lia was at Nyssa's when they found her. She and Iadon tried to fight the raiders off. They were no match."

"And?"

"They struck Nyssa to the ground." Durian's gaze dropped to his boots. "They kicked and beat her, Galan. She bleeds inside. Iadon says the baby and she are lost to us."

Galan staggered. Track his sister or say goodbye to his best friend. I touched my index finger to my thumb, pressed them to my mouth, and blew. Wherever Reign was, he would hear my whistle and come. In a matter of seconds, they were at our side, and we filled them in.

Durian's eyes popped wide when Reign halted his horse and thudded heavily to the ground. In another situation, it would have been funny.

"We'll follow the trail," Reign said. "Talon are arriving."

Tham squeezed Galan's shoulder. "You are needed here, brother mine."

Galan hesitated but nodded. "Durian, where is she?"

"The council's inner chamber."

That's all he needed. He clasped my hand and ran the smoldering streets to a long, two-story stone building. I sucked in a breath as the carved wooden door swung back, and the fecund scents of fear and death hit us like a wall. This was the aftermath of battle: the tang of copper, mingled with the smoke of lamp and candles, and the reek of spilled bowels.

Galan paused in the entry and scanned the room. Heads turned as we scuttled through the dozens of injured and their families. Muffled whispers rose like a misty fog. I supposed we were quite a sight, Galan back from his *Ambar Lenn* with a leather-clad, red-headed human in tow. Either he didn't hear them or didn't care. He was fixated on a cot at the back of the chamber.

"Nyssa!"

The man hovering over the cot pulled back, revealing the woman I'd seen in Lexi's vision. At a glance, it was obvious she was in a great deal of trouble. Aside from the bruising, her unfocused gaze followed the direction of Galan's voice, weak but warm. "Thank the Fates," she sighed. "The raiders spoke of you, and I feared—"

"I am well." Galan fell to his knees. "Iadon, Nyssa, this is Jade." He pulled me to his side. "She is an emissary of the Fae and a powerful healer. Allow her heal you Nyssa, you and your young."

Iadon let out a strangled cry. "A healer?"

Galan turned to him, the muscle in his jaw twitching once again. "Trust me, Iadon. I love them as you do. If Nyssa and the young can be saved, Jade will do it. I have seen her gift."

"Gift? Galan, the elders will never—"

I turned to the confused faces of the Highborne crowd as they parted to make way for the host from Lexi's vision. The fair-haired gentleman, still dressed sharply despite the evidence of a harrowing day marring his pant legs and jacket with dust and blood, strode forward. "What is this, Galan? What say you?"

Galan steeled himself, folding his hands together and pressing his shoulders back. "Jade shall heal Nyssa, Gisir. She works on Castian's behalf."

"Heal? Using magic?" Gisir's ears blotched pink in the span of a moment. "In a sennight, have you forgotten everything we stand for? Galan, even you should know better."

Galan's jaw clenched as another well-tailored man strode into the showdown. He was an imposing man with hard, cold eyes and a cutting tone. Galan ignored his arrival and continued. "Jade *shall* save Nyssa and her young. She healed Tham of magical burns in the cavern of the ancient High Ones and Aust when a Mahogany bear crushed his insides and tore his flesh."

A cry escaped from a woman with warm, wheat-colored curls, weeping in a circle of women. Galan bowed his head and smiled. "Fash not, Elora, I swear to you, Aust is well and will join us shortly. He stayed behind to help an ailing friend." When she nodded, he turned back to the argument at hand. "Jade deserves respect, and Nyssa deserves a chance to meet her young."

Gisir turned to me. "No offense is meant to you as an individual. However, magic—"

"A vast difference separates a natural affinity given by the gods and sorcery."

He does listen. I held back my smile as Galan recited a speech I'd given him almost a week ago. My heart sang to have him stand as my champion for once instead of my accuser.

While their argument continued, a warm hand took my wrist. Iadon's gaze almost broke my heart. Battle-worn and bloody, his red-rimmed eyes were pleading. "If it be within your power and Castian's will, save them. I beg of you."

"And how do we know *what* Castian's will is?" The second man snapped. "My son has never been one to follow rules. He spits in the face of our beliefs more oft than not. Surely his opinion cannot be given any merit."

Oh, so this is the colossal ass-wipe.

"Fighting for Nyssa is not spitting on anyone's beliefs," Galan growled. "I swear to you on Lia's safe return that Jade is not a witch or a sorceress. Her gift works the same way as Aust's affinity for wildlife. It is not magic."

"This argument is taking time Nyssa can't afford." I opened my hands and tilted my head back. "Castian? What would you have me do?"

The air in the chamber swirled as the fetid stench of death dissolved and was replaced by bergamot, mint, and sage. The crowd shrieked and recoiled like frightened mice, and even though I wanted to roll my eyes and tell them all to get a grip, I reminded myself that this was an unknown for them. Oh, and I was evil incarnate. Whatevs.

Both mother and child must live, Mir. *It is essential.*

"That's all I need to know." Bending to the cot, I assessed my patient and then my surroundings. "Galan, I need you and—Iadon, is it?"

"Yes."

"This cot is too low for extensive healing. Gently, move the whole thing onto that table, grab as many lanterns as you can manage, and bring those decorative screens over to give us some privacy." As I rhymed off the list of things, I'd need the two men sprang into action, and Aust's mother, Elora, broke free of her supporters to retrieve the washbasin and linens.

The hand that grabbed my arm squeezed and yanked me back. "You forget your place, *female*." Galan's father spat the word female like it left a foul taste in his mouth. "You hold no authority here."

My inner fire threw sparks. I looked from the man's sneer to where he was cutting off circulation to my arm and back. "I *will* use my gift, and I *will* save them because Castian asked me to. It's you who has no authority here. Now, release my arm and let me work."

"Castian asked?" He laughed. "Just because you can perform some parlor trick—"

"Trust me. You don't want to piss me off right now. Let go of me." Heat built in my chest and I fought to retain an air of propriety. I was their first contact for god's sake.

"Never have I taken orders from a female, and today will not be the day to start."

"Last warning." I pulled at my arm, and when his grip didn't lessen, my temper let loose. The tangle of my hair flew wildly around my face, and energy blazed across my skin, exploding in a wave. Galan's father snatched his hand back, shaking the scalded digits as I pivoted to step behind the screen.

So much for not spooking the townsfolk.

Strong arms grappled me from behind and clasped across my chest. *Fuck propriety.*

With a quick elbow to his ribs, I twisted, thrust my knee into his crotch, and just for good measure followed up with a palm-thrust to his arrogant pie-hole.

Galan lunged around the privacy screen, wide-eyed, and then glanced down at his father writhing on the floorboards clutching himself. The corners of his mouth twitched, and I saw the gleam in his eyes. "Did he offend your womanly abilities?"

I calmed my hair and moved to my makeshift surgery table. "Something like that."

Nyssa was unconscious as Galan kissed her knuckles and squeezed her hand. "Hold on, Nyssa, Jade will take care of you."

I pulled Nyssa's shirt off her stomach and placed my hands firmly on the baby. Bowing over the bulge, I reached out. The baby was in distress. Her little heartbeat was slow and irregular. She was out of position, and Nyssa was hemorrhaging.

"What is it, Jade?"

A freaking mess. "Nothing I can't handle."

Galan searched my face, and though I hoped he couldn't read the truth, his eyes pinched closed. "This birthing will be different. I know you will save them."

"I cannot lose them," Iadon whispered. "I will cease to exist without my mate."

Elora, moved inside the screens, carrying the blankets and supplies I'd asked for. After setting them on the deep window ledge, she gasped at something in the main chamber.

I glanced over. Lexi waved as Aust caught his mother in his arms. Maybe with all the turmoil, the Highbornes would miss the fact that Aust wore sunglasses inside the hall.

"How does she fare?" Galan asked.

JL MADORE

"I need to get this bleeding stopped."

"And if you cannot stop it?"

"Then, I'll take the baby."

"And what of Nyssa?" Iadon brushed his finger down her cheek.

I took a total pass on that one. "She's a fighter, right? Focus on that." With both my hands pressed above the baby, I began to sing.

Galan looked to Iadon to explain. "Jade's healing energy comes from Castian, the patron god of poetry and music. When she sings, the strength of her gift is enhanced." My breath caught as Iadon and Galan sang with me, their voices a harmonized in silken sorrow.

Fully connected, the shimmer of Nyssa's memory filled my mind.

∼

Nyssa and Iadon meandered along a riverbank path, strolling into a golden meadow of wildflowers and hummingbirds. Their feet crunched on tiny stones, and the perfume of hyacinth blooms filled the air. Nyssa waved to a stunning young woman with silver locks, lying on the grassy hill next to Galan. He was sleeping, a look of utter of contentment on his face. With his shirt open, his muscled chest absorbed the heat of the afternoon sun.

Nyssa approached, laughing at what Lia was up to. "You best flee when he wakes."

"He is adorable," Lia said, a guilty smile tugging at her mouth.

"You are both incorrigible." Iadon kept a straight face but couldn't hide his amusement.

Galan half-opened his eyes and eased his arm from behind his head. When he brushed the lavender flowers braided into his hair, Lia and Nyssa burst into giggles. Fully awake now, he rolled over Lia, straddling her waist. He mussed her locks and tickled her sides until she squirmed in a fit of squeals. "What shall I to do with you, little one?" he said.

"Love me forever?"

"As if there were ever a choice."

I pushed away from the images, listening as Galan reminisced about their childhood, whispering into Nyssa's ear. Every now and then, Iadon would nod at one of Galan's memories and chuckle with him.

It was full dark outside when I finally gained control. I was beyond drained, past dizzy, and verging on nausea. I wiped my brow with the back of my wrist. "Iadon, I'm about to wake Nyssa up. I've stopped the bleeding and rotated the baby to where I need her. It's time to push."

"Will they survive?"

"We're doing well." I squeezed in beside Galan at the head of the bed and massaged her temples, realigning her energies. Concentrated on the thrum of her heart, I worked until, after a few minutes, her eyes fluttered open.

"*Melamin.*" Iadon clutched her hand to his chest.

Nyssa looked from her husband to Galan and back. "*My young!*"

All three of us jumped to calm her as she thrashed.

"No, Nyssa." Iadon stroked her cheek, his tears glistening in the lamplight. "The babe is well. I swear it."

As she exhaled, she met my gaze and froze.

"Nyssa, this is Jade." Galan's tone was low and reverent. "She is a healer in Castian's service and has cared for you and your young."

I nodded and moved to her side. "The blow you took caused some bleeding. I've repaired the damage, and now it's time to have this baby. Are you ready?"

Galan straightened. "I shall return your privacy."

Nyssa clamped onto his hand and shook her head. "No, I need you with me."

"Stay," Iadon said. "Please, for Nyssa and the babe."

Galan kissed her forehead and reclaimed his seat.

"Okay gentlemen, ease her up."

Galan and Iadon each slipped an arm under Nyssa and lifted her forward. Once Elora had made her comfortable, we were ready to roll. Initiating labor was easy-peasy after everything we'd been through. Within minutes Nyssa was bearing down.

JL MADORE

"Iadon, come bring your daughter into this realm."

"Is that possible?" His eyes glistened. "Oh, Jade. Verily I would love it."

"Hurry. She's anxious to meet everyone."

Iadon left Nyssa's side, taking two quick steps toward me, then dashed back to his wife to kiss her and then hurried back to my side again.

Nyssa chuckled then grimaced as she clasped her free hand against her belly. "She's impatient, like her *eda*."

I positioned Iadon's unsteady hands to support the baby. A moment later, their baby girl was in his grasp and wailing. Radiation of sheer bliss replaced the worry and despair he'd worn like a shroud all afternoon. "Merry meet, Ella," he choked, "We waited some time for you, little one." When his voice broke, he cradled her to his chest and closed his eyes.

Elora brought a small blanket and basin to the table and busied herself as I took care of finishing things on my end. When Ella was clean and calm, Iadon laid her in Nyssa's arms.

"Hello *neelan*," Nyssa whispered, her cheeks glistening.

Ella wasn't the first baby I'd delivered, though she was the first Elven baby. I couldn't decide if her angelic features were genetic or if she was simply extraordinarily perfect. Tiny blonde wisps framed a cherubic face and curled over tiny pointed ears.

Galan bent over Nyssa and kissed the top of her head. "Congratulations, *Naneth*."

After taking a sec to wash up, a wave of dizziness hit. My hand shot out to catch the wall as the floor of the chamber began to wave. Whether it was the emotionally charged day or the hours of healing, the room just wouldn't settle.

"Jade?" Galan's arms drew me tight against his chest. When the world steadied, he lifted my chin to meet his gaze. "Gratitude, Jade." He kissed me on my nose and stepped back. "I wish to formally apologize to you, once again, before friends and family. True to form, I continue to apologize to you for one thing or another."

I chuckled. "What for this time, Highborne?"

"I am a hypocrite, a judgmental imbecile, an ass even." He winked and flashed me his crooked smile. "I chastised and vexed you for your gift, until the moment when those I love needed help. I cannot begin to tell you... to express how thankful I am for you and your incredible God-given ability. There are no words. I would never have survived this loss. For sparing me that devastation and for giving us this gift, I pledge my eternal gratitude."

He bowed his head, sank to one knee, and fisted his hand over his heart. In response to this, Iadon left his newborn with Nyssa and did the same. Then Tham and Aust silently strode inside the screen, and they too followed suit.

"Blessed be." Their melodic voices filled the space.

I blinked fast and ignored the Highborne crowd staring at me. "That was easily your best apology yet, Galan. Thank you. Now, get up." Galan winked again as he rose, and the touch of his gaze fluttered inside me like a butterfly in my chest. He closed the distance. His hands cupped my face and pulled me against his warm, firm lips.

Sweet gods, I'd missed this. His mouth was heaven. His lips moved with such a surge of passion that my eyes brimmed. My body burst to life, pounded, pulsed, and tingled. A bolt of raw, physical need jolted from my toes, snapped through my cells and burned just under my skin. I grasped the color of Galan's emotions in my mind, a kaleidoscope of swirling hues. I drank in the scent of him. Intoxicating. Then, too soon, he withdrew and pulled me into his arms.

"Thank you, Jade Elizabeth Glaster, for all of your quirks and gifts and uniqueness. You are an exceptional female, an unstoppable force of nature. My life has been blessed and forever altered because you are a part of it."

The fact that he was whispering meant nothing. Every person behind those flimsy screens was leaning forward to catch the show, staring, scowling, and whispering.

The other men stood, and Galan realized Tham was back. "What news have you of Lia?"

"Reign and I followed the trail until its end at the river's fork. Faolan covered the forest. There is no sign. The Scourge must have vanished using one of those magical portals or Flashes to another location. Reign took Puff and Naith and returned to Haven with Samuel while the Talon enforcers remain to take up the search. They said they shall contact us as soon as there is news. In the meantime, Jade and Lexi are to continue readying the village."

I squeezed Galan's shoulder. "Reign will find her. Don't panic yet."

He rounded on me. "The Scourge have my sister. How can I not?"

CHAPTER FOURTEEN

We sat at the newly excavated breakfast table in Tham's cottage, picking at the fruit and sweet bread Elora had sent over for us. Despite his nonchalance, Tham was a very gracious host when put to the task. His place was modest and welcoming, in a weekend by the lake kind of way. And he'd bent over backward to make Lexi and I feel at home.

Most of yesterday was spent occupying Galan, in an effort to clear enough floor space for the four of us to live. Lexi and I were sharing Tham's parents' old room, and Tham and Galan were in Tham's room. The task of organizing and airing out Tham's life had worked well to distract Galan. Now that we were settled, *he* was definitely not.

"*Three days.*" Galan dragged his fingers through his hair. "Three days and *nothing.*"

"It's barely been two, Galan. Try to stay calm." I reached across the table to touch his arm. He pulled back.

"Please, Jade, you must ask Castian to aid us."

I shook my head. "That's not how it works. He's the god of all members of the Realm of the Fair. He won't interfere as long as no Fae gods or members of other Pantheons are involved. If it's a realm problem, he won't get involved." I nudged the tray of fruit toward him and tried to recall when he'd eaten last. He looked at the platter with disdain then flipped the glare at me.

Tham ended the uneasy silence. "So, ladies, were we correct about the elders?"

I pinched the stem of a purple dewberry and set it on the edge of my plate. "Well, nobody has clucked or scratched in the dirt if that's what you're asking."

"Actually, they've pretty much stayed out of our way." Lexi shrugged and sipped her juice. "We established a formal perimeter, training schedules, and worked out our team leaders for ongoing security patrols. They haven't opposed a thing. Either they don't know what to make of us, or they're scared shitless of Jade and her evil ways." Lexi wriggled her fingers, giggling.

"Watch it. I know where you live."

Lexi laughed harder. "Or maybe it's the fear of igniting your blazing hell-fire temper."

"Is that the true reason your warrior comrades call you Blaze?" Tham asked. "I thought it might tribute your hair."

"No. It's definitely her temper." Lexi giggled. "Oh, and her little trick with candles."

"Little trick?"

"No trick," I said, shrugging. "Sometimes, when I lose my temper, candles burn wild." I thought about my little temper tantrum in the inner chamber yesterday and sighed. "Temper or not, I shouldn't have sacked Galan's father. As an emissary of Haven, it was bad form."

"No apologies," Galan said. "He deserved that and more."

Tham broke a piece of pastry off a large loaf and slathered on some mango chutney. "I heard you were fighting to save Nyssa and Ella at the time, were you not?"

I nodded. "Still, it was crude." I bit my berry, and its juice dripped down my chin. I chased the sticky mess with my napkin and picked up another berry, which I held out to Galan. He was having none of it, staring across the room, shoulders stiff and jaw clenched. I pinched off the stem and held it to his lips. "We'll find her, Galan."

He waved away my hand and slid the fruit platter across the table.

"The Scourge took the lives of twenty-eight villagers, including Aust's father. There is nothing to stop them from killing Lia. If she still lives." Galan's chair scraped against the floorboards as he stood.

My breakfast sat like a stone in my gut. I pushed away my plate. "She's alive. They sought her out and left as soon as they had her. There's a reason." I took out my phone for the hundredth time. *Ring dammit.* "How were Aust and Elora at the memorial ceremony last night?"

"Persevering with grace," Tham said. "Apologies again for your exclusion. Aust wanted you to be there, despite the upset it would have caused."

Lexi shrugged. "Traditions are traditions."

"Besides," I said, "we enjoyed taking care of the baby."

Tham ran his fingers over the row of runes embroidered on the black choker he'd worn the past two days. "I detest grieving bands."

"Nonsense. They are a lovely tradition." Galan adjusted the black band where it lay against his Adam's apple. "I pray Aust knows he does not face Cameron's death alone."

"He knows," Tham said, wiping his empty plate with his bread. "Nyssa invited him and Elora for evening repast with us tonight. With his eyes the way they are, Elora wants him to remain in the shadows for now. The elders will never accept his—what? Evolution? Transformation? Well, whatever it is, with the loss of Cameron, the two of them are dealing with quite enough."

I nodded. "If it's ready, Galan and I will go through the portal tomorrow and find out what's happening with the search for Lia and maybe something about Aust's gift."

"I cannot believe the elders allowed a gateway established inside the village."

"Jade can be very *persuasive* when she wants to be." Lexi winked. "Besides, if the Scourge return, help can flood from Haven to your streets in a matter of minutes." She tipped back the last of her juice and checked her watch. "Gotta run. The morning training session starts in fifteen. Wait till you boys see what I have planned. It'll make yesterday's workout feel like a picnic in the meadow."

"Oh, joy." Tham piled the dishes on the buffet and stretched his neck. "Then come along tiny-she-devil and crack your whip." Lexi slapped his shoulder, and he arched away from her touch. "So, Jade, what plans of torture and torment have you this morning?"

"Nothing too arduous." I stood up and straightened the shirt I'd borrowed for the day. "I thought Galan and I would take those llama-horse-things out for a long-range sweep."

Galan turned from the window, the sunlight highlighting worry on his pale face. "Those *renier* would love a long ride. Alas, I am due in the meadow for Lexi's torture session."

"Well, I do happen to have a considerable amount of influence over your trainer." I laughed and held my hand out to him. "Come with me for a few hours. It will clear your head." When he made to argue, I raised my palm. "If Reign calls, we'll come right back."

"I am not fit company, Jade. You might well regret this."

I took his hand in mine and headed for the door. "I'll take my chances."

Galan led me to the western edge of the village where the stables and pens were bustling with livestock: renier, strange cows with double chins, large peccary, chickens...

We found what we needed in an Elven equivalent to a tack room and readied the renier. Galan chose Celeb, a gray and black male who stood about seventeen hands, and I picked a chocolate brown mare named Roch. She would've measured just under fourteen. With their long, thick wool, we didn't need saddles, so all Galan had to do was rig up some ropes to act as a bridle. They whinnied, stomped, and jerked at their tethers, apparently excited for a morning ride.

The soft *clop* of cloven hooves followed us as we led them out of the barn and onto the walk. I skipped to Roch's side, ready to mount.

"May I aide you?" Galan asked, his hands coming to rest on my hips. "Roch is slightly larger than your cat."

Ignoring the fact that I'd been able to mount a horse since I was twelve, I bent my knee for a leg up. "That's very thoughtful."

Galan mounted Celeb in one lithe spring and sank deep. The tension in Galan's brow eased, giving him the first look of semi-calm

I'd seen in days. I bit my lip and took in the sight. In doeskin pants, no shirt, and an open suede vest, it was hard to miss the flex and shift of Galan's muscles as he moved.

Mhmm. My new-found lust overheated my body as much as the tropical climate. I shifted, suddenly very aware that the friction of fabric against my tacky skin brought me toward the edge of combustion. Gods, what I wouldn't give to be back in that waterfall pool with him naked against me.

I swallowed and shook my head. He was dealing with a lot and was understandably moody and withdrawn since Lia was taken. I'd waited twenty-five years to feel sexual attraction, surely, I could rein in my hormones a while longer.

A soupy breeze stirred around us as the renier ambled beyond the boundaries of the village. Roch's full body swayed like a ship at sea, plodding along the sandy path. Galan and I shared a comfortable silence, taking in the brilliance of the forest, the shrill cries of birds above and the pungent sweetness of blooms. When she thought I wasn't paying attention, Roch munched on a passing shrub. It soon became clear she was a problem nibbler when traveling at a slow pace.

"You'll get a belly ache if you eat too many." I pulled at my ropes, tugging her head out of an overgrown elderberry bush. "She seems to have a soft spot for berries."

Galan smiled, reaching over to pat Roch's neck. "I cannot blame you, *wen*, I suffer the same affliction."

"You don't eat the bush, do you?"

He chuckled. "No. I detest brambles in my teeth."

Laughing, I tied my hair back and untucked the blouse Tham loaned me from his mother's closet. Highborne linen was thinner than what Lexi and I wore, and we were thankful for a change of clothes. Although Lexi was tiny and fit into the size zeros or twos Elven women wore, I needed something roomier in the curves. Even this blouse strained across my chest. Unhooking the bottom fasteners, I tied the ends in a knot above my navel.

In my periphery, I noticed Galan's head tilt in my direction. Was he watching me? I might have imagined it. Stretching my hand forward, I stroked a woolly curl that hung down Roch's forelock and slid my glance sideways. Yes, he was watching me. A rush of heat raced across my skin. My damned red hair made it impossible to hide my blush, so I urged Roch to a trot.

"How did you end up with a mount?" Galan chuckled when he caught up with me.

"He was a gift."

"Naith is Elvish. Did you name him?"

I hesitated, having a silent conversation with myself. His one eyebrow rose, and I spoke in a rush. "A former patient of mine was a Dark Elf soldier. You met him a few days ago. You shot an arrow through his chest."

Galan's expression hardened. "Bloodvine? The one who escaped our battle?"

I nodded and swallowed hard past the lump in my throat. "I'm sorry. It was before he became Scourge. About four years ago, he ran into some trouble and needed medical attention. He was denied care in a couple of villages, and when he arrived at Haven, he was in rough shape. As a sanctuary, Haven offers aid to anyone who asks."

Galan glared into the trees, the muscle in his jaw twitching.

"I, uh, I healed him, but his recovery was slow."

"Had you seen him since?"

"No, not until the clearing at Dragon's Peak." Reaching to a branch as we passed, I twisted off a bloom and raised the orange flower to my nose. Again, I faced the repercussions of that split-second decision. Had I killed him, would Lia be missing? Would Aust's father be dead?

"While he recuperated, his mount bore a cub. He gave Naith to me as a parting gift. To settle his debt."

"Naith is not fond of me . . . though I cannot blame him."

I chuckled, revisiting the image of Galan sprawled out in the clearing with Naith standing over him. "You need to avoid first impressions. You're more of an acquired taste."

He pegged me with a sinful look. "Have you acquired that taste, Blossom?"

I blushed again. "It's too soon to tell."

He adjusted his ropes as we crested a small hill and approached the forest. His gaze returned to mine. "Well, be sure to let me know if you hunger for more than just a taste."

When Caleb jolted into a canter, Roch and I matched their gait and crested the next rise, nose to nose. Galan glanced sideways, a hint of daring in his expression. "Azaa!" he cried, leaning forward over the horn of his saddle.

I laughed and pressed my heels into Roch's padded side. When I shifted forward, she lunged into a full-on gallop. We raced across the green hillside, the drumming of eight padded hooves thundering up from the earth, vibrating in my chest. I squeezed my knees, pushing Roch forward toward the wooden bridge, which led over the river. The scent of summer wildflowers filled my senses while a cool wind whistled in my ears and cooled my skin.

Roch and I hit the bridge an instant before Galan, and I cut in front of him, clattering across. He tugged his reins to the side and turned his beast to the open river bed. Celeb's nostrils flared. His soft, round ears laid back as he and Galan cleared the babbling waters. They landed sure-footed with a *cathud* on the opposite bank and tightened behind Roch's hindquarters. Galan attempted to pass, but the lack of space kept him right where he was. In. My. Dust.

Musical laughter echoed amongst the trees.

I set the pace through the narrow forest path. The protective umbrella above held the day's unrelenting heat at bay. Strobe-light patterns flashed over us where the sun penetrated the canopy. We wove and dipped along the trail, under low branches, and over fallen debris.

Roch huffed and snorted, invigorated by our pace. I knew how he felt. It had been too long since I'd ridden full-out. The wind pulled at my hair and ignited my senses. My blood fired, lit by Roch's thundering power beneath me.

Galan's expression spoke volumes, enthralled among the blur of green and brown. The golden light of the afternoon filtered through the trees ahead. Roch broke free of the woods and continued along the western crest of the mountain.

The turquoise sky swirled, entwined with the amber glow of the sun. Galan leaned back, hauling on his ropes. Both renier braced their stride, slowing to a stop. We stared out at possibly the most perfect scenery on Earth, a landscape painted by a master's brush.

"Behold, the Western Summit." Galan swept his hand toward the mountain range beyond.

"It's breathtaking."

"I agree," Galan murmured. "Utterly breathtaking."

Our eyes met. Galan wasn't admiring the skyline. I half expected him to look away once I'd caught him staring. He didn't. The hunger in his gaze radiated sex, and my body knew it. Warmth flushed through me, and I fought to look away. I could almost feel him kissing the insides of my thighs, nipping and caressing me in places no man had ever touched.

Roch waggled her head from side to side, stomping her hoof into the soft ground. As her adrenaline settled, her muscles pinched and twitched. I sighed, thankful for the distraction. "Uh, the animals will need a drink after that run."

Galan chuckled, reining away from the edge. "Over here."

Roch and I followed down the slope to where the water snaked its way across our path. I bit my lip as Galan dismounted. His hair had come loose and swung free as he strode to my side. When his hands reached for me, I kicked my leg over Roch's rump and let him ease me down against his front. At first, his hands gripped my hips. In the course of setting me onto the ground, my shirt rucked up, and they found their way to the skin of my waist.

That inexplicable electrical current snapped between us again. The jolting effect of his skin touching mine raised the hair on the nape of my neck. As quickly as the frenzy invaded, it ceased when Galan pulled his hands away.

I faced him. We were close enough for the warmth of his breath to tickle my neck. Close enough for him to dip his head and claim my mouth, or for me to step up on my toes and claim his. My arms reached around his neck, and I had every intention of kissing him senseless.

"Jade—" He shook his head and backed away.

"What? What's wrong?"

"Nothing is wrong. I simply remember your passion from the grotto. For today, I have too much on my mind to try to be sensible for both of us."

What? "Do you honestly think I don't know that? That I can't control myself? I'm not some hormonal seductress who'd force myself on you against your will."

He scrubbed his fingers through his hair, leaving it tousled. "Of course not. And though I am bodily willing, it would be a mistake to allow you to—"

"Allow me to what? You arrogant *bastard*." I threw up my hands and stepped away. Marching to the water's edge, I glared at a group of black birds holding their wings out to dry in the sun. "You're right, bringing you out here was a mistake."

Stiff fingers on my shoulder had me turning. Though he glared, he had the decency to look abashed. "Apologies. I should have chosen my words more carefully. I never meant to hurt you."

"I'm not hurt, Galan. *I'm pissed off*. I was only going to kiss you." I let out my breath in a deep sigh. "On the quest, I was never sure if you wanted to kiss me or kill me, but I thought we were beyond that."

"We were—we *are*. Things are different now."

"Why?" I lifted my chin and poked my finger at his chest. "Is this really about Lia, or did you get back to your village and realize I didn't fit the mold? I'm not some Elven Barbie doll. I'm not skinny or blonde or elegant. I'm a size 10, warrior's daughter. I argue, curse and am—"

"—nonsensical, trying, and infuriatingly daft—" Galan's fingers clamped around my arms. "I adore the ways you differ from other females. We are simply not a good fit as a coupling."

"Says who?" I struggled against his hold. When it only proved to rattle my teeth, I stilled. "We could be magical."

His expression and his grip softened as his mouth twitched up in a weak smile. "Or we could be a cataclysmic event of momentous proportions."

"That's a possibility too." I exhaled. "I thought Tham said you were good with women."

"Elven females," he said.

"Not so much with the humans, eh?"

"Obviously not." He smoothed the frown line from my brow and sighed. "I am sorry I vexed you. However, in all honesty, I did warn you of my mood."

I nodded. "You did at that."

Galan managed a weak smile and led the animals, knee-deep into the sparkling water while I headed to the shelter of a massive cashew tree near the bank. Once he tied our sweaty beasts of burden, he sprang up the slope to join me. After wiping his forearm across his brow, he cleared his throat and picked at the grass. "You ride well."

"For a girl?"

"No." He fought his smile. "I shall never underestimate you due to gender again."

"See. I told Lexi you could be trained." I knocked my shoulder against his and laughed. "Are you surprised I ride?"

"Mayhap a little, yet you constantly challenge my understanding. It is enormously difficult, not to mention frustrating, to unravel the mystery of what is Jade Glaster."

"Maybe you should stop trying."

"Where is the rise in that?" Galan untied his boots and stripped off his vest. Scooping up a handful of pebbles, he waded into the creek and tossed them one-by-one. The slow current of the water broke around his knees, sending ripples downstream. After a while, his fist tightened, and he threw the pebbles. Stone projectiles ricocheted off trees down the river.

"*I want her back!*" He yelled. "Gods, forgive me, I should never have left her."

When he'd worn himself out, I waved him back to the bank and led him into my shady spot under the cashew tree. "We'll find her."

Settling onto my side, I pulled him down, so we were face to face. His body was rigid, his muscles tense. With the back of my fingers, I drew my hand slowly down his cheek and neck. His tension eased a little.

"Galan, I know what it feels like to have someone you love stolen by the Scourge, to ask why the soldiers walked through a village full of people and pointed their claws at your family, to suffocate with guilt because *you* are the one left standing."

His eyes closed. "Does it get easier?"

"Yes . . . and no. The anger fades, but the injustice of it remains. Why were my parents killed while I survived? That knot tightens in my gut and worsens every summer solstice. I have the right to avenge them, but I want answers and may never find them." I flopped onto my back. Lifting his hand, I watched how perfectly our fingers meshed together. "You still have a chance to get her back."

"What if you are mistaken?" he whispered.

"I'm not." I nuzzled closer and laid my head on his shoulder. "Reign made locating her the Talon's priority. It's just a big world out there. They could be anywhere."

Galan bit his lip and sighed.

"Hey, tell me about her—something happy."

He kissed the top of my head and drew a deep breath. "Near a decade past, Lia set herself on the task to find my perfect mate." He chuckled, and his chest jiggled against me.

"I cannot count the times she and I looked up at the stars as she listed the available love interests in our village. With such a small community, the prospects do not change. She created new criteria to be weighed and measured. She pointed out which characteristics would be a logical match and which would simply prove to annoy me over time. In the end, she would sigh and say, 'No brother mine, she is not the right one for forever.'"

A warm wind stirred the leaves above us, lifting our hair, so it tickled my face. Birds spanning every color of the spectrum, bounced between branches above. They chirped and plucked at blossoms as they swayed.

"Lia is charisma, happiness, and sunshine combined in one incredibly beautiful package. From the day of her birth, she was the center of my world. My universe created a new star, and I was drawn into her orbit. Back then, my father was a compassionate man. He and my mother were perfectly suited and blissfully happy for two centuries.

"Was it the loss of your mother that changed him?"

He nodded. "When he lost her during Lia's birthing, his soul shattered. My sister reminds him of all he believes she cost him. He cannot understand how I demean myself to raise her. He told me if I took on the task, he would never offer me aid. True to his word, he never did."

"So, you and Lia were alone in the world?"

"My *eda* kept up pretenses of being a supportive patriarch, though behind closed doors he was lost to us. No matter. Lia and I fared well on our own while our father focused on community matters and working with the Elders Council. When Tham's parents died, he was alone as well and joined our duo.

"Tham lost his parents too?"

Galan nodded. "The *naneth* of his *naneth* reared him, but while he was young, she too slipped Behind the Veil."

I envisioned Tham losing his parents and then his grandmother. A gentle finger lifted my mouth, and Galan touched his lips to mine. My body burst to life, heart thrumming, skin tingling with heat. It was the taste of him, the scent of clean sweat and wildflowers, the warmth of his arms encircling me. "How do you do that?"

"Do what?" His eyes sparkled, church-glass blue.

"One touch and I'm completely unraveled."

He chuckled, stroking my jaw with his lips. "I rather like you, unraveled."

I moaned as Galan rolled over me and pressed me into the long, thick grass. Morning flowed effortlessly into midday and midday into afternoon. Under the shade of the tree, we looked up at the sky as it peeked through leaves and covered every topic imaginable: friends, memories, dreams, loves, regrets.

When we returned to the village and stabled the renier, it seemed a lifetime had passed.

Galan caressed my hand like I was made of the most delicate

porcelain. "Gratitude, Jade. For letting me speak and laugh and breathe for a few hours without feeling angry."

The sun continued toward the western skyline, the orange ball of fire just visible between two distant violet peaks. The purple and tangerine sky gradually transformed into a mauve grey. It would be dusk within the hour.

"The portal mirror should be ready by morning. We'll find out about your sister."

Galan nodded. "I would like to pack a bag before we go. If we went directly, my father should be with the Elder's Council. We would have the place to ourselves."

"Well then, lead the way, Highborne."

CHAPTER FIFTEEN

*G*alan's bedroom reflected every nuance of the man: elegance, strength, an almost OCD sense of order, and the best part— it smelled like him. A floor to ceiling, built-in ran along the long back wall. To the right, an ornate stone hearth sat flanked by two arched doors. To the left, a window, covered with finely woven drapes, looked onto the forest behind the house. In the distance, raised to overlook the village, I made out the ivory pillars of the ancient ruin site.

Fascinating how, in eight thousand years, the Highbornes had developed along the same path as the rest of the realm. In the center of the room stood a canopy bed draped with more of the gold sheers and a decadently thick pallet. The headboard was planed and inlaid with a carved depiction of a deer drinking from the riverbed. I sank into the fur bedcover and scrunched my fingers deep into the pelt.

"Who carved your bed?" I asked. "The craftsmanship is amazing."

"Iadon's cousin, Maryssa. Where he is gifted as a leather-worker and tailor, she is an inspired sculptress. Anything she sees in nature can be reproduced with perfect accuracy. When my father succumbed to one of his moods, I would lay Lia in her basket and spend time in

Maryssa's workshop." Looking sheepish, he glided across the room. "Sculpting is a secret indulgence of mine."

After picking up a small, wooden sculpture from a bookshelf, he returned to the bed. He held out his cupped hands, and I took the carving. It was a timber wolf fighting with a peccary.

"You did this?" My mouth fell open. "Galan, why would you keep this a secret? You're so talented."

He bowed his head. "Gratitude. Carving is something I do for personal satisfaction. I learned at a tender age not to allow others to voice an opinion on things dear to me. It cuts too deep when used against me."

Whoosh, the candles on either side of the bed burst to life. His words burned in my gut. "Let me guess… your father?"

He shrugged, placing the sculpture on the bedside table. "Unimportant."

"No. It *is* important. The way he treated you and Lia is unforgivable. You lost your mother, had a newborn to care for, and instead of bonding with you, he chose to chastise you?"

Galan brushed his thumb over my lips. "Thank you for being my champion; however, what has passed, has passed."

I rolled off the bed and explored the room.

Everything sat compulsively organized except for the books. Even with enough shelf space to house a small library, books piled high on his bedside tables, hide-covered bench, and every inch of the deep window seat. Leather covers, parchment scrolls, even broad flattened and inscribed with poems.

"Wow, read much?"

He shrugged. "Mayhap a little."

"You'll lose your mind when you see all the books in the instructor's lounge at the Academy. We have enough to keep you reading for centuries."

His smile was brilliant white. "I have wondered a great deal about your world."

I stroked the teak furniture. His bed, chest of drawers, and shelves, finished in a dark stain, were detailed with intricate silver gilding. I traced the smooth carvings on the headboard and noticed three-stringed instruments hung over the hearth. "Would you play something for me?"

He cocked a brow. "We best leave for Nyssa's before my sire returns."

"Please. It won't take long. I'd love to hear you play."

He hesitated for a moment, then tapped me on the nose and turned to the mantle.

While he retrieved his lute and tested the pitch, I explored. He had sophisticated taste, Spartan, but resplendent. A blue, scarlet, and gold woven rug covered the stone floor. It was stiff and resisted my toes as I scrunched into the thick fabric. I lifted the sheer draperies and marveled at their weightlessness.

A hand-painted picture of Lia sat on Galan's bedside table. I recognized her from Nyssa's memory when I healed her. Even from the painting, I saw why she was the sunshine that warmed him. I rubbed my sternum, knowing too well what the Scourge did to women they captured.

Fucking Scourge.

"She is a vision, is she not?" Galan slipped behind me, resting his chin on my shoulder. "She had that painted as a surprise for my birthing day. It was a wonderful evening."

"Tomorrow, we'll talk to Reign. He'll know more." *I hope.* Climbing onto his bed, I shuffled back and avoided his gaze. "For now, play me something."

"How could a male deny you anything?"

"Smart man."

He sat on the side of the bed, propped his leg to support the instrument, and stroked the wooden neck. His devilish smile grew more heated. "I like having you in my chamber."

I ignored the flush of warmth coming over me. "And what will you play for me?"

"*Naiore Atulie,*" he said, his eyes locked on mine. "I believe you know it. I heard you sing it once or twice as you tended to Nyssa."

"As a bard in training, I learned dozens of Elven songs by my tutor, Chiron of Delaran. That is my favorite."

When he began, I swear my heart stopped beating. He sang a quiet melody. It was delicate and painfully perfect. His voice swelled in the air and filled my chest, the sound so clear and pure it made time grind to a halt.

A wave of emotion hit me. First, heat smoldered in my chest, moving lower, growing as it gained momentum. Then a gentle throb started between my thighs. My pulse thundered in my ears, my heart pumped as if it wanted out of my chest. My hands balled in the fur covers, and I focused on Galan's song. The beautiful tenor ascended and descended with the notes.

Breathtaking.

Gods, is this natural? With his gaze fixed on mine, his stare grew erotic and hungry. I felt undone. Again. He closed his eyes, softly grinning. Tilting his head to the side, he held the final note. As it faded, he set down the lute and cupped my face into his hands.

"You liked it?" he asked, wiping the tears from my cheeks.

"It was magnificent."

Galan lifted my chin and dipped his mouth to my lips. His kiss was gentle and tasted faintly of elderberries from the bush by the barn. A warm, strong hand slid behind my neck, urging me closer as he explored my mouth.

I grumbled as Galan pulled back and ended our kiss. "Where are you going? I wasn't finished with you yet."

He laughed and pulled me to my feet. "Having you on my bed, I near the limits of my restraint. We have friends awaiting our arrival and issues awaiting our attention. We need to pack my things and be ready to leave in the morning."

I pouted as Galan grabbed a pile of clothes and led me through one of the closed doors into the adjoining bathroom. He shook out the satchel and gathered what he intended to bring. I packed while he handed me things.

Like Tham's home, the room housed all the things one would

expect from a bathroom in one form or another. Since Lexi and I received training on how to use their toilet system, we were good.

Ironically it was Galan's bathtub, which stunned me into silence—hollowed out of what looked to be one gigantic piece of wood. Tham said Elven craftsmanship and attention to detail rose far superior to human.

I thought he was boastful. Apparently not. The large basin was sloped, sanded, and stained to cradle the bather. Without magic, or advanced tools, the Highbornes used what nature supplied them. Living in exile hadn't been a total sacrifice of comfort like I'd thought.

"I still can't believe you have running water."

"You thought us to be primitive?" Galan raised a brow and pointed to the basin. "Cool water is brought straight in from the aqueducts and catch basins, and for tepid, it passes through the south-facing wall for the sun to warm."

"It's so innovative." I caressed the satiny rim of the tub. "This is the most beautiful thing I've ever seen."

"It is a bathing basin. Not a work of art." Galan buckled his bag.

"No, this is *definitely* a work of art."

A heavy wooden door closing near the front of the house froze us both. Galan quietly slid the bathroom window open. With a sweep of his hand, he gestured for his bag.

"I know you are here, Galan. Alwyn saw you enter with that human female."

Galan slowly lowered the window to rest on the sill.

"Don't worry about it," I whispered. "He doesn't bother me. Ignore him."

"No, Blossom. Not this time," he growled. "I shall not slink away into the night to escape the conflict. If he wants a row, I accept." Slinging his bag over his shoulder, he took my hand and stepped out into the hall.

His father returned from a night with the Elders Council and wore an embroidered, ivory tunic and moss green slacks. "There you are."

Without checking to see if we would follow, he retreated down the hall to the library of the living room. The contrast in the man was impossible to miss. The elegant, upper-class atmosphere of dignity and the guttersnipe attitude Galan's father spit like a viper. "I figured you would have scampered off into the shadows ... mayhap through a window." Cold blue eyes rose to mine. "That is what you may expect, human, him scurrying off like an insignificant rodent."

The fire in my gut flamed to life, steaming in my veins. "Spew your acid, old man. Galan has more honor and class than you'll ever be able to fake for your friends. He stands up for what he believes, even if it brings ridicule from small-minded, self-important peons like you."

"Indeed," he chuckled, turning a lethal gaze on his son. "And your female fights your battles now? Have you no self-respect?"

"Jade possesses the strength to speak her mind. In truth, I find it alluring." Galan wrapped his arm around my back and set his hand on my hip. "Was there something you wanted?"

"When have you bothered yourself with what I want?"

Galan's hold on my hip grew tighter. "I am sorry you are vexed. Jade and I came merely to pack. We are happy to return your privacy to you. Excuse us."

Galan's father stepped into our path. "For once in your worthless life, use logic, son. You hear the whispers. You flaunt this female on your arm as if you give her consideration. A magic-wielding human may seem exotic with her green eyes and her large breasts, yet surely the importance of honoring your community is not lost on you entirely."

I snorted. "You realize my breasts, and I are standing right here, don't you?"

"I do." Galan kissed my temple. "I am acutely aware of where you and your voluptuous curves are at all times."

His father's malevolent stare did not affect either of us. "Galan, son of mine, no matter your current standing, you are a Highborne, one of the Noble Children. It is incumbent upon you to seek a female who will have you despite your shortcomings. We must ensure the population of our race continues. This human will wither and die while you are still a youth. Gods forbid you have children. You would be left raising mixed-race bastards. What will people think then?"

I thought Galan might stiffen right out of his skin. "I consider myself more than a tool for procreation, Eda. When I consummate with my mate, my commitment will be based on many things, race, genetics, and longevity will not be among them." Galan took my hand and, in one graceful motion, strode to the door. "Fash not, father-mine. From this moment forth, neither Lia nor I shall tarnish your shining image within the village. Consider us off your list of obligations."

"Assuming you find the whelp," his father muttered under his breath. "Imagine her at the mercy of those vile raiders. No telling what liberties they have taken. Her virtue will be soiled, surely. Mayhap it is better to leave her where—"

Galan spun, struck as hard as a sledgehammer, and fast as lightning. The crack of fist to jaw echoed through the elegant foyer. Sprawling in a daze on the woven mat, Galan's father looked dumbfounded. Galan shook his fist once then adjusted the strap of his bag on his shoulder. "That is the last time you shall speak of Lia. The Fates may have taken Naneth from us. However, it was you who destroyed this family."

Hand in hand, we stepped out, closed the door, and headed down the street.

Iadon answered our knock and swept his arm into the large, open room. "Ah, Jade, welcome to our home." He kissed my forehead and clamped wrists with Galan. "Nyssa is tending to the babe. She will be right out."

Tham, Lexi, and Aust were already into the spirit of the night. By the flush burning on Lexi's cheeks, I would guess they were on their fourth or fifth glass of wine. Galan dropped his bag and strode to the side table.

Half a dozen crocks and colored bottles were set out for their evening. He uncorked a tall burgundy bottle and poured a glass of clear fluid for each of us.

I took a tentative sip, then drank. "Where's Elora?"

Aust glanced toward an interior door, his unusual eyes filled with sadness. "She is preparing victuals. She will be out in time."

"Jade. Galan. You have arrived." Nyssa floated down the short hall cradling the baby. Her long mane flowed behind her like a shining golden cape. "We were beginning to worry."

"We know better than to come looking for the two of you." Tham smiled as he narrowly evaded Lexi's elbow-shot to his ribs. "We learned that lesson well enough."

Had everyone heard about our waterfall tryst? I glared, but it only made Tham laugh.

Nyssa licked her lips and straightened out the curve of her mouth. "Galan, would you mind?" She raised the swaddled infant toward him, and he cradled the newborn into his arms.

He held Ella as if destined to do so. I didn't wonder how wonderful Galan was with Lia as a child. He transformed the moment the baby settled into his arms.

If I lived a thousand lives, I would never forget the peace Ella brought him. He looked into those tiny blue eyes, and Ella lifted the weight of his fears and frustrations. He traced her cheek as if memorizing every inch of her face.

Iadon surprised me by stepping behind me. He wrapped his arms around my shoulders and kissed the back of my hair. "We shall never be able to repay the blessing you gave us, *neelan*. You are loved beyond limits of measure in our home."

A knock at the door had us all turning. Iadon answered the door to a crowd of half a dozen well-dressed, pompous-looking men. The Highbornes inside the cottage froze.

"Elders." The warmth Iadon's voice held a moment ago morphed to a cutting chill. "What brings you to our home?"

"May we enter?" Gisir stepped inside, not waiting for a response. The others followed. I didn't recognize many of the group, but saw Tham's clucking chicken scenario unfolding.

"Of course. Please do." Iadon snapped, sweeping his arm toward the great room though they were all inside. Galan and Tham moved forward and stepped in front of Lexi and me.

Elora emerged from the kitchen, her bloodshot eyes, rimmed pink.

"Blessed evening, Gisir. What business has the Council here this night?"

Gisir pursed his thin lips and slowly swept a meaningful glance toward Aust. "Apologies, Elora, we need to discuss Aust's situation."

In an instant, Elora transformed from a vulnerable widow to a mother bear defending her cub. She flew across the room, standing between the mob and her son. "*Leave us in peace!* You fine gentlemales have the gall to judge Aust when Cameron's pier still smolders?"

Gisir dropped his gaze to the floor. "Apologies, it was not a unanimous decision, and the timing is appalling. However, the majority of the Council has spoken. Aust is to leave the village at first light."

"What?"

Aust held his hand out to his mother and stepped to her side. "What have I done?"

"You know well what this is about."

"I have lived my life upholding the governances of our race. More so. Do I not aid our community and bear more than my share of the load?"

Gisir nodded. "You do, son. Regardless, your presence has long disturbed the harmony of our beliefs. It was only out of respect for your father and the knowledge that there was no other place for you that judgment was not rendered sooner."

"This is bullshit!" Lexi spat. Tham grabbed her wrist as she started for the crowd, amethyst eyes blazing. "Aust's affinity is a blessing from the Fae gods. Do you have any idea how lucky you are to have him in your community?"

Aust held up his hand. "I shan't leave *Naneth* at a time when she needs me so. No matter the judgment of the community, my place is at her side. Mayhap in time. Not so soon after our loss." Faolan rubbed against his leg, showing her very sharp, white teeth to the Councilmen.

"Then that's settled," Lexi snapped.

"That is not for you to decide, halfling." Galan's father stepped to the forefront and crossed his arms over his chest. I admired the purple shiner darkening his face and beamed with pride. "It is we who make those decisions here."

"It's not," I said, throwing my two cents in and grabbing Lexi's belt as she flew by. "Your little group of wizened old men was all-powerful when your exile was in place, but not now. You are reinstated to the Realm of the Fair. Castian's laws state that everyone, anywhere within the realm, is free to live their lives as long as they do no harm and follow his ordinances. From what I understand, Aust has broken no laws."

"He will leave this village," Galan's father sputtered. "He has until the morrow."

"Or what? What will you do?" As I squared off, a dozen candles burst to life, flaring six inches in the air.

Worried looks darted wildly around the room and then from one elder to another. As the heat of my anger built in my chest, Galan's hand rested heavily on my shoulder and squeezed.

I stretched my fingers out of the fists they were clenched into and exhaled. "If Aust isn't ready to leave his mother, he's not going anywhere."

"And you can bet your pompous, upper-class asses we'll dig in and make sure he doesn't have to." Lexi drew her dagger and twirled it in her palm, pointing the working end for effect.

"No," Elora whispered. "Aust has suffered too much judgment already." With hands clenched in the folds of her ebony gown, she strode, head high to face the elders. "I am deeply ashamed of each of you ... males of worth."

She moved her gaze slowly from one to the next until she had forced each one of them to look her in the eye. "Each of you have eaten from my hearth and accepted the hospitality of our home. Cameron may not have agreed with you, yet he always respected you. Now, while his spirit still walks among us, you treat us thus? Shame. On. You."

Big, fat tears welled in Elora's eyes, but none fell. "Jade, what you said before about your world accepting those with affinities. Would my son be welcomed on your mountain?"

"He would be adored and revered."

She bit her lip and nodded. "Then, I wish for him to join you in your world."

Aust surged forward. "*Naneth*, no. I cannot—"

Elora pressed her fingers against his lips and blinked fast. "A century is long enough to be hated, my beloved. Go with your friends. Make a life beyond the cruelty of this village."

"Will you come with me? We can start anew."

Elora cupped his face. "In time mayhap, but for now, I need to be close to Cameron."

"*Naneth*—"

Elora kissed his cheek. "Come. I shall help you pack." With her head high and her shoulders back, Elora led Aust through the center of the crowd and out the door.

They had barely swung the front gate shut when Iadon strode to the open door. He pointed out into the chill of the night. "Your business here is done," he growled. "*Leave.*"

CHAPTER SIXTEEN

*B*y dawn, the mirror was functional, and the elders were ridding their petty little lives of the evils which descended upon them. I couldn't give a shit if that included Lexi and me, but it pissed me off Aust was on that list.

Galan tossed Tham his satchel and gripped one end of Aust's trunk. "There are those of us who love and admire you for everything you are and marvel at your gifts, brother mine."

Lexi laced her fingers with Aust and pulled him toward the floor-to-ceiling, antique mirror. "Trust us. Dive into your *Ambar Lenn,* and you'll see that starting over is the perfect opportunity to strike a new path and create a life you've only dreamed of."

The portal gate shimmered like a still lake in moonlight. Its glassy depth rippled across the mirror's surface as the magic took hold. A low rumble from the floor built in intensity until the ebony surface began to undulate like waves of evaporating moisture rising under the summer sun.

The Council antechamber filled with blinding, white light followed by the fragrant scent of honeysuckle and raindrops.

I inhaled deep and laughed out loud at Galan's expression. "Stop worrying. Lexi and I have traveled by portal for twenty years. It's perfectly safe."

"Especially with Julian on the other end," Lexi said.

"Why, especially?" Galan looked from Lexi to me. "What might happen if Julian is not on the other end?"

"Stop being such a chicken." I laughed. Lexi and I took their hands and dragged their Highborne hineys through the mirror. "Fate's Journey, remember?"

Safely on the other side, we gave the Elves a minute. They looked faint, but it was more nerves than traveling by portal mirror. Flashing would leave people disoriented the first few times: nausea, the whirling sounds in their ears, the pressure in their lungs, but portal mirrors were no different than walking through an open doorway.

While they settled, I met Julian at the console.

"Welcome home, sistas." Julian knuckle-bumped the two of us. He wasn't the warrior type that made up most of the men in our household. Julian was the brains of the operation. He was fit, but not bulky, and his soft mocha skin highlighted his mint-green eyes.

"Gentlemen," I said, gesturing to my brother, "may I introduce Julian Sandler, gatekeeper and overall network and computer genius."

"And one of our adoptive brothers," said Lexi.

With their focus on Julian, the three of them fell quiet, eying him with curious glances. It dawned on me then that they were responding to Julian being black. After a moment, though, the Highbornes gave him a nod and said. "Merry meet."

Tham strode forward and clasped Julian's wrist. "I am Thamior, and this is Galanodel, Aust, and Faolan." He pointed in turn. "Gratitude for getting us here safely."

"Not a problem." Julian turned to me. "Reign wants to see you and Galan in his office at ten, so you have twenty minutes to drop your bags and get them settled."

"Did he say anything about Lia?" I asked.

"Not to me." Julian picked up a long PVC tube and a small oxygen canister. He didn't have any issues with breathing, so I guessed it was part of the ongoing prank war he was in with Cowboy and Nash.

"What's will this end up being?" I asked, nosing through his box.

"Spudzooka," he laughed. Holding his box to his chest, he backed out the door and held it for the group. "With my own diabolical twist."

Outside, the Elves took a moment to absorb their surroundings. The differences were obvious at once. At Haven, it was warm, not blistering. The forests were green and treed, not impenetrable or tropical. And the air was refreshing, not hanging with moisture.

Lexi swept her hand across the landscape. "Originally, the property housed only the main castle and stables, but over time additional buildings have scattered the grounds: a produce market, bakery, tavern, winery, butchery, observation gallery, guest cottages, hot springs. We're almost completely self-sufficient."

I pointed at the ivory obelisk in the distance. Jutting up above the tree line, it stood stark against the pale blue sky, overseeing the Academy grounds. "Twenty-seven ward towers are disbursed around the mountain perimeter. They offer sentry points and enable us to monitor and block unauthorized activity on Haven grounds."

"So, the mountain is a sanctuary in its entirety?" Galan asked.

I nodded. "Reign established this as the first secured Safe Haven sanctuary when we were kids. That was also when he organized the Talon. The Academy of Affinities came later, about twelve years ago now. He wanted to provide a place where we could train members of the realm with affinities and give them a safe place to learn their craft."

"And everyone is peaceable?" Aust scrubbed his fingers through Faolan's ruff, scanning the surroundings.

"Locals and students can be aligned either Light or Dark. We teach acceptance, but if there is a conflict, Haven laws are absolute. We don't tolerate wrongdoing, and we enforce that. As a rule, our biggest problem is a bar brawl or a domestic disturbance, nothing that can't be worked out."

Following the cobblestone walk, we made our way toward the castle, and I continued my walking tour, pointing down the mountain slope. "The town at the base of the mountain is grittier because travelers come and go freely. For now, it would be best to stay within Haven grounds."

I led them across the courtyard and gave them a minute to soak up the facade of the castle: seven stories of solid stone with leaded glass, turrets, towers, and a formal keep. With their mouths agape, we led them up the broad stone steps.

"Jade?" Aust stopped just outside the threshold. "Is Faolan welcome within the walls of your home?"

"Of course. This is your home now, and Faolan is part of your life." With a gentle tug, I pulled him into the marble foyer. "Don't worry. You'll love it here."

The main foyer had a 'Tudors' sort of magnificence. Built in the days of King Henry VIII, the castle was as impressive as it was impenetrable. Leaving the main entrance, the six of us climbed the gentle arc of winding stairs, following an elaborate mural toward a vaulted ceiling. Without question, the images depicted on our route rivaled the glory of the Sistine Chapel.

The Elves' eyes widened as they took it in. The realism of the murals brought the battles and triumphs of the Fae gods to life. The colors swirled in broad, powerful strokes of Prussian blue, scarlet, ochre, and forest green, the highlights, and accents in silver and gold leafing.

"The *Aina Nosta?*" Tham murmured.

"Yes, the Holy Birth of the Elven race." I pointed ahead. "This one's the battle in the enchanted gardens of the Pixies where Castian was injured by Garekk the Vile, First Power of the Orcs." I climbed the steps and pointed to the next panel. "This is the sunset on the fifth day of their deadlock when Garekk's sword found purchase. Here are the seven drops of Castian's violet blood seeping into the enchanted soil."

"His immortal essence bound with nature itself to produce an enlightened race." Julian said. "Not a bad start for Elves."

We continued upward. "This is Castian's banishment of Rheagan." Scrunching up her nose, Lexi pointed to the image of Castian transforming his sister into a tentacled beast and banishing her to the depths of the sea. "Look how hideous he made her."

"A sore spot for the Highbornes, even eight-thousand years later," Galan said. "Though the artistry is astonishing."

"The only sin your people committed was to follow a batshit Queen," Julian said.

As we followed our ascent to the fifth floor, horses reared, troops were slaughtered, and pools of blood soaked into the soil. The battles captured the Realm of Fair's struggles for justice and the age-old conflicts between Light and Dark. When I closed my eyes, the sweat of men and smoke of battle was almost detectable in the air.

Long ago, I memorized every line of every form, and yet it never failed to steal my breath. We stepped onto the fifth-floor landing, and Julian led the way across the open foyer.

"All Academy lecturers and guests live on the fifth floor," he said. "Reign assigned you three the suite beside Jade's."

After checking my watch, I rushed through the highlights of some of the shared common rooms. Galan stared mouth agape, at the thousands of book spines standing floor-to-ceiling in the lounge. I pointed out the quiet area with club chairs and reading lamps on one end of the room and then turned to the three, wall-mounted plasma screens hanging on the opposite wall.

This section of the lounge was adorned with every electronic toy imaginable. I didn't even try to understand how it worked. The men living on the floor oozed testosterone whenever they discussed the hi-def-surround-sound-media-center-input-blah-blah-stuff.

Whatever.

I didn't have the necessary anatomy to understand the allure. Aust and Tham came to life as they passed the televisions. Julian dropped his box on the table, plunked down on the sofa, and turned on UFC. With his feet crossed on the coffee table, he gave a quick tutorial on how the remotes accessed the satellites. It was clearly nature versus nurture because the three Highborne Elves, straight from an enchanted valley, glossed over with male techno-glaze.

"It is remarkable." Tham moved slowly to stand in front of the UFC action. He tapped the screen with his finger then peered behind the television where it hung on the wall. "What sorcery is this? Are these men trapped?"

Aust joined him. "What is the purpose of having people suspended within your home?"

Julian barked out a laugh. "They're not suspended. A cameraman is recording what they are doing. Images get transmitted to our TV through cables, and we see it."

The Elves didn't look any less confused.

"Julian, pass me the clicker," I said, holding my hand out to my brother. "There are hundreds of programs running all the time, like picture books sent to us. Aust, you'll like this." When I punched in the three digits to bring up Animal Planet, his curiosity ratcheted. "This channel is all about animals of the modern realm. They usually run either half-candle or full-candle and tell you all about animals. See, this one's about the African big five."

"Sweet Shalana's grace." He ran a trembling finger over the cheetah racing across the screen after a gazelle. "And they come to no harm by this process?"

I shook my head. "No. None. It's like a painted picture but instant and constant."

Galan lifted my hand by the wrist and pointed the clicker toward the TV. "Can you make something else appear?"

"Sure. Maybe you'd like this." I changed the channel to Much Music, and they were equally absorbed. "This band is called *The Black-Eyed Peas*."

"Oh, I love this song," Lexi squealed and started dancing around the lounge.

Tham chuckled and cocked his head. "None of them have black eyes."

I shook my head, tossed Julian the clicker, and tore them away from the lounge. "That is the billiards room. Later we'll come back, and Julian and I will show you how to play."

"Do you play this game, Lexi?" Tham asked.

"I'm too short, but Jade's good. She never tires of kicking ass and humiliating men."

I shrugged. "Not my most mature impulse, granted, but amusing none the less."

After a quick shuffle down the main corridor, we ended the tour at their bachelor suite. I opened the arched wooden door, stepped aside, and let them scope out their new digs. Their room was the same large rectangle as mine, minus the turret room, which I used for meditation and the three twin beds against the wall to the left instead of my king-sized canopy.

The large sitting area had a fireplace and two sofas to the right. Directly in front of the door was a small round wooden table with four chairs and behind that, against the back wall, sat a buffet counter with a cooktop and the accouterments to make light meals.

"The dining hall on the main floor is staffed and open, any time day or night. If it's between two and five am, you'll have to go into the kitchen and help yourself."

Tham skated across the floors toward the two doors on the far, right wall. He explored each before bouncing back to the living room, grinning like a kid on Christmas morning.

I fought back a giggle. "The first room is your bathing room, and the second is your dressing room. You'll find clean clothes and toiletries for the three of you. Reign will have anticipated your needs. If we've forgotten anything, let me know." I looked at the clock. "Okay, Galan, we need to go. Lexi will help you settle in, and we'll be back."

Galan dropped his bag on a bed. "Very well, I am ready."

CHAPTER SEVENTEEN

"Who the Christ do ye think ye are? I've done everything ye asked, *but no this!*" Even if the venom in Samuel's words hadn't carried through Reign's office door, the thickness of his brogue told me he was pissing mad.

"Watch yourself," Reign growled. "This isn't about you."

Galan and I stood silent outside the office. Students, hearing the cutting edge in my father's voice, hurried down the halls and out of sight. Everyone knew Reign was vicious when challenged. I couldn't imagine why Samuel would speak to him like that. It was no different than poking a dragon with a spear.

"I don't give two shits about perceived injustice, Samuel. The decision is made."

"Decisions made, eh?" Samuel growled. "D'ye think I'm some mindless eedjit who'll follow orders and lick yer arse after ye've shit on me? *Well, fuck you.*"

"Colorful, yet your outrage changes nothing."

"'Course not." A loud crash rang out. "Never has."

"You made your choice, Samuel. Now, lock it down and get it done."

Heavy footfalls stomped toward the door. We stepped back as

Samuel swung the thing nearly off the hinges. His shoulders stiffened when he saw us, the air crackling with aggression.

"Are you all right?" I asked him.

He glared at me, and his eyes darkened to near black. "No Jade, far from it." After throwing Galan a hostile sneer, he skulked off.

Reign filled the doorway, frame to frame, his muscled arms bulging beneath his black T-shirt. He gave me a sullen look then walked back into his office. "I'm glad you're home. Galan, welcome to Haven." He indicated for us to sit in the brown leather chairs that faced his oversized desk. "I take it the mirror is up and working well?"

"Perfectly," I said, my mind spinning. "Julian's a marvel."

"That he is." Reign sat in his chair and leaned back, rubbing the bridge of his nose. "I'll get right to it. Preliminary reports haven't turned up anything solid on your sister. Cowboy and Savage are working on something, and I'll know more this afternoon. In the meantime, the Queens have requested an audience with Galan ASAP. Can you two be ready in an hour?"

"Of course."

"Good. I'll tell Lexi and Julian to help Aust and Tham get settled." He pulled out his phone and leaned his elbows onto his desk. I made no move to leave. "Is there something else?"

I drew my finger along the seam of the chair arm and tried for nonchalance. "What's up with you and Samuel?"

Reign held my gaze, and his expression blanked out to a calm mask. "Administrative adjustments, nothing to concern yourself with."

Administrative adjustments my ass.

I stared into his charcoal eyes and sighed. Reign wouldn't crack. That didn't mean he wasn't lying, just that he'd never admit it. "I know Samuel is always part of the excursion party, but since he's in a mood, do you think he should stay home?"

My gaze flicked sideways to where Galan sat beside me. Hearing there was nothing new with Lia had him practically vibrating out of his chair. He was back to that perma-scowl he'd worn the past few days. The last thing I needed was him and Samuel to hit head-on.

Reign stared at me, and the hair on the back of my neck prickled.

He had an eerie way of knowing things about my messed-up life long before I told him. He was like Yoda, only way bigger and not so green. *When 900 years you reach, look as good, you will not.* His dark eyes glittered with amusement as my mind-wander spun. Was he tuned into my thoughts right now, or did he just find his flitty daughter strangely bizarre?

"Don't worry about it," he said.

"Mhmm, it's not so much that I'm worried. I don't want Galan and Samuel to wrestle to the asphalt and pound the crap out of one another in front of a bunch of Mundies."

Galan looked at me like he thought that was a fine idea.

"They'll behave." Reign cocked a brow and locked Galan in a stare. He held him pinned in his sights until Galan finally nodded and adjusted the tie of his tunic. "Now, go see if you can make this one a bit less conspicuous. Samuel and I will meet you in the gatehouse in one hour."

I led Galan up to the storage room on the fourth floor beneath the main stairwell. Placing my hand flat over the brass lock-plate, I waited for the metallic *click*.

The closet was twenty feet deep and sloped at the ceiling where the stairs angled over us. Floor-to-ceiling shelves and racks brimmed with clothing and costumes for travel into the Realm of Men or 'the modern realm' as we called it.

After closing the door behind us, I inventoried his body from head to toe. *Uh-huh, who could complain about this assignment?* Addressing the shelves, I selected a few items. I had to admit, I looked forward to seeing Galan wear tight jeans and a body-hugging T-shirt or even better… not wearing them.

"Why must I change my attire?" he growled.

"The Gypsy Queens live in the Modern Realm. They've been trusted oracles and prophetic readers for years. They rarely leave the safety of their home."

"Have they knowledge of Lia? Is that what this is about?"

"I hope so, but we'll have to wait and see."

"And we have to go to a modern city?"

"Yes, which is fine, except dressed like that amongst the human population you don't blend." I ran a hand down his tunic, and my heart pounded erratically. It always amazed me how soft the fabric of their clothing was.

"Is there something amiss with the way I dress?"

His suede skin pants were laced and tied at the front. They were body fitting and showed off his toned perfection from front to back and every curve and angle in between. His tunic dipped low to expose the strong line of his collarbone, a bare chest, and just a hint of the ripples of his abs.

I wiped my moist palms on my pants. "Absolutely not. But for the city, you need to look more Urban Street and less Elven ranger." I handed him a pair of black DKNY jeans and a black cotton-T. His face scrunched up like he'd sucked on a lemon. "Problem?"

"These breeches are . . . will they not chafe my, uh, skin?" He brushed the surface of his doeskin pants then looked at the jeans. He held them away from his body as if contact might infect him with some unwanted ailment.

I thought through his concern. Over the past weeks, I had seen him undress several times, and it came to me. "Ahh, right, you go commando." I glanced down his front. Even bewildered by the term, Galan nodded. It was common for him to miss the meaning of what Lexi or I said, though he generally caught the underlying context.

Chuckling, I ripped open a small plastic package from the bottom drawer and tossed him the contents. "Boxers. The male version of the underpants you've seen me wear."

His eyes closed for a moment, and his mouth crept up to a smile. Biting his lip, he looked me over. "I remember. Black wisps barely enough to hide your most delicate parts."

I took a step back, my cheeks suddenly getting hot. "Yes, well, put these on first, and your delicate parts will be just fine." I gave him my back, drawing a deep breath.

"You need not be concerned with modesty. Elves are not bashful, and you have seen my physique before." I rolled my eyes at the back wall and fought the urge to turn. I might have, if I had a little more

Lexi in me. She wouldn't think twice. "Mayhap, in this private room, you have an ulterior motive for wanting my clothing removed?"

A burst of nervous hysteria escaped before I knew what happened. I was so out of my depths here it was embarrassing. "You're not nearly as charming as you think, Highborne. Besides, we're in a hurry."

"Would you like to look me over and tell me if you approve?" His low, velvet voice was undoing all my careful self-restraint.

I turned for the runway show and was startled. He'd snuck directly behind me and caught me off balance. Gods, he smelled so good. I had to swallow before I spoke. "Wow. You, uh, clean up well." He smiled at my reaction, apparently liking how he affected me. My hand reached toward his chest and ran down the front of his shirt. "This is too big on you. Let's showcase the landscape better."

I handed him a smaller size, then, in a move more forward than I'd ever been, gripped the hem of his shirt. I pulled it up and over his head, exposing the rows of corded muscle I loved.

Bare-chested, he prowled closer.

I stepped back.

He grinned, resting one hand on the coat rail above my head as he sunk his fingers into my hair with the other.

I was trapped. He eyed me with the hungry focus of a jungle cat. "And what will you wear for our little adventure, *neelan*?" He raised a brow, our eyes locked in that touch my soul way we sometimes shared.

Dwinn. Motionless, I listened to that word replay in my mind, lost in the blue depths of his eyes. I licked my lips, wondering if his heightened hearing picked up my quickened pulse.

Galan's body pressed hot against my front, the stone of the wall cold on my back. Cupping my cheek, he leaned in, taking a slow, deep breath along the length of my neck.

I stifled a groan as his nose brushed my jaw. The tickle of his warm breath sent a shiver down my spine. He tilted his head, touching his lips to mine, very softly parting them.

My body ignited. I loved the way his heart hammered against my chest. He held me, gentle yet strained, as if I wasn't the only one fighting for control. I met his kiss and, in a sultry rush, his tongue entered my mouth. He kissed me in the same frantic way he had before, his tongue dueling, possessing—

The diffused sounds of students in the halls flooded into the room.

It took a moment to figure out what happened. Galan turned toward the open door, and I caught the twisted grimace on Samuel's face. It as clearly a wish for Galan's immediate and painful death.

Galan muttered something and began pulling a shirt on when a crashing blow cracked him across the jaw. Staggering, he caught himself against the stone wall and raised his fingers to the blood on his lip. Fists clenched, he lurched forward.

"No!" I forced myself between them. "Back the hell off, Samuel."

Galan's fury eased and slipped into something else. He looked almost amused, either by the depth of Samuel's hatred or by me as his champion, I wasn't sure. With far too much calm, he tested his split lip. His lack of reaction seemed to fuel Samuel's anger like an open flame, which only proved to amuse Galan more.

"Have we a problem, Samuel?" Galan drawled.

"Aye, *you!*" Samuel pressed closer. "Ye've been a spear up my arse since the day ye stumbled into our lives. Do ye think it's proper, drapin' yourself over Jade, half-dressed, in the storage room? Ye've ken her what? Two weeks?"

"Excuse me?" I snapped. "If I remember correctly, you dumped me like yesterday's garbage and moved on to a slutty brunette. We are friends, Samuel, nothing more. I am not your property, and I'm not your bitch to heel when you whistle."

Samuel's eyes flared. "I never treated ye like one, Jade, and ye bloody well know it."

I inhaled, and after a minute, I nodded. "Fine, let's drop it. Reign asked me to get Galan dressed for the Queens. Give us ten minutes to finish up in here, and we'll be out of your way."

Samuel's expression chilled me through. He stormed out, the bang of the door echoing like a gunshot. I rubbed my hand over my eyes then threw a charcoal knit zip-up jacket and a mid-length trench at Galan. He caught it as it flew at his head but didn't say a word.

Shit. It wasn't Galan's fault that Samuel and I didn't work out, still — "Could you look a little less pleased? Believe it or not, Samuel was good to me, and I don't find any of this funny."

"Apologies. I do not understand your attachment to him. However, it is not for me to judge." He trailed his finger along his bloody, swelling lip and took a slow step directly in front of me. "Jade, would you mind?"

I couldn't stop my idiotic grin. Rubbing my palms together, I raised my hand. Allowing my affinity to touch his life again was... everything. Light as a feather, I dragged my fingertips across his bottom lip. I jumped as brilliant white teeth nipped my finger and held it prisoner. Ever so lightly, the tip of his tongue advanced to caress it.

I swallowed, focusing my affinity on our connection. The healing was calmer this time, richer. His passions were still overwhelming, but there was something else. Something dark that I missed last time.

Something he didn't want me to sense.

Violent images struck me then, Galan accepting his father's anger and frustration to save his sister the same fate. He tried to block the thoughts, the pain—both emotional and physical—but I felt the evidence in the tissue and bones beneath my fingers. He had protected his sister the only way he knew how and believed he failed her in the end.

He stared at me, his heart racing beneath my palm.

"Good as new." I swallowed and stepped back. "Reign will be waiting. Do you want to come while I get ready?"

Twenty minutes later, I had regained my composure and left my dressing closet. Galan was in my kitchen, tipping back a second Guinness. "All set?" I asked.

Galan choked, sputtering beer over his hand and down the front of his t-shirt. After setting the bottle on the counter, he grabbed the marble edge and coughed it out until he could straighten. I fought back giggles. His reaction went a long way in boosting my ego. "So much for smooth, Highborne."

"By the gods." His watering eyes were wide as saucers as they scanned me up and down.

I gave him a runway turn and let him take in the sights from all angles. I sported an army green camo-T, cropped to reveal the emerald gemstone I'd just replaced in my navel. My black and silver kilt brushed the tops of my thighs and rode low on my hips. Accessorizing with chunky black leather boots buckled up to my knees and a silver serpent spiraling around my upper arm, and the look was complete.

If I read him right, those jeans didn't leave a lot of space for lust. Good. That was the reaction I wanted.

He drew long fingers through his hair, his ears deepening to scarlet. "Is this what females wear in the city? It is revealing, is it not? I would never allow Lia—"

"Then it's a good thing I'm not your sister," I raised a brow and adjusted the weight of my backpack. Swaying my hips, I headed for the door. "Okay, one foot in front of the other Highborne. Let's go."

CHAPTER EIGHTEEN

Stepping out of a full-length, 18th-century mirror wasn't all that startling to me, but traveling by portal mirror twice in one morning left Galan unsteady. While Reign checked us in, Samuel slipped out the side door to the alley, and Galan leaned heavily against a Gothic cabinet in the back room of the Reminiscence Antique store. Tucked just off Richmond Street in the downtown core of Toronto, the shop served as one of two Toronto gatehouses.

Enchanted by a gatekeeper years ago, it repelled Dark members of the realm, including Scourge and other would-be bad guys who might be passing by.

I dug into my backpack and tossed Galan a black Dobbs fedora. "Keep your ears tucked. Once we get where we're going, you can take it off. Oh. I'm not sure if the Queens will speak Elvish or English. It depends on their mood."

"Very well." Galan nodded and pulled the brim in place. "Tham, Aust, and I have practiced. If I have difficulties with what is said, I shall let you know."

I retied my backpack and let Galan take it when he held out his hand. "Do you remember what I told you about the greater Fae?"

Galan nodded. "Never thank them outright, or they can hold me to a debt owed. Flatter their efforts in a way that expresses my thanks without actually saying it."

"Good. Don't forget. The Queens are nicer than most. Still, you don't want to spend the rest of your very long life in servitude."

"How do I know which members of Fae to be wary of?"

I shrugged. "Magic is the biggest clue. Lesser Fae have minor magical abilities. The more powerful the Fae, the warier you need to be. You'll feel the power of Greater Fae."

Samuel's all-clear whistle brought the three of us out the side door to join him in the familiar corridor between the Chinese produce market and the military surplus store. It was a dirty, rundown, nondescript area that blended in with every other side alley in the neighborhood.

And that was exactly why it was perfect.

As we exited, I scanned the surroundings. Most of the second-story windows in the alley were lost to vandalism long ago and covered with chipboard. Others were opaque with grime deposited over years of neglect. Either way, there were no vantage points for prying eyes to monitor the comings and goings of the alley.

Samuel and Reign led, while Galan and I took up the rear.

Once on Richmond, we headed up toward Queen. People rushed across crowded streets, streetcars dinged, cars honked, and the constant clack and shuffle of shoes tromping their way along the sidewalks added to the din.

An urban symphony of chaos.

Galan's nostrils flared as we passed the silver cart-umbrella-combo, and he breathed in the unmistakable scent of street meat. "Incredible."

"It is, isn't it?" My stomach rumbled, and I made a mental note to grab a sausage on the way back.

"Where do they go in such a bustle?" Galan's gaze pivoted as we walked amongst the foot traffic of the sidewalk headed toward the crosswalk.

"Working, shopping, eating. Who knows?"

"Is it always like this?"

"Mostly." I skirted around a young mother pushing a stroller. She gave my outfit an unflattering scan yet seemed to find Galan's appealing enough. "It's busier during the workday and then again at night, but yep, it's always busy."

Galan smiled at a toddler chucking Cheerios out of the stroller. "And the Gypsy Queens reside nearby? What domain do these women rule?"

"Well, I wouldn't exactly—"

"Wait and see," Samuel said, his daggered glares now holding obvious amusement.

I was glad Samuel's tirade had ended but worried about the Jekyll and Hyde routine. He was rubber-balling between the man I cared about and an angry Scottish arse.

After a few more minutes of Galan gawking, we stopped.

"Here we are." Reign gestured to the facade of a three-story, brick building. A grand marquee was lit above the main entrance while a dozen framed posters glowed with hundreds of little, white, globe lights. It was glitzy now, but much more impressive at night when the crowds mulled around.

"The Diva's Den," Galan said, stepping beneath the dark, burgundy awning cantilevered over the sidewalk. He eyed the colorful posters of elaborately dressed women, and tried to make sense of this strange new world. Little did he know how strange this world was about to get for him.

"After you, Elf." Samuel snickered as he opened the door.

"Reign, *darrrrling*." A husky voice greeted us as we stepped through the double glass doors into the dark foyer. "Where have you been keeping yourself? It's been ages."

Galan stared at the six-foot-four brawny woman wearing vibrant, slime-green, vinyl. She was steady in fuchsia, high-heeled boots, rushing to greet us. His gaze snapped to the light dusting of chest hair peeking out of the low V of her jumper, and traveled south, down to her enormous silver belt buckle.

"Cara," Reign said, accepting a kiss to each cheek. "I've meant to stop by to see the new show, but life gets away from me these days."

Cara pushed out her bottom lip and propped her hands on her hips. "Life, huh? Amanda said you don't love us anymore."

"Nonsense," he said. When he shook his head, his brindle hair swung against his jaw, the strands of gold and copper glinting under the track lights. "You know I adore you, ladies."

She flipped her hair, though it didn't move and pushed out her bright pink lips.

"How could you doubt me, Cara? Haven't I always come when you call?"

After a long moment, she nodded. "Well, yes. Okay, I'll forgive you if you promise to come to our gala next month. It's a theme night—Merry Queens and Scots. Can you guess who the Merry Queens are?"

"I wouldn't miss it." He winked, and she swooned. Reign was an incorrigible flirt when it came to the Queens. Beyond their value as prophetic readers, he found them to be endlessly amusing. "I'll polish my Gillies and press my kilt, but only if you promise to save me a dance."

Ew, not an image I need in my head.

"Now," he said, lifting his elbow for her. "Where are your sisters?"

Cara ushered us down the dimly lit hallway, through the black corral doors, and into the main nightclub. The stage lights were turned on, and Cara *sisters* were strutting across the glossy floor singing a duet. Their costumes and makeup screamed the same vibrant whimsy as Cara's, just on different parts of the color wheel. Standing together, the three of them looked like a Skittles bag exploded. Cara was lime, and these two were happy-face yellow and candy floss pink.

Mmm, taste the rainbow.

Our arrival brought an end to the rehearsal, and the two on stage threw their arms open. "Oh, you're here!" They skittered to the edge of the stage and lowered themselves sideways down the four steps to the main floor. You'd think four-inch stiletto boots would make maneuvering difficult. It didn't seem to affect them in the slightest.

Drawn like magnets to Galan's side, they pawed like cats with a new feathered toy.

JL MADORE

Amanda stroked the definition of his chest through his T-shirt. "Ooh, isn't he yummy?"

"Like a freshly baked cookie," Clare sighed, before biting her lip. "If I nibble on you for a while, I bet you'd melt in my mouth."

"He makes *my* mouth water." Cara winked. Holding Reign's arm, she leaned back to scan Galan's butt. "And the gifts keep on giving."

"Yes, he's stunning," Reign said. "Introductions, ladies. Galanodel Caleblasse, this is Clare Vuoyant, Cara Zmatic, and Amanda Playwith."

If Galan was unnerved by the attention, it didn't show. He was as suave and charming as ever. "It is a true pleasure." He smiled my favorite smirk, the one where he raised one eyebrow and looked totally, sinfully hot.

Clare fanned herself, then pulled off Galan's hat and mussed his hair.

Samuel fought to keep straight faces and failed. Quaking with suppressed laughter, he leaned close. "Do ye think he's into them? Ye know what they say about Elves."

"Stop." I smacked his arm but laughed when I saw the sparkle in his eyes. "Behave."

Amanda put her hands under Galan's leather trench, slid them over his shoulders, and let the jacket drop to the stage.

Galan's glance shot to Reign, who cleared his throat and stepped in. "As intriguing as it is catching up with you girls, we're curious about the reason you requested to meet Galan."

"In good time, Reign." Clare laced her arm around Galan's waist, hooking her thumb into a belt loop. "Are you musical, Cookie?" she asked, moving him toward the stage.

Reign intercepted the two of them and positioned Galan to his side. "I must request we discuss why you asked us here."

"Oh Reign, we want to get to know—"

"I understand," Reign cooed, his voice sweet yet firm. "We can't loiter in this realm with Galan. You know how Castian disapproves of exposure risks."

The three ladies straightened.

"Yes, yes. I suppose we don't want to upset Castian." Amanda huffed, pushing her bottom lip out. "You need to get some grind, Reign. You are usually so much more fun."

"Behave," he said, then chuckled. "How about I send you three an invitation for Lexi's birthday party in February? There will be dancing, and Hugh and his cubs will be there."

"Oh, how purrrfect. We loves us those lion-men. So sexy." Pantomiming the locking of her lips, Amanda threw away the key. "Fine. I suppose we've dallied long enough. Let's retire to our palace of promiscuity where we can talk privately."

Upstairs, the Queens' parlor was even more outrageous than their costumes, stage names, and theatrical makeup put together. The walls hung draped in fuchsia satin with large etchings of nude men in poses, which made me blush. The heavy gilded frames accented the electric-blue velvet curtains, gold and sapphire area rugs, and twin suits of armor sitting on either side of the doorway. The metal men might have seemed stuffy, if not for the French-maid aprons they each wore.

In the center of the room stood a round table with eight chairs. It looked like a do-it-yourself craft bomb had gone off, leaving behind glitter and paisley shrapnel. The table, carpet, wooden floor, and every other surface lay buried in sparkles.

"A slice of heaven, isn't it?" Amanda said, sweeping her hand through the air in front of her. "It screams serenity, don't you think?"

It screams something.

The Queens took their places, and once I settled opposite them, Galan sat beside me, and then Reign and Samuel sat on the other side of him. Cara laid her hands flat on the table. Clare and Amanda, seated on either side of her, took a hand in theirs.

"What do you know about your history, Cookie?" Cara asked.

Galan leaned forward, his leg bouncing under the table against mine. "Solely what we were taught through our lore. Ten thousand years ago, my ancestors were guardians to Queen Rheagan, immortal half-sister to Castian Latheron. He appointed her as a Fae matriarch to oversee the mortals of the Realm of the Fair. She was to govern yet remain impartial and allow the realm to decide its fate. Two millennia later, my Highborne ancestors realized they had unknowingly become part of her plan to control the existence of all races. Though they endeavored to stop her, they were exiled for their part in her destruction."

"Basically, your average dysfunctional family." Amanda winked. "Every family has a few bats flying loose in the attic."

"Ours is Stinky Uncle Pete." Clare looked sympathetic.

Cara smiled at her sister and continued. "That's true, but Rheagan was incredibly powerful even though she was bat-shit crazy. She truly believed weeding out the weaker races would preserve the arcane energies of the Fae. What you might not know is that when she clued in that her noble children didn't have the stones for her plans, she struck up an unholy alliance with a few of the Dark races."

Amanda nodded. "Even then, some were well on the way to becoming the scum-sucking Scourge we know and abhor today."

"When Castian kicked Rheagan's scrawny tukis out of the Pantheon," Cara said, "she gathered what supporters she had and formed a secret society—the *Aina Ohtar*." She paused and looked at Galan. "Did I pronounce that correctly, Cookie?"

Galan's hair swung as he nodded. "Holy Warriors."

Cara beamed, obviously pleased with herself. "So, she held clandestine meetings cultivating plans to skim the scum off the Realm, letting the cream rise to power. It was very 'Illuminati-esque', wouldn't you say sisters?"

"Absolutely," they chimed in.

"Her Holy Warriors gained strength as the uprising progressed. She knew her brother would never stand for a member of the Fae gods altering the lives of his mortal charges and she didn't have the juice she needed to defeat Castian head-on, so she devised her comeback tour."

I gasped. "Do you think Rheagan might come back?"

"We do," Cara said. "She's banished and cursed yet retains her immortality. In theory, the *Aina Ohtar* could free her from the depths to help her reclaim her throne."

"How?" Reign asked.

Cara leaned forward and raised a brow. "Well, we're just speculating on that. At the time of the final uprising, the Highbornes had taken control of the palace. The Queen had no allies. We believe she embedded a resurrection spell amongst an innocuous incantation in her spellbook. According to the records of the Highbornes' sentencing, Aduial, General of the Royal Guard, took that spellbook with him into exile."

"Why would she trust him with it if she knew they were against her?" Galan asked.

"Well, for one thing, she didn't tell him about the spell. And also, for centuries, Aduial was not only her personal bodyguard but her voracious lover. Legend says his endurance and prowess in battle translated to other areas of their relationship. He caught the wanton eye of the Queen, and she never looked back."

Amanda smiled. "From what we hear, he rocked her like nobody's business."

"Oh," Clare sighed, "we need to find us one of those men, don't we, sisters?"

"From your lips to the Fates' ears," Cara said, clasping her hands. "Light a candle and say a prayer, girls."

"Anyhoo," Cara said, shaking her head, "although Aduial lay beside her in the sheets, he couldn't abide with her quest for power no matter how much he enjoyed the canoodling. Unknown to all but the two of them, Aduial and Rheagan had a secret love child. A baby girl named Ezra. They hid the pregnancy, but with her coming fate, Rheagan spilled the beans about the birth to the *Aina Ohtar*. She claimed her daughter was the key to her resurrection to power."

"What happened to Ezra?" Reign asked.

"The babe was exiled with her Highborne daddy and the spellbook. The *Aina Ohtar* had no way of breaking Castian's spell and couldn't resurrect their Queen until he pardoned their sentence and released the exiles."

"Which has happened," I said. "So, what became of the *Aina Ohtar?*"

"Oh, it's still around. It's governed by the leaders of the faction

JL MADORE

uniting the Dark rogues of the realm. In short, it's the foundation of the Scourge hierarchy."

Fabulous. The possibilities of what they meant flopped in my belly like a knot of eels. "Assuming the spell is secured, could they still resurrect her?"

"From what we've seen in the cards, no, but sorcerers are a tricky, sticky bunch."

Galan slid a sideways glare toward Samuel and then shook his head. "How could they know which one of us was Ezra's heir? After eight thousand years, *we* have no knowledge of who that might be."

Amanda brushed a blonde wisp from in front of her eyes, and her Adam's apple dipped as she swallowed. "Ezra was known for a rare genetic characteristic which set her apart from other Highbornes. It was said to be a gift from Castian to his niece at the time of her birth."

"And what was that?" Galan waited, fingers drumming the table. I covered the hand closest to me and squeezed.

Amanda looked to her sisters and let the words tumble in a rush. "Ezra and her heirs were the only Highborne females who were ever, and always, born with silver hair."

Galan's face drained. "Lia?"

"Lia." Cara repeated. "I'm sorry, Cookie, but your sister is the living heir to the Queen and her lover. And there's more." She waited for his attention, her gaze locked on his. "From the time of her rule until now, all male offspring in Rheagan's bloodline had flaxen hair. You are the first male ever to have silver like the females?"

Galan nodded. "My mother said I was a gift from the gods, that she never expected the blessing of a silver son."

Clare's eyes filled with compassion. "I received a poem of prophecy yesterday." She pushed a sheet of parchment across the round table.

Though I couldn't make out the words, the poem flowed across the thick sheet in a flourish of calligraphy. He drew it closer. I'd studied most of the languages of the Realm enough to identify them. This was something I'd never set eyes on.

"What does it say?" I asked.

Galan's stare moved from the black ink to me, then to the three women. His lips pressed tight together as he dragged his fingers through his hair.

"I'm just a messenger," Clare said. "The gist of the images I got while writing it were that there is an uprising coming. From what I gather, the man at the helm of the resistance is you, the silver Highborne male."

Cara leaned closer, her face lined with shadow. "I'm sorry, Cookie, but if Lia is the key to freeing Rheagan, we believe you are the key to stopping her."

Galan jacked out of his chair and paced the glittery rug. "It is a *mistake*. Lia is a sapling and I—I am no warrior. I have no instinct for rebellion. It is ludicrous."

The three oracles looked on steadily as he swirled and spun and paced. "Cookie, you've gone an unsightly shade of mint. Can we get you some tea?" Cara said. "We have a lovely Chamomile that might soothe you."

"No. Grati—"

"*Galan.*" I stomped my foot, unclear if he was even aware of what he'd almost done.

Galan clenched his hands into fists, crumpling the parchment in his grip. "Apologies, I need a moment." Whirling toward the door, Galan made his escape, and I followed.

A few feet down the hall, he braced his hands on his knees. After what I'd lived through, the battles, the healings, and the death of my parents, I thought I'd be immune to this level of suffering. Not even close. One look in those ocean blues and my heart shattered like crystal, nothing but a million shards hitting a slime-green runner. "What can I do?"

Galan's breathing hitched as his lungs took in shallow breaths much too quickly in a disjointed rhythm. His head must be spinning. Before I got under him, his legs buckled, and he fell to his knees, his expression blanking out.

"Galan, breathe slower, or you'll faint." I knelt behind him, not sure he even heard me. "Deep breaths." Rubbing my hands across his back I connected with him and sent out a wave of warmth. It permeated deep into his lungs until they eased open and let in oxygen. As his breathing slowed, his dizzy panic faded. He leaned heavily against my chest and tilted his head into the curve of my neck. I wrapped my arms around his chest and held tight. "It's all right. We'll figure this out. We'll find her and figure this all out."

"Are you certain?" he whispered. "They expect to use her to release their Queen. Even *if* we find her, she will be forever hunted by Dark members of the realm. How do I protect her?"

My arms constricted tighter. "The two of you will live at Haven until we figure this out. You'll stay there and be safe."

CHAPTER NINETEEN

Back on Richmond Street, Galan lowered the brim of his hat, lifted the collar of his jacket, and pushed his Ray-Ban's tighter against his face. The stiffness in his body made me nuts. I opened my mouth a couple of times. No words came. What the hell do you say to someone who finds out he's a descendant of a maniacal Fae goddess and his sister was kidnapped to resurrect her? Is there a Hallmark card for that?

Fucking Fates. They had a way of kinking the road ahead, so you never saw what was coming. Then your life careened over a cliff and landed in a fiery ball of mangled steel at the bottom of some out-of-the-way ravine. Even the best-laid plans blew sky high when those women got bored with their day-to-day.

In one afternoon, Galan was devastated, and Samuel and Reign were stewing about something I missed while Galan and I were in the hall. Turmoil hemorrhaged from the group, but I couldn't do a damn thing to help any of them. *Yippee.*

I caught Galan's arm and hung back. "Are you all right?"

"No," he muttered, his honesty catching me off guard. "My life is aflame. Fire bursts all around me, yet I have no way to extinguish it."

While Galan and I spoke, Reign and Samuel crossed the street and headed down the alley toward the antique shop.

"Give yourself a sec to catch up," I said. "Two weeks ago, you were packing for your *Ambar Lenn*. I've been dealing with this insanity for decades, and it still swamps me at times."

He reached under the glasses and rubbed his eyes. "What will they do if she refuses them? Lia can be strong-willed, trying even."

"She's valuable to them. That will probably keep her safe. I bet they consider her royalty already." Goosebumps covered my arms, and my body was suddenly tingling all over. *What the hell?* I scanned the crosswalk and street. Nothing. "Let's get home. Reign and Samuel are probably already at the shop."

Tires screeched, and two Escalades with blacked-out windows blocked us from the alley. When the passenger doors swung open, half-a-dozen men in black oozed onto the sidewalk. The looked human enough, but the warm summer breeze carried the faint scent of skunk and rot.

Shit. Shit. Shit.

"It's a glamour." Without thinking, I reached for my whip, right, not a weapon for the city. Sending off jolts of magical energy here was a no-go, too. The truth was, the Scourge didn't attack in the Modern Realm. What the hell?

Stopped in our tracks, I searched for an out. In the split-second, I glanced away, the tallest of the group grabbed something out of his belt. A metallic edge glinted blue in the evening sun.

With sickening speed, the man unleashed the dagger into the air. We didn't have time to avoid the hit. All I could do was throw up a quick veil of secrecy and hope it would be enough to conceal our actions from Mundane eyes.

Galan blurred, his reflex nothing short of lightning. Caging me into his arms, he spun us out of the path of the approaching blade. He flinched and, in that same instant, turned with the blade of the dagger in his hand. He'd plucked it out of the air and, without hesitation, sent it end-over-end back to its owner.

The blade sunk true. The attacker's hands grasped at the weapon lodged into his throat as he crumpled. Blood fountained through clenched fingers, pooling like oil onto the concrete. Three others stepped over him and advanced.

"Are you hurt?"

"I shall do." Galan snapped. "We need to leave this place."

I grabbed Galan's outstretched hand and wove through the evening traffic. Dodging cars, cabs and delivery trucks, angry drivers honked and threw hand gestures. When we turned a corner, a bike messenger almost rammed into Galan. We kept running. By the way, he cursed at us, there was a possibility he would come after us too.

Glancing over my shoulder, I saw that there were three men right behind us and two more behind them.

"Castian, come to me." A warm breeze swirled around my face. "Wind, carry my message. *Reign, seal the gate. We've got company. We'll find another way. Trust me.*" When the comfort of the breeze left me, I knew my warning was sent. Reign's first instinct was always to protect his girls, but he knew I could take care of myself. I think.

I dodged a row of street vendors and almost took out a couple of ladies with enough shopping bags to fill the fourth-floor closet.

I pulled Galan down an open concrete staircase leading from the street to the concourse. "I need my backpack." I grabbed it on the fly and pushed through the glass door dividing the stairwell from the shops below. Urging it closed behind us, I touched the handles and locked them with my powers.

"Will that stop them?"

I shook my head. "Just slow them down." We hustled down the polished passageways of people while I rummaged through the pack.

"Where are we?" he asked, eyes wide.

"In the PATH. It's an underground extension of the city's major streets and businesses." The shattering of glass had me glance over my shoulder. "*Dammit.*" Closer than I thought.

After a brief pause to orient myself, I grabbed his wrist and led him through another maze of corridors, restaurants, and shops.

"There." I pointed to the dark shadows down a long dead-end service corridor. "This will do."

When we turned the corner, I began to hum, weaving the incantation. Galan's jaw dropped slack when he turned back, and an identical image of the two of us stood at the opening of the hallway.

With the wave of my hand, the conjured doppelgangers continued up the main corridor the way we'd been running.

"What was that?"

"Not now." I recited an invisibility chant to shield us.

The door to my right was marked *Storage*. With the pass of my hand, a soft, metallic *click* sounded from the lock. We slipped in, but it was tight. The space was nothing more than a reach-in closet. Galan's hips pressed against my butt as I faced the door to close it. After a small struggle, I managed to slide the tumbler back in place and close us in. It was pitch. At the soft rustle of Galan's reach, I caught his arm.

"No lights," I whispered.

I pressed my palms against the cold steel of the door. The tremors were already building. My eyes darted through the black void in front of me. Nothing. *I'm won't lose it. I'm not trapped. I'm not alone. I'm not going to lose it.*

"Jade?" A firm grip on my hips had me turning in place. He secured my face in his palms. "What is it? Your heart races like a hare in flight, and your fear burns bitter in the air."

Memories overtook logic, and that storage closet became a dank, root cellar. Childhood nightmares boiled in my gut and expanded. As the pressure built, I tried desperately not to let a scream peal from my throat. My hands.

They shook like the wings of a hummingbird.

"Blossom, what can I do?" Galan's voice was grounded, calm. He gathered my hands in his. He wasn't rattled. He was just—there with me. The heat from his body was incredible. It barely touched the ice circulating through my veins. Barely. I locked my knees and tried to focus on reining in this fall-apart. The last thing I needed was to buckle to the floor when we were being hounded.

"Jade." His breath warmed my ear. "Tell me what is happening, and I swear to make it right for you."

Instinct demanded I curl up on the floor and wrap my arms around my knees. I swallowed hard, trying to draw oxygen into frozen lungs. "Tight, dark spaces. I, uh, hate—"

Galan tightened his hold on me and stroked my cheek. "Close your eyes and focus on my voice. You are not alone in that terrible place, Jade. The sapling you once were has grown into a force of nature, an incredible, powerful female." He took my wrist and pressed my hand flat on his chest. "Slow your heart to match the rhythm of mine."

His heart beat against my palm, racing. Too fast. This wasn't working. "Galan, I—"

His lips were soft and warm against mine as he pinned me to the steel of the door. The metallic chill behind me seeped through my clothes. The scent of him, his clean, manly spice inched inside me and calmed my nerves. Silky fingers slipped behind my jaw, securing me in his kiss.

This was the best diversion ever. His arms twined around me, ivy reaching for the warmth of the sun's rays. I seized the front of his shirt, twisting the fabric, crushing my body to his. He kissed me in that powerful, possessive way he had.

The stuff of legends.

The panic eased, replaced by something else, something primal and urgent. I wanted to continue, never stopping to eat or breathe or speak to another soul save him, but my survival instincts were back on-line. I slowed the kiss and gently pulled away from his lips. I blinked against the darkness and shook my head. "Um, image projections only work for a short time before they fade. We should keep moving."

"Very well," he whispered in a broken, jagged breath before he kissed the tip of my nose. "Expect to revisit this matter in short order."

I swallowed, turning back to the handle before he saw my reaction. His body brushed down my bare thigh as he picked up our belongings, and I sighed.

When the door opened a crack, a sliver of light illuminated us. He looked flushed. "Focus, Galan." I shot him a playful glare but was just as breathless. "They'll likely have a Shifter, or a Were to track our scents. Once they realize they're following decoys, they'll be back."

"Fash not. I am versed in obscuring scents for stealth."

"In a forest maybe," I snorted, "how are you in the streets of Toronto? We'll double back and stay somewhere safe for tonight." We eased up the corridor and merged into the congestion of the main section of the concourse.

"The night?" He repeated close to my ear. "Are we not returning to your Haven?"

"The other gatehouse is on one of the city's islands. It would be suicide to get stuck on a ferry with Scourge after us. We'll lay low tonight and head to the port in the morning."

Even with his disguise in place, Galan was drawing female attention. Oblivious to the appraising looks, Galan wiped his brow. "And in the meantime?"

"Up there." I pointed to the escalator climbing to the lobby of an office building above. If I remembered correctly, it connected to a hotel further along. When Galan paused, I held out my foot in an exaggerated example of where to step and pulled him along behind me.

Smiling at Galan's uncharacteristic lack of coordination, I placed his hand on the rubber handrail, and we rode the moving stairs to street level. "There are always taxis outside hotels."

A crowd mulled around inside the rotating doors, a sun shower holding them indoors. We jogged passed the fair-weather Mundies, into the rain and up the cab line to the first orange car. Soaked, we slid into the car. "Casa Loma, please."

Our driver nodded, staring at me in his mirror. "They're probably closed for the night."

"That's okay." I dried my hands, unzipped my phone from my pack, and scrolled through my contacts. They answered on the second ring. "Hey, it's Blaze. I've got a plus one. It's hot out here. Yep. Fifteen minutes. Thanks."

"Where are we going?" Galan's voice sounded off.

"To a Haven safe house." I leaned close to whisper and took in his pallor. His skin had drained to bone white and glistened. It wasn't rain. He was covered in a sheen of sweat. "Are you all right?" I brushed a piece of hair away from his face to look into his eyes. They were dilated and roaming. "Galan, wha—?"

I caught his head as it lolled to the side, and he lost consciousness.

Fifteen minutes felt like two hours while we inched our way northward toward privacy. The rain picked up and was pounding on the windshield as the cabbie's watchful gaze bore holes in his rearview. I fought the need to flip him the finger, rip open Galan's shirt, and examine him.

The gate was open, and Kobi, a friend of Bruin's and Talon enforcer, was our welcoming committee. Smoking under the overhang in the courtyard of Casa Loma, the guy was tall, dark, and Goth. His features leaned toward being GQ pretty, but the black Kohl eyeliner and the multitude of silver piercings said otherwise.

As we pulled to a stop, Kobi snuffed his smoke on the sole of his shitkicker and jogged out to meet us. "Hey," he said, opening the door. "What have—" He cursed at the sight of Galan slumped and unconscious in my lap. By the time I'd tipped the cabbie, Kobi had him slung over his shoulder and heading into the servant's entrance of the castle.

"Making friend's in the big city, eh?" Kobi flopped Galan down on the harvest table in the kitchen. "How hot are you? Is his pretty face going to be the lead story on TMZ tonight?"

"Originally half a dozen came at us, maybe more. And no, I don't think there's been exposure." I yanked Galan's shirt up so to feel the energy of his organs. "Galan killed one, and I think we lost the others in the Concourse."

"He *killed* one?" Kobi's eyes glowed scarlet. "In the city?"

I relayed the events of our attack, starting with getting separated from Reign through to Galan passing out in the cab. "Gods, he's on fire. His heart is pumping way too fast."

"Venom?"

"Has to be for it to act this fast. Shit." I focused my gift, working as fast as I could to slow the avalanche of decay, overwhelming all of Galan's organs and systems. Heart, lungs, blood—all of it was compromised.

As the convulsions started, I prayed I wasn't too late.

CHAPTER TWENTY

"Lia!" Galan jacked halfway off the mattress, knocked the side table, and sent my glass of wine toppling to the hardwood. Long, graceful fingers clutched through empty air until the shattering of crystal fractured his illusion. He hissed, clutched his side, and collapsed back onto the bed.

"*Shh* . . . Galan, it was a dream." Lifting his head, I slid a pillow beneath his matted hair and retrieved the damp facecloth from the basin on the bedside table. His gaze skittered around the room before his attention settled back to me.

"Lia," he mumbled. Restless legs stirred beneath the damp sheet as I sponged back the hair stuck to his neck.

"It was a dream. I'm sorry." Palming the smooth rise of his chest with my free hand, I used my gift to ease his panic. His eyes followed my voice and then surveyed the room.

Straight out of the turn of the century, the bed, a huge four-poster draped in a brocaded canopy, was flanked by bedside tables and matching bouquets of white peonies. An oversized desk sat against the mahogany-paneled wall, and in the corner, our clothes lay drying over two mohair slipper chairs that faced the marble hearth of a large fireplace.

Galan's focus shifted to where I was touching him. "Jade?" He winced, struggling to straighten. "Jade . . . I, uh—"

As his eyes rolled back, I stroked his hair, coaxing the silver mess off his heated skin. "*Shh*, Galan, rest. We're safe for now."

Sometime in the middle of the night, Galan started coming around. There were false alarms throughout the day when I thought he might wake up, but between the venom, his grief, and the stress of what had happened with the Queens, his body had decided to take a detour into coma-town for a while.

Uncharacteristically, I wasn't in much better shape. After tightening the lapels of my terry robe, I dried my cheeks with the cuff of my sleeve. "Are you really awake this time?" I turned the bedside lamp on to its dimmest setting and propped up on my elbow to look him over. There was a jolting noise downstairs, and I stilled as hundreds of chandelier prisms jingled like wind chimes, tinkling their song above us.

Galan's eyes widened. "Where are we?"

"We're at a Haven safe house."

A crease appeared between his brows. "Still in the Modern Realm?"

"For a bit longer. When you're well, we'll go back." I reached into the long rectangular pocket of my robe and brought out the crumpled parchment the Queens had given Galan. "I've been thinking. I know someone who might be able to decipher the prophecy."

Galan didn't move, didn't even blink. "Who might that be?"

"Chiron of Delaran, a famous Centaur scholar. If anyone can figure out what this poem says, it will be him."

Galan took possession of the message and scanned the flourishing script. "Will he help us? I have no valuables to barter nor coin to pay him with."

I shook my head. "We won't need it. Chiron was my private tutor for fifteen years at the Academy. He was the one who taught me how to use my bard powers. He knows more about poetry and the written word of our realm than anyone else I know."

"And he will be able to read this?"

I shrugged. "If it's written in one of the lost languages of this realm, or one of the other realms, he'll know it or know who to go to next."

"Good." Galan folded it carefully along its creases and gave it back to me. "And have the Talon come up with anything on the whereabouts of my sister thus far?"

I shrugged. "Not as far as I know. We'll find out as soon as we can get through the Portal Mirror. Rest tonight, and tomorrow we'll know more."

"Can we Flash to this gatehouse now and avoid delay?"

I shook my head and raised my hand in a sweeping gesture. "This is a safe house hidden within a strong glamour. We can't Flash through it. We have to wait until you're well enough to travel."

Galan pushed against his elbows, attempting to straighten. It looked like he'd insist that he was well enough now, but he sagged back to his pillow. A rush of hostility heated my insides. The Scourge were so close to taking his life I could scream.

Galan's eyes closed as his hand rubbed at his forehead. "What happened?"

"The dagger from the street attack grazed you as you pushed us clear. It was tipped with venom, and you collapsed in the cab."

He nodded and examined the faint pink scar on his palm. "I thought it only a scratch when there was no blood."

"Only a *scratch*?" I shook my head. "That *scratch* almost killed you, and I didn't even know you were hurt. There was no blood because Scourge venom cauterizes the wound so the poison can attack your internal systems." *Was that shrill tirade coming from me?* I flopped back down on the bed and brushed my cheeks with my fingers. "You scared me to death. This isn't your valley, Galan. If you're hurt during battle, you have to let me know."

Securing my wrist, he brought my hand to his lips. "Apologies. I was unfamiliar with the protocol of such an event. However, I now stand fully enlightened and properly lashed for my error." He was making fun of me. When I refused to smile, he tugged me closer, tucking me against his chest. His gaze softened. "I regret you were frightened, Blossom, truly, yet I survived. You handled everything, as always."

His apology was so eloquent it pissed me off. I glared at him, which triggered a twitch at the corners of his mouth.

"Don't flatter me, Highborne. I'm *mad* at you."

He dipped his head and kissed the top of my head. It didn't fool me. I knew he was fighting a smile. When I sighed and gave in to his sultry comfort, he flipped the quilt over both of us and cocooned us tightly in the blankets. Soft strokes of his finger raked through my hair and had my eyes drifting closed.

"So, tell me what went on after I lost consciousness. Did those men return?"

"No. We lost them. They'll be tracking us, but we should be good until we leave here tomorrow. When Kobi realized it was me coming in, he called in some extra enforcers. We're locked down tight."

Galan stretched and sank deeper into the mattress. "Then, for this night, *neelan*, you rest, and I shall watch over you." Galan kissed my forehead and hummed while I reined in my nerves.

Huh, a night on the receiving end of the TLC.

"I find I have no recollections beyond entering that orange vehicle."

"You passed out cold in the back seat. I told the driver you were drunk." I shrugged at his disbelieving grin.

"It would take an incredible effort for a Highborne to become intoxicated to the point of unconsciousness."

"Good to know. I'm scratching off drinking games with you and your family."

He fingered my hair behind my ear, his chest rumbling against me as he laughed. "Does Reign know you are well?"

I nodded. "I spoke to him yesterday and told him you needed time to recoup."

"Then we'll be heading back to the castle in the morning?"

I shook my head. "No. I think we should focus on the prophesy and let my father and his men work on locating Lia."

"And what do you think the prophecy will tell us?"

I shrugged. "No idea, but several things are bugging me." I lifted my fingers and began counting off my points. "How did the Scourge know where to find us? Why would they risk breaking Fae laws and attack us right in the middle of a human city? Why would— *Whoa!*" The room rattled as another bang came from downstairs.

"Is it an attack?" Galan asked, trying to sit up.

"No." I pushed him back down and propped up on my elbow. "There's a prisoner in the dungeon that is quite determined to break his confinement. He's being transferred in a few hours when the Mundies in the neighborhood have all gone to bed."

When the tinkling of the chandelier died down, Galan brushed my cheek and breathed deep. "Did you tend to your needs as well? Did you eat and rest after healing me?"

"Mhmm. I pulled a blanket over us and had a long nap."

He kissed along my collarbone as he whispered soft and serious. "You carry too much weight in your basket, Blossom. You are not invincible."

The room bounced and jingled again, and he tightened his arms around me.

"I thought you said I was an unstoppable force of nature?"

"Without a doubt. Still, we must not tempt the Fates." His lips lingered in the hollow of my throat. "I wonder how upset Samuel is about us finding ourselves stranded together."

I tried to ignore the male amusement in his tone. "It doesn't matter. Samuel and I ended before you came along. I'm not sure what his issue is."

Galan shifted to look at me, staring into the depths of what I was sure were bleary, puffy eyes. After a time, he raised one arm behind his head and fell back to stare at the ceiling. Light from the sconces passed through the prisms of the chandelier and danced in dappled whimsy on the ceiling above. "Why do you suppose all of this occurred?"

He reminded me of a carved statue, staring off beyond the boundaries of our room. His skin was soft as the still summer night, his body chiseled in perfect proportions. A part of him, and I had no idea how large a part, was born of the gods of the Fae. *Huh.* Maybe that's why he accessed the spellbook in the cave. What else would it mean?

"Why did I leave her?" he whispered. "Why, of all the Elves in my village, did the Fates single out Lia and me to live this life of turmoil?"

I had no answer, other than, 'That's what the Fates do.' "It wasn't all bad," I said, fighting back a smile. "The Queens were quite taken with you."

The bed shook with Galan's laughter. "The Queens. That was outlandish."

"Um ... Galan, you did realize—"

"They are males?" His smile shone in the candlelight. "Yes, I gathered that early on. I assumed it was merely one of those modern details I am not accustomed to, the dressing as a female part, the sexual component of it I understand."

I hadn't thought about all the jokes before. "Are there a lot of gay Elves?" I explained what I meant and he shrugged.

"I cannot speak for all Elves. Highbornes, however, are a passionate race. Mayhap we differ from humans in the way we look at things. Sexual pleasure and love are two different plains of reality. We enjoy one another based on attraction, mutual affection, or a biological urge to satisfy. Male, female, two, three, four... it matters not. We care for the soul of a person, not their gender."

I'm not sure what my expression betrayed, but he chuckled and leaned closer.

"Love, however, is an altogether different matter. We mate for life, so the intimacy of coitus is preserved solely for those bound for life. There are no partings in our community. Mating is an eternal, unbreakable bond."

My mind sorted through the implications of that. "So, although you've enjoyed a century of messing around, you're technically a hundred-and-ten-year-old-virgin?"

"Yes, in the sense that I have yet to consummate with a female, yet it is quite a bit more complex. It takes years to understand the governances which dictate when and with whom we can be intimate. We only become eligible to take part in sexual activity after our sixtieth year."

"Then, you can pair up with whoever is single?"

"Not necessarily. The pairing could be with those single or mated."

"You said Highbornes didn't... If you're mated, you're bound to your mate."

"Yes and no. As I said, it is complex. We have intercourse with our mates, but mated females often take consorts to—add to their relationship." Galan absorbed my astonishment and chuckled again. "Highbornes live a thousand years or more, Blossom. If we mate in the first or second century, it is an incredibly long time to be with one person."

"You said that mated *females* take consorts? What about the males?" I shook the night's exhaustion away, finding this fascinating.

"Ours is a matriarchy. Females are the cherished members, and males focus their time and efforts protecting, providing, and pleasing."

Oh, Lexi is sooo going to love this.

I nibbled my lip and imagined this in action. "So, have you been a consort to many women?" Galan said nothing, though I waited for a long time. When he didn't meet my gaze, I leaned forward. "That bad, is it?"

Galan shifted under the sheets and exhaled. Kissing my cheek, he put his lips to my ear. "I wish it would not matter. I am eight and a half decades your senior, love. I cannot truthfully say I have locked myself away."

It was hard to concentrate on my agitation while he ran his lips down the side of my neck. My stomach flipped as I imagined countless Elven beauties writhing under his caress, all of them slender and blonde and graceful. All the things I was so obviously not.

"Aside from raising Lia and my camaraderie with Tham and Nyssa, being a consort was my only pleasurable outlet. It is considered an honor to be requested by females."

I locked onto his gaze, ready to read his reaction. "And are you honored, *often?*"

"I would consider myself *popular*, yes."

Enough said. I never expected Galan to be a virgin but didn't like the direction this conversation had taken. He had so much more experience than I. Maybe that explained why the Queens hadn't fazed him. I pushed back at the wave of self-consciousness that washed over me. Thinking about it, I couldn't imagine being with Galan and wanting Tham or Aust or any combination of them sexing me up for an evening, but there you go. I wasn't an Elf.

"You were a good sport with all the shameless flirting of the Queens." I gave him what I hoped was a warm smile.

Galan shrugged, tucking me into his neck. "To each their own, besides," he ran his hand down his bare chest and flashed me a seductive grin, "can you blame them?"

Laughter bubbled up. "Easy, Cookie, you're not half as mouthwatering as you think you are."

"Really?" He rolled on to his side, so we lay face to face. My head swam with the closeness of him. He smelled like suede, sunshine, and musky male. "Then why have you undressed me *twice* in as many days?"

"What?"

"Once in the storage closet and," he lifted the covers and glanced down the length of his body, "apparently, again as I lay unconscious and unable to defend my virtue." He feigned a look of shock so hysterical I burst into giggles again.

"I am a medical professional who needed to examine you." I was amazed I kept a straight face on that one. "Hey, your boxers are still on."

"Mhmm." His eyes sparkled in the moonlight from the window. "I would hazard a guess you examined my body in its entirety while I was unconscious?"

"I am nothing if not thorough."

He traced my burning cheek with his finger, his smile so cocky he beamed. "I am not surprised you were unable to resist. The reaction of the females on campus indicated my outfit was quite fetching."

"Fetching?" I repeated, raising a brow. "All right. Go on."

"On the way to the gatehouse, several women ogling me smelled more than pleased." He captured my hands, his smile shifting to something sultry. "Did you know humans give off discernible scents in emotional situations: desire, fear, anger, stress, all trigger the release of pheromones?" He wet his lips, smirking. "Quite fascinating."

"Fascinating, is it?"

"Yes. My brothers and I first noticed it on our quest. Then, on the way from the gatehouse, three females made less than appropriate remarks to one another regarding what they wished to do to 'our rockin bods.' We were not familiar with the vernacular, yet had an accurate mental image of the intent. Verily, Elven hearing is much more acute than they realized."

I gasped. "When we're together, you can smell my moods toward you?" As his grin grew, my stomach started to squirm.

"I scent when you are angry with me, worried about me or. . ." He waggled his brow.

"You can smell when I'm attracted to you?"

"Mhmm." His eyes drifted down my body, and he inhaled deeply. "Your desire is sweet succulence. As Lexi would say, it has become *my fix*."

"Oh, gods, that's embarrassing." I thought I had conveyed an aloof, composed image, but he smelled that I had the hots for him? "I am officially mortified."

He wrapped me in his arms, and his chest pressed against mine. "Why would you be mortified when, with your touch, you gain private knowledge of both thought and emotion from the moment you lay your hands to heal?"

I shook my head. "That's different, half the time I can't figure out what you're feeling. Your emotions shift around so much I can't get a read on you. You're a twister, taking out half the mid-west. I just try to follow the path of destruction to head you off and save the innocent."

The bed shook as his musical laugh filled the room. "So, the fact that I am an emotional natural disaster has been thwarting your god-given powers?"

"And the fact that you can smell my desire—" I gasped as another thought struck me like a truck in an intersection. "Oh god, they can all smell it, can't they?" I buried my face in his chest. "Tham and Aust? Your friends? No. No. No. How do I face them when they know I want to rip off our clothes and roll around naked?"

Galan chucked my chin, holding it up to meet his gaze. "Verily, pheromones are not as informative as you believe. We simply pick up the scent of attraction. I thank you, though, for the visual. It is nice to know what you've been thinking."

I pinched my eyes closed and buried my head back into his chest, fully intending to hide there for the rest of my life.

"May I ask you something?" His voice was honey-suede, wrapping me in decadence. I shook my head, still buried in hiding. He laughed and ignored my refusal. "Does being a warrior not conflict with your natural passion for healing? I understand the urge to avenge your family, but it seems to me, killing and fighting counters your greatest skills."

I wasn't sure I liked the change of subject. After a deep breath, I raised my head. "I fight to keep innocents safe, Galan, not just for vengeance or to kill. As a kid, I swore I'd never be a helpless victim again. Reign ensured it. He hired Chiron, and I trained for almost fifteen years to become the woman I am."

Galan's smile beamed white in the dim light. "That woman enamors me. But would you have chosen the violence of the warrior's path had the world not turned on you?" The depth of sadness in his voice stole my breath.

"I'll never know, but being part of the fight is everything to me. It's who I am now."

Galan winced as he shifted under the covers, and I became very aware the only thing separating his almost naked body from mine was my thick terry robe and a flimsy pair of boxers. In a fleeting thought, I wondered where this might lead.

I jumped at the rap on the door and the blinding slice of light streaming in from the hall. "I hear voices," Kobi said, swinging the door open. "Is sleeping beauty finally awake?"

I sat up and tightened my robe. "What are you doing here? I thought you headed out?"

Kobi set a tray of food on the desk and pulled the chain on the desk lamp. As the room lightened, he shot me a scowl. "Like I'd leave with Scourge tracking you. If you won't call Reign, you need someone watching your fine ass. And who better for the job than me?"

Galan's eyes shot across to me.

"I *did* call. I don't need a babysitter, so I left a message."

Kobi pulled out a pack of smokes. "This isn't just about you, Blaze. If you get yourself killed, Bruin will kill me, and then Reign will cut off my balls. I'm rather attached to all my male parts, fuck-you-very-much." He winced and cupped himself. "Don't roll your eyes at me like I'm dramatic. You know he will. That man is one seriously scary beast."

"There's nobody like him," I said.

"And thank the gods for that," he grumbled. As I made my way over to look at the tray, Kobi lit his cigarette and looked me up and down. "Where did you find that hideous robe?"

"Inside the armoire."

"Well, it's wacked. It covers all your bells and whistles. You look like a marshmallow."

I scowled. "Kobal, Demon of hilarity, this is Galan."

"Call me, Kobi." He held out his hand, and Galan eyed the large silver thumb ring. "Are you two hungry or what?"

"Yes, and thanks. I'm famished." Freeing my hair from the robe, I looked over the spread.

"You hungry, sleeping beauty?" Kobi asked.

"Yes, gratit—" Galan tried to sit up and winced again. "Kobi, might I trouble you on another matter which is even more pressing?"

"Sure. Shoot."

"Would you object to helping me into the privy? I am not certain I can venture myself."

I strode to the footboard of the bed and ducked under the canopy. "Galan, I would've helped you to the bathroom. Why didn't you say something?"

He threw me a beautiful scowl. "I fancy myself more of a gentle-male than to ask a female I am newly courting to aid me in relieving myself."

"That's *stupid*."

Kobi stepped to the side of the bed. "Kids. Kids. It's not a problem, Galan. Are you ready now, or did you want to get something to eat first?"

"No. Most assuredly now."

Kobi slid under Galan's shoulder and hoisted him off the mattress. Another moment had the two of them shuffling to the en suite. I was unsure if the discomfort on Galan's face was from the poison, being vertical or having to pee-like-ninety.

Elves. Men. Elven Men.

I popped a few grapes into my mouth before the water turned on in the next room. A few strawberries later, and the bathroom door opened. Kobi strode out, opened the armoire by the window, and brought out a pile of fresh towels.

"What's he doing?"

"He saw the shower and begged me to get him naked."

"And you left him *alone*?" I lunged for the door when Kobi met me, towels in hand.

"He's all right. I wedged him into the corner and told him not to collapse and crack his head open on the tile while I got the towels. He said, '*I shall try my best.*'"

I took the towels. "I've got this. Thanks."

"Well, well." Charcoal eyes danced as he grinned like a Cheshire cat. "Has Blaze finally started to smolder—"

"Goodnight, Kobi." I didn't wait for the ribbing I knew he was about to let loose. Stepping into the bathroom, I closed us in. Galan was indeed pressed into the corner, arms braced against the opposite wall of the shower. Even unsteady, he was a vision standing under the stream of warm water.

Tossing my robe onto the pedestal sink, I stepped in wearing bra and panties. *Same as a bathing suit, in theory, and so lacy thin it'll dry in no time.*

Galan's eyes opened. The astonishment that crossed his face was so funny I had to laugh. "You okay? You look faint."

His hands were flat against the tile wall, his arms braced to hold his weight. "Verily, I may. I was expecting Kobi. You jostled the very rhythm of my heart coming in here dressed as you are. In my weakened state, it might be too much."

The shower was spacious for one, but more than cozy for two. I reached under his arm and picked up the fancy flower soap and the facecloth. "I'm your doctor, so I'm sure you'll survive. You're better than you were this morning, and by tomorrow you'll be back to full strength. You said you aren't shy, and I'd much rather be in here bathing you than Kobi."

"True enough. Still, I appreciate your sacrifice."

I lathered the little flower-shaped soap into the facecloth. "I'm all about my bedside manner these days. Someone implied recently that it could be improved."

He let his head drop to rest on his outstretched arm. "I believe you have bettered your services beyond measure."

Moving the sudsy cloth in slow circles, I massaged across the flat plains of his chest, down the curves of his lats, the outsides of his hips, and across the cut ridges of his abs. In another instance, this would have been deliciously sexy, but he was beginning to fade and needed to get back into bed.

"I wish I were fit to enjoy the moment," he whispered, his eyes fluttering closed.

I unhooked the showerhead from its mount and slid in behind him. When his backside rubbed against my belly, a whole lotta warm and wet slid between us. I bit my lip and tried to breathe. *Focus.* Running my fingers through his hair, I forced myself not to press up against all that slick sudsy skin. "Maybe when you're feeling better, we'll revisit this scenario, and you can have a Mulligan."

"A Mulligan?"

"Yeah, a Mulligan. A raincheck. Do-over. A gimme. It means you can have another chance at it another time."

"You are very kind." I heard the smile in his voice.

It was a crime to hurry, but I rinsed the suds down his back, his hips and his smooth, muscular legs avoiding his man parts with all the will power I had. "All done."

After finishing the wash-up, I checked that he was steady and nabbed a couple of towels. Without fanfare, I dried us off and helped him step into his BVD's. With my robe in place, I helped him into a fresh, clean bed. *Huh. Nice.* Kobi changed the sweat-dampened sheets.

When Galan's head hit the pillow, he sighed. Horizontal was good. Nobody fell and cracked their heads open when they were horizontal. I snagged the tray of fruit and propped him up enough to brush out his hair while he ate. When he'd finished, I snuggled in beside him and watched the numbers on the clock flip. 3:23 am.

"Gratitude," Galan whispered close to my ear, his warm breath kissing my cheek.

"For what?" I yawned.

"Saving my life." He wrapped his arms tighter around me, gathering me close to his side. "Lay your head now, Blossom. We shall speak more in the morrow."

"Right. Like I could sleep while you rub up against me."

"Would it be better—" He grinned as I hooked my ankle around his legs and pulled him back in place. "I thought you might prefer space to get some sleep."

I gave him a quick kiss and closed my eyes. "No. You are perfect right where you are." And he was.

He really was.

CHAPTER TWENTY-ONE

Sunshine in my face made it impossible to go back to sleep. Lying motionless across Galan's chest, I soaked in my surroundings: the steady hum of traffic along Spadina, the distant rattle of a breeze through the window, the gentle, even breathing of my Highborne bedfellow.

Opening one eye a crack, I peered through the curtain of my crazy hair. It was strewn like red strangleweed, flailing off in every direction. Galan's eyes remained closed, but the tip of his finger ran a repeating circuit across my shoulder and down the curve of my back, light as the kiss of a feather.

Sometime in the night, I had eighty-sixed my robe and tossed it. We lay together, wearing only our underthings, sharing the decadent warmth of skin on skin. The blankets were pulled low on his hips, exposing a tight six-pack. My fingers, of their own accord, explored his soft, bare skin. It was no secret Elves didn't have body hair, but to know something and to feel it were two different realities.

No manscaping necessary.

Galan's breathing hitched. "Continue stroking me, and you shall experience firsthand how an Elven consort pleasures a woman." His bedroom voice was husky, and the look he pegged me with was beyond X-rated.

I told my heart to calm the hell down as it started to pound. I didn't want to throw off the scent of horny desperation—lusty was bad enough.

When his expression transformed into something wistful, I propped up on my elbows and flipped my hair out of my way. "What are you thinking?"

He fingered a curl out of my face and shook his head. "How did I think to resist you?"

"First impressions." I cleared the morning rasp from my voice. "How are you feeling?"

"Overwhelmed."

I snuggled against his shoulder, once again surprised by his directness. Raised in the presence of warriors, I was accustomed to men having their arm severed and hanging by a ligament, and insisting they were fine and ready to return to battle—only a flesh wound.

"Overwhelmed how?" I asked.

"In every sense. How shall I tell Aust and the others that they found themselves beset and besieged because of Lia and me? If not for us, their loved ones would still live. How shall I live with the knowledge that the scum who took my sister intends to use her as a pawn? How shall I justify allowing people close to me when that proximity endangers them?" He sighed, dragging his fingers through his hair. "Add to that the conflict between what I know in my logical Elven mind and what I feel with every cell in my body."

"Okaaay, a little clarification might help that last one."

He stared up at the ceiling for a long time before he spoke. "Jade, you know your purpose. It is a clear path set before you. My father told me, time and again, that I was a non-committal disappointment with no direction and no prospects to win or keep a mate. His berating never truly bothered me until now."

"Galan, your father is an ass."

"Mayhap," he rolled onto his side to face me. "Yet the truth remains, that I yearn to be worthy of you—for you. You deserve more than a male who cherishes you. You deserve a male you are proud to have at your side, a male with skills and purpose and station. As much as I despise it, a male such as Samuel is the logical choice for you."

I lifted my head and glared at him. "Do I get a say in this?"

He cleared his throat. "What have I to offer? My life is a shamble. I have no home or worth, and it is dangerous to even stand next to me on the street. I have lain here since before the sun broke the horizon and find there is only one logical answer. We should stop this. I would not survive it if the next ambush led to your death."

"I can take care of myself, thanks." I gathered my hair away from my face and sat up. "This crazy magnetic force drawing us together doesn't have anything to do with your dowry or your station in life. It's not Samuel or someone like him I want—"

"Yes, but—"

"—it's you." I pressed my fingers over his lips and held back his objections. "I want the man who went against tradition and raised his infant sister, the man who held his best friend's hand willing her to survive through childbirth, the man who looks into my eyes and touches a place in my soul that has been cold and empty my entire life. You fill that space, Galan. That's what you offer me."

"Yet in reality, I have no direction in my world or yours."

I tucked the sheet tighter under my arms. "I think the reason you haven't figured out your life is because your destiny was so far beyond your valley. Maybe you are Rheagan's heir, destined to save the Realm of the Fair, or maybe you'll simply be a loyal friend to Nyssa and Tham and guardian to Ella. The one thing I am sure of is you, and I *are* meant to happen. If your destiny is simply to grow to love me, would that be so bad?"

His eyes filled with emotion as he reached to kiss me. "To love you is more than I dreamed for myself. However, I will not be a kept man. If Tham, Aust, and I are to live on your mountain, we must earn our keep."

I nodded. "Fine. Hugh and the merchants are working on some new construction projects. They could use some strong, virile men."

"Virile?" Galan chuckled, shaking his head.

"What's so funny?"

He shrugged. "It amazes me that you know about my life and see me as anything but weak and unworthy." His lack of confidence broke my heart. His father was such an ass.

"Galan, you think you're worth less than other men because you took a different path than the elders wanted. I say you're twice the man because you *did*."

His lips brushed across my temple. Warm breath tickled the column of my neck as he traced down my jugular and drew a deep breath. He did that a lot.

"What do I smell like to you?"

He nuzzled up the length of my neck. "*Mmm*, the sweet warmth of spring, delicate white flowers with blush centers." Galan dipped his mouth to the hollow of my throat. "Spring blossoms." He pulled back, his eyes wild with emotion, and leaned in.

Lips met lips. Heat met heat.

Galan kissed me with such exquisite care. Even with his tongue in my mouth, he was all about passionate restraint. It wasn't anything like the wildfire kisses we'd shared before.

This was soft and gentle, unhurried.

Gods he *sooo* knew what he was doing.

Silky fingers traced the curves of my side, moving down my ribs, down to the bone of my hip. In a slow sweep, he brought them back up the same path. He hesitated then sent his palm down again. With each upward circuit, his hand landed tantalizingly closer to the curve of my breast. I moaned as he finally slid his palm over the lace of my bra and held me in his hand. My body roared to life, arching into his touch.

"Is this all right?"

I was famous for daydreaming, but this was beyond even my creative powers. When I nodded, his thumb brushed the peak of my nipple where it pressed against the black lace. His lips moved to my neck, gentle as a breeze. I was lucky to be lying down because my legs would never have supported me. He settled his weight over me and pressed me further into the mattress.

"I love your curves," he groaned. He stared down at me, his hips swaying in a slight rocking motion. "You are a vision."

"Galan?" The conflict between uncertainty and yearning was evident in that one word. He was addictive, impossible to say no to, yet... I needed to focus. "Galan? I'm not sure, I mean—I've never been like this with anyone before."

Galan froze. When he remained motionless, I cursed my stupidity. Of course, he would want to stop. Why would someone like him, with all his experience fondling slender, elegant women want—

"Blossom?" he said, hoarsely. "When you say never—"

"Never mind. Forget I said anything." I clenched my eyes shut and tried to get up.

Galan grabbed my wrists and pinned me beneath him. Restraining me only proved to make me struggle harder. "Blossom, please stop. Shh. Stop this."

"Just forget it," I muttered, not meeting his gaze. My cheeks were blazing, and I wanted to crawl into the bathroom and lock myself in.

"I never meant to upset you, *neelan*. I am simply stunned that you are a Newling. In my world, that is something to cherish. It is extraordinary." His voice was rough as he pulled back to look at me, his eyes filled with compassion. "Allow me the honor of addressing your needs. I swear we shall stay within the boundaries of playful pleasures." In his most formal Elvish, he said, "Trust me to do right by you. Please."

When I relaxed beneath him, he covered my mouth with his own. Oh, god his lips were soft. And warm.

Galan took his time deepening our kiss, getting acquainted with my curves, brushing my hair off my shoulder, skimming down my arm and over my ribs. When my whole body felt loose and sinfully slick, his fingers dipped across my navel, to the lace of my panties. My eyes widened as his intentions flared in his. His fingertips tugged the lace down my thighs, sliding inside my knee, leaving a trail of warmth in their wake.

"*Sweet Shalana*," he gasped.

"Wha—" I squirmed. "What's wrong?"

Galan stretched his leg over my thigh. "Nothing, Blossom. Nothing is amiss. I was simply taken aback. You, oh, you have a lovely thicket of burgundy curls here."

My cheeks burned as probing fingers raked through my damp curls. "You like that?"

"I do." As he drew me tighter to his body, his erection pulsed against my hip. "It is unbearably erotic to me." Lust sizzled in the air between us as he deepened our kiss, and his bare chest pressed against my bra.

My muscles tightened and twitched as his fingers caressed the most intimate parts of me. He seemed to know exactly what ached. Timing, touch, pressure—he read my body as if it were Braille—exactly why he was popular in his village.

Sooo not something to think about right now.

"Blossom, are you well? Tell me, truthfully. Do you wish to stop?"

I was right there with him and ran my palms down his back to the perfection of his ass. Slipping my hands under the waistband of his boxers, I explored what, until now, I had admired only by sight. "I *ache*, Galan. I need you."

"Ahh," he purred, kissing down my breastbone, down my belly, down further still. His movements were slow and smooth as if I was an animal ready to bolt, and he was trying not to spook me. From beneath lowered lids, with his gaze locked on mine, he nipped and kissed his way down my stomach. Warm palms drifted along the inside of my thighs and pressed them open. I shuddered when he slipped his arms under my legs and dipped his head.

"Sweet female," he moaned, the vibration of his words rippling into my flesh. My fingers dug into his hair, and my hips jerked forward. He nuzzled against my core, pushing deeper with each lap and kiss. "Be still, Blossom. Relax," he whispered and then continued working between my thighs. He'd found a seriously erotic rhythm, the friction of his tongue darting and penetrating as his fingers swirled.

I dimly felt one of my legs get thrown over his shoulder, then the other. He blew a long hot breath over my most sensitive skin. I thought I would lose my mind.

"*Galan*," I cried, not recognizing my voice. I clutched his shoulders, the tension building, and clenching, threatening to overwhelm me. "I don't think I can do this."

"Let yourself go, Blossom. Breathe. Allow the sensation to overpower you."

Returning his attentions, his tongue delved deeper and deeper still, his chin and lips and mouth adding to the magic. It was the vibration of a manly moan against my flesh that sent me out of my body. I arched back, my nails gripping the sheets. Wave after wave of blinding pleasure washed over me, burned through me. It seemed endless. I was lost.

Dizzy and breathless, I finally collapsed into the crumpled sheets. Galan climbed up my body and nipped the crook of my neck. His smile lit me up. Never had I experienced anything like Galan. He held me in a full-bodied embrace, murmuring in Elvish as he kissed his way up and down my neck. "Are you well?" He waited until I was able to nod. "Gratitude, Blossom."

"You're thanking *me*? Why? You did all the work."

Galan's laughter vibrated against me and shook the bed. I was ashamed to admit it, but I often wondered what it would be like to want a man to touch me. It was a communion sweeter than anything I imagined. It really was magic.

"It is a great honor for a Highborne to pleasure a woman, though to be your first—" he shook his head. "I am humbled beyond words you chose me."

I cupped his jaw and giggled. "I think I'm addicted to you, Highborne. Suddenly, every female desire that has lain dormant my entire life is throbbing and screaming out for you."

He grinned unrepentantly. "I feel it as well. It is as if the sun has broken through the haze of my life. Everything has brighter colors, richer fragrances, and more succulent flavors than ever before." His smile was glorious, his face glowing in the morning light.

"When a Highborne loves, it is eternal, Blossom. I am yours, body and soul if you should ever choose to claim me." His lips moved soft and silky against mine. When his hips rolled, it became apparent he was still very much aroused. I reached down, but he caught my wrist. "This is about you, Jade, not me."

I pulled back to look at him. "But surely you'd enjoy some attention too."

He shook his head. "I am completely, deliriously sated to focus on you." His kiss trailed down my neck to my collarbone. "May I ask you something personal?" I rolled my eyes, and he laughed. "When you said you have never... I mean, Samuel courted you for some time, and humans have different customs. It would be understandable if the two of you were intimate on some level." Galan's voice tightened as his suggestive ramble began to unwind.

"No," I said. "Much to Samuel's annoyance, I never felt right about advancing our relationship. It's what broke us up in the end. I couldn't bring myself to be physical with him or anyone before you. He hasn't even shared the privileges you enjoyed just now."

"Enjoyed? Past tense?" His sensual smile made my heart jump. "Oh, by no means am I finished yet, Blossom. Our loveplay has just begun."

My body heat rose instantly. He was more experienced, but I was a willing learner. Just the thought of his touch had me pulsing again.

He pulled back to stare at me, a wicked smile playing on his lips. "Your eyes are dancing like liquid emeralds. What are you thinking?"

"I was considering how I'd like to honor you next." I pushed myself up to straddle his waist. With fingers shaky but determined, I unclasped my bra and tossed it. "You have half a century worth of moves I haven't seen yet. I wouldn't want any of them to go to waste."

Galan growled low in his chest and rested his arm behind his head.

A knock at the door brought us up short. "Crap! I never locked the—"

"Jade, are you up?" Without waiting for reply, Kobi opened the door.

I barely made it under the covers as Galan rose to block Kobi's view. I felt like a teenager caught in the act as Kobi eyed the two of us without an ounce of embarrassment. "Nice. Well, It's nice to see that Galan's *up*, and you two are getting a jump on the day."

Kobi was dressed entirely in black: ripped jeans, muscle shirt, boots, and leather bracelets with skulls on them. The only hint of color was the gold and scarlet bands clamped through his ear and the scarlet anarchy symbol on his shirt. I asked him once about the bands and the piercings. The look he shot me was so venomous I never brought it up again.

Ignoring his jibes and double entendres, I pointed to the white heap of robe crumpled on the floor. "Do you mind?"

He set the breakfast tray on the desk and came to my rescue. "Reign's on the warpath. He's been calling you, and you're not picking up." After tossing me the robe, he gave me his back and pulled the drapes open all the way. "You're lucky he's swamped at the Academy, or he would've busted in on the two of you."

Well, didn't that make me want to throw up?

Kobi cocked a brow and laughed. "Not ready for daddy to walk in on your shore leave?"

I resisted the urge to stick out my tongue and went over to my backpack. Pulling out my phone and the charger, I plugged it in. Seven new messages. Great. Without opening any, I set down the phone and left it to charge.

Kobi pointed to the food. "Come eat, Galan. I bet you've worked up an appetite."

Galan's wicked smirk made me blush. He sauntered to my side and winked as he lifted a glass of juice to his lips. He seemed unabashed that his boxers were tented and doing nothing to conceal his current state of arousal.

Kobi looked him over and whistled through his teeth. "You can't be the same half-dead Elven road-kill Jade brought in two days ago. Damn, Blaze, you even managed to get color into his ivory cheeks. Must be those healing hands of yours."

I added milk and sugar to a mug of coffee and palmed a banana chocolate-chip muffin. When I looked up, Kobi was staring at me. I'd seen the look enough times on the face of warriors to know what it meant. "What? Tell me."

He crossed his arms over his chest and exhaled. "Well, first off, everyone's fine." He raised his hands as I began to speak. "Nothing happened, well, almost nothing." He met my glare and shrugged. "A party of Dark Elves took a stroll through the Highborne village yesterday. Apparently, they wanted to reconnect with their long-lost cousins."

"What?" Galan choked on his juice. His face blotched red as I thumped his back. "Are they well? Was anyone injured?"

"No." Kobi tossed Galan a napkin. "It was an intel scout. They came in, looked around, and left without a scuffle."

"Were they working with the Scourge?" Galan asked.

I swallowed my coffee and nodded. "Even if the men weren't transitioned, there are plenty of Dark Fae and Shifters in that camp. It would be nothing for a scouting party to gather info and report back to Abaddon and his men."

"Can naught be done?"

"Sorry," I said. "As long as they make nice, there are no laws against walking through a village."

Galan's scowl said he did not agree.

"I should also tell you," Kobi said, "Reign ordered your sister's things and your friend's newborn onto Haven grounds."

Galan strangled the napkin in his fist. "What has Nyssa's young to do with this?"

Kobi shrugged again. "Reign knows more than he's saying. Big surprise. I hear he's been a beast since the trip to the Queens." Kobi speared a piece of pear with his knife and bit it from the tip. "Anyway, it's time to get you two home. He should settle a bit then, and you can ask him."

"Yeah, about that." I set my mug on the tray and smiled as sweetly as I could manage. "Galan and I are planning a short side trip first."

Kobi's eyes burned red, the metal piercings through his brow, reflecting the scarlet glow. "Fuck, Blaze, don't jam me up. I've got orders to send you straight home."

"No one's jamming you up. We need to make one stop."

"Reign will tear me a new orifice. You know that."

I rolled my eyes. "Don't be so dramatic." He wasn't, and we both knew it. Reign would flip that we hadn't follow orders. The protocol was for safety—everyone's safety. I sighed and softened my voice. "It's important, Kobi."

Kobi scrubbed the growth along his jaw and cursed. "Fine. Get cleaned up, and I'll drive you to Harbour Front in an hour." He headed for the door but paused and turned back. "Unless the two of you would like some company in the shower? You can make up for a little of the pain and suffering I'm in for."

I stared at him, mouth agape, and pitched my muffin. He snatched the chocolaty projectile from the air and crossed the floor, laughing. "Another time then. Two's company. Three's too much for some to handle. Not me—and I'm sure not the Highborne—but some." He looked Galan up and down, smiled, and then stepped out into the hall and closed the door.

"Has he been offended?" Galan asked.

I laughed at the impossibility of that. "Kobi's an Incubus demon. He's just true to his oversexed nature." I glared at the clock. Warm arms wrapped around me from behind.

Sliding a palm under the puffy lapel of my robe, Galan palmed the weight of my breast. "Shall we shower together?" The silk of his voice had my cheeks burning and my insides flaming. "Mayhap, enjoy my Mulligan?"

"Uh, no," I choked. "If we did, we may never leave this room."

CHAPTER TWENTY-TWO

The snow stopped after the second hour of hiking into the Forest of Delaran. Kobi, deciding to shadow our little outing, had sweet-talked the busty blonde at the Portal Gate into lending Galan and me each a Parka for our trek and, since the night was falling here, a lantern, a knife, and a survival kit.

Not a fan of the climate or the prospect of trespassing on Centaur land, Kobi had chosen to stay behind and keep warm with gatehouse Barbie. By the casual stroking of hands down shoulders and arms and the way she bit her lip when he tucked her hair behind her ear, things were going to get very warm at the gatehouse—the minute we were out of sight.

I couldn't blame him. The wind swept through the forest, lung-chillingly cold. Flakes of snow melted in my hair and on my lashes, deposited by the dripping pines and ice-encrusted firs which loomed above us. The walking was easier farther in the woods, the majority of the storm blocked by the ceiling of branches above.

Galan walked head down, our boots crunching through the crest of virgin snow. Looking back the way we came, he smiled at the two rows of tracks weaving through the trees. Exhaling, he reached through the wispy cloud of condensed breath. "Fascinating."

"I guess you didn't see snowstorms in the rainforest."

"No," he said. "Verily, this is my first."

Ten minutes later, I raised my lantern, scanning for some hint of the Centaur city. "Chiron told me Centaurs are private, but I figured we'd stumble upon a sentry or someone."

"Mayhap, they are simply wary."

Possible. After handing the lantern to Galan, I raised my palms and accessed my powers. As my fingers tingled with energy, I reached out. Scanning the trees and expanding to the forest beyond. Only the slightest disturbance came back to me. I saw nothing beyond shadows and the tall eerie silhouettes of trees caught in the lantern light.

"Is your acute Elven senses picking up anything?"

"Honestly, I see naught save trees and snow. My sinuses are filled with cold, and my ears sting with the bite of the wind."

I blew into my palms and cupped my ears. "Yeah, I know what you—"

A blast of wind drove stinging snow into our faces, and I spun and hunched away from its force. Galan pulled me into his side and tucked my face into his shoulder until the air stilled. When he stepped back, he held his head tilted to the side, a deep furrow creasing his brow. I waited as he glanced down at his lacings and adjusted himself.

"Problem?"

His ears were bright pink, but that might have been the cold. "Uh, I am not certain. Never before has my—how shall I describe it delicately?"

"Your ice-cold jewels crawled up into your gem pouch?"

The bewilderment on his face turned to blank amusement. "How did you know?"

I laughed. "That's normal. It happens in extreme cold."

"Fascinating." He blew into his palms and cupped himself.

I giggled. "Yep, all kinds of learning experiences today."

"Verily." He glanced down his front again. "And when might things right themselves?"

"As you warm up." I pressed a kiss to his cheek. "Trust me. It's nothing to worry about."

"Listen to her, Elf," a deeply, graveled voice commanded. "It's when you have to piss, and you can't find your cock, you'll need to worry."

Galan spun in front of me and the lantern light glinted off his dagger's edge as it pulled free from its sheath. Which was actually... sweet. "It's okay, Galan." I tugged his hand down and looked to the deeply shadowed trees. "What do you know about the cold, old man? You're furred from navel to hooves."

From behind a giant mountain ash stepped my mentor and friend, Chiron. From his barrel chest down, he was a stunning black and white gypsy horse with long, thick feathering on his lower legs. Above the waist, he was a burly, powerful man, cut from the same granite mold as my father, muscled, chiseled, and clad in the armor and leathers of a celebrated warrior of his race. His ebony mane hung long and loose, swirling, ice-encrusted, in the breeze. It made him look wild and very much the dangerous bastard he was.

"You're a long way from home, kid." His veiled concern warmed me to the bone.

"What? Didn't you miss me?"

"Oh, I missed you." Chiron opened his arms and scooped me up. The heat coming off him felt terrific. I didn't even mind that he was crushing me or that he reeked of man-sweat and horse. "What I didn't miss is you running off and putting my nuts in a sling with Reign."

"Me?" I batted my eyes. "You handle my father fine."

Chiron barked a laugh and set me back on my feet. "No one *handles* Maximus Reign, my dear, and you know that as well as anyone."

The mention of Reign swamped me with guilt. I'd pulled the GPS chip from my phone and left it in Toronto. But really, why would I go straight back and wait for news at the castle when we might find answers here? I was a Talon enforcer. Why shouldn't I be part of this search? I stepped back from Chiron's hug and caught a faint scent of wood smoke. "Are you going to invite us in?"

"And who would the *he* in the *us* be?" Chiron said, his eyes shifting to Galan. After the introductions, Chiron led us through the maze of trees.

"How did you find us out here in the woods?" I asked.

Chiron smiled. "When the outer perimeter guards called in a human woman with your description, I wondered. When they said you called on bard energy, and they had trouble blocking your scan, I knew." He draped his arm heavily over my shoulders and squeezed. "It's good to have you here, kid, but you should've given me some warning. The City Guard doesn't take kindly to unannounced company. Best if you two keep quiet until we get where we're going."

Walking on in silence, the haze of the moon eventually gave way to the flickering light of lampposts fixed in regular intervals along the massive Wall of Deleran. The ebony steel surface stretched out on either side of an outer gate until it blended with the shadows of the forest beyond and reached upward until it disappeared into the black of night.

It truly lived up to its reputation of the wall with no end.

Without uttering a word, Chiron escorted us past four heavily armed Centaur, City Guard and stood, shoulders back and hand on the battle-ax hanging from his belt, in front of the steel gate. One guard on each side of us grabbed a wide wooden handle attached to a wheel on the wall and began heaving it in slow circles. As their momentum built, an intricate mesh of cogs and wheels began to turn above the gate, lacing the teeth with a low scraping of metal on metal.

When the gate swung open, Chiron placed a firm hand between my shoulder blades and ushered us inside. "Welcome to Delaran, kid."

Walking close to Chiron, we made our way through the dark streets of the city. Steam hissed from grates in the sidewalks, in front of houses, and along the cobbled streets. It rose like a curtain of ghostly mist evaporating into the frigid air of the night. We continued past stone houses with wide steel doors reminiscent of the main gate, shops closed and battened down till morning, then industrial buildings with smokestacks still exhaling clouds from the day's efforts.

At the crossroads of what appeared to be the main intersection, a Clydesdale male was shoveling coal from two large, communal bins into a wide metal cart. When his load mounded well above the sides of the barrow, he speared his spade into his haul and wheeled away.

We continued to the next corner joining the flood of Centaur traffic going in and out of the tavern.

The air inside the tavern was thick with humidity and smelled of beast, beer, and barn. It rang with deep male voices, the rattle of bones and dice, and the music Chiron had tried for years to make me appreciate. It still sounded like war drums and Celtic flutes to me. I winced as my body warmed too fast, and my skin started to sting.

Chiron kept his arm around me and ushered us past the raised brows of the Centaur clientele. From years with him, I knew that physical affection shown by a Centaur to anyone, not of their race, was rare and respected. By the simple gesture of his touch, Chiron made it clear to his people that I was *his*.

Galan pulled two tall stools from against the wall, and we climbed to sit at a private high-boy in the back. Standing with his elbows resting on the surface, Chiron waved to the bartender. "So, what brings you to my mountain, kid?"

I flexed my frozen fingers for a second, and when they moved, I unzipped my jacket and reached into my bra. Chiron raised a brow as I retrieved the folded parchment covered in elegant black script. "It's been a while since we played a game of 'What does this prophetic poem say?' Care to give it a try?"

The corner of Chiron's mouth twitched as a conspiratorial light gleamed in his eyes. "Let's see what you brought." The moment his gaze settled on the parchment, he froze. "Where did you get this?"

I leaned in. "The Oracles of Toronto called in Galan for this. Unfortunately, we have no idea what it says."

Chiron closed the paper as three huge steins arrived at our table. "Bless you, Sluran." He nodded to the bartender and took a long, slow swallow. With our heads lifted, it was obvious we were on the cold side of the welcome mat. Chiron raised his stein and cast a scathing smile around the room. "To those who judge and gossip, this warning should appeal; the steam that blows the whistle will never turn the wheel."

That seemed to do it. One by one, Centaurs stomped their hooves into the packed dirt floor, and heads turned until we were alone again.

Chiron took a second look at the parchment while Galan and I drank our cider perplexed. "When a prophecy comes to an oracle, the language is determined by the energy of the message itself. As a rule, the language of a missive can be translated because most members of the realm live hundreds if not thousands of years."

"And they recognize or read most of the current languages of that time."

"Right, but this is an ancient script coming from arcane powers." He scowled and tapped the folded paper with his fingertips, looking around. "What are you into, kid?"

I shrugged. "We don't know. That's why we're here."

Over the next half-hour, the three of us drank while catching Chiron up on the events since the night of the solstice: the spellbook, the Scourge taking Lia, and everything the Queens had said about the rebellion and the silver Highborne. Throughout the conversation, Chiron studied the parchment and made notes in a small notebook he'd retrieved from the leather pouch he wore across his chest.

"This will take time, girlie, days, or possibly weeks." He folded the parchment and tucked it into his sporran with his notebook. After fishing around in his pouch, he came away with another folded paper pinched between his fingers and leaned in. "Still hunting ghosts? A Dark Elf Scourge slipped this to a friend this week and asked for me to get it to you. Said it was a matter of honor."

The serious edge in his tone should probably have given me pause, but my focus was on the paper. *Bloodvine.*

After accepting the info, I stared Chiron straight in the eye. "I won't stop until I've fulfilled my Right of Vengeance. Every last one will die." The burn in my chest flared and raged. How could something as innocuous as a tiny yellow paper drive me to bloodshed?

"What is it, Jade?" Galan asked, his eyes sharp, and his brow deeply furrowed.

"A lead on one of the remaining men who killed my parents."

Chiron closed his hand over mine and squeezed until the bones rubbed. "You go back to that castle and stay out of trouble, Jade. A

JL MADORE

twenty-year-old vendetta isn't worth getting yourself killed. It won't bring them back."

I squared my shoulders and shifted my gaze to the silver band locked around his wrist. "And how many of Essandra's killers still walk this realm?"

Chiron's nostrils flared. After a long moment, he released my hand and nodded. Draining the last inch of his cup, he slammed it on the table and stepped back. "I'll be in touch."

"Apologies." Galan stood and pointed discretely to Chiron's sporran. "That missive was meant for me. It may well be the only means to find and reclaim my sister."

"It's fine, Galan." I hopped down from my stool and squeezed his arm. "Chiron will take good care of it."

Galan shook his head. "Verily, I mean no offense—"

"You kids having fun?" I stiffened and closed my eyes, praying whoever was standing behind me just *sounded* like Reign—exactly like Reign. Cracking one eye open, I peeked over my shoulder and gritted my teeth. I knew better than to offer a 'hey' or 'I was just about to call.' Instead, I waited. Thankfully, Galan took my lead and did the same.

Reign's obsidian glare had my blood pumping. He was fully armored, as was protocol, and covered in protective leathers from head to toe. He was intimidating at the best of times but amped like this, he was flat out scary. "Thanks for the call, Chiron. I owe you," he growled.

Chiron waved that away. "I think the debts are still heavily weighted in your favor."

Reign inclined his head to my tutor and then turned on me.

"I'm sorry—"

His hand clamped around my arm at the same time he grabbed Galan by the scruff of his neck. We Flashed. Without letting go, Reign rounded on me the instant we were standing in his mint green office. Face-to-face, his ire froze me in place. "You went to Delaran? Unarmed. Without backup? What the fuck were you thinking?"

A blast of cold air lifted my hair and sucked the breath from my lungs. "Both of you go to your goddamn suites and plant your asses.

I'll speak to you when I'm calm." He rubbed his eyes, his mottled jaw clenching like a vice. Both were signs he was about to crack. "Go. Now."

He released my arm, and a rush of warm and tingly flooded to my fingers. We scooted out the door without a word. The broad span of Reign's chest eclipsed the doorway, then disappeared as the deafening bang of the door slammed home. It shook the stone walls of the castle. Dozens of students jumped and scurried down the halls.

"That went well."

CHAPTER TWENTY-THREE

From the landing of the stairs, Galan and I heard the muted roar coming from the fifth-floor lounge. Reclined in leather club chairs, Cowboy, Rue, and a couple of other enforcers were slaughtering each other at Black Ops while tossing back Scotch, insults, and—in Savage's case—glares. Julian and Lexi were playing poker with Tham, Aust, and Nyssa while a harried-looking Iadon paced the room with Ella, squawking like someone was torturing her.

"At last," Tham said as we joined the fun. He hauled himself out of his chair like an old man stiffened from sitting too long. "Reign said the two of you were attacked and Galan was poisoned. Are you well, brother mine?"

"Never better." Galan helped Tham to his feet. "What ails you?"

Tham rolled his right shoulder and winced. "While you gallivanted throughout the Modern Realm, Aust and I have endured grueling torture. Those men pose as peacekeepers, but in actuality, they are beasts." He pointed to the enforcers who hadn't raised their heads from their video slaughter. "Every inch of my formerly glorious body cries in agony, besmirched by bruises and unseen strains."

I tried not to laugh but failed. "Training's tough, but you'll tighten up in no time."

Tham threw me an adorable scowl and sidled up against me. "Mayhap, you might heal my aches, *neelan?*"

Galan patted his shoulder with a heavy hand and chuckled as Tham buckled and pulled away. "I am certain you shall survive, Tham, even without Jade's gentle hands."

As he winked, I blushed, my mind flooded with images of our morning escapades. Yep, other than Reign wanting to strangle me, life was pretty good at the moment. It really was.

Had anyone noticed the tone in Galan's teasing? Nyssa definitely did. A private look passed between the two of them. It was subtle; the corners of her mouth turned up. She threw her glance to Iadon, who nodded infinitesimally to Tham, who smiled and leaned to whisper to Lexi. Aust smiled and splashed his chips into the pot. Thankfully the gossip train passed-right-on-by the others in the room.

Highbornes.

Galan stepped to Iadon, holding out his hands. "*Neelan*, such a raucous is unbecoming," he cooed, raising Ella to his kiss. The baby stared at him, her face red and pouty, her fists balled tight. "Come now, little one. What ails you?" Galan nuzzled her neck and covered her with a dozen kisses as his hair brushed against her cheeks.

The screeching stopped. Ella's blue eyes blinked wide, and her little pout curled into an open-mouthed smile. Galan smiled back, tucking her into the crook of his arm. "Much better, my love. Much better."

"Nicely done," Iadon sighed, sinking onto one of the sofas.

"Fuckin' A," Cowboy shouted over his shoulder and flicked the brim of his hat with his finger. "Where the hell were you an hour ago when she got really rollin', Highborne? That's the last mission you go on, my friend. You're needed here."

"We heard you moved in," I said to Nyssa, scratching my head at the whole exchange.

Nyssa tossed in her cards. "Your oracles foresaw Ella in danger, though not from where the threat stems."

"What did Reign say?"

Iadon crossed his arms over his chest, looking seriously pissed. "In truth, your father said little. However, we would never take a chance with Ella's safety."

"Certainly not." Galan rubbed his lips over Ella's forehead, her heavy lids fighting to stay open. "Has there been any word on Lia?"

"Actually," Cowboy rose from the couch and handed his controller to Sin. It was easy to see the wolf in him as he moved. As a Were, his gait in human form depicted his animal-self. Cowboy was dangerous and predatory. "From what we hear, an Elven woman is being guarded in the caverns of one of the northern compounds. We're working on getting a man inside. If it's your sister, we're on our way to recovering her."

He patted the pocket of his plaid button-down and pulled out a pack of hand-rolled cigarettes. "I know it rots, but this is progress."

"How will you get one of your own to her?" Galan asked.

Sin paused the game and scowled. "Leave that to us."

Galan tickled Ella's belly absently as he moved to the window and stared out onto the grounds. She couldn't fight his touch. Her eyes rolled shut as she drifted off.

"What else have we missed?" I asked.

"A few things," Cowboy said, his eyes lighting up. "The old horse arena is the new Highborne training center. The team leaders you set up in the village are coming to train with the morning session."

"Maybe by next year, they might be able to defend their own village, and we can get off babysitting duty," Sin sneered.

Cowboy shook his head. "Reign's keeping at least four enforcers on-site at all times in case anyone comes after Galan or his family. He's right pissed about something and—" Cowboy stopped mid-thought and scrubbed his hand over the stubble of his darkened jaw.

"And what?"

"Maybe I shouldn't bring it up." He propped a cigarette between his lips and fingered into his pocket for a lighter.

"Spill it, Wolf. Bring what up?"

Cowboy flipped open the silver lighter and rolled the flint wheel. It hissed and fired to life. After a deep inhale, the end of his hand-rolled glowed orange, and he snapped the thing shut. "Well, Reign and

Samuel have lost their god-lovin' minds, is all. They won't say what's up, but something bad is brewing between the pair of them."

"They've been fighting? Again?"

"Fighting doesn't quite cover it." Cowboy's gaze shifted to the baby as he exhaled a cloud of sweet-smelling smoke and turned for the balcony. "It's messed, whatever it is."

Reign commanded a great deal of respect and a healthy dose of fear, but the aggressive side of my father—the ruthless, tough-as-steel warrior—was something, present situation excluded, I rarely faced. The chosen few who basked in the privilege of his more tender side, if you could call it that, were Lexi, Bruin, Julian, me, and a few others. It was an extremely elite circle; those within it were in it for life.

Or so I assumed.

Four months ago, Samuel and Reign were tight. Now, they fought at every turn. *Is it about me?* Whether or not I was dating Samuel, he was a great guy, an inspired lecturer, and a powerful wizard. It sucked that he was at odds with my father.

Deep in thought, I sensed his concern before I felt the warmth of his hand on my shoulder. "Blossom?" Galan whispered close to my ear. "Are you well?"

"Sorry." I forced a smile. "Are you ready for dinner?"

"The repast can wait." Galan eased Ella into her bassinet and moved us into the privacy of the reading nook on the far end of the lounge. "What is it?"

"Nothing. I'm fine."

He raised a brow and frowned. Sliding his hand around my waist, he pulled me close. At some point in the past few days, my body had found its home—it was folded in Galan's arms. "You are far from fine, Blossom. Now, trust me."

"It will make you angry."

"Regardless, I wish to know."

It was the warm silk of his voice that undid me. His brows grew tight when I paused to think, but I wanted to get this right. "Something is happening between Reign and Samuel, and neither of them will say what it's about. They're seriously upset with one another. I have a bad feeling—a gut instinct—it has something to do with me. Somehow I'm the cause." I couldn't bear to look at him, so I studied the lines of his abs where they peeked out of his tunic.

Galan brushed his lips back and forth across my forehead and sighed. "You are a compassionate female. I am certain you shall figure it out." He laced his fingers in my hair and tilted my face to look at him. "Meanwhile, I could try to make you feel better. Are you up for a little distraction?" He smirked and kissed my temple. "Unless you would prefer to keep our relationship to ourselves for a time?"

I rolled my eyes. "Our privacy lasted all of thirty seconds once your friends saw us together. Are we that transparent?"

He chuckled, kissing down my neck. Gently grabbing my backside, he pressed his hips against me. I was pinned between Galan and the stone wall of the castle, literally between a rock and a hard place. "Nyssa knows me well."

The hair on the nape of my neck stood on end. One look at him, and Nyssa seemed to know exactly what was going on with him. It was unnerving. "Did you two ever date?"

Galan pulled back. There was nothing in his eyes except for genuine amusement. "No. Elves feel emotional connections more intensely than other races. From a human perspective, mayhap, it seems like more." He kissed my nose, the corners of his mouth twitching.

"But you *have* been her consort, right? You've spent time with her—with them—behind closed doors?" My chest tightened at the images in my mind.

"Of, course. Why does that—" His expression grew wary as his eyes narrowed. "You are not envious, are you?"

Yes. I raised my hand and tried to sound confident. After drawing a deep breath, I met the concern in his blue eyes. "I'm not jealous in the way you mean. I'm not thrilled that you've been naked with practically every female in your village, but with Nyssa... it's just... I envy how well she knows you."

He smiled and ran a finger down the side of my cheek. "Iadon had his sights on her since we were saplings. The moment they were eligible to be together, they consummated their union. To everyone's astonishment, when they bound as mates, they Recognized. Our lore spoke of Elves Recognizing since the beginning of the Highborne race, though it had not occurred in millennia. It is a rare bonding of mates where the union is blessed by the gods. They share a synergistic connection beyond all others. Two halves of the same soul. There is nothing for you to be envious about."

I peeked around the corner where the two of them watched Ella sleep. "They are great together."

"That is what it is to Recognize," Galan said, returning to the column of my neck.

"Apologies." Aust stepped around the corner, with his head bowed to give us a moment. "If I might interrupt, *Naneth* ventured through the mirror this morning and has toiled in the kitchen. If the two of you would join us for evening repast, I would appreciate your support to her."

Galan stepped back and took my hand. "It would be our pleasure, brother mine."

Little more than an hour later, Aust helped Elora clear the dinner plates, and our intimate dinner group moved to the main floor lounge.

"You knew, didn't you?" I whispered to Nyssa as Iadon refilled our glasses. We thanked him, scanning the dessert plates lining the buffet. "What was happening between Galan and me?"

She slid two flan-custard things covered in honey onto plates and chuckled. "Of course. The two of you are as obvious as the sunrise each morn. You simply needed to steady your footing." She handed me one of the plates and paused. "You love him?"

The directness of the Highbornes kept things honest.

Galan sensed my attention from across the room. His gaze lifted from his conversation with the men and met mine. My skin tingled hot, and I blushed, knowing they smelled my need for him. "Hopelessly."

Nyssa beamed. "We could not have chosen a better mate for him if

Iadon and I tailored you ourselves. The two of you shall be extraordinary together."

"Even though I am the most illogical, infuriating, confounding female he ever met, who does not possess the grace or etiquette of any of the females he's courted?"

Nyssa recognized the tone of the words. Her mouth fell open as she drew herself up. "He said that to you? I cannot believe—"

I shook my head. "It was a shimmer of memory, a conversation between him and Tham. I saw it when I healed Tham in the cavern at Dragon's Peak."

She laughed, tipping back her glass of cider. "His opinion was moot regardless; Tham said he was lost to you even then, from the moment he lay over you in the forest scrub."

"Nyssa, may I ask you an extremely personal question?" I hesitated, taking a deep breath. "What did you and Iadon do for your first night together, to make your bonding special?"

She studied my expression and leaned closer. "Are you planning a night of bonding?"

Heat flushed to my cheeks. "Not right now, but maybe once Lia is home."

CHAPTER TWENTY-FOUR

Galan downed his fifth flagon of dark mead like he didn't even taste it. Alone amongst our group and the rowdy Hearthstone dinner crowd, he stared out the picture window watching the brilliant sun sink behind the violet mountains. After three long days of training and waiting to hear about Lia, Galan's mood had hit a wall. The rest of the Highbornes had taken my challenge in good humor, venturing beyond the meals at the castle or what Elora prepared to try something new.

Fast food.

I wished I had a video camera as Galan stared down at his untouched platter. "I don't understand. Why would one grind vegetables to make them appear as meat? If you wish to eat meat, eat meat. If you wish to eat vegetables…" Galan cocked a brow and raised an onion ring. He scrunched his face up and dropped it back to his plate.

I sighed. "It's a veggie-burger. Don't try to understand it. Just try it."

"Indeed," Tham said, chipmunking his way through the entire menu. "Strange as it seems, it is quite flavorful. This is our *Ambar Lenn*, Galan. Live the adventure."

A crash at the next table had the Highbornes jumping to their feet.

"*Duck.*" I dropped below the table just as two quarreling Lightning Sprights flew through the air. A mass of colorful fire and sparks, the size of a bowling ball, shot out as the two tumbled and twisted in their struggle, ricocheting off the lantern above our table. "Don't let the sparks touch you."

Tham dove forward and saved his plate as Iadon turned Ella's carrier and gained some distance. The snap and sizzle of the altercation filled the air with the pungency of potatoes burnt to the bottom of a copper pot. The shriek of angry Spright chatter was as biting as a Banshee cry.

"Stand down and move off, ye wee miscreants. Ye ken, there's no feudin' in my pub." Hugh barreled out from behind the bar. The sea of patrons parted, tripping over themselves to let the burly Were Lion Prime pass. Even in a dirty cook's apron with a bar rag hanging from his back pocket, Hugh was an intimidating sight.

"Got it, Hugh." Nash stepped into the skirmish from another table, wand extended. With a dip and a twist of his wrist, the fireball froze. "You want them outside?"

Hugh's wavy mane of gold swung as he nodded. "Aye, that's a good lad. Take 'em outside and let 'em calm down a spell." He held up his hands and turned to the other diners. "Sorry for the commotion, back to yer business." After righting Galan's chair, Hugh tucked mine under me. "Bree." He waved thick fingers at his ward, and she strode over from behind the bar. "Bring Jade and her friends some dessert, would ye lass?"

Bree, a lone coyote pup raised by Hugh's pride, was built like a miniature marathon runner. Sleek and wiry, she'd come a long way since Hugh took her in. Her gunmetal eyes still held a warning of the animal she was made at a young age, but coyotes were bred from tough, predatory stock. They were also cunning, and Bree was no exception. "Sure, Da. The usual, Jade?"

When she headed to the kitchen, we watched Nash out the window. He released the spell, and the flaming ball of Spright fury resumed its flight. It tussled and sparked in the dusky sky all the way to the forest beyond.

"What was that?" Nyssa asked.

"Lightning Sprights. They're fairly common. They keep to themselves as a rule but get them drunk, and they're just plain nasty." I picked up a fry and popped it in my mouth.

"You have sauce on your face, Tham." Nyssa offered him a napkin as she sat down. "What did you call it, Jade?"

"Mustard." I grinned at the mess Tham made with his burger and how well they were learning English. "Wait until dessert. I'll introduce you to the weakness of our race."

"Truly?" Iadon set the carrier on the chair beside him, dipped an onion ring in his mead, and gave it a taste. With a shrug, he tossed it into his mouth. "And what might that be, *neelan*?"

"Chocolate."

The clatter of someone tripping over a chair caught my attention. Samuel staggered toward the door and stumbled to catch the frame. As he gripped the handle, he glanced back and threw me a look so cold it chilled me to the bone.

Galan followed my gaze and made to stand.

"No," I whispered. "I've got this." I hustled between tables and pushed out into stale night air. Samuel was trying to put some fast distance between him and the tavern, but his feet weren't cooperating. He was pissed—in more ways than one.

"Ah, sweet Jaysus," he growled when he saw me. "Jade, I'm in no mood. I had the brutal pleasure of watchin' your domestic bliss all night. I canna stand much more." He threw a disgusted scowl toward the tavern window.

I cringed at our audience of Elves and sent Galan a warning glare. I didn't want him anywhere near a drunken and angry Samuel. The two of them were a powder keg ready to blow without adding booze and poor judgment into the mix.

"Let me walk you home." I nudged his arm and moved to slide under his shoulder.

He jerked as if my touch scalded him. "Feck, Jade, I'll manage. I'm no bloody bairn."

"I know you're not, but I care about you, Samuel."

"Ye don't say! Ahhh, grand." He staggered to the side and steadied before he fell. "Am I like a brother then? Or a BFF?"

"It wasn't your fault," I choked. "I told you. I was the broken piece in the puzzle."

"And everything's the mutt's nuts now, no?" His gaze flew over my shoulder, back to the window. "For him? Yer miraculously whole and in love and ready for a life with him after what—a couple o weeks?" The agony in his eyes was unbearable. It clawed at my insides. "Well, balls to ye, 'cause never once did ye look at me like that."

He turned to the tree line, rubbing his chest.

Something about the energy in his stare kicked my instincts into high gear. An Arctic chill shot up my spine, and I scanned the tree line. Something was off. The sun setting across the horizon was too bright, the heat too intense. The hair on the nape of my neck prickled.

"I'm sorry," I whispered. "Tell me how to make this better for you?"

He recoiled, his eyes as dark as night. "Tell me ye've been holdin' out on him too. Can ye do that?" My heart cracked wide open. He winced at my reaction and swung toward the forest, shoulders stiff. When he turned back, his gaze was hollow and unrecognizable. "I may be thick as a stone, but I've got it now." His mouth twisted in some dark moment of dawning. His voice was too calm, too quiet. The turmoil churning in him was palpable. "I wasted two years being a sound man. That's not what gets ye, is it?"

I stepped back. "What's wrong, Samuel? Tell me what's happening."

Samuel grabbed both my arms, pinching my biceps. He pulled me crashing against his chest. Hot breath washed my face with the rank stench of his afternoon's binge. "Ye like the angry, wounded prick, no?" His eyes were frantic, darting unfocused. "What a grand arsehole I've been. You and your Elf must have died laughing."

"*No!*" I grunted. "That's not true." I struggled against his steel hold, wrenching my arms. "Samuel, you're hurting me. Let me go."

The seam of my blouse couldn't withstand the strain, tearing under the tension of his grip. Samuel's eyes were dead black. I don't think he heard me. He released one arm and grabbed a fistful of my hair. White-hot pain tore from my scalp as he pulled my face to his.

"Tell me. How do ye like, the misunderstood prick now?"

"Samuel stop. What are you—"

The hammering in my ears drowned out my voice. I squirmed, pushing against his chest with all my force. He tightened his hold on me. Strong fingers dug into my scalp, and he crushed his lips against mine.

The stale aftertaste of his stupor churned my stomach. I shoved with both hands clawing at his chest. With his lips forced against mine, my temper ignited. I opened my mouth and bit. Hard. Warmth seeped into my mouth as I twisted free. Reeling, Samuel's arm connected with my cheek, launching me backward.

Dazed and disoriented, I spun from the force of the blow. My feet left the ground, and I threw my hands out. Everything happened so fast. A blur of silver flashed in my periphery, and familiar arms caught me before I hit the cobblestone.

In the next instant, I was surrounded.

Aust, Iadon, Tham, and Faolan became an ominous wall of protectors, separating me from Samuel. Hugh's two oldest cubs, the bouncers working the door, filed in too. With arms outstretched, everyone braced for a fight.

Galan's heart pounded against my chest, his arms wrapped around my shoulders. I shook my head, and salty tears stung the scrape on my cheek. "Stop. Stop this, everyone, please."

Galan helped me stand, but held my shoulders, his hands trembling. "Is this how you treat a female, Samuel?" he growled. "They bow to your advances, or you assault them?"

Samuel's lip curled. "I'm the last man ye want to end up in a mangle with, Elf."

"Actually, wizard, you are the first."

I pressed at my wall of protectors. "Back down, boys. This is between Samuel and me." I half-turned and braced a hand flat on Galan's chest. His eyes were wild, stormy, and ice-blue. "Calm down. Let me handle this. Please."

"No." Galan shook his head and grabbed my wrist.

He didn't just say that. "Galan, I get you're upset, but you are *not*, nor will you ever be, my lord and master. If I say I will speak with Samuel, you and your well-meaning family will back the hell off and let us speak." Sparks fizzled from my fingertips. "Something's not right here, and I'm going to figure out what it is."

Galan's glare narrowed. "Jade, I am looking at what a few moments alone with Samuel have done, and it is a macabre sight. You owe him nothing."

I caught my reflection in the tavern window. It was grisly.

My cheek was a violet patch. My mouth and chin were stained with Samuel's blood, and my blouse was ripped and falling back to expose bruises already blooming on my shoulder and neck. Okay, I looked like shit.

Drawing a deep breath, I softened my voice. "It looks worse than it is." No one moved to let me pass. I closed my eyes and steadied my nerves. Not waiting for a reply, I built up some juice and pushed past them with a jolt. Thankfully they parted and gave me some space.

Samuel looked spooked, like a cornered animal about to bolt. I walked slowly, gauging his mood with each approaching step. The emotions on his face didn't make sense. He was so conflicted. "I am sorry you're hurting," I whispered. "But I don't understand. You said you needed more than I gave you. *You* broke it off. You said we were over."

Samuel's expression contorted, and he rocked on the balls of his feet.

"Why are you doing this, Samuel? You're my family."

"Family?" he snorted. "Are ye that blind? Ye think ye know the people around ye—what's going on. Ye've no idea. Castian. Reign. It's all a fucking charade." He glanced at the trees in the distance and seemed to gain focus. He moved directly in front of me, glaring through glossy eyes to where Galan was standing behind me.

"Take her Elf, for all the good it'll do ye. She's a honey, I give you that. Though I wouldn't have wasted so much time if I'd known her silken thighs are locked tighter than a vault. Two years for nothing but bursting bollocks and a broken heart."

Samuel spat. Saliva hit my eye and ran warm, down my cheek. In a fog, I raised my hand to my face. I didn't see when he lunged, but I felt the force of a truck hit my chest. I gasped, staring down at what was left of my shredded blouse. Pain ripped through my body before my mind understood.

Samuel whispered something and disappeared.

Stunned, I clutched the hilt of the dagger protruding through my chest. Wet heat washed down my belly. I crumpled.

"NO!" Galan cried. "Oh, no, no. *Jade.*" Warm arms lowered me to the cobblestone path. His hands fluttered over me. He gathered my hand, cradled it to his chest. "Blossom, if I remove the dagger, can you heal the wound? Jade, can you?"

"No." I coughed. Blood spewed from my mouth. "Too much... can't focus."

"All right," he sobbed. "What can I do?"

All sounds receded from my mind as a hazy, cold fog enveloped me. I was struck by the desperate love brimming in those glossy, blue eyes and the soft lines of his chisel-cut face.

Everything went black.

CHAPTER TWENTY-FIVE

Through the fog, I strained to focus. My body was blurry, detached. I wanted my arms to move, to pull myself up. I couldn't find them. My eyes refused to open. I tried to remember. Stabbed. Samuel stabbed me. *Shit. I'm dead.*

Dead was uncomfortable. I didn't want to be dead.

The blanket of fog drifted. I felt my feet, then my knees. Inch by inch, limb by limb, I became more aware. Soft breathing close to my ear. Sweet, warm breath brushed my cheek. I listened through the foggy mist, fixated on the rhythm in my ear. I tried to find my eyes again. They fluttered open a sliver. I searched for something—anything—to settle on.

Nothing. They closed.

My head spun. My eyes remained closed. The scent of lilacs drifted in on the breeze from an open window. My fingers twitched, tracing the detailed embroidery on the bedspread—my bedspread. I sighed. Warmth skimmed across my cheek. Liquid sunshine washed over me. My skin tingled with the touch. Someone was with me, holding me, stroking my face.

"*Au' laccer en lla coia orn ne' omenta grantha.*" The silky voice whispered, but I couldn't translate the Elvish. *"Cormimen niuve tella' tue les lla au'."*

That voice. What was it saying? I tried to rouse. My head was cradled. My eyes opened. Church-glass-blue. I knew that color. "Galan?"

"Blossom," Galan exhaled on a sigh.

"What happened?"

"Shh, Blossom." His voice was shaky, his eyes swollen and bloodshot. "Are you well?"

"Am I dead?" I struggled to sit. A stab of pain broke through the last of my fog.

He laid his arm across my shoulders and held me still. "No love. You were hurt and lost a large amount of blood."

My hand fumbled to my chest. Everything felt normal. "Oh," I mumbled.

"Yes, oh," he said, closing his eyes for a long moment.

"You look like shit, Highborne."

He barely chuckled. "You scared the life out of me." Slowly, as if he were afraid to touch me, he cupped my face in his hands and touched his lips to mine. I closed my eyes, gathering what focus I had. With my eyes closed, the world spun uncontrollably. Black fog blanketed me again, and Galan's arms wrap tighter. I couldn't hold on.

"Jade?" Galan cradled my head.

"*Mhmm.*" I didn't want to pass out. I focused on my breathing until it steadied.

"Do you know how desperately I cherish you?"

"*Mhmm.*" Did he know how sexy his voice was? With my eyes closed, his words wrapped around me like fur on bare skin. It stoked the fire smoldering in my soul.

"How's my girl?" A graveled voice asked from across the room. The voice echoed hollowly as if he stood down an empty corridor far away.

"Improved, though she is still groggy."

Someone kissed my forehead. The touch of his chin was scratchy and smelled of Dolce and Gabbana cologne. *Reign.*

"Look at her wound site," Galan said. The slightest brush of his fingers touched my chest. "The scar is completely gone."

"She's a healer, Galan. By morning she'll be one-hundred percent. Trust me."

Somewhere in my fog, something didn't ring true. How had I healed myself? Pain interfered with my focus and the pain that ripped through my chest— "Samuel! Samuel stabbed me."

I raised my hand and cringed as my movement sent spears of agony ricocheting through my chest.

I moaned and tried to breathe.

"It's being taken care of," Reign said, pressing a flat hand on my chest. The bed creaked and dipped under his weight, shifting me toward him. "We'll bring him home to answer for this. You worry about getting better."

Galan ran his thumb over my hand. "This should never have happened."

I forced my eyes open. "Not your fault, Galan. I'm fine."

"Fine?" he said, his brows arching. "You were a breath from death because I let him too close to you."

"No." My tongue felt gigantic in my mouth, a huge, dry pillow taking up all the space. "It doesn't make sense. He was acting crazy." Reign listened calmly to my garbled ramble. Calmly? Getting a dagger rammed into my chest should have Reign tearing down the castle. I pegged him with what I hoped was a serious stare. "What do you know about this, Reign?"

He met my gaze, his mask of innocence perfectly in place. "And what would I know?"

My eyes rolled closed. "Why were you two fighting? Why is Samuel so upset?" I couldn't piece my thoughts together. Something wasn't adding up. "Galan, may I have a drink?"

Galan poured a glass of water and tipped it for me to sip. It was fresh and washed down to my belly. "Rest now. Address your questions when you are stronger."

My focus was a mess, true, but I knew my father was the key. "Reign, what's doing?"

He placed a whiskered kiss on my forehead and strode for the door. "Nothing, love. Galan, don't take any shit from her. Keep her in bed until she's one hundred and ten percent. Tie her down if you have to."

"Don't leave." I tried to sit up but didn't make it. "Reign! I want to know—"

As Reign eclipsed the doorway, Lexi tucked in around him. He didn't even acknowledge her as he blew by, thus signaling the end of that discussion.

"Hey girlfriend, what did I miss?" Lexi skipped over and set down a plate of brownies.

"Reign knows something about Samuel stabbing me, but he's gone mute."

Lexi flopped onto the bed beside me. "You've had a shitstorm couple days. Don't try to make sense of everything the moment your eyes open. Give yourself a break. I'm sure he'll come clean when it's time."

"Honestly, if it upsets you, let it be," Galan said. "Rest."

I crossed my arms over my chest. "I don't want to rest. I want to know what the hell is going on. There's more to this. Why was Samuel so upset this week, and why did he stab me?"

Galan scowled. "Why? He is a jealous *Ud 'Raan*,"

"No. He's not."

Galan's nostrils flared, and he held up his hand. "Do. Not. Defend. Him. He spat in your face and rammed his blade deep into your chest. Have you any idea how that image haunts me?"

"Yeah, I was there," I snapped. "I was the one choking on my own blood."

Galan stiffened.

When the silence continued, Lexi eased off the bed. "On that note, I'm outtie. Just came by to check-in and drop off the chocolate goodies. You two obvi need a moment. Don't worry about your classes, sista. Julian, Aust, and I have you covered."

"Thanks, Lex. You're my rock."

"You know it." She smiled, springing on her way. "I'm locking the door. Try to remember you love each other, and you just stopped fighting a few days ago."

Galan sunk onto the edge of the bed and rubbed the back of his neck. His whole body was vibrating with fury.

"I'm sorry," I said.

Galan shook his head, refusing to look at me.

"Galan, we're not always going to agree. Actually, with us, we'll be lucky when we do. Samuel is a topic we should avoid. You feel strongly one way, and I feel equally strong the other."

He didn't move, just stared out the window from my bedside. "How can you possibly give him consideration? I am honestly trying to understand. For the life of me, I cannot."

"I'm still alive." That got him looking at me. His eyes burned, and I sighed. "Enough. Samuel doesn't have it in him to want me dead. I know him. I've healed him. I would have felt it if he wanted to hurt me. He didn't. Doesn't. There's more to this."

He pinched the bridge of his nose, his eyes closed. "He does not deserve your compassion, Jade."

"Look." I sat up and gritted my teeth as the room did a Tilt-a-Whirl. When the ride stopped, I met his anxious glower. "Samuel is important to me. I know what was in his eyes when he stabbed me. It wasn't hatred or anything malicious. It was raw horror. He was terrified."

"He was inebriated and out of his skull." Galan pressed his palms on the mattress beside my hips. Hovering close, his expression softened, and he reined in his frustration. "Can we stop discussing him, Blossom? Please, if not for your sake, then for mine. Rest now, recover, and when you are well, we will revisit this. Please."

How do you stay mad at a man who looks at you like you're the very reason he walks the Earth? He looked so tired and sad. "Okay, consider me calm." When he lay down beside me, I snuggled close and breathed him in. "Congrats. You win the gold medal for stubbornness."

His chest gently bounced against mine. "Oh, I think you put me to shame. Now, close your eyes and get some rest." He kissed the tip of my nose and stroked my hair, playing with my locks while his breath tickled my skin.

"Galan?"

"Yes, Blossom." His breath hissed out of him as I twisted my hand between our bodies and cupped his crotch. He stilled and then eased away. I kissed the line of his jaw. He tasted salty and warm. "You need rest, love."

I shook my head, surprised when it didn't spin. "I need *you* and a little of your TLC. Please, Highborne, I just need your skin next to mine." After a moment, his lips covered mine, tentative and tense at first, then the stress of the past few days seemed to drain out of him.

Fire smoldered deep inside me, and I reached under his tunic. Just like that, our fight was over—for now.

CHAPTER TWENTY-SIX

"Feeling better, Jade?" Iadon asked. He, along with the other Highborne men, stood as Galan, and I entered the lounge. I signaled for them to sit, and they settled back to the table. Iadon flipped the turn card and smiled.

"Much better. Thank you." I had to laugh. Lexi, Tham, Aust, and Iadon were all sporting mirrored sunglasses, and baseball caps spun backward. "Nice look. Texas Hold 'em?"

"Yes." Tham tapped the table to check his bet. "It keeps us from losing hold on our sanity while waiting. Is it always like this? Days and days of no news?"

I shrugged. "It can be. The world's a big place and magic makes it difficult to find people who don't want to be found. It sucks, but our guys are the best. You'll find the warriors of the Talon are very creative in ways to distract ourselves, which reminds me, I heard I missed a potato war."

Julian jumped up from the couch, rubbing his skull trimmed afro as he laughed. "Oh, man, Jade. You should have seen the look on Cowboy's face when Nash's Spudzooka shot wide, and his russet smashed through Reign's office window. He shifted to a wolf, tucked his tail, and booked it as fast as four paws would take him. Didn't see him for two days."

"I heard you're all in the doghouse."

"Shit." He waved my words away, his mint green eyes swimming with laughter. "It was so worth it."

"So, is Reign around? I've left him messages and swung by his office, but he's MIA."

Julian opened his mouth to respond when the air crackled behind us, and a fissure opened. The electrical charge made my hair stand on end. Galan spun, withdrawing his dagger. His body blurred as he pulled me behind him and hit a ready stance. My heart stopped dead, and I grabbed his hand. "*Stop.* It's not Samuel."

Standing in the center of the room, was my gorgeous best friend and adoptive brother, Bruin. He materialized in a surge of power I was very accustomed to and missed more than I realized. Shaggy brown hair flopped in front of his face, hiding the turquoise peepers that women died for. Wearing his trademark worn blue jeans ripped at the knee and sloganed T-shirt he was the most beautiful site I'd seen in ages. His shirt read: *It's all fun and games until someone loses an eye. Then it's a critical hit*

Every inch of my body vibrated even before he flipped his hair and looked at me. Gods how I'd missed the man under that beautiful shaggy mop. "Hey Blaze . . . Princess!"

Lexi and I launched ourselves across the lounge and into his arms. "You're home!" Our squeals and giggles filled the lounge as he crushed us to his chest with one massively strong arm swooping around each of us.

Lexi covered his cheek with a million kisses. "Gods, we've missed you."

"How are my girls?" He squeezed tight, lifting us like feathers into the air and spinning us in a slow circle. His familiar scent of pine and wood-smoke filled my senses. He leaned down to nuzzle the tops of our heads, growling deep in his throat.

The sound of someone clearing his throat brought us out of our love fest. The muscles in Galan's jaw twitched as he moved forward, his dagger still in his hand. By looking at him, I'd swear he was back to being that angry, mistrusting Galan from the enchanted valley, but with an added edge of possessiveness.

Bruin locked into his stare. "Something I can do for you, buddy?"

"You could remove your hand from Jade's backside."

Bruin held his gaze and took a deliberate step forward.

Shit. I wriggled free of Bruin and stepped between them. "Galan, look at me." His eyes were locked on Bruin's as the two men advanced on a collision course. I grabbed his face and dug my fingers into his jaw. "Look at me, *now*."

When Galan's gaze met mine, Bruin's energy eased behind me.

"Galan, this is Bruin, my brother. I told you about him, remember?" I turned to my brother. "Bruin, this is Galan,"

"Blaze? What did I miss?" Bruin asked.

"Too much," I said. Bruin was still standing his ground. "Galan and I are together, the Highbornes were released from exile, and Samuel stabbed me—"

"*What?*" He breathed out a gust of air and spun to glare at Julian and Lexi. "Why the fuck wasn't I told? How could—"

"I'm fine," I assured him, stepping in to hug him again. "Actually, I'm over the moon."

Bruin eyed Galan from the tips of his ears to his suede laced boots. "Well then, congrats." He kissed my cheek and extended a hand to Galan. "You're one hell of a lucky man. This woman is as good as they come, you feel me?"

Galan nodded, and the tension dissipated—a little. "Gratitude. And yes, she is."

With that settled, I smacked Bruin on the chest. "Do you know how long you've been gone? Seven months. What the hell?" I drank in the sight of him and, at the same time, punched him in the shoulder. "Would it kill you to come home once in a while?"

It was a good thing he was looking sheepish. "That's what undercover means, right? Cutting off ties and being, umm, oh yeah, *undercover*."

Galan studied Bruin, and his tension ratcheted. *Fabulous.*

"Reign didn't mention any of this when he told me to come in. This is big news."

"When does Reign ever give up the deets?" Julian said, meeting Bruin chest to chest, arms clapping on broad shoulders. "Good to see you, my man."

"You too. Gods, I've missed being home."

I nodded toward Tham and the others who were gathering. "Bruin, this is Nyssa, Iadon, Aust, and Tham. Everyone, this is Bruin, our brother."

In true Tham fashion, he sauntered over and clasped Bruin's wrist. "Merry meet. How long are you home for?"

"Not sure. Reign asked me to watch over the campus while he's at an emergency Talon summit. It seems I've got catching up to do."

"Emergency Talon summit?" I asked. "Bullshit. He's ducking me."

"Maybe, but there was some kind of fallout from an incident in the modern realm—risk of exposure, questions about an attack—that sort of thing. The Fae Authority has demanded a hearing. He said to haul my ass back here ASAP because the shit's about to hit. We're planning to raid a Scourge compound?"

"Yep. We're waiting for word on Galan's sister, Lia. We should hear anytime."

Aust's head cocked to the side, his expression showing a whole-lotta confused concentration. Faolan whined a soft whimper and laid her head on the floor. Bruin's attention was drawn to Aust a moment before I spoke.

I held up my hand toward my brother. "What are you sensing, Aust?" I was impressed by both his sensitivity and the fact that Bruin was letting him meet his stare.

"I am not entirely certain." He strode to my side. Bruin seemed equally intrigued. "It is similar to what I sense with Cowboy's wolf, yet not."

I nodded. "Bruin, Aust has the strongest natural druid powers I have ever seen. Without training, he communicates with all wildlife he comes in contact with and has an unbelievable sensitivity to nature."

Bruin smiled with warm admiration of a brother. Subtly he raised his head and sniffed the air. "Can you shift forms?"

"No . . . you?"

Bruin looked to Lexi and me. "I'm insulted that my reputation hasn't preceded me, girls. My talents should have come up with a new druid in the castle."

I turned to Aust, ignoring Bruin's feigned distress. "Yes, he shifts. He's a Were."

"What breed? Would you show me?" He looked quickly to me. "Is it rude of me to ask?"

"Nah," Bruin said. "Weres love to show off." Bruin flashed a dazzling boyish grin before stepping into an open space and falling forward onto all fours. His clothes disappeared as his body exploded into his animal form. Muscles expanded, bones lengthened, fur appeared where a moment ago there was bronze skin and shaggy brown hair.

"He is a bear," Aust mumbled.

"A Silver Kodiak," I clarified. "His family sleuth came from Alaska."

Bruin lumbered over and nudged his massive head into my side, nearly knocking me over. His head was wider than my rib cage. He growled long and low as I scrubbed the thick fur between his ears. He'd loved that since we were kids. Galan strode to my side, looking anxious. He was trying not to lose his cool, but he was just this side of a total meltdown.

"Relax, Galan, s'all good. Just don't meet him eye to eye again. Bruin is the Alpha, King of all Weres. He's as dominant as they come, and his bear considers staring a confrontation. He's pretty good at control in his human form, but you can't get so possessive of me."

Aust's look of sheer fascination warmed my heart. "What a miracle it would be to run as one of my animal brothers in the wild." He studied Bruin's massive frame, and I recognized the look as soon as Aust started speaking into his mind.

Bruin changed back into human form and materialized in his clothes. "Sounds great." He nodded as the two clamped wrists. "How about tomorrow? I'll join the morning training, and we can try out a few things."

"I look forward to it," Aust said, a genuine grin lighting up his face.

Lexi huffed, shifting her feet, and Bruin brought his attention back to our sister. "What's doing, Princess?"

"Did you bring us presents, because I haven't seen any?"

Bruin raised a brow, and it disappeared under his shaggy bangs. "Have I ever forgotten to bring a token of my love?"

No, he hadn't, and Lexi knew that as well as I did. She bounced in front of him, wriggling her fingers, and closed her eyes. Bruin chuckled and winked at me as he magically produced two gift bags bursting with color-coded tissue. He placed the mauve one into Lexi's hand and handed the emerald one to me. We'd been doing that since we were kids. Bruin's color was turquoise, and Julian's was mint.

I reached in and pulled out a cute midriff T-shirt that said *Tank 'n' Spank*. Lexi's said, *Well behaved women rarely make history.*

"There's one other thing. Dig a little deeper."

We did as instructed and came out with something smooth and curved. I examined the mystery gift, and a rush of pleasure surged through me. It was a bear claw pendant on a woven cord. The claw was almost three inches long with the tip cut, hollowed, and a small hole bored near the top. It was polished to a deep chestnut and was smooth as satin. Lexi's was identical.

I stroked the lustrous sheen with a light, gentle touch. "Are they your claws?"

He nodded. "I researched clan traditions and learned about these. These are an ancient gift called talisman skirls. If you blow into them, I will hear the call no matter where I am in this realm or any other and will come.

"Our very own personal Bruin whistle?"

He wrinkled his nose. "It's a hell of a lot more masculine than a whistle, but yeah, that's the gist." He reached into his pocket and tossed a third skirl to Julian, who inclined his head and settled his skirl around his neck.

Lexi put hers to her mouth. Her cheeks ballooned even though no sound was made. She pulled it back, looked at it, and started to pout. "Mine's broken."

Bruin shook his head and tugged at his ears. "No, it's not. It's like a dog whistle, Princess. Only I hear it. And please don't blow it so close to me. You almost busted my eardrums."

"Thank-you." I kissed his cheek and laced mine over my head. "I love it."

Lexi wrapped her arms around his neck. "Okay," she laughed wide-eyed. "Put them on me." Bruin laughed again, and an instant later, Lexi stood wearing her new T-shirt with her claw necklace hanging in its place.

"Nice trick," Tham muttered, glancing over to a stiff and stern-looking Galan.

"Yeah," Lexi said, "Weres can do lots of neat little tricks."

CHAPTER TWENTY-SEVEN

The next morning Galan and I left the Highborne training session at the old horse arena and went behind the barn to the archery lanes Savage and Cowboy had set up. My head was still a little fuzzy from the wine we drank in honor of Bruin's return, but the warm, morning air was clearing the cobwebs.

Standing perpendicular to the targets, Galan brought his arms around to my front and placed his bow in my hand. "This time feel for the wind. The farther the target is from your arrow, the more its path will deviate. The instant before release, hold your breath and loose the string between the beats of your heart. Even those two tiny movements can alter your shot."

I nocked the arrow, stretched my arm until it started to quiver and let it fly. *Thunk*, it sunk into a bale of straw supporting one of the closer targets.

"Acceptable," Galan said. "Did you close your eyes again?" I shook my head, and he chuckled at my hasty denial. "I thought as much. Would you close your eyes when you are under attack?" He kissed up the length of my neck while I pulled the next arrow from the quiver.

The touch of his lips on my skin sent me to another plane of existence. From one breath to another, my body heated. His hands skimmed upwards from my hips to cup my breasts. My entire body tingled. I shook my head. "Like I can concentrate when you do that."

"Chaos and distraction are part of battle, Blossom," he whispered. "I am dedicated to furthering your training."

"*Mhmm* . . . will you show me again?"

"If you like." He chuckled a deep velvet rumble, then stepped in front of me and took the bow. "How many would you like this time, *neelan*?"

I bit my bottom lip and swept my hair behind my shoulders. Gods, he was gorgeous when he was all warriored up and holding his bow. "Three."

"My female wishes to see three arrows in the bull's-eye. Are you watching carefully?" He smiled his crooked, cocky smile, and I had to lock my knees to keep from falling.

"I am, but first. . ." I leaned in and kissed him with all I had. As I moaned into his mouth, my hand ran down the front of his suede pants. His laces were already bursting, and as I palmed his arousal, he pressed his hips forward. He kissed me again, harder, deeper. When I knew he was turned-on, I stepped back. "It's only fair that you get distracted too."

Galan smiled, drew a deep breath, and let it out fast. "What a glorious distraction you are."

"Fair's fair. Let's see what you've got Highborne."

Galan winked, and in an instantaneous blur of motion, he struck the center of the target. Once. Twice. Three times. Each arrow split the one before down the length of its shaft. I sucked in a gasp. I don't know what it was about this man in action, but gods he was sex-on-a-stick.

Handing me the bow, he established his position behind me. "Relax your bow arm."

With the tip of my arrow aimed and both of my eyes open, I was loosing my shot when Galan nipped my bare shoulder. Every hormone in my body burst into flame. Dropping the bow to my side, I pivoted and lunged. He caught me in his arms. His hands tightened on my ass and swept up my back until my breasts were firm against his smooth, muscled chest.

Cheers from the training session on the other side of the arena reminded me we were far from being discreet. Damn. My hormones were raging, and we had no hope of finding privacy.

I forced myself to step back. "Be good." When he started to prowl toward me, I held up a finger. "We're changing the subject now. *Sooo*, Galan, how'd you get so good at archery?"

Thankfully played along. "My father, I suppose."

"Your father? You must be kidding?"

Galan looked surprised at my reaction and then, damn him, amused. He took possession of the bow. After nocking the next arrow, he let it sail straight into the farthest target's bulls-eye. "For the first half-century of my life, my sire was a loving, supportive male. He instructed me as any father would, and I practiced to become a great ranger and a male of worth." Galan's hands dropped to his sides as he stared into nothingness. "After *Naneth* passed, and I began to care for Lia, I used the practice to escape being berated."

And beaten. I fought back my anger before Galan smelled it. He was a proud man and obviously wouldn't want the abuse I'd found while healing him to come to light. "Does he have any idea how good you are?"

Galan shook his head and loosed another arrow. It flew straight on target, splintering the shaft of the first. "In truth, I have never felt the need to share it with him. Besides, my shot is not as true when others are watching. Lia, Tham, and Nyssa can watch me for hours, and I shall never falter, but for some reason, I do not retain my accuracy when others are around."

"Sounds like stage fright. How are you in battle?" He stared at me —glared at me, actually. "Right, sorry. You've only been in that one battle on Dragon's Peak. But your aim was true then."

He frowned, turned his back, and drew another arrow. "I realize I am not the seasoned warrior you are accustomed to." His voice hardened, and his body went stiff as a lamp-post. "You have every right to point out my shortcomings."

"What? Galan, I wasn't—"

"I have little to offer a female warrior, such as yourself."

"Stop that!" I grabbed his jaw, forcing him to look at me. His gaze was hard, but I saw the hurt behind the veil of anger. "I wasn't saying anything about your worth. Don't put words into my mouth. It's rude."

Galan stepped closer, looming over me like an ominous shadow. I glared back at him, digging my fingers deeper into his jaw.

"Oh, look, a party," Lexi said.

"And us left uninvited?" Tham wiped the sweat from his brow and fingered through his wet hair as he and Lexi strode around the end of the barn. Appraising glances ping-ponged from Galan to me and back again. "We wondered where the two of you had run off to."

I released my grip on Galan's jaw, and he turned away, adjusting his bow.

"What's the story behind that?" Lexi pointed to the far end of the arena. My practice arrows were sticking out of the straw on the close target, and Galan's splintered bulls-eye shots were there too. Nothing worth wondering about.

"The story behind what?" I sighed, flexing the stiffness out of my hand.

"That." Tham pointed well off the flight path of the targets to where one arrow stuck out of the side of the arena wall.

Even in my mood, I laughed, remembering Galan nipping my shoulder as I shot. "Oh, that one got away on me. I was, uh, distracted."

"Distracted?" Tham discretely sauntered toward Galan.

I cleared my throat and turned to my sister. "Well, what did we miss?"

"Quite a bit. Come check this out." Lexi grabbed my hand and skipped around to the front of the arena. Aust was standing with Bruin on the track of the outdoor ring. The two of them were practically glowing, a matching expression of amazement on both of their faces.

Bruin nodded once and took a step back. "Okay, Aust, like we practiced."

Aust closed his eyes and raised his hands from his sides. As they moved higher, a whirlwind picked up. It swirled around us growing in intensity, the higher his hands raised. Hair whipped, clothes pulled in every direction, and we were forced to squint to shield our eyes from the dirt of the track. After a moment, he lowered his hands, and the whirlwind dissipated. When he finished, the air was calm, with only the trace of a warm summer's breeze.

"Oh, my gods," I gasped. "That was exceptional, Aust. Whirlwind is an upper-level spell, and you learned it in a couple of hours?"

"Not even." Bruin shook his head, his shaggy brown bangs falling over his eyes. "He had it down pat right away, and then we worked on this one."

Aust reached into his vest pocket and produced a carnelian carving of Shalana, Goddess of the Woodlands figurine. My stomach flipped. It was one of the icons recovered from the Altar of the Ancients, at Dragon's Peak. It was the one we believed caused the surge in his affinity and the beginning of his evolution.

Aust inclined his head and regarded the heavens. A look of concentration crumpled his brow, then his shape shimmered and disappeared morphing into a sleek, muscular white tiger.

"Holy shit!" My jaw dropped. "Polymorphing at his first training session?"

"I know," Bruin said. "He's a beast. And of course, I'm an exceptional trainer."

Aust padded once around us, his head low, his ice-blue gaze sharp yet his own. When he returned to his natural form, Bruin materialized Aust's clothes and gave him a minute to gather himself. When he straightened, he was smiling from one pointed ear to the other.

I threw my arms around his neck and practically tackled him to the ground. "You are amazing, Aust. You should be so proud." I kissed his cheek, then looked up to find that Galan and Tham had joined us.

"I am in awe of you, brother mine." Galan glided forward to embrace him, chest to chest, thumping his back with his palm. "If you can do this in just a few short hours, imagine what you shall accomplish on your second day."

"Tell me," Tham said. "How is it to be a creature of such strength and power?"

"It is the most incredible sensation," Aust said. "I retain my wits and senses just in the altered form. I feel the beast's basic instincts, his keen senses, his strength and, of course, his ferocity. I cannot hold my form long, though it is unbelievable to experience a oneness with a creature so primal. A dream come to fruition. One day I shall see the countryside the way Faolan and my wildlife family see it, running on all fours."

"Not if we slack off, you won't." Bruin's voice was stern, but the twitch at the corner of his mouth told us he was joking. "Back to work. Don't you girls have classes to teach?" After giving us the proverbial boot to the ass, Bruin pulled Aust back into their training session, and Tham and Galan walked us to the forest path.

"Can you believe that?" My head was buzzing. "He morphed on his first day. It's unheard of. Elora is going to pee her pants when she sees him turn into a tiger."

Galan's scowl softened. "We can only hope you are wrong."

I crinkled my nose at him. "You know what I mean."

"Yes. I do." He tugged my hair, and we let Lexi and Tham get a bit ahead of us.

"Are we okay?" I caught his hand. "I mean, I want you to know—"

"I know." He took a deep breath and squeezed my hand. A stiff, uncomfortable silence fell between us. My heart raced as I waited for him to say more, to look at me, to smile—anything. After what seemed an eternity, he nodded. "Fash not, Blossom. All is well."

Sadly, I didn't believe that for a second.

CHAPTER TWENTY-EIGHT

*W*ith classes over for another week, I peered through the doorway of the fifth-floor lounge. Everyone was still riding the adrenaline rush after a grueling training session. Savage sat alone, sharpening his blades, while the rest of the group fidgeted in their seats, stretching out tweaked muscles, cracking knuckles and rolling necks.

Amped atmosphere aside, everyone bore the stress of waiting with a great deal of humor. Lexi, Tham, Rue, and Cowboy were cheating at Euchre, cracking up at the thinly veiled attempts to table-talk their suits to their partners and throw lame-ass signals.

Iadon, Aust, and Nyssa were over by the televisions, playing the instruments they'd brought back from the village. The harmonizing of Iadon and Aust's smooth, deep voices sent shivers through me. I laughed out loud, realizing they were singing Phillip Phillip's *Home*. I didn't even know they were American Idol fans.

And then there was Galan.

He lay, stretched out on the leather sofa with Ella lying flat on his chest. They were both sound asleep, Galan's hands splayed protectively over her back, a chenille throw over them both. After another of his fitful nights, it seemed Galan had succumbed to Ella's soothing effect.

"Jade, are you supporting the doorway, or would you like to try your luck at cards?" Tham winked as he shuffled the deck then started dealing out the next hand.

"I'll pass. I suck at cheating."

"Cheating?" Tham feigned insult. "Harsh words, female. We are simply…"

"Creative with the finer points of rules," Cowboy finished for him.

The four of them laughed and nodded.

Aust set his lute down against the marble hearth of the fireplace and joined me by the door. Pulling back from kissing my cheek, he slid the wide strap from my shoulder and set my bag on the floor just inside the room. "How was your class this afternoon, *neelan*?"

"Good, thanks." I shuffled over to the buffet and poured myself a glass of soda. "Naith and I took a group of fourth-year students to a clearing near northern ward seventeen to harvest the Purple Pollida. The lavender flowers are almost three feet tall this time of year."

"And for what shall you use them?"

"A couple of things. Both the spiny heads of the flowers and the roots are used in different natural remedies." I pointed to my bag, and when he brought it to me, I retrieved one of the cuttings from the pocket. "Aust, if you're interested in my Phytotherapy classes, you're more than welcome to sit in."

He smiled wide. "If our training schedule should allow, I shall. Gratitude."

Aust gave off such beautifully pure energy I couldn't help but be drawn to it. "I'll make sure your schedule allows it." I winked at him. "I do have a little pull around here."

"Gratitude, Jade. The natural world of Shalana—"

We both swung around when Galan—still clutching Ella to his chest—stood bolt upright. Looking at all the watchful eyes upon him, the energy of the room changed.

A cold tingling clawed at me. "Galan, what is it?"

"Something is wrong." He growled, moving to Iadon and handing off the sleeping baby. He drew his dagger, tensing as he spun it in his hand, obviously trying to focus on whatever it was that he was sensing. Cards fell in a flurry, weapons and daggers took their place.

Then we felt it too, the crackle of the electrical fissure opening up in the room. Bruin materialized into the center of the lounge, bruised and bleeding from a gash across his shoulder. He met my gaze and nodded once. "Saddle up."

Every person in the room was on their feet. The Elves slung quivers, cinched belts, and unsheathed swords. Cowboy, Savage, and Rue heaved on their battle-vests and dusters, which were each stocked full as an arsenal.

"The majority of Scourge raiders are out on a raid. The compound is guarded by a skeleton force of fifty or so." Bruin looked to Iadon, inclining his head. "Did you finish that little project I gave you?" Iadon laid Ella in her chair, then retrieved his satchel from the floor.

"Blaze and Princess, come over here for a sec."

I looked at Bruin while Iadon laid out two black chest harnesses. They looked like Army Surplus had ravaged Victoria's Secrets and sired hybrid Kevlar, tank-top-sport-bras.

"Battle vests for girls?" Lexi squealed. "Cool."

"Iadon sized them to fit you and will show you how to get them on."

With Iadon's help, Lexi and I slipped into our new assault apparel. They were lightweight and strong as steel, covering our chest and bellies. And what do you know, we rocked the look. Small Velcro pockets ran down the front and along the bottom edge with two slim blades sheathed crisscross for a stealthy retrieval.

"In a tight jam, these babies might keep your girlie parts protected, you feel me?"

I patted my pockets and activated my communicator. With that done, I checked how the others were doing. Though I thought Lexi and I had ceased to be female in the eyes of our fellow Talon enforcers, the men stood, transfixed on our new bad-ass vests.

"Down boys," Tham said, smacking Lexi on the butt as he grabbed his dagger.

"Sorry, Tham. At this particular moment, *down* is not an option." Cowboy adjusted his leathers and waggled his brows. "How hot is a woman in battle gear?"

Bruin turned to the group. "Those who can Flash grab hold of those who can't and follow my vapor." Bruin nodded once toward Galan, who was sporting a greenish hue and paying no attention to the banter. "Galan. We need you tight if we're going to get your sister back, right?" When Galan nodded, Bruin scanned the group. "Everyone ready? Okay, don't let go until we're in the belly of hell, and you're surrounded by Scourge scum."

Iadon stood with his arms around Nyssa, her gaze locked on Galan. They were doing that silent communication thing the two of them did. It didn't take much to figure out what was said. With my pulse racing, I clamped Galan's hand. "I love you soul-deep, Highborne."

"Stay close and stay safe, Blossom." He closed his eyes and squeezed my hand.

"Ready?" Bruin grabbed hold of us and inclined his head. "Here goes everything."

As promised, we Flashed into the eye of a storm of soldiers. The air hung heavy between the forest trees, pressing against my skin like a heavy blanket. Fanning out along the edge of the Scourge encampment, we joined the battle already in progress. Scourge often lived below ground, and beyond the treeline was a small outbuilding that marked the entrance to the underground caverns.

Reign and a dozen men were clashing hard with a defense force hell-bent on keeping us out of those caverns. Sizing up our surroundings, Galan muttered in a low oath and pulled me behind his body. He nocked his bow in repeated succession, releasing a tidal wave of arrows one after another after another until the fight drew too close. Then he drew his short sword and engaged in the melee.

Aust sliced the air with duel scimitars wearing his look of concentration. He was stunning to watch in action, moving as though his weapons were an extension of his own limbs.

Lexi dove in and faced off like the hellcat she was, blades gleaming. Within seconds she scrambled up a mountainous raider, then flipped off and watched him fall to the ground. The guy never knew what hit him.

"Castian, come to me." While my powers strengthened, I dove away from a Scourge barbarian the size of an oak tree. He was an unnatural mass of muscle and brawn. It was lucky his mouth was filled with stained, jagged teeth because it drew attention away from his tiny silver eyes and his chewed-up face.

On a roar, he thrust forward, swinging his flail. He was big but slow. I ducked when the spiked ball came at my head and heard the dull *thwack* when it sunk into a tree behind me. The ballad I hummed focused my energy, and I slammed him with a pulse.

The bastard didn't even budge.

He came at me again. The metallic *whoosh* of chain links hissed in my ear as the metal spikes zinged past my head again. I ducked the blow, escaping decapitation by a sickening few inches. Adrenaline burned through my veins, and I upped my voltage to critical-mass. My next bolt came off like a crack of lightning. It sent his head into a tree with a hollow *thud*.

His expression shifted. His jaw dropped, and the whites of his eyes showed. That split second of disorientation was long enough to wrap him in an incantation and lock him down. Ramming my new slim-blade dagger through his chest, he disintegrated into a pile of black ichor.

Dispatched.

In my periphery, Galan raised his sword. *Too high.* His side was exposed. I whirled, my dagger hand about to release when I realized he'd intentionally overextended. His attacker took the bait, and Galan lunged forward, bringing his sword down, two-handed onto his opponent's shoulder. The crack of bone was followed by a brutal curse. The Dark Elf collapsed, his head bouncing off the forest floor, his collarbone crushed.

The shriek of a giant bird harmonized with the keening metal of battle. A raptor swooped from the trees, talons extended. Wickedly sharp hooks targeted the lime-green eyes of the Dark raider battling Aust. He dodged and swung at the bird, but was no match for a duel attack.

When the raider fell, Aust whistled to the trees. A pack of wolves made short work of him and three other Scourge soldiers—good eating.

Aust caught my glance and flashed a smile.

The gleam on his face darkened at the same time the hair on my neck stood on end. I spun to raise my guard as a hiss of steel cut through the air behind me. In a slow-motion moment, you'd see on a Hollywood screen, a dagger blew by my face. End over end, glinting in the gold afternoon light until it found purchase. My attacker's head snapped back, the hilt of a dagger stuck in his skull. With flailing hands, he grappled me, and we toppled together like a felled tree.

Stunned, I struggled under the crush of his dead weight.

"*Blossom!*" Between one impossible breath and the next, the weight pinning me down vanished. "Are you well?"

I raised a shaky hand to his cheek. "Fine." I looked from the emotion in his eyes to the fallen barbarian and what do you know, I got a rush of the warm and tinglies. Galan helped me to my feet and then stomped on the body to yank his dagger free. And wasn't I just the proudest girlfriend around. "Let's go find your sister."

Cowboy met us on the fly, the amber eyes of his wolf glowing bright and reflective. "Reign and his team secured the entrance. We're headin' in. Scouting shows four dissecting tunnels leadin' away from the main courtyard. Join your teams and activate your comms."

High pitched *beeps* chirped as Talon touched their earpieces and lowered the mics. Galan broke off with Rue and his men in the first tunnel. Savage signaled Tham and his team straight along the corridor. Sin, Lexi, and a few others took the hard veer to the left, and Bruin, Aust, and I moved with our group along the winding left passage.

We raced down the damp, stone corridor, following the dim glow of lantern light. No. It wasn't lantern light. It was the flicker of dying Lightning Sprights trapped in glass prisons. Sick. The corridor seemed endless. There was no way we could unlock every latch and set them free.

Trying not to hear the pitiful whimpers coming from the Sprights I caught up with my group. Bruin paused every few hundred feet to check for activity. Nothing. No movement. No sounds. No scents that might hint at where they were keeping Lia. We pushed on, deeper into the bowels of Scourge central. The reports coming over the comms were the same.

Where is she?

The thundering crack of stone exploding had me spinning. Directly behind me, where I had stood just a second ago, the tunnel crumbled away to rubble. A blue energy bolt lit the tunnel, and then Samuel staggered through the jagged opening. He coughed on rock dust, hunched over something in his arms—no, someone. I saw the blood-drenched, silver locks, and I knew. *Lia*. Gods, she didn't look good.

Bruin's voice rang in stereo from behind me and from my earpiece. "Target acquired. Left passage. Pull back!"

"Jade. *Hurry*." Samuel looked down at the bloody mess, which was Galan's baby sister. "We need to be free of the tunnels to Flash."

"Haul ass, people," Bruin said. "I've got point."

Fighting broke out over the comm while we made our way back to the main corridor. At least one of the other teams was intercepted. *Gods protect him.*

When we got back to the central passageway, Rue came barreling into us with Galan and his squad close behind. Galan was bloody but gloriously alive. In the narrow, bottlenecked opening of the cavern, his head snapped toward me—and then on Samuel holding his sister.

Galan charged. Bruin and Rue saw what was coming and lunged to catch him around the waist. Galan's bloodied dagger swiped the air, the arc falling just short of Samuel.

"You putrid bastard," he snarled. "You backstabbing son-of-a-Scourge-whore." He reached for Lia, struggling against the strength of

Bruin and Rue. "Give her to me, or I shall run you through, as you did Jade."

"Galan stop," I said. "Galan, look at me." Up in his grille, I was stunned by the feral look he was throwing off. "Get Lia home. Be angry later."

Galan's stare hardened and simmered. I knew that look. Betrayal. He thought I was choosing sides. I opened my mouth to explain but was knocked sideways into the stone of the tunnel wall. Chaos erupted, and a dozen Scourge charged through the mouth of the tunnel.

They all zeroed in on Lia.

With my head ringing and white spots dancing behind my eyes, I staggered to my feet. All four teams were back and cutting Samuel a path toward the exit. The hilt of a sword blindsided Aust, and a hell-bolt caught Rue in the chest. As the two of them were knocked on their asses, a mass of bodies—ours and theirs—hurtled to follow.

"Go!" Galan bellowed, diving to help Aust. "Save her!"

The moment the night air hit our faces, I slid my hand around Samuel's bicep, and he Flashed Lia and me to the clinic in the castle. Her skin was caked with blood and dirt, her skirting hung heavy and torn. I tunneled beneath the layers of sheer fabric and examined her fast and furious.

"She seems fine. Whose blood is this?"

"Some mine. Some Scourge. It wasna as smooth a rescue as we'd hoped. How is she?"

"Not sure yet." I looked down the table, scanning Samuel. "How badly are you hurt?"

"Oh, I'm peachy," Samuel deadpanned. "Are ye good? I wanna get back."

"Iadon and Nyssa are in the lounge. Can you Flash them here in case I need a hand?"

"Aye." But he hesitated. "Jade, about what happened. I'm sorry, that wasna me. Whatever happens, I want ye clear on that."

His eyes brimmed with emotion, and my gut twisted in knots. "I am going to kick your ass for stabbing me. You *should* have told me."

"Sorry."

"I'll consider forgiving you *if* you bring everyone home." I tilted my head from side to side and amended that. "*And* after I kick your ass."

He wiped his brow, smearing blood across his grin. "Done deal. I'll be back."

Iadon and Nyssa appeared in my clinic within seconds. After setting Ella's carrier on one of the two recovery beds in the corner, they rushed to my side.

"Gods," Iadon gasped. "She looks… How can we help?"

"She needs fluids. Iadon, behind that door, is a cabinet. Grab me two of the bags with clear liquid and blue writing."

Nyssa and I stripped away Lia's clothes and rolled her over. Other than the filth of her hands and face, her skin was beautifully unmarred. No bruising. No sign of trauma of any kind. She was wearing an ornate silver ring with a Princess cut, blue diamond the size of a postage stamp, and even her fingernails were unbroken. I accessed my gift and assessed her physical health. She was aces on that front, but—

"Jade? What is it?" Nyssa's sharp gaze locked on mine.

"No memories." I adjusted my palms against her warm skin. "I'm connected with her, and I'm getting nothing."

"What does that mean?"

"I have no idea."

The exam was textbook, no obvious indication Lia was abused. I had no idea about Highborne physiology, but maybe Abaddon and his men really did consider her the royal heir and had treated her accordingly. Why wasn't she giving off any shimmer of memories? Why wasn't she waking up? *She will. She has to.* If she didn't—if something was done to her—

Gods, where was Galan?

I shook my head. Any minute, he would to Flash in, kiss his sister, and her eyes would open. I'd seen enough Disney specials to know how the happily ever after shit was supposed to go. I tapped my headset. Nothing. I chucked the thing across the clinic floor. I must have lost my connection to the teams when I got knocked in the tunnels.

What if he doesn't make it back? I banished the thought.

Nyssa brought a small stack of towels and washcloths from the closet as Iadon retrieved the IV pole, and I hung the saline. The three of us worked in busy silence and waited.

Waited for the others to return.

Waited for Lia to stir... even a little.

Nyssa filled a basin and washed the blood and grime from Lia's hair and off her face and hands. When she was freshly gowned, Iadon carried her to a recovery bed and tucked her under a quilt. Bruin and Samuel Flashed Galan and the others into the clinic. Lexi cradled her wrist, Aust's head was gushing, and he was leaning heavily on a battered Tham, but they were alive.

Galan's bow and quiver clattered to the floor as he bolted to the bed. Throwing himself over his sister, he stroked damp hair away from her face. "Tell me, Blossom. Is she well?"

"I'm hoping she'll be up and braiding flowers in your hair in no time."

The group chuckled. Galan didn't. "Hoping? Have they . . . did they hurt her?"

I looked him square in his beautiful blues. "I don't know. I examined her. She seems fine. My concern is this." I indicated two small puncture marks on the side of her neck. "It looks like they injected her with something, but I can't find anything in her system." I rubbed my hand across his back. "We'll know more when she wakes up."

"Uh, Girlfriend? I hate to break up the family reunion, but Merlin isn't looking so hot."

I followed Lexi's gaze to where Samuel had braced himself against my herb table. Barely. He was bone white, the sheen of sweat glistening on his face. As I bolted around the table, his eyes rolled back, and he sank like a stone.

"He's burning up." I pulled his duster open and pressed my fingers to his neck.

Bruin dropped to his knees and ripped away the sopping T-shirt.

"What is it? Venom? Spell?" Bruin's claws extended past his nail beds, and he sliced up the length of Samuel's jeans.

It hit me then.

When I asked about the blood, Samuel said, 'Some mine. Some Scourge.' "He was hurt getting Lia away from her captors. I forgot. Shit, his entire system is shutting down. What the hell is it with men ignoring poisonous wounds?"

CHAPTER TWENTY-NINE

By the angle the light hit my face, and how my stomach grumbled, it was early afternoon when I woke. Galan was there. I felt him even without opening my eyes and imagined him clearly in my mind's eye. His angelic face would light up when he realized I was awake. He'd stalk toward me in his graceful prowl and then trace the line of my cheek with the softest touch. I sighed and stretched, excitement fluttering in my chest.

What would happen now with Lia home? Once she woke and Galan helped her through whatever happened to her, he and I would be free to enjoy our new lives together.

My stomach rumbled again. The deep growl interrupted my daydreams and told my post-healing body to wake the hell up. There he was. I smiled, watching Galan pad around the clinic, meticulously straightening my remedy bottles and crocks, lining the labels up to face front.

Once he adjusted them and then re-adjusted them, he scrubbed his fingers through his disheveled silver hair and paced toward the kitchen, mumbling wordlessly to himself.

Gods, he looked awful.

"Did she rouse at all in the night?" I croaked, my morning voice in full force.

He shook his head and stepped over to the small bar fridge. "No, though, neither did you." After pouring me a glass of pineapple juice, he brought it to the second recovery bed where I'd crashed last night. "You sleep like the dead after a healing. It is unnerving."

The thought of the healing last night brought Samuel to my mind. I was reeling over what I'd learned while stabilizing him. All the missing pieces finally fell into place, but I had Lexi, Aust, and Tham to fix up, so I couldn't act on it.

Galan rubbed the back of his neck and stretched from side to side. He seemed stiff, probably the result of fighting yesterday, followed by sleeping in a chair beside his sister all night. My imagination fired up again with images of giving him a full body massage.

I sipped at the juice, letting the icy sweetness wash down my throat. The bags under his eyes were an alarming purple against his alabaster skin. "Did you get any rest?"

He shrugged, looking toward Lia lying in the other bed. "I watched her for hours, wondering if she truly lived. She never stirred. It is eerie how still she has been."

I eased myself up against the headboard and set my glass on the side table. "Why don't you take a ten-minute break and wash up? I'll sit with her."

He shook his head, dragging his chair between the two beds so he could be with both of us. I reached to cover his free hand, but he slid it away to adjust Lia's quilt. His mood hadn't registered at first, but his face was grave. "Galan? Look at me." He studied the appliqué on the quilt and ran his palms up and down his thighs. My heart accelerated. "Galan? What is it?"

When he finally raised his head, I studied his face. His mask was in place, numb blankness covering a deliberate calm. A sickening wave of nausea swamped me, and I kicked out of the covers.

"I sat here for hours," he whispered, "watching Lia, revisiting yesterday's battle...." His jaw twitched, and he gave me a stern look.

"Through no fault of yours, I am forced to admit I am simply not a good match for you."

"What? What are you—"

"You are a warrior." He spoke the words slowly and precisely, watching as I absorbed what he said. "I believed I could accept that part of you. Verily, I tried. Yet seeing you yesterday, charge into danger—" He shook his head. "Cowardly as it is, I need my female safe. What if the Scourge took you or killed you? What if they left you in the same lifeless state as Lia? I could not bear losing both of you."

"So, you'd dump me instead? That's insane." The words exploded out of me. "Yes, I'm a Talon enforcer, but I train like a machine. I'm surrounded by skilled warriors. They're bigger and stronger than I am and would give their lives for me."

"I am aware of that." He absently picked at a loose thread and nodded. "I come from a different world. Highbornes live and love. We do not train to battle and kill. If not for Lia, we would never have taken part in an offensive."

"Your world is changing, Galan. Pacifism doesn't—"

"I am aware of that as well. Yet, Lia is home now. I must be true to myself, to her."

"So, fine. No one says you have to fight."

He shook his head as if I was missing something. "You are going to continue with the Talon and seeking those who killed your parents?"

"Fucking right I am."

"And if I asked you to give up that quest, to stay on the mountain and dedicate yourself to your teachings and your healing, would you —*could* you do that for me?"

My lips were numb, along with the rest of me. I stared at him, my heart pounding in my throat. I couldn't think in a straight line. "You'd ask me to give up avenging my parents?"

"I ask if you could allow the past to stay in the past and look to the future."

"I can't do that. My mother was violated, Galan. Those men need to pay."

His eyes grew shiny as he nodded. "In that case, it would be best if

I focus solely on Lia's recovery and building a new life for the two of us. The added complication of—"

"*Complication?*" The hellfire in my chest washed away the cold chill of my skin. "Now I'm a complication? *Bullshit.* You sat up all night worrying about your sister and convinced yourself the world should be safe and simple and sweet. News-*fucking*-flash, Galan, *it's not*. It's messy and cruel. You have to grab happiness wherever and whenever you can."

"I disagree."

"Well, give it time, Highborne. You're new to this world."

He refused to look at me but made a quick swipe at his cheeks. "Lives are what we choose to make of them."

I took a breath and edged toward the end of the bed. "Your mind is made up, then?"

"It is."

My pulse roared in my as the room phased in and out of clarity. "Fine. You park your ass and focus on Lia. Tell yourself you're happy until you realize you're old and lonely and a total fucking idiot. Then, you'll see what a colossal mistake you made today."

"Mayhap." He nodded. "Our time together has been nice. I shall treasure—"

"*Nice?*" My entire body began to shake, my vision clouding red. Sparks began fritzing off my fingertips as I bit my lip. "Look, I need you to get the hell away from me before my temper gets loose." I fought between needing to put my head between my knees and slamming his head through the stone wall. "I feel like hell, and you look like it. So, if you don't want to frighten your poor sister when her eyes finally open, go have a long, hot shower and pull yourself together. I'll try to do the same." Without waiting for his answer, I stumbled to Lia's bedside and hung on to my fall-apart. *Nice?*

Galan and I were amazing, electric, life-altering. Not *nice*.

When the muted splash and trickle of the shower started in the bathroom, I let my tears fall. He didn't want me. Oh. Gods. I sobbed until my whole body went numb. Life without Galan? I didn't even know what to do with that.

Somewhere in the back of my mind, I heard the knocking, but couldn't quite grasp the thought. "Blaze, you up?" Bruin lumbered in, dragging Kobi and Savage behind him. Judging by the unusual shift-n-fidget of the demon and the very usual glare Savage was throwing off, they weren't thrilled to be there. Bruin sniffed the air as I swiped my cheeks and was at my side in two strides. "What? Tell me."

I shook my head, wiped my cheeks again, and nodded to Kobi and Savage. "What's up?"

Bruin threw me a wary glare but didn't push. "Kobi and Sav came to have a boo at Lia."

"Why? What are you thinking?"

"Let's hold off on guessing. I'd hate to be wrong and get Galan worked up for nothing."

"Worked up regarding what exactly?" Galan strode from the bathroom, wearing only his pants and toweling his hair. The muscles of his smooth, bare chest glistened and danced as he back-and-forthed over his rumpled hair. The sight of him, even disheveled and exhausted, sent a dagger through my chest.

He didn't want me.

"Oh, uh, just an idea Samuel came up with when we were discussing Lia."

Galan stopped the hair drying. "I would appreciate if Samuel was not included in conversations regarding my sister. His input is unwelcome and untrustworthy."

Bruin opened his mouth, but when I shook my head, he let it slide. "Go ahead, guys."

Savage released the tie-back of the privacy curtain and swept the heavy drape along its track to encircle Lia's bed.

Kobi bumped knuckles with Galan and joined Savage. "Sorry about this, my man. You three give us a sec, and we'll see what we can figure out." With a tight smile, Kobi pulled the drapes closed, leaving Bruin, Galan, and me on the outs.

"It's okay," Bruin said, squeezing Galan's shoulder. "Finish getting dressed. By the time you're back, they'll be done what they're doing."

"What are they doing?" he snapped, pointing at the curtain. "Have I no right to know?"

"Relax. They won't hurt her. They want to check out her neck and use Kobi's abilities to pinpoint any kind of magical juju that might have been used on her. I swear."

Galan scowled. "And what are Kobi's abilities?"

"You'll have to ask him. That's not my story to tell." Bruin shifted his attention to me. "Hey, did you have it out with Reign yet? Does he know Bloodvine got a name to you?"

"No. He's avoiding me. I thought sending a text saying, 'I'm pissed you've been manipulating me, but you can make it up by helping me kill one of my mom's rapists' was a bit much. The Scourge compound was the first I'd seen him, and he was a little busy cutting raiders in half to bring it up."

"Maybe a little," Bruin agreed. "Well, I saw him ushering half a dozen enforcers into his office ten minutes ago. You might take advantage of the opportunity." He tugged on my hair and let it spring back into place. "How long till Julian verifies the deets?"

"He said a few days."

"Cool. Let me know, and we'll roll out and nail the bastard together."

"You *cannot* be serious." Galan's voice was harsh as he spun on Bruin. "You love her, yet you encourage her to instigate an attack on a man who kills and rapes for sport?"

"Fuck yeah," Bruin said. "It took me twelve years, but I killed every bastard involved in the slaughter of my people. Jade deserves the same satisfaction. That's what the Right of Vengeance is all about."

Galan cursed. "Am I the only male who thinks it wrong to put females in a situation where they are almost certainly going to suffer injury?"

"Yes," I snapped, "but don't *complicate* your life by worrying about what I do."

Galan surged toward me, his eyes blazing. He raised his hand to capture my arm.

Bruin lunged between us, his low growl echoing through the

clinic. "Galan, step the fuck off my sister before you and I have a problem." The two men met chest to chest. Bruin had him by a couple of inches in height and a good seventy pounds, but Galan was fast and angrier than I'd ever seen. Thank the gods he had the sense to focus on the wall behind Bruin's head.

Bruin's nostrils flared. "I smell that you're twisted in knots right now, Highborne, but instead of coming after Jade, maybe you should hammer back hooch until you black the fuck out. That's what the rest of us do when the Fates deal us a ball-gnasher."

No response. Galan's chest rose and fell. His jaw muscles twitched, and his eyes bore a hole in the clinic wall.

"Go finish in the bathroom," Bruin mumbled. "When you come out, we'll discuss what's doing with your sister." The air crackled between them until Galan peeled away and stormed across the clinic. The bathroom door slammed behind him with the boom of a cannon. Bruin turned a look on me. "What the fuck did I miss?"

When my vision blurred, Bruin dropped a heavy arm across my shoulder and pulled me in. Gods, he felt solid and warm. Rubbing my cheek against his T-shirt, I let the tears go. It was a mini-meltdown, but it did the trick. I straightened and accepted the box of tissues he offered. "Galan broke it off. He says the way I choose to live my life is too dangerous for him. He's got enough to worry about with Lia."

"Fidiot." Bruin shook his head. "It's his—"

The slide of the curtain had us both turning. I didn't know a lot about Kobi or Incubus demons in general, but he and Bruin were tight. In the past few years, Bruin had been away a lot, and the two of them worked together.

Savage, on the other hand, was a fierce fighter and a downright scary man. With his dark black eyes, the tats and the piercings, the mute warrior threw off a do-not-approach vibe like you read about.

I didn't know how Bruin thought they'd figure out what happened to Lia, but I hoped he was right.

Galan skulked over at the same time the two of them stepped away from Lia. Kobi studied the hardwood as he reached to his back pocket and slid a pair of dark sunglasses over his eyes. His brow pinched, and his expression cast a whole lot of shadow.

"Tell us," I said.

"It's a form of spirit wound." He scrubbed his hand across his jaw, the light glinting off the multiple piercings through his eyebrow. "The Scourge fissured her soul."

Bruin cursed, shoving his hands deep in his pockets.

Galan looked from Kobi to Bruin to me. "Explain. I am not following."

I drew a deep breath. "He's saying that the Scourge used dark sorcery to capture her soul. Even though her body is well, her spirit is vacant."

"How is that possible?" he choked.

Kobi pulled out two cigarettes and flicked open his lighter. Passing one to Savage, the two of them drew hard until their vices flared to life. After a long pause, Kobi let out a heavy exhale. "Soul Entrapment is a despicable spell that holds a person's soul hostage in a sorcerer's crystal. As long as the Scourge retains possession of that crystal, your sister's spirit is suspended in the nether region of the Veil. She can't find her way back to her corporeal self but can't move forward into the After either. She's trapped."

Galan recoiled. "If I recover the crystal Lia can be restored, yes?"

"In theory," I said. "But we don't know who has the crystal. If they see us coming—"

"If they destroy the crystal," Kobi continued, "Lia will be trapped forever. She'll become an undead."

CHAPTER THIRTY

It was absolutely pissing down. Fat, cold raindrops pelted down from an angry dusk sky, seeping under my battle vest and pooling in the mud around my boots. Murphy's Law, I supposed. Bruin and Cowboy didn't seem to notice, but Lexi and I were rocking the drowned rat look. It didn't matter. Squatting in the dark, behind a rusted-out John Deere and some rotting fence rails, was where I wanted to be. Needed to be.

Stuart 'the skull' Skelly, the bastard Julian had confirmed was part of the death squad that killed my parents, had gone into the dilapidated barn on the back of his remote property two hours ago and hadn't come out since.

He wasn't alone—and that was our problem in a nutshell. Right of Vengeance gave me the go-ahead to confront and off Mr. Skull but didn't extend to snuffing out the budding potential of his Scourge pals. Not unless they attacked us first—which was what Bruin, Lexi, and Cowboy were jonesing for.

"O-two-thirty," Julian's 'military voice' sounded over our headsets. "Sit rep."

"No change," Bruin reported. "Just the four of us doing our best rubber ducky impressions, while the pigs are cozy and dry inside the barn."

"Girls?"

"S'all good," I whispered into my mouthpiece.

"Quack, quack," Lexi said.

Not for the first time, I wished this was over. After Galan had obliterated my hopes for a future, three days ago, I'd considered giving up my fight. That thought lasted as long as it took to picture the scene of slaughter at my farmhouse. I couldn't ignore my parents' suffering. But if Stuart Skelly gave me the final name, I could end this once and for all. Would Galan come around if I finished with my vengeance? He would if he was truly my destiny.

After leaving Galan and Lia in the clinic that afternoon, I had paced the corridor outside Reign's office, waiting for his enforcer meeting to end. I'd worn a path up and down the hall until I thought I'd explode. Taking the offensive had probably been the wrong tack, but I hadn't been firing on all pistons. The half-dozen Talon enforcers gathered around Reign's desk actually looked amused when I barged in.

"Sorry for the interruption, I need a moment with my father."

"Now is not the time, Jade," Reign growled.

"Funny, I've been trying to get face-to-face with you since my recovery and have had the damnedest time, locking you down. It's as if... oh, I don't know, you're avoiding me."

Reign's dark eyes were calculating yet calm. "Give us twenty, gentlemen."

While Rue rolled maps, I had roamed the office. Aside from the charged atmosphere, that room hadn't changed in almost twenty years. Rows upon rows of irreplaceable grimoires lined the bookshelves, filling the space with the earthy smell of leather and parchment. My fingers traced across their spines while everyone cleared out. Reign had spent a lifetime amassing his collection, yet even as clumsy children, he'd encouraged his four orphans to explore the fragile pages. If you counted the hours, I'd bet he sat with us for years, flipping through those books.

JL MADORE

"All right, missy, let's hear it. Get it off your chest." He sank into his chair and leaned back, fingers tented. Even oversized, the leather, desk chair groaned under his weight.

"Get it off my chest? Hmm, where should I start?" I planted both hands on his desk and faced him head-on. "Should I ask why my boyfriend of two years was only supposed to be acting as my bodyguard, or how you ordered him to break up with me and break my heart, or how you arranged for him to stab me—cause *fuck*, I could have used a heads-up on that."

Reign's expression gave nothing away. "I have to speak to Samuel about the confidentiality of orders. It seems he's been opening his mouth."

"Samuel didn't say anything. I healed him after Lia's rescue and saw for myself."

Reign sighed. "I made a tough call, Blaze. It got Samuel into the Scourge compound, and we got Lia back. Don't expect an apology."

"Of course not," I snapped. "Why order him to dump me? You saw what that did to me."

"He wasn't the one for you. He knew it. I knew it, and if you're honest with yourself, you knew it. Your destiny lies elsewhere."

"With Galan?" A flare of hope flickered in my chest. With a wince, I doused it. "He broke it off. I'm not Stepford Wife enough for him." I brushed my hair away from my face and narrowed my sights on Reign. "How long have you been lying to me?"

He'd grunted at the question, his jaw tightening. "Since the day I found you in that cellar."

My whole life? I shook my head. If there was one thing I would have laid coin on, it was that Maximus Reign loved me. But at that moment, the first in seventeen years, I didn't trust him. The blow of that reality was like losing my foothold and dangling over a precipice. Everything I considered a given in life teetered on lies.

That's when I'd stormed out. I hadn't told him Julian was verifying a name and getting the kill sanctioned through the Seelie Court. I hadn't trusted Reign enough to let him in.

The grind of metal on metal snapped me back to the barnyard.

Someone was hefting the barn door open, the weight of it fighting to slide in its rusty track. I touched the hilt of my dagger.

"Naptime's over, y'all." Cowboy drawled, thick as molasses. "Up and at em."

My backup waited outside, covering Mr. Skull's guests as they dispersed and hopefully Flashed straight to hell. I slid in the side door, unfurled my whip, and called on my bard powers. If Mr. Skull heard me walk up behind him, he didn't let on. He seemed wholly focused on the maps and papers pinned to the wood on the inside of the barn wall.

"Stuart Skelly?" He jumped and spun. "In accordance with the Right of Vengeance, I sentence you to death for the wrong you inflicted on me and mine seventeen years ago."

The bastard had the gall to look relieved as he assessed me up and down. Coughing up a gob of phlegm, he spat it on the ground between us. Wiping his mouth on the back of his sleeve, he sneered up at me. "Be more specific, dollface, I was rather active in my thirties."

Tightening my hold on the braided leather grip of my whip, I stepped within range. The barn was a long rectangle with an open center alley and closed off pens running up either side. "On a small farm, the afternoon of the summer solstice, you and your raid party eviscerated my father on the front porch of a yellow farmhouse then proceeded to follow my mother into a barn very much like this one."

I glanced at the bale hooks, pitchforks, and halters still hanging on their rusty pegs. Beyond the musky skunk of Scourge, the place held the sweet smell of straw. There was no room for animals in the stalls, though. Each cubicle was packed from the plank floor to hayloft with wooden crates. The days of this being a working farm long forgotten.

It was some kind of Scourge depot now.

"My mother was tortured, raped, and killed because she wouldn't tell you where I hid."

A light of understanding lit in dark eyes, and he laughed. It was a chunky, wet sound. He spit again. "Ah, I do remember that. I was so green then I felt bad about the way that woman was ravaged." He took a step closer and dropped his hand to the dagger sheathed on his hip.

He winked, and his face distorted into a hideous smile. "Well, until it was my turn. Then I fucked her hard and deep. I swear I nearly ripped her in two."

"*You bastard.*" My whip cracked through the air, narrowly missing his neck as he barreled at me, drawing his dagger. The edge of the blade glinted blue in the light. I sent out a sound burst. As the air exploded in a cacophony of eardrum splitting chaos, the bastard dropped his dagger and grappled me.

I staggered under his weight, fighting to free my hands. Shuffling through loose straw, I connected my knee to his crotch and freed myself enough to press the handle of my whip against his throat. As we struggled, my mind flipped through the macabre pages of my family album, revisiting scenes from that afternoon in the barn. Rage boiled in my gut. I was a scared little girl back then. I wasn't now. Every last one of them would pay.

Skelly's shoulder rose as his fist swung. Before I reacted, white spots exploded behind my eyes. He yanked me back by the hair until I was staring at the crumbling boards of the hayloft above. By sheer weight, he forced me skittering to the back of the alley, struggling toward *the trap door.*

Built into the floor of the barn was a door leading to the cellar below. With the door propped open against the back barn wall, the black rectangular opening sucked at us like a black hole. As we struggled, I had a feeling he envisioned me becoming his guest down there.

Screw that. With trembling hands, I clawed at his face and drew one of the daggers from the bottom edge of my battle vest. As he hefted me over the opening, I twisted, thrust the blade into his sweet spot, and pulled him in tight. If I was going down, he was coming along for the ride. As he exploded into a mass of black goo, I tumbled backward. Pain seared the back of my head, and everything disappeared.

At some point, I became aware. Aware of a throbbing in my skull, which made me sorry I was no longer unconscious. Aware of lying sprawled on my side, my face mashed into the dirt. The grit of moldy soil caked the inside of my lips and lodged up my nose. Rolling to my back was a big no-go. There was a pile of Mr. Skull on top of me. I tried to shift under his weight, and fireworks went off inside my eyes. A fiery sting licked across my shoulder and down my side.

With either sheer grit or red-headed hellfire, I forced my body to twist the other way. Bile slammed the back of my throat. There was no preventing my lunch from fertilizing the dirt. My eyes watered and my shoulder screamed. I wretched. And again. And once more just for fun.

After my vision cleared and my eyes adjusted to the blackness, I studied my surroundings.

Oh gods, the root cellar.

As my heart really got pumping and my airways closed off, I fought the urge to blackout. Galan. I needed him. I thought about that storage room in Toronto and how he soothed my crazies. Then I remembered the blow-out we'd had hours ago. He was livid I let my past endanger my life. I reminded him my life was none of his concern. I was a warrior.

Although, at that moment, giving up the fight didn't seem like such a bad idea.

The crash and thud above me brought me back into focus. Someone was battling in the barn above. The growls and deep approving laughter told me Bruin was having some fun. The wafting stench of skunk and rotting death told me he wasn't alone. I imagined Bruin slicing through Scourge bastards with one of those bale hooks in each hand, goring them, staining the barn walls black with their tar ichor.

Kick their asses, Bear.

More footsteps above. Bits of straw floated down between the cracks in the floor. I raised a shaky hand and wiped at my face. *Shit.* It was sticky and warm, the result of my free-fall tango through the trap door with the late Mr. Skull. *Get up.* Nope. There was something wrong. The good news was the searing pain was holding off my usual trip down panic alley.

"Blaze, *Check in*. Where are you?" Julian shouted. It wasn't in my ear.

I fumbled with my good hand, fingering across the dirt floor until

I found my comm. I pulled it to my mouth and tried to speak. Nothing. I swallowed. The iron grit of soil and aftertaste of vomit made me gag. "Jules," I croaked. "Cellar… trapped…hurt."

Bruin swore above me now, long runs of colorful obscenity punctuated by the rhythmic pounding of a man getting a beat-down. "I'm coming, Blaze." Bruin let out an ungodly, animal bellow. More footsteps and another crash.

"*Shit*. Julian, somebody phoned a friend. We're getting swarmed here. *All call.*"

Julian sounded an all call in the background and then spoke to me. "Blaze, how bad?"

The fire in my chest expanded, boiling up through my body. "Need out," I whispered.

This was my fault. I couldn't be locked in this stupid cellar while my family fought for their lives—not again. I'd already lost Galan. I wouldn't lose them. The *Scourge* needed to pay for Lia and Aust's father and my parents. Not my family.

My head swam. The burning in my gut grew. It coated my skin with incendiary heat and sparked from my fingers.

Fucking Scourge. With a whoosh and crackle, it escaped. I wasn't a powerless child anymore. The scent of burning barn-board filled my sinuses. The barn ignited like kindling, as if the old wooden structure wanted the battle to end.

Well, all right then. Let it be over…

~

I woke in a panic, my heart pounding in my ears. Reign's obsidian stare locked on mine. Sitting on the edge of my king-sized bed, he looked tired, and his eyes much too glossy.

"Bruin and Lexi—"

"Fine," he said, pushing me back down. "What the hell were you thinking?"

I meant to apologize, but my voice didn't come.

He nodded. His brindle hair flashed copper and gold in the dim light of my candles. "I almost didn't get you out of that cellar in time. That was quite a bonfire you started."

"Couldn't help—"

Reign placed his hand against my cheek. "Tight spaces have never been your best event."

His calloused hand against my skin erased the fight we had and went a long way to ease the hurt of him keeping things from me. I drew a deep breath. "Did everyone get home safe?"

"It was close but other than a few singed eyebrows and some smoke inhalation s'all good." He rubbed the bridge of his nose and sighed. "Seems, that barn was a Scourge war base, and you four stumbled right into their lap. While Bruin and I got you out, Cowboy, Lexi, and the team salvaged what they could from the barn."

"How'd you get there so fast?" Julian's all call wouldn't have reached Reign in time to get to me. He must have been on the move.

His eyes grew serious as he squeezed my shoulder. "Galan. He demanded a head-set from Julian. He listened in, and when the shit hit, he came gunning for me."

I wasn't sure if I was excited or pissed about that. "He needs to mind his own."

"He loves you."

"No. He loves part of me. He rejects the other."

Reign's jaw twitched as he leaned closer. "Love is not an exact science, Jade. People make mistakes, even when it's for the right reasons."

The way he squeezed my hand, we weren't only talking about Galan. That was the closest I'd ever gotten to an apology from the mighty Maximus Reign. We sat there in silence, staring at each other. Gods, I wished he'd tell me what was on his mind. Just once.

"Your mother was the closest friend I ever had," Reign said, as if he'd read my mind. His voice trailed off, filled with a dark sadness I'd never heard before. "I loved her."

"You knew her?" I choked. "Why is this the first time I'm hearing this?"

Reign blinked fast and cleared his throat, staring into nothingness.

"She had the gift of speaking over the wind, like you. She called to me that afternoon. I Flashed to the farm. When I got there… when I rounded the corner, and those motherfuckers were bent over her body, I lost my mind. I ripped them to shreds, but it was too late to save her. Before she died, she told me where you were. She made me swear I'd take care of you. I tried to be the best father—"

I pressed my fingers over his lips. "You were stellar."

He scooped me into his arms. Holding me close, his heart pounded against my chest. "Funny thing about forgiveness," he said. "Sometimes, it frees you up to see where the other person was coming from."

CHAPTER THIRTY-ONE

I watched the ball of orange fire sink in the distant sky and sent up yet another prayer of thanks. I was alive, Reign and I were back on track, and Julian, Lexi, and Bruin were making strides in deciphering the intel from the barn. Killing Stuart Skelly and almost dying in the process made me realize Galan wasn't all wrong. He had a point—at least about some of it.

A bad past wasn't worth destroying my future.

I ran a hand down the smooth stone column in the ancient Fae ceremonial circle. I hadn't been here for years. Reign used to bring me when I was younger. He said it was my special place, its existence known to only a few of us that grew up on the mountain. Like many other ceremonial sites, it was shaped like a horseshoe with two concentric circles made up of standing stones, lintel stones, and monoliths. Our very own Stonehenge.

In the light of day, it was impressive. In the darkness of night, it was different. The power of the Fae gods flowed in currents underneath the site. These Ley-lines were invisible and usually undetectable by anyone who wasn't Fae, but I'd always been able to feel their power. It was even stronger at night.

Traditionally, offerings were made under the blanket of darkness. Tonight, would no different, except I was the one up for offering.

My Highborne family had prepared me, in secret over the past week setting the stage for the evening. They draped the offering table in white gossamer, midnight blue silk, and orchids. Hundreds of pillar candles sat along the tops of the stones, fifteen feet above the ground. Without my fire affinity, they would have been a pain to light, but as it was, I had the whole place glowing golden in a matter of seconds, hundreds of stars flickering in our own little sky.

Platters of food and bottles of wine were lying in wait on a fur pelt atop one of the fallen stones. For luck, Nyssa had set out the wine glasses she and Iadon had used for their mating ceremony. She had also prepared all of Galan's favorite foods. In hopes of either softening him up or wearing him down, I wasn't sure which.

Iadon took my request for something sultry to wear and created a gown beyond my imagination. It reminded me of the gowns worn by ancient Fae royalty from Reign's books. The flowing, ice blue dress was an inspiration. The sheer chiffon was slit from my ankle up to my hip, showing a lot of skin as the summer breeze caught the fabric. Subtle draping of the neckline wrapped over one shoulder and barely contained me. The fabric gathered in an elegant knot over my heart, secured by a jeweled, silver arrow brooch.

I laughed at the precariousness of that arrow.

My silver, vine armband, and the amethyst choker were given a thumbs up by Nyssa. Amethyst was worn by healers for centuries, recognized for focusing spiritual power. Wearing it always made me strong, and I was counting on that again tonight.

The only missing element to the evening was Galan. He should have arrived by now. Tham was told to pry him away from Lia's bedside, get him dressed, and delivered here. That was ages ago. He hadn't come to visit me after Reign brought me home from the barn, and for the first time, I wondered if he truly was done with me. Maybe I was already too late.

As if the Fates heard my thoughts...

"Merciful gods," Galan breathed, stepping amongst the ruins.

Tham blew me a kiss and disappeared back the way he'd come. Galan stood mouth agape, looking anguished. "When I am certain I have seen the pinnacle of beauty, you reach new heights. You are exquisite, Blossom."

"Thank you." I tamped down the butterflies tickling my insides. "You're quite stunning yourself."

Galan's midnight blue jacket was embroidered with silver olive leaves and hung perfectly over a crisp white tunic. "If your aim is to tempt me—"

"Relax, Galan." My voice quivered. Dammit, I didn't know how to do this. I drew in a deep, unsteady breath. "Don't close doors on me yet, Highborne."

Galan walked slowly around the pillars. He paused when he saw the silk-draped offering table, staring at it in silence. "I should go."

"Galan, stop. Word on Lia's crystal might come tomorrow or in six years or six decades. You can't live in a vacuum. You love me, no matter what you say."

"I never denied it." The ache in his voice broke my heart. "Yet, a coupling based solely on love would be a mistake."

"How can you say that?"

He stepped in front of me, his jaw set. "You know how. You are reckless with your life. If the Scourge were to come after Lia or me, where would you be?"

"Standing right by your side."

"Exactly." He brushed my cheek with the back of his fingers. "Do you know what it did to me to hear that Skelly male beat you? You were nearly killed, Jade. *Again.*" His fingers closed around my wrist and brought my knuckles up to his lips. "I have no idea how to reconcile my fear for you. If what your oracles predict is true, Lia and I may be targeted by every Scourge raider in the realm. You are sure to be hurt, and since you refuse to value your own safety—"

"I'm not helpless, Galan. Danger was in my life long before you."

His brow tightened as he stared passed me to the gossamer canopy. "I am inconsolably aware of that, yet the Scourge will consider you my weakness. What if they come for you?"

"*Let them.* I am not your weakness—I'm your strength. You want me to live a long healthy life. Well, the two of us being apart isn't living. A few things became clear to me while lying on the dirt floor in that barn." I fisted my hand over my chest. "You brought me to life, Galan. I belong to you, and you belong to me."

Galan scrubbed rough fingers through his hair and raised a pained gaze to the heavens. "I cannot—"

"I'll give up being on the front lines." I steadied my hands, swallowed, and let the words fall in a rush. "I'll go on raids as back up for the injured and focus on teaching and healing at the clinic. You said that's what you wanted, right?"

Galan's vivid blue eyes locked on me.

"I would do it. For you," I said, through an aching throat. I held out my hand. He made no move to take it. His expression emptied until there was nothing left, his mask firmly in place. My eyes brimmed. "You truly don't want this?" I clasped at the pain ripping through my temples. I couldn't breathe. My vision sparked white as the world spun, and my knees buckled.

In the next moment, I was against Galan's chest, his arms strong as steel around me. "Blossom, your life was full before the Fates thrust me in your path. Return to that life again."

I leaned into him, shaking my head. He smelled amazing, familiar, and warm. It steadied me. It strengthened my resolve. "You told me that a male's mind, body, and soul were claimed by his female." I brushed my lips against his throat as my hands flattened on his chest. Grabbing his lapels, I pushed his jacket over his shoulders, and I tossed it over a stone. "True?"

"Yes."

"Well, I am your female, and unless you can say you don't love me—unless you flat out deny me—I'm claiming you." My heart thundered as I undid the tie on the side of his tunic, and it fell open. He sucked in a breath. My hands weren't steady, but I was determined. My fingers splayed across his exposed chest, down his navel to the waistband of his leather pants. With my eyes locked on him, I waited for our electricity to surge. "I'll give up fighting. I'll do what you ask.

We'll work it out, so you're comfortable with my life. Just tell me you want me."

"Of course I want you, Jade. You are the blood that keeps my heart beating." He groaned. The sound was deep and hungry, and my body ignited. "I never wanted anything more."

Destiny. I knew that as concretely as I knew my name.

With his gaze locked on mine, I pulled the silver arrow pin holding my dress in place. With one motion, the sheer fabric fell to the stony ground and pooled around my feet.

"By the love of all things holy," he gasped, his eyes rolling back. Galan sank to his knees and wrapped his arms around my waist. "Have you any idea how you tempt me?"

I laced my hands into his hair and pulled his head back to look at me. "I hope so."

Strong fingers spanned my hips, my ribs, and my back while he nuzzled his way up my front. When he stood, he hesitated a moment, then cursed more eloquently than I would have believed possible. The passion in the kiss that followed ignited our bodies like dried grass in a wildfire—crackling and burning—consuming everything in its path. His embrace was masculine perfection, hard as steel yet soft as silk. I moved to his cheek and then angled his head to nip the peak of his ear.

He hissed. "How am I to remain of a logical mind when you seduce me so? Verily, you steal my strength of will." My hand slid down the front of his leathers, cupping the swell. "Oh, Blossom," he growled. His hips rolled forward, pressing into my palm.

"Fight if you must, Highborne, but you said you're mine, and I'm taking what's mine."

Galan's eyes grew dark and hooded. Light fingers traced my shoulders, continuing down my arms until he grasped my wrists and wrapped them around his neck. With one elegant motion, he swept under my knees and lifted me against his heaving chest. Carrying me tight against his body, he walked to the offering table and laid me under the billowing canopy.

"Be certain, Blossom. If we succumb to our passion, we are committed."

"I love you, Highborne. Now shut up and get naked. I have things I want to do to you."

In a blur of silver, he shed his boots and pants and stalked up the silk draped, stone slab. He was a panther on the prowl. "How could a male deny such a heartfelt overture?"

"Hopefully, he can't," I breathed.

"Indeed." He crawled up my body, his erection bobbing proudly between us. He licked my navel, nipped up my ribcage, sucked my tight nipple into his mouth with a growl. With slow, lazy pushes, he moved his hips in and back, stroking his arousal against my thigh. The friction sent shafts of heat down my spine, through my nerve endings, until every cell of my body inflamed with it. "If you are certain, my succulent Blossom, I am yours evermore."

"I am."

"Then, prepare to be mated most thoroughly."

A cry tore from my throat as his fingers pushed into the hot, moist core of my sex. It was too much, and yet not nearly enough. I arched off the mattress as his lips suckled, his fingers stroked, and his hips rocked against me. I tugged him, shifting my legs to get closer, wanting him to push inside me.

Husky laughter vibrated against my breast. He let go of my nipple with a *pop*. "Easy, love. I read about human coitus, and it can be quite uncomfortable on the first encounter. Let me service you first and ready your body."

I giggled. "You read about human coitus? Oh my, you are the sexiest bookworm-geek ever."

"A geek, am I?" What he did next with his fingers had me hurtling into an orgasm fast and hard. I was still flying outside myself when he shifted over me and pressed between my thighs. With my core still pulsing in heated waves, he rocked his hips, demanding more space. "*Amin mela lle*, Jade."

I gripped his shoulders, and he thrust forward.

The pain was raw, and I froze at the invasion. When he made to withdraw, I held him still. "No, give me one sec." I closed my eyes and focused on my breathing. I could have healed, but I wanted to keep every sensation our mating. After a moment, the sting faded, and I relaxed. "Okay, I'm good."

Galan arched a brow. "Are you certain? If it is painful—"

"No. I'm sure." As his arms flexed and his hips began to sway, the feeling of invasion transformed into amazement. "You're very big. It feels like you fill every inch of me."

He barked out a laugh, the vibration creating a peculiar tingle inside me. "You say the sweetest things." Galan pressed and retreated, a teasing rhythm at first, but gaining in fervor.

"*Amin mela lle, Dwinn.*"

Something flashed in Galan's eyes as the words left my lips. With no warning, Galan became a maelstrom: his mouth, his hands, his body, his heat. It was good we were on stone because my bed might not have withstood the wildness he released. Muscled shoulders blocked the stars and thrust in abandon. I gripped onto him, digging my nails into his flesh to hold my place as our bodies meshed together.

Galan roared, pressing so far inside me, I felt our souls crush and unite as one. "*Mine,*" he vowed in Elvish, "now and evermore you are my female, my love. *My beloved mate.*"

Hands and legs entwined as our bodies rolled in sexy waves. My breath came hard and fast. "*Oh gods,*" I cried, overcome by a sense of transformation—metamorphosis.

Suddenly I felt what Galan was feeling.

It was more than a heightened awareness of two bodies. It was a physical sensation of touch. As I ran my hand down the contours of his side, I felt the caress tingle down my skin. Our bodies were linked, sharing sensation, doubling our pleasure. I struggled to breathe. It was incredible but too much.

A firestorm shot through me, hurled me careening out of body and mind. I cried out his name with what little breath I had, shaking, shuddering, aching for him.

It wasn't gentle or calm. The desire that exploded inside me was as wild as the hunger that raged in his eyes. Galan couldn't hold out. Pitching his shoulders forward in one great thrust he collapsed, whispering in Elvish. He wasn't making coherent sense, but the tone was reverent almost devout.

It was a long while before either of us moved, then Galan shifted and pulled me over his chest. "Are you well, Blossom?"

"More than well." I swiped my hair out of my face and smiled at him. "And the moment I can breathe, we are *sooo* doing that again." I circled his smooth, pink nipple with my fingers. "So, after a long and tortured century, was it what you expected?"

"Not even close." Galan exhaled, cradling my head. "I have hungered many times and burned for you until I thought I might not survive it. Never would I have—" He laughed, biting my shoulder. "I have not but left you, yet there is nothing I need more than to be inside you again. I wonder if I shall always burn so, or can I be stated?"

I stroked my hand down the front of him. "Only one way to find out."

After what seemed like a lifetime, but surely was no more than three or four hours, Galan sank back onto the silk of the sheets with me draped across his chest in a delicious sensual fog. His hand caressed a long sweep down my back, resting on the rise of my hip. When I had recovered enough to think, I rolled onto my side to find him staring at me.

"You look so proud of yourself, Blossom." He chuckled, propping up on his elbow. "I was not much of a conquest. Seductress. My resistance was lost the moment I saw you." He glanced down to my dress, lying in a crumpled heap. "Nyssa and Iadon were co-conspirators in this, I presume."

"Guilty."

Glancing to the stars in the velvet night sky, he ran his hand through his hair. "This is perfect, Blossom," he whispered. "You have given me the most memorable moment of my life." He kissed my palm and wove our fingers together.

"Galan? I'm not complaining, but what happened? When we first made love? One minute, you were loving me, and the next, you were possessed. Don't misunderstand, the intensity had me unhinged, but what was that?"

Galan brushed my hair back from my face, and I couldn't stop grinning like an idiot. "Elves are given two names at birth, one by our parents which we use publicly and one which is imprinted directly onto our soul, given to us by the gods. That name, our soul name, is shared only with the most intimate lover, family, or friend."

As a cool breeze blew through the canopy, he gathered the sheet and draped it across my body. "When an Elf's soul name is spoken, it touches him to the depth and breadth of his emotions. Each of us instinctively knows our own and can share it with those we love and trust. It is the greatest honor a Highborne can bestow. Mine is *Dwinn*." He laughed, shaking his head. "In one century and ten, I have shared my name with my *naneth*, Lia, Tham, and Nyssa. They are the only four to ever speak to my soul until you spoke it tonight.

"How did I know to say it?"

Galan's smile widened, and the starlight sparkled in his eyes. "That is the incredible thing. It is part of Recognition. Elves experience a telepathic sharing of soul names when they find their perfect other half. Ordinarily, we fall in love, bond, and give our soul names to our mates. It is accepted and wonderful in its own rite. When Nyssa, Tham, or Lia speak my name, it is deeply personal and private. I never imagined anything could touch me more deeply."

"But it did?"

Galan laughed then flopped on his back. "When you called to my soul." His voice caught, deep and husky. "I have no words. It was a hundred times more intimate, mayhap a thousand."

"But I'm not an Elf."

"True, and I wondered about that myself. I believe that since you worship Castian Latheron and he has shown his favor for you as well, he gave you my soul name because he approves of our union."

I delighted in that and met his lips for a kiss. As I pulled back, I held his face to mine. "I told you we were destined to be together."

"You did, and you also told me you didn't believe in destiny." He rolled over me, pressing his hard body into the softness of mine.

"That was before I met you."

He hovered, his eyes glittering in the dancing candlelight. "I have something to give you." He shuffled over to where his jacket lay over a rune stone. Fishing in the inside pocket, he withdrew a small cloth bundle tied with a silky ribbon. "For our *Ambar Lenn,* we were each to carry a talisman until we found our way. This is mine, and by all rights, it now belongs to you." He unwrapped a silver pendant and held it for me to look at.

"My mother's ancestral grandmother, Rheagan, as we now know, handed down this pendant from the time of the exile. In each generation, the oldest male inherited it to give to his true love. In my memories of my mother, I remember how beautifully it hung over her heart. She had no brothers, so it remained in her possession, becoming mine after her passing, and now it belongs to you."

"Galan, it's beautiful." I traced the graceful, silver lines. The pendant was a flower, its stem wrapped and woven with delicate silver ribbons. Five teardrop cut, hematite stones made up the petals surrounding a garnet center. "It's spectacular. Are you sure you want me to have it, it was your mother's?"

"I have loved it my entire life. It symbolizes the love she had for me, my father, and Lia as well. Now it symbolizes my love for you. I would be honored if you would wear it."

Galan hung the pendant over my heart and beamed as it shimmered against my skin. "As of this moment, you belong to me as I belong to you."

I couldn't decipher the emotion swirling in his eyes but felt his turmoil roiling in my gut. "What's wrong?"

The muscle in his jaw twitched. His voice was nothing more than a whisper. "Nothing, love. I am merely emotional." I arched a brow, and he sighed. He picked up my hand and kissed it. "I was thinking of Lia. How excited she would be that I have found you and Recognized."

"You'll get the chance to tell her. I am sure of it."

"When you say the words, how can I believe anything other?"

"Please. I'm far from perfect." When he shook his head, I flung my hair out of the way and brushed my lips over his. "Shut up and make love to me, Highborne." I giggled as his body reacted to my request. "*Dwinn.*" He shuddered and pulled me tight. "*Dwinn.*" He moaned, and I ran my fingers over the tips of his ears. "*Dwinn.*" He seized me and lost himself again.

Just before the sun pierced the crest of the summit, Galan woke me with a kiss. He laced his fingers with mine, his voice thick and smooth. "Do you still wish to watch the sun rise on our first day as mates?"

As we lay together in our gossamer haven, we watched as the sky lightened. Crimson and pink swirls rose with the sun's light, painting the canvas for the day. I was lost in the sensation of Galan rubbing against me, his hands, his lips, his hair, tickling my skin. After being out of step, our lives had finally synchronized. "Are you really mine? Forever?" I asked.

"Forever, love." He traced the dragon tattoo on my hip then expanded the circuit up my back. Invisible patterns made a creative exploration of our new bond. Who knew sleeping naked could be so decadent? My body arched as I stretched awake, and Galan nipped my shoulder. His tongue danced across my skin as his hair dangled and tickled my neck.

I closed my eyes and just let it all wash over me. "*Mmm* what a glorious way to wake up. You're going to have to sleep in so I can wake you up like this tomorrow."

His body shook against me. "Elves do not sleep like you lazy humans. Four hours of quality reverie is as revitalizing for us as eight hours of sleep for you."

"So, what did you do with all those extra hours?"

"I watched you sleep, listened to you breathe, and drank in your beauty." He winked, a faint blush coloring his ears. "You are enchanting when you are still."

I studied his expression. His smile was provocative but didn't look like he was joking. "So, have I missed anything interesting this morning?"

"Nothing." He smirked, looking terribly guilty. I raised a brow, and his ears flushed brighter. "In truth, you might have missed a *few* things." His smile gave me goosebumps. "I would be happy to catch you up."

"You're terri—"

The air stirred around us. A golden light accompanied the sensation of a fissure of power opening around us. Galan watched my gaze harden. I sensed a presence behind him.

One of absolute power.

CHAPTER THIRTY-TWO

*G*alan launched to his feet, and I followed, arms raised. After my heart skipped a beat, it pounded back to business. I shook my head. Galan was fully dressed and so was I.

What the— "Where are we?"

We'd Flashed from our romantic rendezvous to a palace throne room like none I'd ever seen. The long, open chamber put shame to even the finest parts of Haven castle. Draped in shades of autumn, the ochre walls were accented in butter, crimson and green. Woven tapestries, Fae art, and ancient artifacts were lit by the warm golden brilliance of fireflies flitting and frolicking in the fading light of afternoon sun.

A movement drew our attention toward the seat of power. The semi-circular altar on the far side of the room terminated with a vaulted ceiling above an ostentatious, gilded throne.

A man—indescribably handsome—sat askew. With one knee bent over the arm of his perch, he bobbed his foot, looking almost bored. Almost. He watched us with cunning alertness, his aristocracy as obvious as his omnipotence.

He was power incarnate.

And we were, what—two mice caught in his maze?

JL MADORE

"Castian come to me," I hissed. My hair swirled as the warm breeze filled my senses with bergamot and lavender.

"I am here, child." The melody of the stranger's voice was home to me. He rose from the thrown and glided down the steps of the altar, arms open. "I am always with you, *Mir*."

Grappling with understanding, I looked at him again and stumbled to my knees.

Galan grabbed my elbow and tried to hold me back. "Are you implying—"

"I needn't imply, *Dwinn*. I am." His words rang like bells tolled by the heavens.

Although beautiful, Castian's features were unmistakably masculine. Long, wavy chestnut hair framed a square-cut jaw and set off the brilliant emerald green of his eyes. It was easy to see that he had fathered the creation of the Elves. They had his grace. Even though his feet were bare, he glided across the inlaid marble as if he hovered above the floor.

"Castian Latheron, my Lord." Galan took a knee by my side and lowered his gaze.

When Castian's hand rested on my head, an electric charge tingled from my scalp through my body and sent goosebumps prickling along my skin. He placed his other hand on Galan's. The instant the circuit was connected, a white-hot fire spread across my shoulders. I gritted my teeth until my jaw ached, and my vision fritzed. Galan's fists tightened and pressed hard against the floor. The scent of bergamot grew until it was rife in the air.

A moment later, the burn was gone. I glanced over my shoulder and saw the edges of a tattoo inked onto my skin.

Castian raised his gaze, his expression serene. "I bless your union," he said, his eyes swirling with emotion. "With all my heart."

I swept my hair to one side. We'd been branded, marked by the ruler of the realm—the God of the gods.

Galan traced the design across my skin with the pad of his finger. "It's intricate Elven scrollwork of vines and leaves from shoulder to shoulder." He looked to Castian. "Is mine the same?" Galan beamed when Castian nodded, then returned to my back. "Oh, Blossom, it is stunning."

"As is your coupling," Castian said. "You cannot grasp the importance of your bond, but the ripples of your union will reach still waters across the Realm of the Fair." Castian stroked Galan's hair before looking at me. "Rheagan's heir. A worthy and wise choice, my child."

"I didn't choose him because of ancestry."

The gentle smile Castian wore made me think he was privy to some inside joke. "Every queen needs her guardian, *Mir*." He placed his hands under my elbow and raised me to my feet. With a nod to Galan, my husband rose as well. *My husband.*

"Reign has done well as your guardian until now. You have grown into an incredible female. Your father's heart swells with pride and adoration."

"My father is dead," I whispered.

Castian stroked my cheek with the slightest of touches, a caress of velvet on my skin. "Not all is as you perceive it, *Mir*. Events were set in motion long ago, which brought you to where you are now. Finally, you two have the opportunity to set things right."

"Why have you brought us here, Lord?" Galan put his arm around my waist. "What are we to set right?"

He pointed toward an archway leading outside. "It is time, please, come, sit."

With a hand against the small of my back, Castian escorted me to a multi-tiered terrace. My mind spun. Was it real? Scanning beyond the rail of the balcony, the lush green and aqua grounds were home to birds singing tunes I'd never heard, flowers blooming in colors I'd never seen, and the warm breeze carrying scents I'd never smelled. *Behind the Veil.* Galan and I were Behind the Veil.

My heart thundered in my ears as I absorbed everything about... everything.

"Sit." Castian pulled out a chair that overlooked the grounds.

The heat of the afternoon was blocked by the trellis above. Overgrown with dense vines and laden with bunches of grapes, flowers, berries, and little creatures hustling and hiding amongst the greenery, the lattice provided a secluded shelter with a surreal charm.

Beyond the balcony, a herd of deer grazed lazily on the rolling grounds. "They don't even look timid," I said.

Castian's brow furrowed. "Why would they? They are my guests; therefore, they live confident and unguarded lives."

I studied the setting as a whole. "So, this is Behind the Veil."

"To you, yes, but others call it something different." He turned and pointed to the dark hazel peak of a mountain. That is Mount Olympus, and there is Elysium." He walked to the end of the balcony and pointed out over the lands. "That island is Tir na nOg, there is Valhalla and those golden pavilions there are in Vaikuntha. It is breathtaking, is it not?"

"It is. But why bring us here?"

His smile was devastatingly charming. He took my hand in his and rubbed his thumb against my palm. "I have waited for this moment for years, Jade, to disclose truths about your future and your past."

"What truths?" My voice cracked, but when I swallowed, my mouth remained dry.

"Truths about childhood and destiny." He hesitated, looking out into nothingness. "Your mother, Abbey, was a gifted woman. She wasn't a healer like you, but shifted form and possessed strong prophetic abilities." Castian brushed my cheek and met me with his gemstone gaze. "She didn't discuss her ability to prophesize, but your father knew, and so did Reign. It came from her gypsy heritage, you see."

"My mother was a gypsy?"

Castian nodded. "From the Carpathian Mountains. She wandered the mountains one spring with her caravan, and your father found her praying by a riverbed. His soul was hers from the moment their eyes met. They were never meant to be together, but their love exceeded reason—they Recognized."

"Like Galan and I?"

He nodded. "When Abbey became pregnant, your parents were thrilled. They knew, given your parentage, you would be gifted.

However, as a toddler, it became obvious that even they had underestimated your powers. You called on enormous stores of power without instruction. Your control was astounding and grew stronger each day. They tried to keep your gifts private, but one night, your mother was overcome by a vision. She witnessed Scourge soldiers coming for you. They knew what you were going to be capable of."

"And they killed her because of me."

Castian brushed my chin with his finger. "Abbey was desperate to protect you—to hide you from the evils of our world. Because of his station, your father could not go with you. Instead, he assigned a guardian, Drew Glaster, to accompany your mother and take his place as your protector."

"He wasn't my father?" My heart ached as a million childhood images raced through my head. *Was any of it real?*

"Reign refused to let your mother leave." Castian shook his head. "That man is stubborn as rocks."

I nodded. "Especially if someone he loves is in danger."

"True. So, Reign insisted your father assign him to accompany them. Even then, Reign was a warrior with legendary fighting skills. So, those three men dedicated themselves to protect you: your father, Drew, and Reign. With your identities altered and gifts bound, you ventured off to live a normal life in a provincial town."

"So, it was all a lie?"

"Your father's hands were tied. He'd seen your future woven in the tapestries of the Fates. For your destiny to be fulfilled, he had to choose his love or his child."

"Well, that's a shitty choice." My voice hitched. "So, my mother was sacrificed for me?"

"She wouldn't have it any other way. Your father—"

"Enough. Stop saying that! That doesn't tell me anything." I turned, my hair starting to rise with the heat of my temper. Galan placed his hand firmly on my thigh under the table, but I couldn't stop now. "Who is my father?"

"The only man, other than Reign, who watched over you, loved and protected you. The man you turn to whenever you need help."

"I... uh, are you saying?" I froze, lost in the impossibility. "Oh, gods, give me a second." I dropped my head to the table to stave off the blackout rushing up on me. My stomach spun while I tried to hold it together.

"Yes, Jade, that's what I'm saying." I looked up into his emerald green eyes, *my* eyes. Galan had turned that sickly shade of mint I'd seen in the hallway at the Diva's Den. I was probably close to the same shade. *Castian is my father?*

Part of me wanted to collapse into his arms. Part of me wanted to scream that he left me an orphan. Part of me was pissed that the two men I considered my fathers, my whole life, were only bodyguards lying to me. No.

I would never regret my life with either of them.

I tried to think of something intelligent to say, my mind one giant void. I was blank except for the collapsing pain in my chest for the family I'd lost. I drew hard, trying to pull air into my lungs. His choice to let me live had cost my mother her life.

What kind of choice was that? I swiped at the tears streaming down my cheeks with the back of my hand. Tasting their salty warmth, I fought the hitching sobs about to overtake me and walked to the railing.

Castian ghosted to my side and paused. "Now that you know, do you hold me in your heart with love or hatred?" The quiver in Castian's voice broke the dam on my sobs. I squeezed the rail as my knees buckled. He caught me against his chest. "Jade, say you forgive me."

"Are you really my father?"

"I am." He hugged me tighter and pressed his lips to my forehead. Power surged through me, tingling just under my skin. That's when I felt it unlock. *Our bond.* Castian was my father, my true flesh and blood father. And he'd been watching out for me my entire life.

Childhood memories filled my mind. Moments locked away— moments with him before I became Jade Glaster.

"I am sorry for the secrecy, *Mir.* I pray you were as happy as you always seemed."

"My dad and Reign were both wonderful. They loved me, and I never wanted for more."

Connected as we were, I felt the hurt and jealousy that never appeared in Castian's perfectly chiseled face. As quickly as I detected it, it was gone.

Shit. "But now that we've found each other, I couldn't be happier." I started to breathe again when his smile grew softer. "Why did you send us away? Wouldn't we have been safer with you than left alone in the Realm of the Fair?"

Castian looked defeated. "Your mother believed the danger to you stemmed from someone within the Fae Pantheon working to free Rheagan. I could not protect you from another god within my family while you were still vulnerable. I had no choice but to try to hide you until your mating triggered your god powers."

My mating. I pivoted to Galan, who sat wringing his hands, staring out at the animals. The muscle in his jaw twitch, and I knew the look. He was having a meltdown of his own.

"I'm ashamed to say that me being your father put your life at risk, *Mir*. Everyone knew what you and your mother meant to me. Your status as a demi-goddess wouldn't be acknowledged until you turned twenty-five. Until that time, you were vulnerable. Your mother made me change your appearance to allow you to hide. Your skin, hair, and features were altered. Every trace of your heritage erased."

My mind stumbled over that one. Who the hell was I if I wasn't me?

"Now, we're at a place where I may finally claim you as my child— if you'll have me."

Was he asking me? There went the tears again. "Of course I want you to claim me, but *demi-goddess*? I don't even know what that means. How do I wrap my mind around that?" Galan was way too still, his face pale and unreadable. I touched his arm. "You didn't agree to this. Does it change how you feel about bonding yourself to me?"

He shook his head. "Blossom, you are the same woman now that you were an hour ago."

There was tension behind his words. "What aren't you saying?"

"Do you realize that you will no longer grow old and leave me in fifty years? You will be by my side for centuries. We will raise our children and live our lives together."

"That is not the only benefit," Castian said. "Now that you have bonded, both your Fae powers will be unlocked. With time and some training, you'll be true forces."

"*Both* our Fae powers?" We said in unison.

"Yes, Jade is my daughter, and Galan is blood of my blood, son of my sister's line. By bonding, the Fae DNA lying dormant in you both will become dominant. Over the next few weeks and months, your abilities will grow more powerful."

"What abilities have I, sire?"

"You, my son, sense an innocent soul's need for care. The increase in that ability, along with your physical speed and skills, will make you a great protector. Together with my daughter's gift of healing, you will make quite a team."

"Sire, since you mentioned the innocent," he said, joining us at the railing. "Might I ask you about my sister? Lia?"

"Truths are better learned in small doses, *Dwinn*." He squeezed Galan's shoulder. "You and Jade have the answers to what must be done to bring Lia back to you. Once your reality settles a bit, you will come to the answer without my interference."

"Sire—"

He cut Galan off with a look and took my hand. "Will you come with me? I have one more thing to show you."

CHAPTER THIRTY-THREE

"Oh. My. Gods." I didn't know what else to say. The woman was lying on a raised platform in a small alcove off Castian's bed-chamber. With hair the color of burning embers and an ankle-length champagne chiton, she looked like a mirage. I might have thought she was merely sleeping. She wasn't. The similarity between her and Lia's state was eerie.

"Is she dead? Soul Entrapped?"

Castian shook his head, walking over to adjust a wayward lock of hair by her shoulder. "No, though she is not truly living either." He smiled and motioned for me to join him. "Don't be alarmed. Her rest is quite peaceful."

"Who is she?"

"Jade. Do you not recogni—" Castian's eyes widened. "She is your mother."

"My *mother*?" Galan caught me as my legs gave way. Grappling around my waist, he lent me his strength and held me upright. "No. I know my mother, and she isn't—"

Castian nodded his head. "You grew up looking at her altered appearance. When I brought her home... after she was hurt, I restored her appearance to the woman she was born. This is Abbey, as I fell in love with her."

I took a step closer, then another. *My gods, she's beautiful.* I picked up an unruly red curl, and memories of a forgotten past flooded my mind. "I have her hair."

"When I altered your appearance, I left you with something of your mother and, of course, something of me." He smiled at his reflection in my eyes. "It was terribly vain, yet I needed you to have some small part of us with you, even if you were unaware."

"I'm glad." I stroked the back of her hand, where it sat folded over her gown. Her skin was warm and silky soft. Her image blurred behind my tears. "Does she ever wake?"

"No. Her body is mended, but her soul shattered by the atrocities inflicted upon her and the horrors she believed they would do to you. Until those wounds heal, she will remain in stasis. I believe, when she is ready, she will come back to us."

"I hope so." Carefully, I picked up her hand. The moment I touched her, I felt a glimmer of power, either hers or mine, I wasn't sure. "Hello, Mommy." I force down the lump, blocking my throat. "I didn't know, or I would've come sooner."

"You're here now, *Mir.*" Castian squeezed my shoulders from behind. After a kiss to the back of my head, he floated to my mother's other side and perched on a stool. Leaning over her, his eyes swirled like liquid emeralds. "Wait until you see her, Abbey. Our baby girl has grown up to be everything we dreamed. Her husband's here too, Galan. He's one of the Highbornes like you saw." Castian held his hand out for Galan to join us. "It's safe to come back to us now, my love. You did it. Their powers are unlocked. Your sacrifice kept her safe."

In a Disney movie, that would be when her eyes flittered open. My mother just laid there. "I've avenged her death with all but one of those bastards who hurt her. I hunted them down and took their lives as they took hers. But I have to stop now." I glanced over my shoulder at Galan. "I'm looking—*we're* looking—forward now, not back."

"I shall finish it." A dark shadow blanketed Castian's gaze. The room went cold as a violent menace rolled off him. "I've dreamed of nothing else since that day. Don't you worry, I shall finish what you started."

"Can you do that? Would that be interfering with the lives of the realm?"

"I will take the life as a husband, not as a god. When the time is right, the last of the men who attacked her will be exterminated." Castian's gaze hardened and menace filled the air between us. "Enough of anguish, today is about new beginnings. I have a gift for you, *Mir*, something I created for your mother when she told me she was expecting." Castian put his hand in his pocket and produced an ornate, silver ring. He slid it onto my finger.

The design reminded me of how Galan described my tattoo. Tiny leaves and vines entwined around three perfectly shaped stones. I touched the stones, thinking how, if things were different, we could've been a family. It made my heart ache for what I missed with them.

"We are a family, Mir." Castian's words whispered in my mind. *"You have only been separated from us for seventeen years. Over the eternity that you will live, that time will seem like nothing. We have a lifetime to love each other."* He kissed my ring and hugged me tightly.

I hugged him tighter. "When can I come back and sit with her again?"

"Whenever you wish. This palace was your home once. You will always have a place here. With your abilities unlocked, you can Flash here under your own power." Stepping back, he laughed at my expression.

"*Really?* You might get sick of me."

"Never." He shook his head, then sobered.. "*Dwinn*, your entire world will tilt and tumble. Only if you put your trust in *Mir*, will you survive. Your spirit can soar boundlessly if you let it. Guard Jade's soul as the most precious treasure I entrusted into your care thus far."

"I shall, my Lord."

Castian's gaze was that of a doting father. "It was no accident that you are drawn to nurture, Galan. Lia, Ella, and all the others you aided over the past century were put in your care for a reason. The depths of your love for innocent souls is your greatest gift. It is why you are the perfect choice to be their guardian."

He focused on Galan's expression and took him firmly by the shoulders. "*Dwinn*, you are mistaken. You are the perfect match for my daughter. As time passes, the two of you will stand together, equals in life and battle. You are the man for her. I have seen it."

Galan looked stupefied. "Thank you, my Lord, I hope only to live up to your praise."

Castian's voice softened as he cupped Galan's neck. "You will, son, have no doubts. But would you do me one honor?"

"Thy will be done." Galan straightened, pressing his shoulders back.

"Address me as *Nimithil* or Father if you prefer. You are my son now. I give you my soul name freely and with no doubts that you will guard it with your last breath."

I read the vacant disbelief on Galan's face.

Castian chuckled softly. "You will need to harness your inner monologue if you are going to be spending time within the Fae gods, *Dwinn*. Most can hear thoughts. Some might take offense to you thinking they have lost their sanity." He smiled as Galan's ears flushed red.

"Yes, Lord, I shall."

"Lord?" Castian raised a brow.

"Yes . . . *Nimithil*." Galan whispered.

"*Dwinn*, why do doubt your union with Jade?"

Galan's brow furrowed, he didn't look my way. "Your daughter is beyond spectacular. She exceeded my worth when she was a healer, teacher, and bard Priestess." Galan looked crushed. "Now she's the daughter of the God of Elves, and the heiress to his Realm? I am overwhelmed."

"No," I protested.

Castian glanced to me, unaffected by Galan's concerns. "Jade was never whole until the two of you collided in that forest. Now she radiates joy and contentment. It suits her. You are destined for more greatness than you know. Your *Ambar Lenn* will transform you into one of the truest souls and greatest males to walk the Realm of the Fair. I have seen it."

Galan didn't look convinced.

Sadness blanketed Castian's face. "I deeply regret that your father's influence has scarred your self-image, son, but listen to me. I know more than he about the man you are."

Galan stared at his feet. "Thank you, Father."

Castian accepted that sad show of confidence. It was probably all he'd get for today. "Before I return you to your celebration, indulge me once more."

Castian caught a strand of my hair between his fingers and drew his touch down to its end. After resting the piece beside my face, he repeated the action in Galan's hair. When he pulled back, my father wore a look of smug satisfaction. "I love you both. If you need me, I will come no matter the consequence." With a blinding shower of delicate golden sparkles, we returned to our pallet.

For a long moment, I studied the dappled morning light the forest cast over Galan's naked body before reaching for the braid hanging to the right of his face. The deep red of my hair hung woven into Galan's silver hair in a thin intricate braid.

The contrast in color was amazing.

"It is a Binding Braid, a symbol of being united in the eyes of the gods," Galan whispered. Hesitantly, he lifted his hand and touched the braid in my hair. His eyes sparkled with wonder as the ribbon of silver slid through his fingers.

"Like a wedding ring?"

"The silver of mine is exquisite when woven into the rich burgundy of yours." I heard the emotion folded in his husky voice. It was there too, behind his eyes, unmistakable despite his attempt at composure.

"You like this, don't you?" I raised a brow. "I mean, you really like that I am marked as yours. Like some kind of alpha male, marking his territory thing."

"You have no idea," he smiled, pulling me against his chest. "Let me see your markings again."

I rolled onto my stomach and swept my hair out of the way. Galan ran his fingers across my shoulders, following the contours and curls of my tattoo. The sensation sent tingles across my skin. "What does it look like?"

He nipped at the nape of my neck. "There is an intricate vinework surrounding a crest with ancient Draconian runes. The primary symbol is the crescent moon representing Castian and is interwoven with the symbols for the body and the soul."

"Okay, my turn . . . let me see." I sat up, sweeping Galan's hair over his shoulder, exposing his markings. His were just as he described mine to be. "What do they mean?"

"Castian has branded us mates, body and soul." Galan's voice broke.

Instinct told me there was more—the symbols signified something more profoundly crucial than our bonding. But what it meant, I had no idea.

CHAPTER THIRTY-FOUR

*A*s I walked barefoot up the stairs of the castle a couple of hours later, I wrapped an arm around Galan's back in blissful exhaustion. Hooking my thumb in the back of his leathers, I smiled. "I could get used to this." My cheeks ached from the dumb-ass grin now permanently on my face. "Would you mind if we didn't say anything about Castian being my father for a bit? I'd like a chance to let it sink in before everyone knows."

"As you wish." Galan nodded. His absent look of anguish had returned.

"Thinking about Lia?"

"Day after day, we wait for her to awaken, yet we are no closer to finding the crystal. What if she never wakes? What if, like your mother, decades pass and she fails to rouse?"

I stopped on the landing of the fourth floor, thankful that classes wouldn't interrupt us for a while. "I know it sucks, but we'll know something as soon as there's something to know. Besides, Castian said we could bring her back. We need to figure it out." Reaching beneath Galan's hair, I massaged the muscles of his neck. "And we will." Greedy hands ran up my back, pulling me into his embrace.

He kissed me—like only Galan could—and I was so on board with distracting him. His mouth settled over mine, owning me, possessing me with an ardor that took my breath away. Shifting his weight to lean against the wall, he settled in as if he had no intention of going anywhere anytime soon.

"How hot is that?"

Two fifth-years stepped out of the weapons room. Nash was sheathing his wand, while a steady stream of blood dripped from a gash across his left cheek. It sat below the tribal tattoo encircling his eye and gaped enough that he needed attention.

"Is this an example of sparring gone wrong, boys?"

Nash probed his cheek. "Nah, just an extra close shave from Clay's scimitar." He chuckled and ruffled his roommate's short ginger hair. "Lesson learned."

"Lessons are easily learned when blood is drawn. Let me fix you up."

"It's nothing, Jade. It's only leaking like a tap because it's a face wound. I don't want to get blood on your dress."

I handed Galan my shoes and waved Nash closer. "Nonsense, it'll take me two seconds." I touched the wound and knitted the tissue back together. He had the beautiful, bronze complexion of his Inuit people, and when I laid hands on him, I felt the power of the Great Spirits run through him.

"Here, give me your hand," he said, grabbing my fingers. After wiping his blood on his muscle shirt, he poked at his cheek. "Thanks, Jade. Don't think this is inappropriate, but *hot damn*, you're rocking that dress." He held his knuckles out to Galan, who knew enough to bump them. "Special occasion?"

"One might say that." Galan winked at me.

Nash chuckled. "Well, you're a seriously lucky man."

"I am indeed."

Trying to ignore my heated cheeks and avoid the appraising looks, I untangled my hair from my pendant and set it flat against my chest. "We should be getting upstairs." I slid my hand into Galan's, lacing our fingers, and turned to the steps. "If the two of you will excuse us."

Clay, who was unusually quiet, eyed me. His unblinking focus had me staring back, waiting for him to remember himself. After a moment, Nash pulled him staggering down the landing to the stairs and smacked him on the back of the head.

Galan chuckled then stared at the length of my leg, showing out the slit of my dress. "Mayhap, we should get changed. You seem to be distracting the students." He brushed his lips gently down my jawline, inhaling deeply. *Though this dress does make me one very hungry male, mayhap it is best enjoyed alone.*

My heart raced as his velvet timbre spoke directly into my mind. I wheeled around, my hands landing on his chest. My body flamed to life, and his nostrils flared. "Did you mean to do that? Use telepathy? Cause *wow*, that was sexy."

Galan's brow rose in a sinful arch. *Your student was correct. You are rocking this dress.*

I moaned and licked my lips. "Think we can get to our suite without anyone noticing us?"

"It is certainly worth the effort." Galan tightened his grip on my hand and jogged up the last flight of stairs. At the top, we made a quick left down the hall, the skirt of my dress billowing behind us like a cape.

"Tham, they're back," Nyssa called over her shoulder from what must've been a sentry position to the lounge. "We were about to come looking for you two."

"I am relieved you refrained," Galan laughed, almost choking. He sent me an apologetic smile, then waggled his brow and kissed her. "No telling what you might have walked in on."

She searched his expression, then broke into a wide grin. "Come inside. Everyone is waiting to hear about your evening."

Damn. I sighed and eyed the hall toward our suite.

He chuckled, kissed my pouty lip, and followed Nyssa into the lounge. "Has there been any change with Lia?"

"No. Elora is sitting with her now."

"Hey girlfriend," Lexi said, pointing to the vine and leaf design twining out from under my hair. "What have you two been doing all day? Getting inked?"

Galan wrapped his arms around me from behind and swept my hair to expose the bare skin of my shoulders. "Last night, Jade and I Recognized as mates, and this morning our union was blessed by Castian, in the Palace of the Fae."

Eyes grew wide, mouths dropped open, and then they broke into a chorus of questions and congratulations. As the chatter died down, Galan turned to the reading nook, where Iadon was sitting with Ella. "I owe you an apology, my brother." Iadon raised his chin. "For the oaths and expletives, I sent your way when I saw Jade in this outfit last night."

"And you gave in to good sense, did you?" Iadon hid his smirk by fixing Ella's blanket in her bassinet.

"The way you and Nyssa know me is frightening. One look at her and I knew you two conspired against me."

Iadon's head fell back in laughter. "I have no idea what you mean. However, I am sure we conspired *for* you, not against." Iadon strode in front of me, lifting my chin gently with his finger. "Nyssa and I already considered you family after everything you did for us. We are delighted the gods made it official." He bent and pressed his lips to mine. He tasted like honey and sunshine and smelled like fine leather.

When he pulled back, I floundered for a minute and looked to Galan. He was beaming.

Tham was next in line. His kiss was playful, and he twisted me down into a dip while everyone laughed. Aust, however, was reserved and sweet. He touched his lips briefly to mine before he kissed my cheek and whispered his blessings in my ear. Dazzled by the whole affair, I decided that lip-locking the bride must be a Highborne thing.

"I am surprised you made it home so soon," Iadon said, moving beside Nyssa.

"Oh?" Galan inclined his head in question.

"When Nyssa and I Recognized, we did not see the light of day for a week. Even now there are times when emotions overwhelm."

Galan stroked his hand through his hair. "In truth, we were famished." He stepped behind me, running his palm across the flat of my stomach. "We need sustenance."

"Well then, we must take care of—"

The room fell silent as everyone turned toward the door. I knew even before I looked. Samuel was frozen mid-step halfway in the doorway to the lounge. He looked like he wanted to back out unseen. Too late. His agonized gaze locked on me then onto the silver braid in my hair. "So, it's done then, is it?" His expression broke my heart as he stormed from the room.

"Samuel, wait." I lifted the delicate layers of skirting and jogged up the hall to grab his hand. "Please."

"I get it, Jade. Believe me. I just came to say goodbye."

"*What?* Don't go. This is your home."

He shook his head. "Aye, well, it doesna feel that way anymore. Every time I turn a corner, I run into a Highborne or a place I kissed ye or some other reminder of what I lost, and he gained. Sorry, I'm not a sound enough man to swallow it."

I pulled him to the end of the hall and into my suite. "We're going to get through this."

He stared at me with sad, brown eyes. "Why should ye care, *a nighean*? I lied to ye for years, pressured ye for something ye couldna give me, spat in your face and plunged a dagger in yer—"

"I don't blame you. Bruin said the Scourge approached you knowing we'd broke it off. He said it was the only way to get to Lia. You had to betray us. They needed to trust you."

Samuel shoved his fists deep into his pockets. "Yeah, what else did Bruin tell ye?"

"He said that you're still one of the good guys."

"And ye believe him?"

I waited until he met my gaze. "*I never had any doubt.*"

"And ye can honestly look at me without despising me for what I did?" His jaw clenched so tight I heard a crack.

I closed the distance between us, cupping his newly shorn face in my hands. "I don't want to be stabbed again, but after what you did for Galan and me, as well as Lia, I forgive you."

Samuel eyed my gown. He ran a finger down my pendant and looked again at the long silver braid beside my face. After a long moment, he forced a smile. "Well, marriage agrees with ye. Ye never looked so beautiful." I heard the pain hidden in his tone, though someone who didn't know him as well probably wouldn't have caught it.

"I'm sorry. I... I don't know how to make this better for you. Tell me what you need me to say."

Samuel's expression became even more tortured. "It's no your fault, Jade. Castian's enchantment saved ye for yer destined mate. Ye loved me the best ye could." He pulled his fingers through his hair and sighed.

"What?" As that little tidbit sunk in, all my guilt boiled into anger. "That's why I could never be intimate with you? I've been guilt-ridden for years because I couldn't connect. I thought there was something fundamentally wrong with me."

"Aye, that's why."

I crossed my arms over my chest. "Was dating me your idea or my father's?"

"Which father cause that water is getting a bit muddy?" He shrugged when I glared at him. "Reign wasna pimping ye out or anything. I courted ye because I fell for ye and wanted to be the man by yer side."

"And pressuring me to have sex, was that part of the plan . . . some bizarre test of my virtue? Was Castian checking if his chastity belt was buckled tight enough?"

He looked genuinely offended. "No! Everyone in Reign's service is painfully aware of his position. He beat it into us—literally." Samuel shrugged and had the good sense to look ashamed. "I held out some stupid hope that the Fates were wrong, and ye could love me."

"So, you knew the whole time? Did you know about Galan and me?"

His chestnut eyes clenched tight. "A bit. It snapped me in the arse, though, when I saw the two of ye together at Dragon's Peak. What I wanted... what I thought we had, wasna real."

I shook my head. "It was real. When you dumped me, you broke my heart. I loved you. Part of me will always love you."

"I appreciate that." He picked up my hand and rubbed my palm with his thumb. "I had to try. If I'd obeyed orders and never gone all in, I would've wondered." He dragged in an unsteady breath and looked to the door. "I need to clear out before I make this worse for the both of us."

As I'd done a thousand times, I brushed his bangs out of his eyes. "Where will you go?"

"I dinna ken. Maybe I'll be a Mundie tourist in the modern realm. Running with the bulls sounds fun. Maybe I'll visit the seven wonders or search for the lost city of Atlantis?" His joking didn't lessen the regret in his eyes. "In truth, I've been ordered to stay on Haven or Fae grounds for a while. Your fathers are worrit about backlash from me screwing Abaddon and making off with Lia. The Scourge had evil plans for her. They'll not be happy."

I placed my hand flat on Samuel's chest and felt its steady rise and fall. He had sacrificed everything for me: his heart, his home, his freedom, and his friends. "Thank you for Lia's return. I will never be able to thank you enough."

Movement in the corner caught my attention. Galan stood staring at Samuel, obviously warring with himself. "I am forced to agree with Jade on that point, Samuel." Galan's voice was too calm. "You jeopardized your life for my sister. You risked everything to bring her back. I shall evermore owe you a debt of honor."

Samuel's shoulders stiffened. "I didna do it for your sake, Elf. If I could have done right by Jade and Lia and screwed ye over, I would have."

The corners of Galan's mouth fought not to turn upward. "Regardless, my gratitude remains."

"Do ye have any idea how much I despise ye?" Samuel growled. "If it wouldn't destroy Jade, I'd wish ye dead with everything I have."

Galan took off his jacket, matched the shoulders together, and slowly laid it flat on the kitchen table. "I cannot blame you. I was welcomed into your home, stole the affections of your love, and now share the bed you imagined sharing with her. In return, you were ordered to destroy that relationship and sent to risk your life to give me what I wished for most."

"And one day, I'll even the score. Ye won't see it coming, but I'll take something precious from you, and you'll know the sting of it, I swear."

Galan sighed. "I choose to believe better of you, Samuel. If you decide to call the Academy your home once more, I will endeavor to co-exist. Unlikely as it seems when you saved my sister, we became allies."

"S'cuse me if I'm no ready to sing Kumbaya and call ye, brother mine."

"Understandable. If you will excuse me, I shall go sit with Lia for a time." Into my mind, he said, *Blossom, take this opportunity to say your goodbyes. Give him what he needs to begin to heal. I do not fault him for loving you. What male could know you and not want you?*

Did I understand what he was saying?

He bowed his head. "I return your privacy." He stepped back into the hall and bowed his head. "Safe travels, Samuel. Blessed be."

I choked on my tears. "Galan, are you sure? I would never—"

Galan's smile was soft and genuine. "I am certain, Blossom. It is the very least he deserves and all I have to offer for his journey." Inclining his head, he closed the door.

Dragging my attention from the door, back to the room, I took a deep breath.

"I'm no sure what he was getting at, Jade. I canna take anything with me."

"Nothing? Not even a memory?" I stepped closer, nipping at my lip.

Samuel watched each step as I approached. "What are ye doing?"

"I'm giving you a proper farewell. Something you deserve. Something we deserve."

My heart pounded when our faces were inches apart. It felt wrong to be close like this with Samuel now that I was with Galan, but at the same time, it felt perfectly right. I couldn't wrap my mind around Galan at times. I didn't understand the way Elves looked at things.

Warm breath tickled my cheek. Samuel's arms wound around me, hesitant at first, but then he secured me against his chest.

He'd held me a thousand times. This was different. With my enchantment lifted, my heart and soul were whole, and my emotions were heightened. Samuel brushed his cheek against mine, breathing in deeply.

"I'll miss ye, *a nighean*." When I kissed his jaw, his body tensed, and his shoulders stiffened. "Jade, ye dinna have to—"

Without hesitation, I stretched up to claim his lips. I knew how he would taste, how his lips would feel pressed against mine. And yet I was shocked by the newness of it. His kiss started warm and tender, but as it deepened, it became more.

His lips danced with mine, eager and loving. He'd wished for this connection, desperately trying to free my bound emotions, while knowing he never could. This moment was for him, and I'd make it count. I would miss him. My heart physically hurt from the pain of it.

I felt as Samuel opened himself to me. With his secrets exposed, he was completely unguarded. He needed this connection between us. I tried to keep a clear head to remember that I belonged to someone else. I reminded myself that these arms and these lips—no matter how heavenly—weren't destined for me.

I failed miserably.

As our kiss continued, my heart raced, and my skin flushed. Samuel's arms constricted around me, crushing me against his muscular body. Strong fingers ran up my back, fisted my hair. A tiny piece of my brain acknowledged that if my father hadn't enchanted me, I would've given myself to Samuel, and it would've been wrong. I loved Samuel, but it paled to the depths of love I shared with Galan.

Galan was my destiny.

Samuel slowed the kiss as if he understood. Cupping my face in his hands, he moved his lips to my forehead, kissing it once, twice, and again. When he pulled back, his eyes were bright and alive and, at the same time, dark and dying. I felt his anguish in being separated from everything he loved, but watching me start my life with Galan would be agony.

"You okay in there?" I circled my hand over his heart.

"I'm no sure," he whispered. "This was supposed to be a duty served. It became *everything*. I'll miss it. I'll miss you."

"Stay safe."

"You too." He kissed me softly and stepped back. "And tell that Elf of yours that if I come back and yer no gloriously happy, all bets are off. There's nothing I'd like more than an excuse to kick his Highborne ass." He blinked quickly and forced a laugh.

"Love you, Samuel."

"Love you more," he whispered. Then he was gone.

CHAPTER THIRTY-FIVE

I'm not sure how, but I made it across the room to climb onto my bed. Slumping into a heap, I grabbed a pillow to muffle my sobs. For years Samuel had been my rock, and now he was gone, and his heart was broken. It was my fault.

I'm so sorry, Samuel.

I wasn't alone in my anguish for long. Familiar hands pulled me into warm arms. As much as I longed for his comfort, I didn't deserve it. "Galan, go to Lia. I'm fine."

"No, Blossom, you are not. You suffer."

I tried to wriggle free. "This isn't fair to you. You're going through enough without wiping tears I shed for another man."

"My only responsibility is to ensure that my reason for living is well. You mourn the death of your relationship with Samuel, and his absence will hurt you."

I sighed when he pulled me tighter into his arms.

"You knew him better than anyone, and he proved me wrong. I am not so proud that I cannot admit that."

Galan's endless ability to love had me coming undone. He would bear anything to soothe my aching soul. He truly was a guardian, and I was a selfish piece of—

"OH, MY GODS!" I jacked myself up and launched off the bed. "That's it!" I ran into my walk-in closet and unpinned the arrow broach. My dress floated to the floor in a soft hiss as I snatched and grabbed something to throw on.

"Blossom. What is it? What—"

I spun wide-eyed. "*Oh!* Galan, I think I've figured—No. It's crazy." I pulled on my panties and bra and stepped into my jeans. "Castian said you were my guardian. See?" I pulled a top over my head and freed my hair. "Is it even possible?"

"Is what possible? Jade, you are frightening—"

I spun back to Galan. "You're not getting dressed. Galan, *get dressed!*"

While Galan changed his shirt, I tried to remember which book it would be in. It had been years since I sat turning the pages of those old—

"Jade, what is this about? Are you well?" Galan looked ready to hit the panic button and call in the white-coats.

I raced across the suite for the door. "I think I've got this Lia thing figured out."

"*What?* Jade, what have you figured out?"

I barely registered his question. I was running barefoot up the hall to the lounge. "The guardian thing. Castian said you were their guardian." My feet squeaked on the floor as I ran straight to the reading area and moved the ladder along its track to the section of ancient legends.

"Blossom, calm down and be careful, please." The tension in his voice had me looking down, way down.

How did I get to the top of the ladder so fast? The worried faces of the other Highbornes, Lexi, and Bruin followed me.

"What's doin' Blaze?" Bruin's bright turquoise eyes sparkled up at me. "You look like shit. Why are you crying?"

"Am I?" I swiped at my face. My cheeks were wet. "Oh. I didn't know. I was upset about Samuel, then—hey, when did you get here?"

"Blossom, please come down and speak to us about what you are thinking."

"Oh yeah. One sec." I fingered over the spines dozens of old books trying to remember which one I needed. They smelled of stale parchment, dust, and leather. It tingled in my nostrils and made me want to sneeze. In the end, I pulled two oversized books, dropped them down to Galan one at a time, then climbed down myself. "Put them on the table and gather round. Bruin, I need a coffee, French vanilla, please?"

"Yeah, like you really need caffeine right now."

"Coffee!" My hair flew from my face in heated tendrils. Medusa had nothing on me. When a mug of French vanilla appeared in my hands, I nodded and darted to the table. "Good Bear, thank you. Okay, we're starting with a history refresher. Highbornes, what legends do you know about Castian?"

"Many," Tham said. "Castian is a powerful warrior god who created our race with drops of his blood. He protects with gentleness yet possesses the unequaled power of a master swordsman. He stands ever-vigilant, dedicated to the members and lands of his realm."

"Okay, what else?" I stood over the first book and pulled back the leather-bound cover.

Tham continued as I flipped through the thick parchment pages. "Only when his charges pass from this realm to the Meadows of Mara does he cease watching over us and allow Alyssa, the guardian of the dead, to take a role in caring for us."

"What do you know about those in Castian's service?"

Iadon pointed to the colored sketches on the pages in front of me. "Castian's primary delegates were the identical twin spirits Lashrael and Felara. Held in some lights by Elves as demi-powers, Castian's representatives served as Protectors of the Realm of the Fair. At the time of their deaths, Castian vowed that their stations would remain vacant until he found the perfect successors. Once chosen, they would be dispatched to defend the innocent whenever our corporal selves or souls were threatened."

Lexi shifted to get a better view. "What does this—"

I held up my hand. "Iadon, keep going. You're on a roll."

"Very well. The two had distinctive personalities. The male of the coupling, Lashrael, was the Sentinel of Souls, given to emotional extremes. He spoke with unwavering conviction and enormous fluctuations of joy and sorrow. His depth of love and compassion was immeasurable and equaled only by his speed and skill in battle."

I sucked back a huge gulp of coffee and winced when I burned my tongue.

Iadon continued. "Felara, in contrast, was the very image of rational detachment, treating situations with logic, strength, and calm reason. She spoke in an immensely reassuring voice and gave direction where there was chaos. She was known as the Queen of the Flesh. This great healer was said to breathe life into those who, by all rights, ceased walking amongst the living—" Iadon's words choked off mid-sentence, and his mouth dropped open.

Galan's expression turned to sheer, dark horror. "Sentinel of Souls?" he gasped, looking at the depiction of Castian with his previous emissaries. "You think Castian—God of gods—has designated *me* as the next Sentinel of Souls?" I didn't need a physical connection to pick up the storm brewing inside him. It rose closer to the surface every second.

"That's the real meaning of the symbols on our tattoos, Castian's crescent moon, and the symbols for body and soul. I'm the guardian of the body and you—"

"Oh, *come* Jade!" Galan twisted away from the group, stalking across the floor and back. "You cannot possibly… how could I?" He stood staring at me. Through me.

I fought the urge to touch him. He was in no mood. "Think about it, Galan. He called you his guardian and said he entrusted the souls of Lia, Nyssa, and Ella to you. He told me that every queen needed her guardian. I'm right about this. You know I am."

Galan's gaze dropped to the floor and pinched shut. "How am I to know *anything* anymore? Gods Jade, how much can you expect me to endure? Since I met you, I have reacted to whatever tempest overtakes me, trying to ride the hurricane which is now my life."

"What are you saying?" I crossed my arms over my chest. "Do you regret meeting me?"

"Of course not, I cherish you. Can you truly say I should be Sentinel of Souls? Your father has lost—"

"He said, 'Your entire world will tilt and tumble around you, but the only way for you to survive it—'"

"Was to trust in you," he choked, waving his hands in front of his chest. "I cannot do this, Jade. It is too much."

"Even if it means not getting Lia back?" I frowned at him, shaking my head. "Galan, I think it is part of your destiny to reclaim her soul so she can wake up."

I rubbed my temples, trying to push away the deep, bass pounding taking root in my skull. Why was I constantly getting clocked in the head with a cosmic beat stick? Just once, I'd like simple, happy, and healthy. "Okay, get ready for the shock of your lives, people." I raised my arms, tipping my head back to call to the heavens. "Father, come to me, please, I need you."

Whoosh. Castian appeared. "To see you twice in one day. I am blessed, *A'maelamin.*"

Everyone in the room froze stiff.

No one moved. No one breathed.

"Surprise." I shrugged and faced Castian—my Father. Wow, that would take getting used to. "Galan and I figured out the whole Sentinel and Queen thing. That's how we'll get Lia back, isn't it?"

"Well done, *Mir*. You were quick to piece things together. You get that from your father." He winked and looked over to where Galan was leaning against the window frame. "Galan? What can I do to ease your anxiety?"

"I cannot think of a thing, my Lord."

Castian tsked. "I thought we agreed you were to call me by name."

"He's having a bit of a crisis of faith," I said.

Castian glided to his side. "Bear with me, Galan. I think I can make you understand." My father led him to the center of the room and snapped his fingers.

An ethereal woman appeared in a golden mist of light. Waif-like, elegant, she was dressed in a filmy lavender gown, and her mahogany hair drifted to her hips in waves. Her skin glowed with a faint iridescence, her eyes, and lips a deep midnight blue. Wide-eyed, she scanned our group. When her gaze settled on Castian, she gathered the skirt of her dress and strode to him.

"Uncle?" she said, bowing her head. "How can I be of service?"

Castian lifted her from her bow and shifted her hair behind her shoulder. "Zophia, I summoned you from Behind the Veil to explain to Galan and Jade what we discussed a few weeks ago. Do you remember?"

She nodded. After a moment of hesitation, Zophia reached her hands out to Galan, a piece of fabric the size of a folded table cloth appeared in his arms.

"What is this, my Lo—Castian?" Galan asked.

"Zophia is one of the four Fae Fates." Castian said. "She is the keeper of the lives in progress and tends to the tapestries. As the youngest of the four, Zophia dedicates her time to ensure your lives are well cared for. I'll let her explain the rest."

Castian gestured for Zophia to take the conversation.

Zophia swallowed and seemed to gather herself before she spoke. "As destinies weave, a tapestry is strung on the looms of the Fates. The colored threads in the fabric of the design represent family, friends, events, and decisions all woven together to create a rich textile. Your life with my cousin, Jade, has knit into something as beautiful and warm as it is strong and durable." She smiled warmly at both of us then helped him lay the cloth flat on the table while we gathered around.

Zophia ran her delicate fingers along the colored threads as she spoke. "This is a replica of your current tapestry, Galan. Notice this upper portion, these rich earth tones, the browns and gold, and greens? These represent you: strength, purity of spirit, and honor. The silver strands mark the divine gift of silver hair he gave to his baby niece a lifetime ago. Those strands represent you and your sister. Your *Naneth* is gold. Thamior the blue. Look at this beautiful strand. Who do you think this one represents?"

Galan touched a shimmering champagne-colored thread. "It is a soft, lovely color. Elegant. This must be Nyssa."

Zophia nodded. "Now, this section is beautiful in its own, is it not?"

Galan nodded. "It is."

"Good, now look here. Look how the Earth tones come to life with the introduction of deep red, copper, and emerald strands. This is where your life begins to twine together with Jade. It is opulent, don't you agree?"

"It is."

"Where am I?" Lexi asked, pushing to the front. "What color am I?"

Zophia pointed to a violet thread woven with the emerald. "This is you, Alexannia Grace. See how long and interwoven your threads become? And this is where Aust becomes part of the weave as well."

"But if we're already part of each other's lives, what does the rest of the tapestry represent?" Lexi asked, fingering the loose threads at the bottom four inches of the edge. "Why are these loose?"

"The tapestry is still being formed. New people, future battles, loss of loved ones, births; all these things will affect the final composition of the fabric. Nothing is set."

"Tell me," Galan said, pointing to a sapphire blue and a sage green tightly woven with his colors and with mine, "what are these colors?"

Zophia's eyes sparkled in the light as she looked to Castian. He nodded, and her smile grew wide. "Those are your children Galan, twins, yours, and Jade's."

I gasped, transfixed with the colors mapped out before us.

"I peeked in my sister's watching pool for the future, and they will be talented and vibrant and adored by all." Zophia clasped her hands together, her smile beaming like sunlight.

"They need a safe place to grow up, Galan," Castian said. "You are the one meant to guard innocent souls. Your struggles in life have taught you acceptance and compassion. Your children need you to accept your station. Lia needs it, and I believe you need it."

I touched the sapphire and sage strands. "Twins?"

Castian nodded. "Take some time. I'll speak to Alyssa about an introduction. If you accept your roles, Galan will have to form a working relationship with her. Only the Sentinel has the right to reclaim a soul once displaced."

Castian strode to Iadon and held out his hands. "May I?"

Iadon hesitated for a second before laying his sleeping baby in Castian's arms.

"You have nothing to fear, Iadon. It is not so long since I held Jade that I forget a father's need to keep his child from harm. You are Jade and Galan's family. In turn, you are mine."

Iadon sunk to his knee, bowing his head. "You honor us, Lord."

He smiled. "With your permission, Iadon and Nyssa, I would like to be the one to implant Ella's soul name." They nodded their consent. Castian pulled back her tiny sleeve, dipped his head, and kissed Ella on her bare shoulder blade. When he finished, he by-passed Iadon and handed Galan the baby. "You were born to protect the innocent, but I will await your decision."

He held his hand out to Zophia, who practically floated to his side. "It was lovely to meet you." She held up her hand as Galan picked up the tapestry and offered it to her. "No, please, it is my gift to you. Congratulations on your Recognition. I wish you great love and happiness."

"Gratitude."

In the next moment, they disappeared in a showering golden mist.

It took a minute, after Castian and my cousin, the Fae Fate, left before the dam broke. Gasps, questions, and colorful expletives flew through the air like a hail storm.

Lexi strode straight through the heart of the chaos and pulled me in for a hug. "So, big day in the world of you, huh? Castian is your daddy?"

"*Mhmm*. Galan and I found out this morning."

"How could Castian be your father?" Tham threw his arms in the air.

I looked over at Lexi, waiting… waiting…

"Well, when a man and a woman find themselves attracted to one another—" She squealed and slapped Tham's fingers away as he poked her. When the assault ended, she gave me a worried smile. "You losing your mind, girlfriend?"

"Yep. I've been thinking of running for mayor of crazy-town. And the day's not over."

"The way you were babbling when you rushed in here, I would vote for you."

"Thanks."

Nyssa brought over a tray of sandwiches and veggies from the buffet table. "You have yet to eat anything substantial since yesterday. If there is more to come, you need sustenance."

"Thanks, Nyssa." I took the tray but couldn't imagine eating anything. Galan clutched the tapestry to his chest. "If you guys don't mind, I need some alone-time with Galan to sort some of this out." It was a silent walk as we numbly made our way back to our suite.

"*Twins?*" I croaked as I closed the door. "Twins?"

Galan looked at me with his mouth open for a long while before he found his words. "The thought of you carrying my young is so far beyond—"

"I need to look at it again."

Galan laid the tapestry flat on the surface of our table, and I ran my fingers along the sapphire and sage threads. His grin grew broader and brighter, the longer we stared at it. "Blossom, do you truly believe I am the right male for this honor? Do you think, in the service of your father, I can help make the Realm of the Fair safe for young ones and innocents?"

"I don't think it, Highborne—I *know* it. Call it a woman's intuition, faith, or my remarkable intelligence. Call it whatever you like, but believe me, you are the Sentinel of Souls."

Galan slid around the table and swept me up into his arms. "Then, we must bathe and ready ourselves. We have a precious soul to rescue."

CHAPTER THIRTY-SIX

"As Bruin would say, here goes everything." I took a deep breath and focused on the two of us standing in the throne chamber of the Fae palace. It was strange to Flash without someone else taking me, and I wasn't sure I knew how to do it. Somehow, though, I did.

My father was perched where he'd been this morning only this time he was plucking away at an electric guitar. We listened while he played a bluesy tune I didn't recognize. Not my usual kind of music, but he was really good.

"*Mir, Dwinn,* you arrived on your own power. Well done." He set the instrument on the throne and met us in the center of the room. Gliding barefoot across the marble floor, his sky-blue robe billowed out behind him. "Have you come to guide Lia's soul back to her corporeal self?"

Galan nodded. "Have you spoken to Alyssa?"

"I have, and she is open to welcome you to Mara. May I escort you?"

Galan's face lit up. "I would appreciate it."

"This is your first official act as my Sentinel, Galan. Are you ready?" When Castian raised his hand, his robe switched to a white button-down and a full-length blue leather duster. His chestnut brown hair pulled itself back into a neat ponytail, and his bare feet were covered with kick-ass leather boots with silver buckles.

Galan's grin grew wicked as he glanced at Castian's boots.

Instantly, Galan was wearing a matching pair. "You have good taste." Castian's glance moved to rest on me. "But we already knew that."

Crossing the manicured lawns Behind the Veil was like walking on an Aubusson Rug, soft and silent under our feet. When we descended to the lower lawn, the deer we'd watched this morning raised their heads and assembled. In a matter of moments, we were surrounded. Long velvet muzzles nudged and prodded our pockets as ears and tails flicked.

"What do they want?" I giggled as a fawn licked my arm with a long, strong tongue.

"They're hungry," Castian said. "Do you mind if we take a moment?"

Galan shifted his feet, but how do you say no to the God of gods? "Of course."

A small satchel of beige and purple berries materialized in each of our hands. The air, thick with the aroma of spring blossoms, encircled us as we doled treats to my father's pets.

"I can't believe how breathtaking it is here," I said.

Castian smiled, leaving our furry friends behind as he ushered us through a maze of rose gardens. "This land is the backdrop for Utopia for almost every Pantheon and every religion: Heaven, Eden, Arcadia, Zion. . . It doesn't matter what you call it. It is home. I'd like you to spend time here, Jade, maybe meet your siblings at some point."

Siblings?

Castian ushered us through the opening in the hedges at the far end of the garden. "This is the passage between life and afterlife, the road to what you call Mara or the After."

Tall elm trees, in measured intervals, lined both sides of the quaint country trail as far as my eyes could see. They reached to the sky and arched over the road, creating a living colonnade of foliage. Castian smiled to himself when we came to a crossroads and changed our path.

There was a sandy, nondescript path leading to our right and a clearing beyond that. The clearing lay surrounded by a maze of manicured boxwoods, arbors, and reflection benches. Topiaries, trimmed and nurtured, brought the species of Fae to life: Weres, Centaurs, Dragons, Griffons, Nixies, Sirens, and more. Some trees swirled up like soft-serve ice-cream cones, and others seemed manicured to resemble Tootsie-Pops.

Songbirds chirped and hopped amongst weighted boughs of fruit trees. Delicate blossoms sweetened the air as the breeze stirred. Sunlight glinted off a circular fountain in the center of the clearing. In its center, carved marble wildlife stood drinking and frolicking in the water with Shalana, goddess of the woodlands. The ivory stone was honed to a satiny sheen, cool to the touch even in the mild afternoon sun.

Captured in stone, a doe and her fawn timidly lapped the surface of the fountain. With ears perked and eyes wide, they watched a grizzly flip an arcing salmon toward two cubs waiting in the shallows.

Above us, a huge red-tailed hawk circled the fountain, her russet feathers black against the sunlight. The way it moved, I would swear it was watching us, its intelligent, dark eyes fixed on our group. I moved to point it out to Castian and Galan, but they were focused elsewhere.

I followed Galan's gaze to a young girl with silver locks sitting on the fountain ledge. With her back to us and her feet dipped into the water, she splashed her feet gently on the surface. He took a small step forward and hesitated. "Little one?"

Lia spun, a glorious grin lighting her elegant features. "Galan, you came." She lifted the folds of her skirt, stepped out of the fountain, and closed the distance, her wet feet slapping against the stone walk. When she reached us, she threw herself into the air, and he caught her as if he'd done it his entire life. "Alyssa said you would. She said I was to be patient, though goddess knows I am not one for waiting idly."

"Certainly not." Galan kissed the top of her head and eased back. "Lia, are you well?"

His shoulders relaxed as she nodded, then he seemed to remember I stood next to him. "I have someone I wish you to meet. This is Jade. My mate. We Recognized last evening."

"What?" Lia squealed and jumped into his arms again. "I have a sister? And she is so beautiful. Blessings to you both. Oh, let me look at you. Such striking eyes, the color of gemstones. And your hair. It is like elderberry wine."

"Yes." Galan pulled her back from me and mussed her hair. "You might say greetings before you take inventory."

"Oh, apologies, Jade. Merry meet. I am very pleased to welcome you into our lives."

"Thank you," I giggled. Galan said she was sunshine and charisma, and he wasn't wrong.

"May I embrace you, sister mine?" Lia had a natural bounce to her as she spoke, sending her silver ringlets bobbing.

"Of course," I said. "It's wonderful to meet you. Galan's been heartbroken without you."

She pulled back from our hug and pouted. "As have I. My heart has ached every minute of every day."

"Likewise." He took her back into the circle of his arms. "I feared I lost you e'ermore."

"Those rancid Scourge males snatched me up and dragged me back to their compound. They prattled on about me being the Queen's heir and said I belonged to them. They were looking for you too. It was ludicrous."

"We can discuss the finer points once we get you settled back home." Galan smiled. I don't know if it was having her back, alive and well, or the sing-songy chime of Lia's voice, but a light lit behind his eyes. "Castian, how do I do this?"

Castian stepped forward. "There's nothing to it. You are the Sentinel of the Souls. It is your right to claim Lia's displaced soul and return it to her body. You and Jade will simply escort her back to her body, and her eyes will open."

JL MADORE

"What about the spell the Scourge cast over her? What happens when we take her?"

"Your powers supersede sorcery, *Dwinn*. The moment you return her to her body, the crystal will dim, and they will cease to have power over her."

The approach of a woman caught our attention. Her mahogany hair was pulled back in complicated braids composed of many small plaits. It flowed down her back and draped over her arm like an expensive wrap at a formal event. Her gown skimmed the courtyard stone, like smoke curling in lazy wisps as she floated to join our group.

"The Guardian and his Queen, I presume." Her voice was like music.

Castian raised his hand. "Alyssa, this is Galan and Jade. You've already had the pleasure of meeting Lia, I presume."

Her smile seemed stiff as she stroked Lia's silky hair. "Yes, Lia and I have spent some wonderful moments getting acquainted. Haven't we, sweeting?"

"Yes, goddess, you were very kind."

When Alyssa held her hand out for Galan, he bowed low and kissed it. "It is an honor."

"*Mmm*, Lia neglected to mention how handsome her brother is." She bit her bottom lip, running her fingernail down the front of his tunic. "Lucky for me, you and I will be spending a great deal of time together in the future."

"I suppose that is correct, yes, goddess." Galan's mouth tightened into a stiff smile as he stepped back to stand beside me.

"And tell me, Guardian, do you recognize your duty as consort to service those in the royal matriarchy who request it of you? It is a longstanding law of the land. I know your maternal ancestor, Rheagan, always loved her Highbornes."

I fought the urge to hurl myself and yank her mahogany hair off her head.

Galan, however, was much more refined. He spoke in an even tone. "You honor me with your consideration m' Lady, however, bound by Recognition to my Queen, the decision is not mine own."

"I see. Pity. I don't imagine your Queen wishes to share if I'm reading her demeanor correctly." She eyed me with no effort to disguise her disdain.

"I believe you are."

Alyssa nipped her bottom lip and eyed Galan again. "However, I do have the authority to demand servitude." She smiled and trailed her hand along the waistband of Galan's leather pants, pausing at the tie.

Castian cleared his throat and threw her a sideways glance. "Such a demand hasn't been enforced in millennia, and you know it, Alyssa. The Fae Authority would hardly appreciate you wasting their time. Stop stirring."

Alyssa didn't show a response, one way or another. "I simply wanted to know if he *would* acquiesce." She smiled, looking all too innocent. "I am not without reason. To seal our new relationship, today, I ask only for a kiss among friends."

"Oh, you wish." I stepped forward, clenching my fists.

Galan grabbed my wrist. *Jade stop, please. Do not anger her. She is a goddess.*

So am I. Pulling my arm back, I shot him a look which screamed, this is *sooo* not okay.

Alyssa moved closer, running her fingers over her upturned lips. "You consider yourself a goddess? By what stretch of your overactive imagination, human?"

Eavesdrop much. Castian had his arms crossed over his chest, his mouth twitching at the corners. I, however, was not amused. "I suppose demi-goddess would be more accurate, wouldn't it Father?"

Castian's growing smile broke my tension. "Indeed, it would, my child, though you are certainly more powerful than most demi-deities, sired by the God of gods. I happen to be a bit of a big deal in this realm." He laughed, moving to my side to kiss the top of my head. "Alyssa was just getting to know the two of you. I'm sure she meant no offense by soliciting the services of your husband."

"Yes, I'm sure," I said.

"So, the long-lost half-breed returns." Alyssa didn't show any sign of being ruffled. She turned her attention back to Galan. "I look forward to *knowing* you, Galan, when we have a bit more privacy, of course." She tossed a dismissive glare at me. "I take it you will be leaving now and taking my little friend with you when you go?"

"That is my intention, yes," Galan hesitated. "Are there arrangements to be made before taking Lia from here?"

"If she were within my gates, yes, but as she is a temporary visitor, she is free to go."

"In that case, goddess, we will take our leave. Grati—I mean, it was a great pleasure." Galan bowed his head and backed away.

"The pleasure was mine." She smiled, her gown swaying softly to the side.

Galan took Lia's hand and mine and turned to the path where we entered the clearing. I felt his tension dissolve the further we got from the Gates of the After.

I glanced at Castian and the unholy laughter in his eyes. "What's so funny about her trying to mount my husband?"

"I was thinking how long it's been since someone, other than myself, denied Alyssa of something she desired. In my experience, it never bodes well. You have drawn a line in the sand, *Mir*, and she will not abandon her quest easily."

Great. "And what have you denied her?"

Castian smiled, and unfortunately, I knew. "Oh . . . ew."

"Alyssa and I have an entangled history. Three of your siblings were born of our union over the millennia. She is currently disgruntled over my affections for your mother. I regret that relationship will again impact your life."

"I'll survive. I am my father's daughter."

Castian smiled. "You are, but until you learn the nuances of our hierarchy, tread lightly. It is wiser to have Alyssa as a wary ally than a formidable enemy."

"I'll remember." Squeezing Galan's hand, I looked at my husband. "Promise me, when you come here you'll, bring someone with you and always have your boots laced tight."

"My boots? Whatever for?"

I glanced over my shoulder, glad Galan was out of the lion's den, for now. "So, when she tries to get into your pants, you can run. Fast."

Galan's chest bounced as he bent and kissed the top of my head. "I so swear it."

"Good." I looked at my new family and felt the warmth bloom in my chest. "Now if it's all right with everyone else. Let's go home."

CHAPTER THIRTY-SEVEN

*B*lind to my surroundings, Galan guided me toward the trees. The silk scarf tied over my eyes effectively prevented me from discovering the surprise he'd been working on for over a week. "Have you any ideas, Blossom?"

I raised my fingers to the blindfold as images of him filled my mind, erotic, sensual images of his hair trailing down my body and silk ties and pounding need. "I have a few, yes."

As my body bloomed, he drew in the scent and groaned. "I love that thought process, love, but sadly that is not what this is about—unless you wish to return to our suite and forget the whole thing?" He gently tugged me back the way we'd come.

"Not on your life," I said, refusing to budge. "I'll behave if you will."

He nuzzled my neck, kissed me once, and resumed our original course. My step faltered when we left the warn cobblestone path and continued on what felt like flagstone. It was flat, uneven, and made an echo under my heels.

"Don't let me fall. I'll never forgive you if I get grass stains on the ass of my new dress."

"I would never allow it," he said. I heard the smile in his voice.

"Rest assured, your dress shall remain intact until I strip it from your body and toss it to the floor."

"You better not let Iadon hear you say that. This dress gets hung when it comes off."

"I will never be able to wait that long. I already picture the navy panties you have on and how easily I could lift the hem of this skirt."

I smacked his groping hand away from my butt, laughing. "How about draping it over the back of the chair? Do you have the restraint to wait that long?"

There was a momentary pause as if he were considering that. "Possibly, though I make no promises. Now, Blossom, you promised to behave. We are within the hearing range of others. Are you ready for the unveiling?"

"Yes?"

We walked on a little further until Galan behind me and untied the scarf. I kept my eyes closed until he was ready. With his hands wrapped around my waist, and his chin rested on my shoulder, he whispered, "Open your eyes, Blossom."

Nothing could have prepared me, and no amount of guesses would've brought me to this. In the middle of the forest, not far from the castle, from out of nowhere, nestled amongst the trees, stood a massive, four-story, stone mansion. Front and center was a courtyard with a marble fountain similar to the one I loved Behind the Veil. Across the courtyard sat a regular, two-story gatehouse which was attached to the stone wall surrounding the entire property. Above the wall ran laser ward-markers hissing with a low hum of power.

I looked again at the main house and up the steps to the first-floor porch. I stared in confusion at a staff dressed in traditional livery. They appeared to be standing for inspection. At the front of the group, Elora stood looking very official in a sleek black gown.

I hadn't noticed at first, but my family of Highbornes, as well as my Haven family and a large group of Talon, had filled in beside me. I stood, open-mouthed, unable to absorb the meaning of it all.

"I think she likes it," Tham laughed as he stepped from behind us, dressed to the nines.

"Close your mouth, girlfriend," Lexi chuckled.

I looked around as smiles overwhelmed me to the point of dizziness. Everyone looked like perfection. It was as if we were going to be on the cover of some exotic magazine. I shook my head. "What am I missing? What is this, Galan?"

"No need to panic, love. This is an engagement party of sorts, and this house is your mating gift from your fathers."

"My *what?*" I spun toward Reign and Castian, who both sported an unmistakable look of fatherly pride. "It's too much."

Reign patted Castian on the shoulder and urged him forward. "My darling, *Mir*. You deserve a place befitting the goddess you are. As much as it saddens me that you chose not to live in the Fae Palace, I understand. Reign and I have given you the next best thing, a home of your own, so that you may begin your new life.

"But it's huge. I'll never be able to find anyone."

"With the future uncertain, you and your new family need a secure home. I insist it be more defendable than the castle. There are too many students and staff stalking about. Anything could happen, as you well know."

Reign nodded and pointed to the walls. "Julian has gated and wired the entire property with the leading-edge security technologies from both realms."

"You bet your ass." Julian winked, tugging the cuffs of his shirt from under his jacket.

Reign patted my brother on the shoulder and continued. "As you know, the Talon's effectiveness has been pissed away on political bullshit. It's time we refocus on our directive to protect the realm and battle the coming Scourge offensive. From now on, Castian will handle domestic squabbles and exposure, and we'll focus on warrior duties."

"And in exchange," Castian grinned. "The west wing of your home is now headquarters and home base for all Talon enforcers."

Ahh, and nothing could happen to me with a couple of dozen warriors living under my roof.

Castian chuckled and swept his arm toward my house. "Everything was designed by Galan and your siblings, with you in mind. Reign and I have selected and interviewed the staff, and Elora has agreed to head the household."

Castian scanned the crowd then grew serious. "This home belongs to my daughter and is to remain secure. No one brings outsiders or anyone not given clearance by either me or Reign. No sexual conquests for the night. No friends for the weekend. If anyone compromises her safety in any fashion or by any slight, I will take it as a personal attack on my family and will unleash my wrath. I will twist off your balls, sauté them in lemon, and feed them to Aust's wolf friends on the end of a bonfire roasting stick—then I'll get nasty. Understood?"

The crowd shifted, and a few men cleared their throats. Everyone nodded. Castian turned back to me and smiled. "Congratulations, *Mir*."

Blinking in rapid-fire, I forced my throat to swallow. "Thank you."

I moved to Reign and laughed at my 'Reign of Terror' welling up. He chuckled, pulling me into his arms.

"I love you." I looked from Castian to Reign and back again. "Both of you. How did one girl get so lucky to have two such wonderful fathers?"

Castian laughed. "I'd say it was the Fates, but I swear other than Zophia, your halfwit cousins don't know what they're doing most of the time." A chorus of laughter joined in.

"I don't know. They got this right." I held out my hand to the man the Fates had given me. Galan took it and led me to sit on the edge of the fountain.

Retrieving a little wooden box from his jacket pocket, Galan sank to one knee and held it out. It was the box he'd carved for me in his valley that first week, the one with my name engraved in its top. He eased it open. My eyes widened, dazzled by the etched platinum band and the princess cut, champagne diamond displayed inside.

Galan brushed his thumb across her cheek. "Rings are a customary symbol of bonding for humans, and since you have my mother's pendant, I thought you might like this as well. I chose it because it was all the things you are to me: flawless, authentic, unbreakable, and stunningly beautiful. You would honor me by wearing it as a symbol of our union."

"Like she'll ever take it off." Lexi laughed somewhere beside me. I didn't look over, though, because I couldn't tear my gaze from Galan.

"Jade," he continued, "though technically we are bound for eternity, I wish to honor your traditions. Be mine, now and evermore, in marriage as well as mating."

His essence strengthened me–mind and body–filling me with a glow of warmth. He belonged to me. I belonged to him. Two halves of the same soul found each other and merged.

Speaking directly into his mind, I replied. *'I will stand at your side as long as we draw breath. I will marry you today and a thousand times over, proud to take you as my mate. Amin mela lle, Dwinn.'*

Out loud, I whispered a breathless, "Yes."

ALSO BY JL MADORE

Find Me:

Social Media – Facebook, Twitter, Instagram

Web page – www.jlmadore.com

Email – jlmadorewrites@gmail.com

Reader Group – JL Series Updates

JL's Reverse Harem Titles

Guardians of the Fae Realms

Guardians of the Phoenix – Calli's Harem

Book 1 – Rise of the Phoenix

Book 2 – Wolf's Soul

Book 3 – Bear's Strength

Book 4 – Hawk's Heart

Book 5 – Jaguar's Passion

Darkness Calls – Keyla's harem

Book 6 – Dark Curse

Book 7 – Dark Soul

Book 8 – Dark Crown

Guardians of the Crown – Honor's Harem

Book 9 – Honor Restored

Book 10 – Honor Guards

Book 11 – Honor Bound

Book 12 – Honor Empowered

Rise of the Amberloq – Lark's Harem

Book 13 – Find the Fallen

Book 14 – Rise from Ruin

Book 15 – Trust and Triumph

Exemplar Hall – Jesse's Harem

Book 1 – Captured by the Magi

Book 2 – Jesse and the Magi Vault

Book 3 – The Makings of a Magi Knight

Book 4 – Clash with the Magi Council

Book 5 – The Unstoppable Storme

JL's More Traditional M/F, M/M, or Menage

The Watchers of the Gray Series (Paranormal)

Watchers of the Gray Boxset – Complete Series

Book 1 – Watcher Untethered – Zander

Book 2 – Watcher Redeemed – Kyrian

Book 3 – Watcher Reborn – Danel

Book 4 – Watcher Divided – Phoenix

Book 5 – Watcher United – Seth

Book 6 – Watcher Compelled – Bo

Book 7 – Watcher Unfeigned – Brennus

Book 8 – Watcher Exposed – Taharqa

The Scourge Survivor Series (Fantasy)

Scourge Survivor Series Boxset - Complete Series

Book 1 – Blaze Ignites

Book 2 – Ursa Unearthed

Book 3 – Torrent of Tears

Book 4 – Blind Spirit

Book 5 – Fate's Journey

Book 6 – Savage Love – epilogue novella

Aliens of Atlantis Series (Sci-Fi)

Book 1 – Taryn's Tiderider

Book 2 – Kai's Captive

Book 3 – Alyandra's Shadow

Printed in the USA
CPSIA information can be obtained
at www.ICGtesting.com
LVHW092134300823
756812LV00023B/136

9 798201 244040